M000158146

RELICS OF
ETERNITY

BOOK SEVEN
OF THE DUCHY OF TERRA

RELICS OF
ETERNITY

BOOK SEVEN
OF THE DUCHY OF TERRA

GLYNN STEWART

FAOLAN'S PEN
PUBLISHING
faolanspen.com

This edition published in 2020 by:

Faolan's Pen Publishing Inc.

22 King St. S, Suite 300

Waterloo, Ontario

N2J 1N8 Canada

ISBN-13: 978-1-989674-06-2 (print)

A record of this book is available from Library and Archives Canada.

Printed in the United States of America

1 2 3 4 5 6 7 8 9 10

First edition

First printing: April 2020

Illustration © 2020 Tom Edwards

TomEdwardsDesign.com

Faolan's Pen Publishing logo is a trademark of Faolan's Pen Publishing Inc.

Read more books from Glynn Stewart at faolanspen.com

CHAPTER ONE

"Good morning, Commander Rogers. What's the daily?"

Commander Bethany Rogers looked up as Captain Morgan Casimir stepped up to the side of the command dais at the center of the ship's bridge. The raised dais was positioned so the Captain—or officer of the watch, in this case—could easily rotate and see what was going on anywhere on the long oval bridge.

The main holotank was positioned directly in front of the Captain's seat, with fifteen of the bridge's fifty seats wrapped around it. *Defiance* wasn't at battle stations at the moment, so most of those seats were empty. The night watch only had sixteen officers and enlisted, soon to be replaced by the twenty-six of first watch.

"The system is as empty as the back of beyond, which it is," Rogers told her blonde Captain. Rogers herself was a young redheaded woman, with the odd distinction of being one of the first hundred humans born outside of the Solar System. She was from Alpha Centauri, the colony founded less than two years after humanity had been annexed.

Morgan, on the other hand, had been four years old when the A!Tol—the ! was a glottal stop, a human attempt to approximate the beak snap of their squid-like overlords—had arrived in Sol. Thirty-seven now, she served the A!Tol Imperium as *Defiance*'s commanding officer.

"The back of beyond isn't always as empty as we'd like it to be," she reminded her First Sword—executive officer in the militia parlance Morgan had first trained in. She was early, but Rogers readily ceded the command chair, allowing her to take a seat. "My stepmother found a lot of secrets buried out past Sol after we joined the Imperium."

"You'll forgive me, sir, if I'd rather have less excitement in a thirty-year career than your stepmother had in one year as a privateer," Rogers said with a shake of her head. "We've got survey probes in orbit of all eleven planets and the star. Standard patterns; I'm not expecting anything unusual, so we should wrap up in about another thirty hours."

That was about what Morgan had expected. The probes had been en route when she'd gone to bed the previous evening, but they had the same gravitational-hyperspatial interface momentum engine as *Defiance* herself. The "interface drive" gave the probes a cruising speed of seventy percent of lightspeed. The farthest planet was only six light-hours away.

"Anything at all worthy of note?" Morgan asked as she pulled up the automated reports that gave her a bit more detail than Rogers's verbal summary.

"Delta looks like an absolute hell-hole for humans or A!Tol but slots neatly into the middle of Ivida comfort zones," Rogers told her. "Whichever investment corp bought the rights to K-Seven-Seven-D-N-E-Five is going to get some nice change from the Ivida colony corps."

"Ten marks says it was my father," Morgan said with a sigh. "That's probably being rude. There's a lot of people on that speculation market. Regardless, if that's the most important thing we see, it's going to be a long, boring day."

Rogers gave her boss an odd look.

"You sound almost pleased, sir," she said.

Morgan smiled.

"I am pleased, Commander Rogers," she admitted. "I know what *exciting* days look like in the Navy, Commander. I have no interest in seeing those anytime soon."

Twelve years before, Morgan had seen rapid promotion from tactical officer of a Duchy of Terra Militia battleship to executive officer of an A!Tol Imperium *superbattleship* during the course of a very exciting year. She'd seen the genocidal Taljzi fanatics besiege Earth—and served in the largest fleet the A!Tol Imperium had ever gathered when they'd returned the favor.

Her promotions since had been far slower and much more relaxing.

"I'll take over being bored for you," she told her First Sword. "Go rest. If something interesting manages to appear, I promise to wake you up."

K77DNE5 REALLY WAS the back of beyond. By Morgan's back-of-the-envelope math, she was three hundred and forty light-years from Earth and four hundred and thirty from A!To, the imperial capital. Of course, hyperspace was far from an exact science in either consistent time or easy translation to realspace.

It would only take her a few weeks longer to reach A!To than Earth, but she was somewhere between two and three months' travel from her theoretical home on humanity's homeworld.

Defiance was her real home, though. Morgan had enough connections—her family, her girlfriend—to keep her tied to Earth, but she'd decided over a decade earlier that her life was the Imperial Navy. The A!Tol had done well by humanity in the long run—and humanity had done well by them in turn.

Many of the key technologies that underpinned Morgan's command had either been developed by humans or reverse-engineered in covert facilities hidden in Sol. Much of the rest had been taken from the wreck of a warship belonging to the Mesharom, generally regarded as the galaxy's elder race.

Taken by human technicians via favors owed to human officers... including Morgan herself. There might be consequences for that still, but no one had seen the Mesharom since the Battle of Arjtal.

The Imperium was enjoying an extended period of peace, but Morgan was reminded of the price for that as she ran through her morning reports and briefings. One of those briefings was flagged as urgent.

Tapping a command, she closed a partial privacy field around her and activated the briefing.

"This briefing is prepared for all command-rank officers of the Imperial Navy."

The speaker was a Pibo neuter, a hairless gray alien that resembled certain myths from Earth's history. None of the Pibo had ever, to Morgan's knowledge, addressed those myths.

This particular Pibo was known to her. Echelon Lord Iros was the usual talking head for briefings coming out of the main intelligence archives on A!To. Anything they were presenting was important but probably not as urgent as they'd flagged it...to Morgan, commanding the heavy hitter of a survey task force on the edge of nowhere, at least.

"High Warlord Shairon Cawl's forces have routed the True Theocracy Fleet at the Torell System," Iros told them, confirming Morgan's assumption that the briefing was about the Imperium's age-old rivals, the Kanzi Theocracy. "This marks the third major victory for the High Warlord's forces in the last long-cycle. Our current estimate at this point is that the True Theocracy is functionally out of deployable warships.

"The High Priestess and the High Warlord may make another round of diplomatic overtures in an attempt to end the civil war, but intelligence does not expect the rebels to surrender at this point."

Morgan snorted. The Kanzi civil war had been ongoing since the

Battle of Arjtal, where a joint Kanzi-Imperial fleet had overcome the Kanzi's xenocidal cousins and ended the Taljzi threat.

Orders from the capital had told Fleet Master Shairon Cawl to betray his allies. Apparently, he'd already known the High Priestess had been kidnapped and had been expecting the treachery, as he'd turned his fleet's guns on the traitors and then moved to rapidly secure control of most of the Kanzi Theocracy.

The twelve years since had been a bloody, grinding civil war, with Cawl claiming victory after victory as the "True Theocracy" were pushed from system after system.

That the Imperium's largest neighbor and traditional enemy had been tied up in a civil war for a decade had helped the Imperium's period of peace—as had the fact that the side that appeared to be winning that war was an Imperial ally.

Morgan privately suspected the reason the war had gone on as long as it had was so that High Priestess Reesi Karal and her adoptive father could keep a free hand to reshape their society. Slavery had been a major part of the Kanzi economy, and now...it wasn't. It was a lot easier, she suspected, to do that reshaping in the middle of a pseudo-religious war than in a time of peace.

"All vessels along the border with the Theocracy are to increase their level of alert," Iros's image told her. "Units in the Arjtal Security Zone are to watch for potential refugees fleeing Rimward from the True Theocracy.

"We believe significant portions of the Clan fleets that supported the True Theocracy have abandoned the cause as well. We expect to see a notable increase in pirate activity and weight of metal over the next few months to years as the warships from those provincial forces try to support themselves."

Iros continued, but Morgan was checking the rest of her messages as she let the recording run. That there was a chance of rogue Kanzi warships ending up in her area of operations was relevant to her, but most of the rest was the usual guff.

Plus, the Kanzi weren't going to show up there. The Kanzi border was by Earth, which meant she was over three hundred and fifty light-years from the nearest Kanzi system—which seemed like a good distance to keep the blue-furred slavers at, in her opinion. You could reform a slaver, but part of her didn't see how you could ever *forgive* a slaver.

And, well, there was *nothing there.*

"HYPER PORTAL ALERT; WE HAVE A CONTACT!"

Morgan turned her command chair to focus on the speaker before they were halfway through their report.

"Contact?" she demanded. "Any details?"

Lesser Commander Thu Nguyen was her Vietnamese tactical officer and the next senior officer on *Defiance*'s bridge. Technically, Nguyen commanded first watch, but Morgan preferred to spend as much time on the bridge as she could.

"It's over a light-hour away, sir, well outside range for any detailed scans," Nguyen reported after a few seconds' digging through her data. A new red icon, blinking to show the lack of detail, appeared on the system map in the main holotank.

"We picked it up from the probes surveying Hotel," she continued after a moment. "Standard-sized hyper portal, but the probe really doesn't have the sensors to resolve many details of the ship without drawing attention to itself."

In theory, that wasn't a problem. But there wasn't supposed to *be* anyone out there with hyperdrives. Scans hadn't shown any sign of indigenous intelligence, and the area was well outside normal Imperial shipping lanes.

They were even well outside normal Imperial surveying distances. The Imperium was pushing its surveys out in this direction for very specific, very *classified* reasons...which made Morgan nervous about strange ships.

"Get what you can from the survey probe," she ordered. "If there are any more ships, I want to know about them."

She was already running the numbers for a hyperspace intercept. She could run *Defiance* through hyperspace, drop out behind the strange ship and make sure they didn't run. Depending on what she was looking at, she could then send first-contact protocols...or shoot to disable and board.

Morgan considered the situation for a few more seconds, pulling up the data they were getting from the probe. Nguyen wasn't wrong in her assessment of what they were getting from the survey probes. Their primary purpose was to map a planet. If they flipped a probe in place and fired its active sensors at the ship, they'd get more data at the price of it being very clear just what they'd done.

There was only one other easy option—and there wasn't supposed to be anyone out there.

"Once El-Amin is up here, I want a target jump plotted to make sure we cut them off from any escape route," Morgan told Nguyen. "Start prepping it now."

"El-Amin isn't on shift unt—"

Activating general quarters from the Captain's chair was more than pushing a big red button, but not much. On the bridge, it was mostly noticeable by a dimming of the lights and a slight cooling of the air.

They could still hear the battle stations klaxon that rang through the rest of the ship.

"He'll be here momentarily," Morgan told Nguyen calmly.

CHAPTER TWO

HYPERSPACE WAS A GRAY, EVER-SHIFTING VOID THAT DEFIED both human consciousness and all but one sensor system. Even the tachyon scanners that provided real-time information around Morgan's starship were limited to a single light-second of useful information in hyperspace.

The sensors that picked up distortions in hyperspace were longer ranged but completely lacking in details. Right now, they told Morgan there was no one else in hyperspace within a few light-years of the system.

"Emitters online, emerging in fifteen," Lesser Commander Hadi El-Amin reported. Morgan's navigator was a man approaching her own age, a Mars native who wore a headscarf with his standard A!Tol Imperial Navy uniform.

"Stand by guns, stand by maneuvering, stand by coms," Morgan ordered calmly. "We'll talk first, but they aren't supposed to be here."

She considered the situation as the seconds on El-Amin's countdown ticked away. If the strangers were true strangers, an unknown hyper-capable civilization, shooting first was an unquestioned violation of Imperial protocol and her own conscience.

If they were Imperials or one of the Imperium's neighbors out this far, the scenario was very different.

The main holotank showed the cruiser's hyper portal emitters flare to life and tear apart the strange grayness of the reality around them. True reality, reality the human brain could comprehend, was visible through the hole in space El-Amin had opened.

And *Defiance* flashed through it, back into normal space. The transition wasn't comfortable—and Morgan was hit worse than most —but there was a definite relief to being back in normal space.

"Nguyen, what have we got?" she demanded.

"Tachyons online; give me a moment," the tactical officer replied calmly. "Bogey Alpha is in the sweep, on the vector picked up by the probe. They're heading toward the second-largest moon at half lightspeed.

"Bogey *Bravo* is new," Nguyen continued. "They're moving to rendezvous with Alpha at half lightspeed. Speed suggests civilian vessels, but we are continuing to resolve data."

"El-Amin, position us to cut off their maneuver cone," Morgan ordered. Assuming the bogies were limited to the point-five *c* they were showing, she had a tenth of lightspeed on either of them without even straining *Defiance*.

On the other hand, all three ships had interface drives and could reach their maximum speed in roughly six seconds. Even a civilian drive could dance on the head of a pin in the hands of the right pilot.

"We have them locked down," her navigator confirmed as the maneuvering zones of all three ships appeared on the holotank. "There's a couple of zones where we'd need to go to full sprint to catch them, but they can't evade us without flying *through* Hotel."

Morgan smiled thinly. If anyone out there was capable of flying through a gas giant twice the size of Jupiter, she'd never met them— and she'd served alongside Mesharom warships.

"Move us in, get me better details, and let me know the moment they react to our presence," Morgan said calmly. *Defiance* vibrated as her own engines came to full power, gently accelerating at a pace that played fair with no one's scientists.

The A!Tol Imperium's scientists—which now included humanity's entire scientific community—were still baffled by hyperspace and its interactions with realspace. They could see its effects, calculate them and predict them—but they would admit, when pushed, that the hyperspace interface itself was probably the single least understood phenomenon in physics.

"We have twenty seconds before they see us," Nguyen reported. "If they had tachyon scanners, they would have already reacted."

"Nystrom, do we have a first-contact package ready to go?" Morgan asked.

Passang Nystrom was her communications officer, a half-Tibetan, half-Swedish woman with a ready smile and brilliantly green eyes.

"We do," she confirmed. "I also have standard channels ready. Any idea what we're looking at?"

"Yes," Nguyen replied instantly. "Bogey Bravo is still close enough to Hotel to be hard to define, but Bogey Alpha? Alpha's one of ours, an Imperial-built medium freighter. Half-c drives, million tons cargo.

"She's not flying ident codes, but we can't enforce that reg out here," she concluded. "Definitely one of ours."

"That does change things, doesn't it?" Morgan said. "Is Bravo ours or an unknown?"

"Still breaking her down, but I don't think she's an unknown," Nguyen told her. "Seventy percent likelihood Imperial, ninety-six percent likely they're at least a known signature."

This side of the Imperium didn't have a massive cold-war enemy like the Kanzi. There were a dozen smaller single-species territories belonging to people who'd been hyper-capable before the A!Tol had arrived along this flank of the Imperium.

The Imperium, for all of its active expansionism, tended to focus on uninhabited systems and species they felt needed their protection. Morgan had her doubts about the true necessity of Imperial annexation, even for Earth, but she was forced to admit they at least tried to do good by the subject races.

And, well, there were twenty-six human legislators on A!Tol between the three Houses of the Imperial Legislature.

"They see us; they are evading," Nguyen reported. "Alpha is making a run around Hotel and Bravo is diving back to try and hide behind Hotel-Eight."

"Do we have an ID on Bravo?"

"Nothing solid," she admitted.

"Is she armed?" Morgan demanded.

"Unsure," Nguyen admitted. "Size and energy signatures suggest another mid-sized freighter. She's probably not unarmed but most likely doesn't have military-grade weapons."

"And Alpha is the same," Morgan concluded aloud. There was an easy solution to the situation available to her, but it put her people at risk.

"Get me Battalion Commander Vichy," she told Nystrom. "Then stand by for an omnidirectional transmission."

"UNIDENTIFIED VESSELS, you are operating in an unsecured region under the authority of the A!Tol Imperium," Morgan told the ships' crews. "I hate to lean on the cliché of *only the guilty run,* but your actions are extremely questionable and my authority over Imperial vessels in this system is complete.

"You will activate your beacons and stand down your engines. Depending on the conversation to follow, I may require my Marines to inspect your ships. I wouldn't expect that, but I'll admit that the chance increases the farther you run."

The message was going out on both hyperfold communications and regular radio. Hyperfold communicators weren't unheard-of on civilian ships, but they were still uncommon.

Morgan eyed the screen that was assessing whether they'd received her message, then shrugged.

"El-Amin, ready a course for Target Alpha, sprint speed if you please," she ordered. "Hold on executing but continue updating. Vichy?"

"We're ready." Battalion Commander Pierre Vichy was probably Morgan's least favorite of her officers, but the Frenchman's voice was calm.

Alpha was closer and had definitely got her message. Bravo might still have missed it.

"We'll drop you off at closest approach," Morgan told Vichy. "I don't think we can slow down."

"Bays and birds are designed for it, sir," the Marine replied. "Bravo might end up a bit roughed around the edges, but we'll bring her in."

"She's almost certainly armed, Battalion Commander," she warned him.

"So are my shuttles."

She concealed a sigh.

"Understood. El-Amin? Execute. Vichy? Stand by to drop."

The course change wasn't much, just enough to make sure they intercepted Alpha's current course. The *velocity* change was more dramatic, as *Defiance* went from sixty percent of lightspeed to seventy.

She couldn't sustain the pace for more than twenty minutes at a time, but the freighter couldn't evade her at that speed either.

"Closest approach to Bravo in thirty-six seconds," Rogers informed them. As First Sword, Rogers was in secondary command, watching and silently listening in case something went wrong.

"Shuttle bays confirmed ready," she continued. "Vichy can launch on my mark."

"Handle it, First Sword," Morgan ordered. "I'll focus on Alpha if you manage the Bravo takedown."

"Understood."

They were in range of the vast majority of *Defiance*'s weapons, but even the faster-than-light hyperfold cannons would be inaccurate at best at this range. Morgan could *destroy* both Alpha and Bravo with a word, but she needed more to go on to do that.

"Nystrom. Any response?"

"Negative," her com officer confirmed. "Both of them have almost certainly received the message, but they're rabbiting instead of talking."

"Shuttles away," Rogers's voice murmured in Morgan's ear. "Holding one platoon aboard for Target Alpha."

New icons spilled across Morgan's holotank as nine assault shuttles took off after Target Bravo. They couldn't match their mothership's full sprint capacity, but sixty-five percent of lightspeed was more than enough for this.

"Let's give them one more chance," Morgan said aloud. "Nguyen, best guess at range for a clean disabling shot?"

Morgan had done Nguyen's job and knew what the answer should be...but Nguyen's comfort with the precision levels of her weaponry wasn't Morgan's, and better the job done at all than done the way Morgan would have.

"Two light-seconds at most, sir. Five hundred thousand klicks would be better."

"I don't believe a difference of a few seconds is going to bankrupt us, Lesser Commander," Morgan replied. "Stand by to disable Target Alpha's engines at five hundred thousand kilometers."

They were gaining at twenty percent of lightspeed, but they were still twenty light-seconds behind their target and over a light-minute from Bravo.

Morgan could run through half of the possible scenarios at a glance. There was no way Bravo was evading her shuttles or Alpha was evading her.

She tapped a command on the screens around her chair, activating the transmission Nystrom had prepared.

"Unidentified ships, this is Captain Morgan Casimir of the A!Tol

Imperial Navy warship *Defiance*," she said, any pretense at friendliness gone. "Neither of you can escape me. Neither of you had anything to fear until you tried.

"You have twenty seconds from receipt of this message to cut velocity and prepare to be boarded, or I will fire to disable your vessels and you will be boarded regardless."

The message flashed into space and Morgan leaned back in her chair.

"Standing by to fire on your time stamp, sir," Nguyen told her. "Lines up neatly with the five hundred thousand klick mark." She paused. "Do you think they'll stand down?"

"If they were going to, they already would have," Morgan replied. "No, Commander Nguyen, the only question that remains is whether they're armed and stupid."

"No, they're both," Nguyen sighed in response. "I have missile launches on the screen. I make it six standard interface-drive missiles. Point-seven *c*."

"Inform Commander Vichy he'll have incoming fire shortly," Morgan replied. "Disable those missiles, Commander Nguyen. Then disable that ship."

IT WASN'T EVEN A FIGHT. *Defiance* had an entire arsenal of deployable parasite, antimissile drones, plus onboard antimissile plasma cannons and a dozen other antimissile systems. If Morgan hadn't been making a point, she would have simply taken the missiles against the cruiser's shields.

Instead, she left it to Nguyen. Hyperfold cannons vaporized all six missiles easily a million kilometers from *Defiance*. More hyperfold cannon shots pecked carefully at the freighter, bracketing it again and again.

Morgan half-expected them to surrender during the ten seconds Nguyen toyed with them. Instead, they were still grimly trying to run when *Defiance* crossed the half-million-kilometer line and the hyper-fold cannons fired one last time.

Target Alpha stopped dead in space as Nguyen destroyed her power generators. The shots were perfectly calculated, triggering safety mechanisms that blasted the fusion reactors into space before they could gut the vessel they supported—and without power, the velocity provided by the interface drive vanished.

"Target Alpha disabled," Nguyen reported calmly.

"El-Amin, bring us up next to her. Nguyen, disable any weapon systems that twitch. Rogers—which platoon commander is left aboard?"

"Speaker Marquez, sir," Rogers told her over their private channel. "Vichy's most experienced platoon commander."

"Good choice," Morgan conceded. "Get him moving. Does he need support?"

"He doesn't think so," the First Sword said drily. "I've got Speaker Susskind assembling the MPs for a second wave if needed."

"Good choice," Morgan repeated. "Keep us in the loop. I need to check in on the Marines."

CHAPTER THREE

"OH, LES CRÉTINS," PIERRE MUTTERED TO HIMSELF.

Target Bravo, which they knew almost nothing about, had apparently decided that her sister ship's example was a good one to follow. Instead of near-suicidal idiocy.

"Pilots, evasive maneuvers," he ordered. "Gunners, target those launchers."

The assault shuttles couldn't fight a real warship, but the one advantage his weapons *did* have was precision. Proton beams had once been the main beam armament of the Imperial Navy, but in the era of the plasma lance and the hyperfold cannon, they were entirely obsolete.

Except for in the hands and tentacles of the A!Tol Imperial Marines.

The helmet of the Battalion Commander's power armor was showing him a three-dimensional model of his assault wing. The computer happily drew in white lines as the shuttle's spinal proton beams fired.

None of the launchers on Target Bravo got a second shot off, and none of their missiles even hit.

Crétins indeed.

"En avant, vite," he ordered. His Marines' translators could handle French easily enough, though he'd switch to English if he was giving complicated orders. He didn't *like* the crude language, but it was humanity's international tongue and had become their interstellar tongue.

The shuttles responded to his orders promptly, lunging in toward the freighter.

"Watch sector six," one of the pilots barked. "I've got what looks like a heavy plasma cannon turret."

"Then take it out," Pierre snapped. A moment later, the turret opened up, spitting heavy fire toward his shuttles. It was a ground-support installation that had no business on a starship—but the rounds could give his shields a headache if they hit.

His enemies weren't the only crétins around, it seemed!

"Someone shoot that, s'il vous plaît," he barked. The turret vanished while he was speaking, two proton beams intersecting on the weapon platform.

"Watch for other weapon systems; they clearly expected someone to be boarding them," he ordered as they swept in.

"Or were planning on boarding someone else," a pilot muttered. Pierre intentionally didn't register which one.

"Conceivable," he agreed. "That turret would make fine support for boarding a civilian ship. Either way, faites attention. Be careful."

Two more plasma turrets emerged as they approached, this pair extending from behind concealed plating to try to take his people by surprise. Pierre Vichy would have been *quite* upset if any of his people had been so lackadaisical as to get themselves shot, but they lived up to his basic expectations and vaporized the new turrets in prompt order.

"Contact in ten seconds," his shuttle's pilot reported. "Brace."

Pierre grinned behind his power-armor helmet, confident that none of his people could see his momentary burst of anticipation. It would never do for the soldiers to think their commander *enjoyed* this kind of thing.

"Shuttle six, contact." One of his other pilots had made it in first, and Pierre's grin faded. He'd have to talk to his shuttle pilot later.

"Shuttle one, contact."

At least his shuttle was second.

"Allez! Vite, vite!" he barked.

His Marines were already moving and Pierre followed the first squad out, a plasma rifle in his own hands.

"Incoming fire," the lead trooper reported. "I don't think I saw armor, but they've got at least a few bipod-mounted plasma rifles."

"Species?" Pierre demanded. "Do we have an ID?"

"Saw at least three," the trooper replied. "Suit identified humans and Pibo. Didn't get a good enough visual to ID the others."

"Understood." Pierre was reviewing the maps his people were feeding him, and his system was matching them against documents in the assault shuttle's database. "Computers have identified the model of the ship," he told his people as the match popped up.

Merde. His command platoon wasn't close to anything of value, though he at least had platoons near the bridge and Engineering.

"All platoon commanders," he barked, switching to the command channel. "Your suits should have identified the vessel. Move to the closest critical components. We are facing resistance from human and Pibo armed crew in the central deck. Maintain communication and secure the vessel. Advise if your situation becomes fraught, mes amis. En avant!"

He studied the map near him.

"We are closest to the cargo bay," he told the Marines. "That they are defending as strongly here suggests that the cargo is valuable to them. We must progress. Grenades, s'il vous plaît."

Pierre had no illusions about what his soldiers thought about him. He was "that prissy French fuck." So long as his men didn't say that to his face and followed his orders, he didn't even care.

A dispenser in his suit popped a grenade into his hand as the three troopers with grenade launchers stepped forward.

"Minimum dispersion," he ordered as he set his own grenade. "We want to remove the barricade, not damage the cargo or where we must walk.

"Now. *Throw*."

Each of the launchers sent a burst of grenades around the corner, and Pierre and the other Marines followed up with thrown grenades. The suit guided his throw to make sure it ricocheted into his target, though he refused to let the computers take over.

The systems could and he was *told* it would be more accurate, but he wasn't going to trust it.

Three dozen plasma grenades went off in the space of a few seconds, and Pierre didn't even need to give an order for his people to charge in their wake. The first squad of his command section was around the corner when he turned it himself, plasma rifles flashing in the hallway.

Their grenades had destroyed whatever lighting had existed, leaving the fight in an eerie darkness lit only by the blue-white flashes of modern plasma weaponry. Pierre had no trouble following what was going on—and it was very clear the fight was already over.

"Hold fire," he snapped. "Secure prisoners."

They probably weren't getting any from this lot, he knew. The grenades had probably been overkill—but, on the other hand, all of his Marines were still alive.

"No life signs," the squad leader reported. "Area secure." She paused for a moment before continuing carefully. "Enough of them were still shooting when we charged that we might have overreacted, sir."

"That's for the debrief, Squad Leader," Pierre snapped. It was entirely possible that only some of the defenders had been shooting, but none of them had been actively trying to surrender, either. There'd be a review later, but that was for *later*.

"Move up on the cargo compartment; squad three take the lead," he ordered. As the power-armored figures swept around him, he cycled his coms to the command channel.

"Platoon commanders, report," he snapped. "Bridge?"

"Bridge has a bit more than I'd expect for a civvie ship," the Marine in charge of Alpha Company's Third Platoon reported. "Deployable fortifications, heavy weapons, some power armor.

"No losses yet and we're pushing them back. We'll have the bridge in fifteen minutes, sir, but I can't promise it's going to be very intact."

"Understood. Engineering?"

"In our hands," his Second Company commander, Oghenekaro Hunter, reported. "Not much left after the shuttle shot the power cores to hell. They didn't defend it, and I have three platoons with me." He paused. "Bravo-Four has life support as well. Permission to send Bravo-Three to reinforce."

"*Oui,* do it," Pierre replied. His display showed him his other platoons as they checked in. Alpha Company was spread all over the ship. Alpha-One was with him, and Alpha-Three was assaulting the bridge, but the other three platoons had landed all across the front half of the ship.

Bravo Company had landed closer together, but one of their platoons was still aboard *Defiance*. If Company Commander Hunter had pulled three of his platoons together, he was doing better than Alpha was.

Unacceptable, really. Pierre was going to have to talk to his First Sword, Company Commander Mikko Comtois, later.

"Alpha-Five, Alpha-Four, converge on Alpha-Three," he ordered, assessing those two as closest to the bridge. "They're going to defend the bridge hardest. Alpha-Two, join Alpha-One; we're en route to the cargo section and the crew seems determined to protect that region."

A chorus of acknowledgments echoed in his com, and Pierre turned his attention back to the situation around him. He'd kept up with the command platoon half-unconsciously, and his map showed they were approaching the main cargo compartment.

He had no idea what the ship might be carrying, but he also had no idea what the hell the damn thing was doing out there. They were a long way from anywhere of importance.

"Contact! Multiple contacts—power armor closing!"

PIERRE HADN'T TRULY REGISTERED that his Alpha-Three Platoon commander had mentioned power armor. No civilian ship had any such thing. Power armor was licensed and restricted. Even planetary and ducal militias had problems getting enough.

There shouldn't be *any* of it aboard a random civilian ship on the edge of nowhere. If he'd taken the time to think about it, he would have guessed that Alpha-Three had encountered something rigged up from civilian heavy work suits or something similar.

Fortunately, Pierre and his people were professionals, and even as he was arguing with himself over whether the strange ship's crew could have proper power armor, he was giving the correct orders.

"Danger close! Set guns for minimum range, minimum dispersion. Pull Third Squad back!"

He *probably* should have left the orders to Company Commander Comtois or Speaker Olimpia Newport, but given that he was in the middle of the firefight himself, he couldn't not be involved.

It took him a moment to consciously recognize the reason why he'd given the orders he had, too. Third Squad had moved out in a careful column of pairs, scouting the doors as they passed them.

What had allowed them to safely progress when they assumed they were facing lower-tier opposition left them extended and vulnerable facing enemies with similar gear. The scan data suggested that the power-armored troopers were closing on them *through* the walls, with a cavalier disregard for their own ship's infrastructure.

Pierre didn't need to give more orders, though. Newport was already in motion, organizing the two squads into a receiving formation with an equal disdain for minor obstacles like walls and doors.

There was a gap for Third Squad to fall back into and a series of interlocked lanes of fire that took advantage of the fact that a plasma beam intended to take down power armor wasn't even going to be slowed by standard steel walls.

"Targets clear," Newport's voice said calmly. "They're adjusting to intercept Third Squad. On my mark, Marines...Third Squad...*drop*."

The armor wasn't really designed for the men and women in it to hit the ground, but the ten Marines in Third did the best they could. Their profile was cut at least in half, clearing the lines of fire to the soldiers closing in around and behind them.

No one waited for a second order from the officers. Their sensors could pick up the power armor through the walls, and their comrades were out of the line of fire. Pierre picked his own target and opened fire with the rest of the platoon, the maximum-focus, maximum-power burst hitting in the center of his target's torso.

Not every species known to the Imperium was humanoid, and not even every humanoid species kept vital organs where humans expected them to be—but very few beings still functioned if you vaporized the core bits keeping their limbs attached to each other.

His target certainly didn't. Icons flashed on his heads-up display, and the power signature the platoon's sensors were tracking went dark. There'd been sixteen power-armored soldiers closing on them, presumably trying to take Third Squad out without dealing with the rest of the platoon.

They'd underestimated the sensor capabilities of Imperial power armor, and that was the end of their short-lived attempt at tactical brilliance. Eighteen plasma rifles fired at sixteen targets. Two stayed up long enough to attempt to return fire, but they clearly didn't have sensors that could target through the ship's walls.

"Bien, so they have merde power armor," Pierre observed aloud.

"I'm still concerned that they have power armor at all. En avant, Speaker Newport. I am now *very* curious as to what these people are carrying."

———————

THE CARGO COMPARTMENT had been reinforced with heavier armor than the rest of the ship's interior. That was probably a good thing, Pierre reflected as he touched the scar marks from his people's plasma fire.

They hadn't exactly been checking their backstops when they opened fire, and bolts that went through power armor kept going a *long* way when they missed.

"Casing is intact; we didn't damage anything," Newport told him. "Standard schematics of the class show the entrance here, though."

"Which it clearly is not," Pierre confirmed. "Split into squads, Commander. One goes up and sweeps the floor above us to port. One sweeps to port here. Alpha-Two will be here momentarily and they will sweep to starboard.

"One squad remains with myself and Company Commander Comtois," he concluded. "We will relocate when we have located the entrance."

He studied the casing. It wasn't quite up to the same standard as his Marines' armor, which suggested other possibilities.

"While the other squads search for the proper entrance, the squad that remains here will work on an entrance of our own," he told Newport and Comtois, adding the Company Commander to the channel as an afterthought.

"The suits' blades can get through this," Comtois agreed. Like Pierre, Comtois was from France. Unlike Pierre, Comtois didn't properly value his heritage and had acquired the same more-American-than-anything-else, near-accentless English as most humans in Imperial service.

"It'll take us a few minutes; finding a door would be faster, but we can do it," he concluded.

"Exactly the plan," Pierre confirmed. "One squad remains here and makes a door; the others sweep for the original entrance. I refuse to be locked out by these crétins."

CHAPTER FOUR

THE PANEL OF ARMORED HULL HIT THE FAR WALL WITH A resounding clatter. At some point while they'd been hacking the wall apart, the freighter's artificial gravity had failed. Given the mess the battle for the ship had created, Pierre wasn't even surprised.

"Move in!" Comtois barked. Four Marines were through the hole before he'd even finished shouting.

"Clear!" one of them reported after a moment. "Looks like we cut into a bloody museum. The fuck is this?"

Pierre forced himself to wait until at least a full squad had gone through the hole before following his Marines in. Leading from the front was all well and good for motivating people, but the Imperial Marines were also clear that leading from the *very* front was damn stupid for an officer.

The Marine's comment on the space they'd entered wasn't wrong. Shelves and benches were spread around the space they'd entered, each covered in bits of stonework and metal. Each piece had a tag, presumably including an electronic component Pierre couldn't read yet, but they looked like random debris to him.

So long as none of his people touched anything, it would all stay where it was. Anything that was touched was going to go flying in the zero gee, though.

"Record everything," Pierre ordered. "We're probably going to hand this over to actual scientists to study, but if something happens, I want every piece of data we can get."

There was no logical reason for there to be a ship this far out with a cargo hold full of archeological artifacts. It made no sense at all.

Pierre crossed to one of the shelves as his people checked on the exterior of the compartment they were in. It was too small to be the entire hold, which meant someone had parked a container in the main hold and they'd cut into that instead of the main space without knowing.

Some of the pieces looked familiar to him, but the coding wasn't. He scanned a tag into his system and inhaled sharply.

"Baise-moi," he snarled. "These are Imperial initial catalog tags. They didn't rob a museum. They robbed a *dig site*."

"There are no dig sites out here, sir," Comtois told him. "That makes no sense."

"Check what your system reads of the tags," Pierre retorted. "They're ours, which means all of this"—he gestured at the stacks of cataloged debris around them—"is from an official Imperial archeology site. So, either there's one around here that you and I don't know about, or this got hauled a long way for a covert handoff."

"Covert handoff would explain why they're out here and why they tried to run and then fight," his Company Commander noted. "What did we stumble into, sir?"

"J'sais pas," Pierre replied. "But I think we're going to find out. Crack this container, Comtois. I want to know everything that's in the cargo bay and everything that's on the damn ship ASAP."

"Understood."

Pierre grimaced and switched channels.

"Hunter, report," he ordered.

"Engineering and Life Support are secure," his other Company Commander reported. "We've secured the entirety of the rear third of the ship. Base ship class schematics were useful, but this ship's been modified beyond belief. Missile launchers, boarding shuttles... this is a pirate, sir."

"I'd got that," Pierre ground out. "Are we in control of those systems?"

"Her weapons are wrecked or unpowered, sir. It looks like there might be one or two with local capacitors, and I have squads on their way right now. I shut down all power to see if we could keep the computers intact."

"That's why we don't have gravity, is it?"

"Doesn't hurt us. If they're half-competent, it won't bother them either, but it seemed useful."

"Keep it down for now," Pierre ordered. Hunter wasn't wrong, even if Pierre hadn't thought of it himself. "Keep sweeping forward; let's get this ship locked down. Have you secured a location to put prisoners yet?"

There was a long pause.

"We haven't managed to take any yet, sir," Hunter said slowly. "I don't know who the *fuck* these people are, but they're all armed and none of them are surrendering. They're all Imperial—I've seen humans, Pibo, Yin, and Ivida so far—but I'm not used to seeing even pirates fight like this."

"Understood," Pierre said. "Let's *try* to take some prisoners, Company Commander. We've neutralized most resistance outside the bridge. Have your people deploy suit stunners when it's safe to."

The power-armor suits had two built-in weapon systems: the extendable force-blades they'd used to open up the walls, and a set of stunners that were definitely able to non-lethally take down any Imperial member race.

Strange new aliens would be far riskier, but if everyone aboard the pirate ship was from the Imperium, the suits would auto-adjust and take them down safely. Whether the crétins wanted to be taken prisoner or not.

"Bridge status?"

"Hold one," Speaker Tahira Qadir replied. Pierre bit back a hot retort as the audio channel recorded the sound of multiple plasma bolts being fired.

"Sorry, sir. Bridge is still in hostile hands," the woman said grimly. "We hit the final interior defense and they have heavy positional weapons. It's like they expected to be facing some kind of onboard mutiny at some point."

She paused.

"Bastards even have a portable anti-grenade system. Lost two Marines trying that. We're down over two squads, sir, though most are only wounded. Three dead."

"Understood," Pierre said grimly. "You're up to three platoons?"

"It's not helping as much as I'd like," Qadir told him. "The hull here has been reinforced; even cutting through isn't opening up options." She sighed. "They've got to be nearly out of crew to resist at this point, but they're defended against grenades and stun fields, and I don't see any secondary approaches.

"Permission to assault, sir."

Pierre muted his microphone for a moment to curse in French. A frontal assault would be the fastest way to resolve this, but even with power armor, charging into fixed heavy weapons was suicide. They could easily lose an entire platoon taking the bridge.

Qadir could launch it without his permission, but she hated the idea as much as he did.

"Denied," he finally decided. "Let me get Hunter and Comtois on this channel." He linked the two Company Commanders in.

"Qadir, brief them," he snapped. "Let me think."

"Sirs, we have three platoons investing the bridge, but even the base interior walls around here have been heavily reinforced," she laid out. "The bridge itself has warship-grade compressed-matter armor. There is only one direct approach, and that's protected by built-in heavy weapons with localized power supply."

There were several seconds of silence before either of the commanders spoke.

"This isn't a pirate, sir," Hunter said into the quiet. "This is a fucking slaver. *Ex*-slaver, I hope, but...the ship's too clearly built for it."

"I concur," Comtois added. "We're in the rest of the cargo compartment, and it is definitely set up for prisoner transport. Some of it's been repurposed for more of the crap they pulled from the dig site, but scans suggest at least one section has prisoners, sir."

Pierre's people had shot a lot of holes through the ship. Atmosphere was only slightly more reliable than gravity—and they'd turned the gravity off.

"Please tell me it's locally sealed," Pierre said.

"All six prisoner compartments are sealed with local atmosphere," Comtois confirmed. "At least one is populated, and one other might be. We're checking, but it looks like they might be set up to be gassed or even have the air evacuated individually."

Slaver, all right.

"That gives me an idea," Pierre said softly. "The bridge has lost control of the ship, yes?"

"The ship has no power until I turn the auxiliary generators back on," Hunter replied. "But the moment I do that, the bridge has as much control as ever."

"Then cut them off," Pierre ordered. "Seal them up in their little armored box. No life support, no gravity, no control of the ship. Cut off everything.

"Even if they're in full enviro suits, that only gives them a few days. We are a long way from anywhere, mes amis. If the bridge crew can't break out, then they're not a threat worth spending lives to break into. Vous comprenez?"

"Yes, sir," Qadir said gratefully. "I'll get the platoons here busy cutting. What about the main access?"

"You've got barrier foam grenades, oui?" Pierre asked. The tools were designed to create a plasma fire–resistant chest-high barricade, since power armor didn't lend itself to prone firing positions.

"We do."

"Set them to maximum height and then use them all," he ordered. "Seal them in until someone finds a radio and asks for us to let them out."

That got him surprised chuckles from his people.

"Once that's done and the bridge is neutralized, we'll sweep the rest of the ship and bring power back up. Comtois, have some of your people bring portable airlocks up from the shuttles. We need to talk to the prisoners and free them, but let's not risk losing atmosphere in the prison containers."

Hopefully, the prisoners could even tell him what the hell the pirates had stolen or who they were.

"REPORT, BATTALION COMMANDER."

Morgan Casimir's accent had always set Pierre's hackles up. A woman who had spent as much time around the world as *Defiance*'s Captain shouldn't, to his mind, sound like a moderately educated American.

Even the verbally beige accent most Imperial officers affected would be better to his ears.

"We have mostly secured the vessel and are in the process of neutralizing the bridge to finalize that status," Pierre said calmly. "The vessel had significant internal fortifications, and the crew has fought like maniacs.

"We have secured the cargo bay, which appears to have been rigged for the slave trade. That minimizes my guilt over the defenders' casualties," he admitted, "especially as there appear to be at least thirty or forty prisoners in the bay, along with a large quantity of properly cataloged archeological artifacts."

"Archeological artifacts, Commander?" Casimir asked with an odd tone to her voice.

"Yes, Captain. I'm uncertain of the source, but I'm hoping some of the prisoners will be able to assist me in locating it," he told her.

"The tagging system and details are definitely Imperial Archeology Institute Standard. I'm sending you a sample."

And he wasn't going to admit to Casimir that he'd needed his computer to recognize that.

Her pause stretched longer than he was expecting and ended in a grim-sounding sigh.

"Understood, Battalion Commander," she said in harsh formal tones. "Inform all your people that the existence of the cargo is classified. It is *not* to be discussed with the rest of *Defiance*'s crew."

"Sir?" Pierre asked, stunned.

"That is an order, Battalion Commander," Casimir told him. "None of your people are cleared for this. I'm probably going to have to change that, but it depends on who the prisoners are. How quickly will we be in touch with them?"

What the merde was that debris?

"I understand, Captain Casimir," he replied slowly. "I suggest, however, that at least *I* have need to know now."

"That's my decision, not yours, Battalion Commander," she said harshly, then sighed. "You're probably right, but I might even need to kick it upstairs. Secure that ship, Vichy. We don't have much else to go on."

"Sir? What happened to the other ship?" Vichy asked.

"They self-destructed, attempting to take shuttle ten with them," she replied. "Your people are fine, they underestimated the survivability of a Marine assault shuttle, but we only have *one* set of evidence now. Given what you've found, that makes me very, *very* nervous. Whatever happens, Battalion Commander, those prisoners and those artifacts must be extracted intact. We're on our way to you, ETA ten minutes."

"Yes, sir."

The channel dropped and Pierre stared off into the air for several seconds.

What the merde was going on?

CHAPTER FIVE

Morgan stood off to the side as the rescued prisoners were ushered aboard *Defiance*, wrapped in blankets the Marines had produced from their emergency stores. Vichy's people had pulled thirty-seven people from the pirate ship...and taken exactly four prisoners from the crew.

"Susskind, I want IDs on these people ASAP," she told the young man standing at her left elbow. The Speaker—equivalent to a full Lieutenant in the Duchy of Terra's Militia—wore a blue uniform that contrasted with her own black and gold or the Marine's dark green, marking him as one of the Imperial Navy's military police.

The senior cop on *Defiance*, in fact. Morgan was grimly certain the cruiser really needed more than a single overstrength platoon of forty cops. In theory, Susskind could second bodies from the ship's three hundred Marines, but *Defiance* had eleven hundred and fifty souls aboard.

Forty MPs didn't seem like much against eleven hundred military personnel with all of the trouble they typically got into.

"We have some tentative IDs from Battalion Commander Vichy's people," Susskind told her. "I'm...hitting security barriers when I try to figure out where they're supposed to be though, sir."

Morgan sighed.

"That's what I expected," she admitted. "You're not cleared, Speaker. Get the IDs and send them to me. Commander Rogers will conduct the interviews and the prisoner interrogations."

"With all due respect, Commander Rogers is—"

"Cleared for this affair and you aren't," Morgan said grimly. "I've already got a note up the chain to request a broader clearance for *Defiance*'s crew, but I don't have that authority."

"Sir, they appear to be from an archeological dig," Susskind pointed out.

"I know," she confirmed. "And more than that is classified. Get those IDs, Speaker."

She left Susskind behind as she saw Vichy emerge from the latest shuttle. There were no more rescuees or prisoners on this one. The Marine CO had apparently sent them back first, along with his wounded and dead.

"Battalion Commander," she greeted him.

"Ma Capitaine," he replied smoothly. Morgan had heard that some women found French accents sexy—it was apparently part of why her youngest half-sister was studying in Paris—but her first experience with them had been with a family friend she'd called "Uncle Jean" for fourteen years...and then "Sir" until he died defending Earth.

And in her mind, Pierre Vichy was a poor substitute for Jean Villeneuve, the man who'd successfully defended Earth against the Kanzi and Taljzi.

"Report," Morgan ordered.

The Marine paused to consider the situation.

"Vessel is secure but crippled," he said crisply. "Thirty-seven prisoners were rescued; all appear to be archeologists of some kind. The ship's cargo holds contain a large quantity of cataloged debris presumably retrieved from a site of some significance and value.

"It all looks like rocks and broken metal to me, sir," he concluded. "What is classified about all of this?"

"That's classified," Morgan snapped instinctively. "Commander Rogers and I are the only people on this vessel cleared for those operations."

"Sir, five of my people died today," Vichy said, very, very softly. "I believe it is reasonable for me to have need to know now. Especially if we will need to act on this data."

As usual with Pierre, Morgan wanted to shut his pompous ass down. But he was right.

"Go get out of your armor and cleaned up," she told him. "My office, at the eighteenth twentieth-cycle."

Hyperfold communication was vastly faster than light but it wasn't instantaneous. *Defiance* wasn't large enough to carry the starcom receiver that would at least mean her answers could come instantly. Her communication loop was nearly two full cycles long— forty-six and a half hours.

She could see in the Frenchman's eyes that he was aware of the same math. She was reading him in on her own authority.

"Fuck this up, Battalion Commander, and I will end your fucking career," she told him flatly. "But you're right. So let's talk."

"I won't fail you, sir."

To Morgan's shock, the French accent was almost gone.

MORGAN WAS on her fourteenth coffee cup of the day when Rogers and Vichy joined her in her office. She gestured them both to seats and studied them carefully.

Rogers looked beat. She'd spent the tenth-cycle since everyone had come aboard talking to the prisoners. Vichy, on the other hand, looked *pristine*.

Morgan could, intellectually, see that the Marine was attractive. He was tall and broad-shouldered, with perfectly defined muscles readily visible against his uniform. Neatly swept-back dark hair and aristocratic features completed a package that she knew had several of the junior women on her ship swooning.

She found him *too* perfect, almost fake. But she'd grown up in the household of the Duchess of Terra, surrounded by heavily muscled, attractive men and women whose job was to die so her stepmother didn't.

Muscles didn't do it for her, in either gender. Her somewhat doughy red-headed second-in-command was more to her taste, though Bethany Rogers was probably the most off-limits person on the ship. And no one aboard the ship *wasn't* off-limits to the Captain.

"System, seal the room under Lost Dragon Protocols," she ordered aloud. Nothing visibly changed, but she could feel the moment the Faraday cage closed.

"We are now fully disconnected from the ship's electronic systems," Morgan continued. "This meeting is now being recorded on an isolated system that is physically present in this office.

"Rogers has been read in on Lost Dragon previously, but for the record, I am reading Battalion Commander Pierre Vichy in on my authority in the aftermath of today's events, as recorded in the primary mission report for *Defiance*, Cycle one seventy-eight, Long-Cycle eleven hundred after Ascension."

Also known as September 9, 2219. Even aboard an entirely human-crewed ship, the A!Tol Imperial Navy ran on Imperial time and calendars, not Terran.

"Are you familiar with the Dragon Protocols, Battalion Commander?" she asked grimly.

"I am, sir," Vichy told her calmly. His accent was back but he'd eased off on it. She was starting to suspect he'd actively played it up around her in the past, which did *not* make her less grumpy with the man.

"Each of the individual Dragon Protocols covers a different set of secrets," Morgan told him. "The penalties for breaching secrecy on a Dragon Protocol remain the same."

The Imperium didn't go in for the death penalty, but breaching a Dragon Protocol would see someone spending the rest of their life working at hard labor in a hostile environment.

It wouldn't be a long sentence.

"There is background information to our operations that is blatantly not included in the Lost Dragon dataset," she told Vichy, to a confirming nod from Rogers.

Unlike Rogers, Morgan knew *that* information as well. She was *definitely* not allowed to share that one.

"Lost Dragon is a particular subset of what I suspect to be a series of operations along our rimward frontier, digging into information we've acquired from unknown sources about Precursor sites and, potentially, further Precursor megastructures."

Neither of the other two officers in the room had been involved in the Arjtal Campaign that had brought down the Taljzi. They'd seen images and sensor data of the planetary-scale constructs of the race that had flourished in the galaxy before any current known civilization and then suddenly died off fifty thousand years before Morgan was born.

Morgan had seen the structures herself, stood aboard ships in the presence of shipyards that had drawn on gas giants to fuel their power reactors, entire planets carved into pieces to access their metal-rich cores—and watched a Dyson swarm's power transmission system go mad and destroy any ship that entered its range.

"We have no illusions that these megastructures are safe for us," Morgan concluded her thought aloud. "But the potential value of studying Precursor sites and artifacts is immense. In the past, such study would have been prevented by the Mesharom, and we are not entirely certain the Mesharom will stay in retreat if they learn the extent of our efforts out here."

The Mesharom had once been slaves of the Precursors. Now they were the galaxy's preeminent race, the "wise elders" among the Core Powers that the A!Tol Imperium was not yet able to challenge. Losses in the Arjtal campaign had gutted the forces the Mesharom had available to project power outside their borders, and they had been missing from the Imperium's space for a decade now.

"We did successfully locate a Precursor facility about three long-cycles ago, and the Imperial Archeology Institute convened a special team of archeologists who have studied Precursor artifacts and are read in on everything we know about the Precursors.

"Speaker Susskind has confirmed IDs on our new passengers," Morgan confirmed for her two senior officers. "All of them are members of that team. None are senior scientists, and we're looking at about a third of the dig team.

"There are still a hundred people, ranging from A!Tol to human, out there somewhere. Potentially, some of them were on Alpha, though it looks like we intercepted them before they could transship anything...or anyone. I'm waiting for confirmation from home whether the dig site is still in communication with anyone."

"If a third of the people from the site are currently in our guest quarters, it can't be, can it?" Rogers asked.

"A lot of people, even military people, will say what they're told with a gun to their head," Vichy noted. The French Marine looked thoughtful. "These pirates could potentially keep the site on the air to avoid suspicion. That might even explain why we only have junior members here."

"I'd love to know what they were planning on doing with them," Morgan said. "The unquestioned good news out of the Kanzi's little civil war is that the slave market is finally dead."

"Mostly dead," Rogers said grimly. "It's underground even in the Theocracy now, but let's not assume that assholes stopped being assholes just because one blue-furred priestess told them to behave."

"Or that all assholes have blue fur," Morgan conceded. "Any luck on the interrogations?"

"Nothing so far," her First Sword admitted. "My training on this is pretty rusty, sir, and we've confirmed they've been immunized against most of the standard Imperial chemical interrogation tools."

"Does that seem odd to anyone else?" Vichy asked. "Pirates don't normally have access to that kind of gear."

"My stepmother managed to buy advanced weapons technology on the black market once," Morgan reminded them. "Tortuga won't deal in slaves anymore, so far as I understand, but they're still host to a thriving black market."

Tortuga was a massive mobile space station belonging to an exiled faction of Laians, the closest Core Power to Imperial space. Exiles from those exiles had settled on Earth and become productive members of the Imperium, but the black-market shipyard refused to come in from the cold as an organized entity.

"That still speaks to a level of resources I wouldn't expect two random pirate ships on the edge of nowhere to have, n'est-ce pas?" the Marine asked. "I accept that much is available if the money exists, but this does not suggest an organization with that kind of money."

"Unless we are simply seeing a tiny portion of that organization," Rogers countered slowly. "They blew up their own ship and, from your own reports, fought suicidally to defend the one you boarded."

"A ship which I must presume did not have a nuclear suicide charge," Vichy admitted. "Or that we were beyond reasonably lucky."

Nguyen had been far more precise in disabling her target than the Marines had been with theirs. There'd been a lot more holes in the ship they'd captured, and Morgan agreed with Vichy's assessment: they had quite possibly accidentally shot the suicide charge.

"I have to assume we're looking at the tip of the iceberg," Morgan told her people. "Potentially even someone who knew we were trying to carry out a covert research expedition out here. We're a long way out from anywhere, on a daisy chain of hyperfold transmitters that only exists because we knew the Precursors had a cluster of installations out here.

"Our closest support is at Kosha—and *we* are Echelon Lord Davor's heavy firepower," she reminded them. The Ivida flag officer based her operations on the mixed civilian-Imperial resupply facility in orbit of Kosha's fledgling colony, leaving her Captains to deploy independently.

Kosha was also sixteen light-years and two hyperfold relay stations behind them and didn't even have a starcom of their own.

"How far are we from the dig site itself?" Vichy asked. "I am guessing it is between us and Kosha?"

"No." Morgan shook her head and gestured a map into existence. "About the same distance from Kosha, with a slightly longer travel time due to the densities. We're six light-years away, three cycles or so, given local hyperspace. Anyone leaving from Kosha would be at least seven or eight cycles."

"They'd only be nine cycles if they came here and swung around," Rogers observed as she looked at the map and the blinking light of the dig site system. "I've seen worse hyperspace densities, but that's still a barrier."

"As of my last messages from Kosha, the Echelon Lord has two destroyers on station," Morgan told them. "I don't see a point in calling for reinforcements that can't make a difference."

She smiled as the decision became obvious.

"We can't haul the pirate ship with us, so we'll take a few hours to empty her cargo bays of the artifacts. We'll flag the location to Echelon Lord Davor for further investigation, and *we* will move to K-Seven-Seven-D-L-K-Six to investigate the fate of the dig site.

"Battalion Commander Vichy, we will almost certainly need to make a forced landing of a captured Imperial facility," she told the Marine. "We need the archeological crew alive. I'd like prisoners from their captors, but preserving our people is the priority. Can you do that?"

"Pas impossible, mais difficile," he replied. She glared at him. She didn't usually wear her translator earbuds aboard *Defiance*—and she wasn't going to *admit* she understood French perfectly. "Not impossible but difficult," he clarified.

"Make a plan," she told him. "Depending on the vagaries of hyperspace, we're looking at as little as two cycles en route. We'll drop out of hyperspace about half a cycle out of D-L-K-Six to pick up our messages, but that's it."

"I wish we had more data on what we can expect for resistance," Rogers said. "If it's more light pirate ships, I'm not worried—but given some of what we're hearing about the Kanzi Clans..."

"Whoever these people are, everyone we've seen so far has been Imperial," Morgan pointed out. "Eleven different Imperial species, according to Vichy's reports, but Imperial."

Their prisoners were three Pibo and an Ivida. Morgan was half wishing she had a member of either species aboard.

"Given that breakdown, I don't expect to see Kanzi out here." She shrugged. "There are heavier ships that end up in pirate hands, but none of them are a match for *Defiance*. Duchess Bond smashed a pirate fleet with a single cruiser with compressed-matter armor and Laian guns. My impression is that pirates haven't upgraded much since then...and *Tornado* is a museum ship these days.

"We'll handle anything that hits us in space. I'm more concerned about getting our people off the ground intact."

"Leave it to the Marines, sir," Vichy promised. "If we have any details on the ground site in the Lost Dragon files that I can use for unclassified training, it will make my life easier, but I will work with whatever I get."

Morgan nodded and ordered her system to disgorge a data chip.

"This goes on your personal device while severed from the ship network only," she warned him.

"Not my first Dragon Protocol, ma capitaine," the Marine told her calmly as he took it.

That raised a mental eyebrow for Morgan. She hadn't known that her Marine CO had been involved in that kind of situation before. Dragon Protocols, after all, were reserved for the things the Imperium was hiding from the Core Powers.

CHAPTER SIX

"I FULLY VALIDATE YOUR DECISION TO READ BATTALION Commander Vichy in on Lost Dragon," the recorded image told her. Echelon Lord Davor was a tall humanoid with dark-red skin and double-jointed limbs. Like all Ivida, her face was motionless and hairless—the race had never evolved the complex array of facial muscles of most humanoids.

"I am explicitly authorizing you to read in as many of your officers as necessary, presuming you follow proper protocol for doing so," Davor continued. "The D-L-K-Six dig site does not report in to me, but I had an agreement with !Lat that he would advise me of any problems they encountered and check in every five-cycle.

"My last report from !Lat was sent only a cycle before your report from D-N-E-Five. I do not assess any reasonable possibility that the Lost Dragon site lost a third of its team and had them moved to D-N-E-Five in a single cycle, so either !Lat is being held prisoner or is part of whatever is going on."

Davor paused and gave a strange one-shouldered shrug, the equivalent to a human shaking their head.

"!Lat is even worse than most of his race at concealing his feelings, in my experience, so either he has been plotting a very long course or they are digitally altering the images to hide his true skin tone."

The A!Tol that ruled the Imperium looked like a mix of Earth's squid and octopi, and their skin changed tones with their moods. They *could* lie, but it was obvious to anyone who knew their race.

If !Lat was speaking under duress, his skin should have made that extraordinarily obvious. If the hyperfold transmission to Kosha had been digitally altered, though, that should show up to an investigation.

"I have our cyber people on the video already," Davor told Morgan, "but I don't expect to get a final answer in time. Based on the physical evidence already in your possession, we must assume that the D-L-K-Six dig site is compromised and has been compromised for an extended period.

"The first objective and clean view of the system we're going to get is when you arrive. I trust your judgment, Captain Morgan Casimir. I have deployed one of our destroyers to D-N-E-Five to pick up the pirate ship and bring it to back to Kosha.

"Your survey mission is officially cut short," the Echelon Lord concluded. "Regardless of what you find at D-L-K-Six, I expect you to bring the personnel you've already retrieved from the pirates back to Kosha for counseling and potential return to our core space.

"I await your report from the dig site, Captain. Warm tides to you."

The recording ended and Morgan sat silently at her desk for a few seconds. *Warm tides* was a strange idiom to come from a species born on an overheated world with no oceans, but that was why the Ivida were an "Imperial Race" rather than an Imperial subject species.

The A!Tol had grown very good at uplifting cultures without destroying them, but their first few attempts had not been so success-ful. The Pibo, the Ivida and the Tosumi had all lost most of their original culture, replaced with an amalgam of their culture and A!Tol culture.

Some parts were inevitably different—A!Tol reproduction was best described as *parasitic*, whereas the Tosumi and Pibo both laid eggs and the Ivida were pair-bonding live-birthers like humans—but the Imperial Races were far closer to the A!Tol in culture than to their ancestors.

Even the A!Tol regarded the Imperial Races' privileged position in the Imperium as poor recompense for that.

Shaking away the vagaries of thought, Morgan deactivated the Dragon Protocol seal on her office and took another swallow of her coffee. The message from Davor hadn't changed much, though the official support from her superiors was valuable.

Defiance was a half-cycle of hyperspace flight from their target— plus or minus a twentieth-cycle or so; hyperspace defied exact calculation.

K77DLK6 was probably going to end up being a human colony. The habitable planet, Beta, was slightly warmer and wetter than Earth but had a perfect atmosphere and gravity. Even without the Lost Dragon site on Beta, Morgan would have paid close attention to the system.

She pulled up the data. The star was on the cool side of the F-series, with the habitable zone closer in than in Sol. One burnt-out cinder in a close orbit, three gas giants and a massive ball of ice beyond the habitable zone...and two decently sized planets *in* the habitable zone.

Beta would make for a tropical paradise colony, warm enough to almost completely lack ice caps and cold enough to be habitable even at the equator. Gamma was much less congenial, but the ice sheets floated in salt water and the atmosphere suggested an active ecosystem underwater and on the couple of less-frozen continents.

Beta's moon was more appealing than Gamma to Morgan, and while that rock's atmosphere had enough oxygen for humans, there was enough chlorine in it to make the moon a toxic mess. With only a third of a gee for gravity, the moon wasn't appealing to most people—but the records showed there was an old Precursor installation on it, too.

For some strange reason, the dig team had started with the Precursor colony site on Beta.

Morgan tapped a command, double-checking that she'd dropped the Dragon Protocol seal before she did so.

"All department heads, this is the Captain speaking," she told her senior officers. "Check your people, check your systems. I'll be on the bridge in two hundredth-cycles—thirty minutes—and if there is *any* reason *Defiance* should hesitate to go into battle, I need to know by then.

"Start the clock, Rogers. We go to battle stations before we enter D-L-K-Six. I'm not taking any chances with this ship."

CHAPTER SEVEN

RIN DUNST WAS NOT, IN HIS CAREFULLY CONSIDERED OPINION, cut out to be a prisoner. Enough of their jailers were human for him to be certain they *knew* they were underfeeding the captives, but the archeologist would also freely describe himself as "plushly upholstered."

Twelve hundred calories of Universal Protein a day was not cutting it. He stared down at the unappetizing bar for a long moment as his stomach growled...and then he heard the coughing from the next cell.

A cold was a common-enough problem, even in the twenty-third century, but it shouldn't have been life-threatening. Even without the medications in the infirmary, Kelly Lawrence was an athletic young woman who'd been in decent health.

Except that same athleticism meant she didn't have the body fat reserves for a starvation diet, and her metabolism expected more. He glared at the bars of the improvised cage he'd been stuffed in for several seconds, then tore the UP bar in half.

"Lawrence, come here," he told the sick woman as he crouched by the bars between them. There was no privacy in the setup their captors had stuffed them in. He supposed they were lucky that the pirates—or *whatever* the hell these people were!—had even put roofs over the outdoor cages.

"Take this," he told her, offering half the UP ration through the bars. "Calories should help you fight that off."

"What about you?" Lawrence said, then coughed again. Looking at her was painful. They'd only been imprisoned for a few weeks at most —though Rin would admit he'd lost track of time—and he could already see her ribs through what had been a tight-fitting athletic tank top.

He smacked his stomach.

"I've still got some dieting to do," he said with false cheer. "*You* need to eat."

She took the bar without arguing further, scooting away from him like she expected him to change his mind.

"Hey, back from the bars!" a voice barked. One of their guards had apparently come around while Rin had been focused on Lawrence.

Rin obeyed. He'd done what he needed to, so he turned to face the speaker and spread his hands to show he wasn't hiding anything.

His translator earbuds had been taken when they'd thrown him in, so the humanoid in the hooded cloak was using a speaker for their translator to produce English. The long black cloaks did a good job of hiding the species of the wearer, but Rin could pick out the people using translators from the people speaking English naturally. About a quarter of their captors were human, which just pissed him off.

This particular guard was a Yin. Rin couldn't speak their language—like the A!Tol language, it required a beak—but he under-stood it just fine without a translator.

"You Dunst?"

"Who's asking?" Rin demanded.

He discovered that the guard was hiding a neural projector under his cloak the hard way, his nerves exploding in a blast of superheated pain. Rin hadn't even known the things *existed*, though if he'd thought about it, he'd have assumed something similar had to be used by the various slaver scum of the galaxy.

"Are you Rin Dunst?" the Yin guard asked again.

"Yes," Rin ground out. "What do you want?"

The cell door swung open.

"You're coming with me," the Yin told him. "We need you to talk to somebody."

That was not a good sign. He knew !Lat had been forced to send the usual messages back to their people in the Imperium from his one conversation with his boss. If they were grabbing Rin, the expedition's theoretical second-in-command...

"Where's !Lat?" he demanded. That, of course, sent him back to his knees in pain.

"They're alive," the guard told him, a surprising moment of mercy. "But we want you this time. Are you coming or bleeding?"

"Coming," Rin conceded. At least out of his cell, he had options. Depending on what they wanted, he might even be able to negotiate a little bit...Lawrence was one of the better computer archeologists he'd ever known. She was no good to anyone dead, not when cheap-as-dirt medicine could kick the cold.

Or maybe he'd just get nerve-shocked into doing their will regardless. Who knew?

Certainly not Rin Dunst, PhD.

———

AS RIN WAS LED out of the rough prison camp, he noted that the enveloping cloaks appeared to be a general fashion statement, not merely a disguise for interacting with the prisoners. They shrouded the identities of the people wearing them, even if some species were more obviously present than others.

The being waiting for him at the entrance to the prefabricated communications tower was one of those. A black cloak could only do so much to conceal the fact that Rin was facing a mobile stack of fungus, a Frole.

Frole speech was a series of burps and color changes that would have been uninterpretable through a cloak, but the sounds were clear enough as the translator set to work.

"There is a ship in the system," the Frole told Rin. "They are attempting to make contact. You will get them to leave."

The thought of a deal vanished from Rin's mind.

"I don't see that as being overly helpful to myself or my friends," he replied. As expected, he was shocked to his knees, hissing in pain as his nerves insisted he was on fire.

"If you do not convince them to leave, we will be forced to treat you as hostages," the Frole told him, the translated voice perfectly calm. "Including executing at least one of your 'friends' to demonstrate our seriousness.

"We do not want a fight today. Convince the ship to leave, and no one needs to die."

"We're already dying," Rin snapped. He still hadn't risen from his kneeling position and braced himself against another nerve shock. "If you start shooting us, that's practically a mercy."

This time, he didn't get shocked.

"The neural projector cannot kill you, Rin Dunst," the Frole reminded him. "It can make you desire that we had killed you instead. Or would you prefer to watch us demonstrate that function on one of your companions?

"Convince the ship to leave, or the Womb will guide me to the ones you care about most. You will watch them die as painfully as we can conceive. This is our duty."

Frole weren't usually psychopaths, but it seemed every rule had its exceptions. Rin wasn't sure what "the Womb" meant in this case, given that the Frole didn't *have* that organ, but he doubted he wanted to find out.

He struggled back to his feet, glaring at the robed mound.

"Fine," he spat. "But you give us the medical supplies from the infirmary. People are going to start dying from things we can treat in less than a minute, for Christ's sake."

Rin had no idea where the Frole was currently positioning their eyes, but he hoped he was glaring right at them. The Yin who'd dragged him out there raised the projector again, questioningly.

"No, my brother," the Frole told the Yin. "We are not without mercy in our duty. It shall be done, Rin Dunst. Once the ship has turned away, we will allow you access to a medkit and your fellow prisoners."

"I'm not a doctor," Rin objected.

"Perhaps not, but you are the only one who has an opportunity to earn some measure of our trust," the robed Frole told him. "The Children will do their duty, but I will leave your fate to the Womb, not the hands of my siblings.

"Come, Rin Dunst. You play for lives now. Do not test my patience."

The sentient fungus didn't really "turn around." They just started moving backward, readjusting their appendages as they did so.

The Yin behind Rin poked the projector into his back.

"You heard. Move."

———

THE COM TOWER was a prefabricated installation with a twenty-meter-tall building acting as an anchor to a ten-meter-radius transmission dish. The bottom third of the building doubled as a computing and administration center for the site, the middle third was the hyperfold communicator, and the top third was the computer data center and more conventional radio-communications equipment.

!Lat's office had been repurposed as the big squid's prison, and Rin got a solid look at his boss as he passed the A!Tol. !Lat was over two meters tall fully extended, with four locomotive club tentacles and sixteen delicate manipulator tentacles. Normally, the archeologist and administrator was colored a mix of blue and red, since his entire life was driven by his curiosity and excitement.

Rin liked !Lat a lot—and it hurt to see the A!Tol lying listlessly on his couch, his skin the gray-black of exhausted fear and pain.

Even if Rin hadn't already begun to scheme on how to use the situation against their strange captors, any idea of cooperation would have died at the sight of his friend.

More black-robed aliens were in the building, clearly going through the Institute files on the site. Rin wished them luck with that —everything they were doing was secured under Dragon Protocols. Lost Dragon, this particular expedition, was treated relatively openly there.

The background and supporting information the raiders must have been looking for? That wasn't in the base computers. The only computer in the expedition that contained *any* copies of the Forge Dragon, Fallen Dragon, or First Dragon protocol information that underpinned the expedition was implanted in Rin's lower back.

Even *he* couldn't regularly access that data, requiring very specific mental triggers and a state of near self-hypnosis to unlock the implanted computer.

"Here." His Yin guard shoved him into the coms center and forced him into a chair. "You know the system?"

"I do," Rin confirmed, checking over the screens in front of him.

The screen should have had some sensor data, but their trio of survey satellites had been taken out by the attackers in the first wave. It did, however, give him the ID of the ship in system: the A!Tol Imperial Navy ship *Defiance*. The name sounded familiar, but the important part was that it was Navy at all. If it was a *civilian* ship, Rin would have hesitated to drag them into it.

A proper warship? These cloaked escapees from a high school Lovecraft production weren't going to stand a chance.

He tapped a command to play the incoming message.

"D-L-K-Six dig site, this is Captain Morgan Casimir aboard the Imperial vessel *Defiance*," the familiar blonde woman on the screen informed him. Rin knew Morgan Casimir's face—he doubted anyone from the Duchy of Terra didn't know Duchess Annette Bond's stepdaughter.

Her father had given humanity the hyperdrive and the interface drive even before the A!Tol had arrived. Her stepmother had bought humanity the semi-independence of a Duchy after the A!Tol had annexed them, and then led multiple defenses of the star system against external threats.

Morgan Casimir stood in mighty shadows, which had only drawn Earth's paparazzi to her. Rin was only a year older than her, and she had been *the* political celebrity for his age group as a teenager.

"Dig site, please respond; we have been transmitting for ten minutes. Given the security of your expedition, we are now extremely concerned and I am setting a course for Beta."

"Not acceptable," his guard hissed. "Stop them."

"Get out of the camera zone," Rin ordered, uncaring now if the Yin listened. If he got shocked, it wasn't hurting *his* goals there.

Instead, the Yin obeyed. Rin Dunst was now alone in the field of the multiple cameras that would send his holographic image back to Captain Casimir.

"Captain Casimir, this is Dr. Rin Dunst of the Imperial Archeology Institute," he introduced himself. "I am the deputy administrator of this facility and I must warn you not to approach."

He lifted one finger, then lowered it. Up, down. Up, down. Up, down.

"We appear to have picked up a virulent contagion on our way to the D-L-K-Six System," he continued. "Containment protocols have failed and I cannot guarantee the safety of your personnel."

Two fingers this time. Up, down. Up, down. Up, down.

"We're unsure where the contagion is sourced from and I'm unwilling to trust the usual protections as they have already failed. Everyone in the dig site is infected. I believe we can handle this internally and I don't want to expose your crew to potential hazards."

Again with one finger. Up, down. Up, down. Up, down.

Morse code and the SOS signal had been a historical curiosity for Rin. He could only hope that Casimir, who'd been trained in the Duchy of Terra Militia before transferring to the Imperial Navy, had learned it somewhere along the way.

"I am denying you landing permission," he told Casimir. "With the loss of hands, we aren't even in control of our satellites. Beta orbital space is going to be dangerous until the situation is contained."

He cut the recording and leaned back in his chair. If he was very, very lucky, Morgan Casimir had at least someone on staff that would recognize the SOS—and from that, hopefully draw the right interpretation of the *rest* of his message.

Pirates of an unknown source *definitely* qualified as a contagion, in his books.

CHAPTER EIGHT

Morgan and her officers finished watching the recording for the second time, and she shook her head at the sheer gall of the chubby scientist in the hologram.

"We've sent back an acknowledgment and broken off from our course for now," she told the senior officers. "I look forward to meeting Dr. Dunst. Even if I *hadn't* known there was a problem, I would now."

"SOS with his hands and then that dancing around exactly *what* kind of contagion he was talking about," Rogers agreed. "Clever man. What are people picking up from what he's saying?"

"The entire camp is interned," Nguyen told them. "No one escaped. Potentially, something happened to Administrator !Lat."

"Most likely, they aren't up to editing !Lat's skin to be non-damning in a reasonable time frame," Nystrom suggested. "We'd be hard pressed to do it, and I imagine we have better software and hardware than they do."

"And it is perfectly reasonable for the deputy to be talking to us if we didn't already smell a rat," Morgan agreed. "Of course, Dr. Dunst made sure we knew there was trouble. If his 'contagion' is still present and orbital space is still unsafe, we have a problem."

"Pirates on the ground, armed vessels in space," Vichy concluded. "If they see us coming, they will use the prisoners as hostages."

"Which is our biggest problem," Rogers said. "I'll back *Defiance* against every pirate in the Imperium at once, but we want to get those people out."

"Especially Dr. Dunst," Morgan agreed. "For reasons even I am apparently not cleared for, he's flagged as a critical priority in our databases."

He was also in her covert systems as being cleared for two Dragon Protocols Morgan was officially in on. She figured that meant he was probably in at least two more—if nothing else, she didn't *know* the official protocol for distributing the information around how the Precursors had died.

She was under orders to never tell anyone. Ever. No matter what.

"I believe this is mostly going to be a shuttle operation, Battalion Commander," she told Vichy. "I mean, I suppose we could insert shuttles directly from hyperspace, but I've been told the Imperial Marines don't *like* it when I tell them to do that."

It was possible to retrofit the systems from *Defiance*'s hyperspace missiles to allow a shuttle to enter normal space through a gravity well. *Possible* didn't mean *easy*—and it was a hellish ride for anyone on the shuttles in question.

Morgan had been the first officer to suggest it and had joined the Marines on the first of those hellish rides. Operating in a zone where an interface drive meant death-by-malfunctioning-Precursor-technology, they'd been looking at a long ride back out when they'd made the jump, too.

"While your personal specialty has value in many cases, here it would only get us to orbit," Vichy pointed out. "However, *Defiance* took delivery of six of the newest assault shuttles before we began this tour.

"While they are mostly identical to the rest of our shuttle fleet, these six have been equipped with the newest version of our minia-turized stealth field."

Morgan had probably known that, but she'd forgotten. She had enough involvement in the shipbuilding community in the Imperium —through her father—to know that there'd been a fierce debate whether the *Armored Dream*–class ships like *Defiance* should carry a stealth field.

The end conclusion had been that *Defiance* and the other classes of her era were being built to fight Core Powers—and Core Power sensors found even the latest iterations of Imperial stealth technology laughable.

Against a random group of pirates on the edge of nowhere, though, Morgan was regretting that decision.

"How good is it?" she asked bluntly.

"Tests suggest the shuttles will remain invisible to our scanners to ranges as close as half a million kilometers, if we reduce velocity," Vichy told her. "Assuming the pirates are limited to something comparable to the satellites the expedition started with, we should be able to land without being detected."

He shrugged.

"Of course, once we are on the ground, we are extremely vulner-able to orbital fire," he noted. "We would require *Defiance* to secure the orbitals as rapidly as possible."

"If you can get boots on the ground and protect the prisoners, *Defiance* can deal with whatever's in space and send in the rest of your Marines," Morgan replied. "It's your people taking the risk, Battalion Commander. If we're trying to be subtle about it, we're launching you from at least five or six light-minutes away.

"That's a long time for something to go wrong."

Including landing, Morgan eyeballed it at fifteen to twenty minutes. *Defiance*'s hyperspace missiles, her longest-ranged weapons, only had a range of three light-minutes.

"It is, but we have no choice, do we?" He smiled. "Au-delà du possible."

Beyond the possible. A French paratrooper's motto, of course.

"Then the Marines lead the way, Battalion Commander," Morgan confirmed. "We'll be as close behind you as we can, but you're looking at almost ten minutes before we're in orbit once the rocket goes up."

"And three until you're in HSM range," he pointed out. "If my Marines are wiped out in three minutes, Captain Casimir, I will have very strong words for God."

EVEN FROM *DEFIANCE'S* BRIDGE, Morgan could have almost missed the shuttles slipping away. She was specifically watching through some of their more standard sensors as they were supposed to be launching, and the stealthed shuttles were barely a blip even on the tachyon scanners.

They *were* still a blip and she could have tracked and targeted them, but she had a lot less data on what she was looking at than she was used to. It was still clear to her scanners that she was looking at six small craft heading away from *Defiance* at half the speed of light, but it was vaguer than she'd have expected.

"I think our stealth systems have improved more than we give them credit for," Rogers said softly. "Most officers I know wouldn't expect we could conceal a full ship that well, let alone a shuttle."

"Size of the vessel is at least as large an impact as the size of the generator," Morgan pointed out. "If you can get the generator small enough, it's easier to hide a shuttle than a cruiser."

But Imperial stealth tech had definitely advanced by leaps and bounds over the last ten years. The A!Tol Imperium had chosen to focus on other areas than stealth for their own tech development, working up new power sources, shields and weapons. The new generation of battleships being laid down would finally be based around contained black holes.

They'd been working on *that* since Morgan had joined the Navy, and she still wasn't sure she wanted one of them on her ship. She already had a power core at the heart of *Defiance* that could be fed any matter available to hand and convert it directly to energy with about seventy percent efficiency.

Her understanding was the singularity reactors used a version of that which drew on the black hole's own mass, creating a near-infinite fuel supply operating with near-perfect efficiency. She *still* didn't want a singularity on her ship.

The singularity core advancements came from the same source as the new stealth systems though, and she wondered if the Core Powers that had fought the Mesharom would recognize the devices shielding her shuttles.

That was classified under the Fallen Dragon Protocol. She was the only person on *Defiance* cleared to know that they were reverse-engineering Mesharom technology, and that was only because they couldn't hide it from the woman who'd retrieved the tech database they were using.

"It's been a decade of change," she finally conceded to her First Sword. "We got our first stealth systems from the Kanzi, and they sucked. We stole Taljzi systems during the occupation, and we've been working on them since. Still..." She shrugged. "I wonder if the argument over whether *Defiance* and her sisters should have a stealth field should have gone the other way."

"Sir, we are two minutes from the logical point we'd enter hyper-space," El-Amin told her. "What do we do?"

"Bring us to a halt, Commander," Morgan ordered. "We'll wait here for a moment. If they get Dr. Dunst on the line again, I'm sure I can keep everyone talking long enough to let Commander Vichy land his shuttles."

"What does *au-delà du possible* even *mean?*" Rogers asked grumpily. "Prissy Frenchman can't even brag in English."

"'Beyond the possible,'" Morgan told her First Sword. "Motto of one of the French Army's parachute regiments; I don't know which one off the top of my head. One of the ones that survived into the

Franco-German Army. His family traditionally served in the Army before the Annexation."

"Huh. I like it," Rogers admitted. "Wait, you speak French?"

"My honorary uncle was Admiral Jean Villeneuve, who was French to his bones," Morgan reminded Rogers. "I speak French fluently. I'm just not going to give Vichy the satisfaction of admitting that."

She'd learned French to please her "Uncle Jean." She'd learned Cantonese, Japanese and Korean because she'd grown up in Hong Kong. Everything outside those four and English she'd need translator earbuds for, but tradition made the working language of a human-crewed Imperial ship English.

Tradition, it seemed, that hadn't made an impact on Vichy.

"We've completely lost track of the shuttles, sir," Nguyen reported. "They were reducing velocity as they crossed the half-light-minute mark. Estimated landing time is four minutes from...*now*."

CHAPTER NINE

Despite his understanding of the system and his confident front to *Defiance*'s senior officers, Pierre was honestly surprised when his shuttle hit atmosphere without even being shot at.

"Did we pick up anything in the atmosphere?" he asked his pilot. "We can still send a pulse back to *Defiance*."

"I don't know about the Navy, but I find the fact that I didn't see anything suspicious," the pilot told him.

"Oui. C'est pas bon." Pierre shook his head. "Nothing at all?"

"The expedition's satellites are gone and there's nothing in orbit to replace them," the woman confirmed. "I'm gonna guess the pirates are parked on the surface."

"We find out in moments," Pierre noted. "Stand by the weapons, Marine. I believe we can disable a sitting duck before it launches."

Their weapons were designed to disable civilian ships in space. He was quite certain they could disable a ship parked on a planet, regardless of its defenses.

"Horizon on the target in five. Stand by."

It was the moment of truth. This particular version of the stealth field was effective enough in an atmosphere, but it wasn't going to conceal the wake pattern of six shuttlecraft flying at several thousand kilometers an hour.

Pierre gave the pilot a firm nod then put on his helmet and returned to the main cargo bay.

"Marines, there are Imperial citizens on the ground," he reminded them all. "We don't have reliable target identification as to who is and isn't hostile. Stunners first, plasma second. Prisoners are almost as handy as rescued hostages, n'est-ce pas?"

"Oorah!"

That particular Americanism, it seemed, was unavoidable with Marines. Pierre wasn't a fan of it, but he was a fan of the enthusiasm it showed.

He checked the charge on his suit's stunners and accepted a plasma rifle from Company Commander Comtois.

"Ready, Comtois?" he asked.

"We're out of time for that question," the other officer told him. "I make it twenty seconds to the ground."

"Agreed. So, we must be ready."

Comtois's response was cut off by the bottom dropping out of Pierre's stomach.

"Sorry, team, it appears our unexpected infection brought along some antiaircraft guns and is finally awake," the pilot replied. "Please...hold on."

There was an audible *crack* as the shuttle's shields collided with something, presumably a tree. How low had the pilot *taken* them?

"Mon dieu," Pierre murmured to himself as he brought the external cameras up. They were *among* the trees, and only the size and separation of the local arboreal life had kept them to a handful of impacts.

Blinking lights ahead announced their destination, and he inhaled sharply and steadied his grip.

"Ready," he barked, as unnecessarily as his querying Comtois. His Marines were *his* Marines. They would no more be unready than he would go unshaven.

THE SHUTTLES WERE STILL invisible as they tore into the encampment, opening their bays and dropping power-armored Marines as they went. Pierre and his command platoon dropped next to what had appeared to be a motor pool of some kind, covered in multiple sheets of plain tarpaulin.

"Not a motor pool," he observed as he turned to see what was under the rough cover. "We have found the prisoners. Alpha Company, perimeter around the cages. Bravo-Five, the com tower, if you please."

Six shuttles meant he'd only brought one of Bravo's platoons. So, of course, he'd brought Bravo-Five under Speaker Lebeau, both his most experienced platoon commander and another Frenchman.

Sort of. He had a good French family name, anyway.

Even through the suit, he could feel stun fields sweeping the site. Most of the prisoners in the cells were unconscious, which was probably the safest state for them. Their guards, all in a uniform strange black robe-like garment, were less disabled.

Plasma fire started to respond to the stunners, and Pierre was watching everything take shape. He took a shot with his own rifle as he picked out a shooter, a cloaked pirate who had *definitely* been hit with a stunner.

"Those cloaks are stun-proofed," Comtois reported as Pierre realized it himself. "Prisoners are contained and stunned. Our hostage-takers are not."

"If stunners won't work, that's why we carried plasma guns," Pierre replied. "Neutralize them, Marines. We know that Dr. Dunst, at least, is in the tower. We need him alive. Speaker Lebeau—bring him home."

The invisible sweeps of stunfields faded now, and his Marines were returning fire with the precision of the elite soldiers they were. The cloaked defenders were well equipped and determined...but they were not elite soldiers.

Pierre spotted one popping out of cover to try to line a shot up on Comtois and calmly shot the being down. He stepped over and pulled the cloak off the corpse. The hard red face of an Ivida stared blankly up at him.

"All Imperials still," he muttered. "Comtois, are the prisoners secure?"

"The prison compound is under our control," his subordinate confirmed. "There were only a few cloaks moving around; I think the rest are either in the barracks or in the tower."

"What about the dig site itself?" Pierre asked, gesturing toward the set of tents around the edge of the city. He could barely make out the buildings amidst the trees, but the trees didn't conceal everything.

"Possible. I'll detach two platoons to sweep the dig site and the barracks. What about the com tower?"

"It isn't big enough for Lebeau's people, let alone reinforcements," Pierre admitted as he turned to study the prefab structure. "Let's hope this was most of them. It's possible there were only a few people down here."

"If that's the case, sir, we may have another problem. There's no ship down here."

Pierre grimaced.

"Get a pulse out to *Defiance*," he ordered. "It's possible that the ship we encountered was the only one that was here, but I doubt it. Casimir needs to watch her back."

CHAPTER TEN

"No contacts, no contacts," Nguyen repeated softly, the words hanging in the deathly quiet of *Defiance*'s bridge.

"We are three minutes from orbit," El-Amin added. "Under two light-minutes and closing." He paused. "Shouldn't we be seeing something?"

"If there's anything in space, we'd see it," Morgan agreed. "Shouldn't there at least be the expedition satellites?"

"I see a debris field in a decaying orbit that might be one of them," Nguyen replied. "There is nothing in orbit of Beta, sir. Beta-A orbit is clear as well."

"Rogers, do we have an update from the Marines?" she asked her First Sword.

"They've secured the main compound and what appears to be the primary prison site," her First Sword told her. "There are no ships, not even shuttles, landed at the site. Hostiles have dug in to the coms tower and are continuing to resist there, and Vichy has Marines sweeping the edge of the dig site itself."

Everything sounded and looked like the situation was under control, but it didn't smell right.

"Not even shuttles, huh?" she asked aloud. "And nothing in orbit? If their only ship had left, wouldn't they have left behind at least a shuttle?"

"I would have," Rogers agreed. "The moon, sir?"

"Most likely," Morgan agreed. "Nguyen, move the probe net. I want eyes on the far side of Beta-A ASAP."

The drones weren't that much faster than *Defiance* herself. The cruiser was moving toward the planet at sixty percent of lightspeed, and the drones were moving at seventy-five percent.

Even their sublight missiles could only move at eighty-five percent, which seemed to be a hard cap for the interface drive. "Long-range" combat was a question of light-minutes, and the main problem was still often getting into range of an opponent that didn't want to fight you.

"I'll have eyes in thirty seconds," Nguyen reported. "Three drones are already en route; I'm adjusting the pattern to send six."

They were now well within range of every long-range weapon known to Morgan. Her hyperspace missiles had a range of five light-minutes. Her sublight interface-drive missiles had a range of two.

Her shorter-ranged weapons were *much* shorter-ranged, with both her plasma lances and her hyperfold cannons maxing out at fifteen light-seconds. The Imperium had designs for even more powerful weapons than those two—but *those* guns had a range of less than a light-second.

As the Imperial Navy had demonstrated again and again in the Taljzi Campaigns, no modern warship was going to let an enemy they knew had a disrupter inside that range.

"One light-minute," El-Amin reported. "Contacts?"

"Nothing," Nguyen reported. "Drones are getting us visibility on the back of the moon...now."

New data flashed across the screen, but it was mostly what Morgan and her people had expected. Beta-A had a native ecosystem, even if most Imperial biologies would die painfully within minutes of breathing the air.

"What's that?" Morgan demanded, pinging a location.

"Matches up with our listed location for the secondary Precursor station," Nguyen replied, "but...yep. Refined metals, energy signature. That is definitely a ship."

"Get Company Commander Hunter," Morgan ordered. "We want that shi—"

"Contact!" Nguyen snapped. "I have...*something*?"

Morgan didn't bother asking for more details. If the tactical officer had known what she was looking at, she'd have reported that. Instead, she pulled up the data and looked at it herself.

Her first impulse was that she was looking at stealth ships. The signatures were very similar to the ones Vichy's stealth shuttles had shown when they were heading toward the planet, but that wasn't right.

"What am I looking at, Commander?" Morgan asked.

"I really don't know," Nguyen admitted. As she was speaking, new energy signatures flared to life. "Well, *that's* a bunch of fusion engines, but I can't find a source for them."

"That's not possible, Commander," the Captain said. "Give me what you can."

"I *think* we're looking at between twenty-four and thirty contacts," the tactical officer told her. "Engine signatures are mixing together. Looks like about a thousand kilometers per second squared in acceleration."

Even with those godawful heat signatures, the ship's computers were having problems resolving the targets. Radar, visual...even their tachyon scanners were insisting there were only ghosts attached to the engine plumes.

"Energy and acceleration suggest about a quarter-million tons apiece, but I've got nothing on the main sensors," Nguyen confirmed. "Radar is going right through them. I've got vague shapes on visual and a *suggestion* of contact on tachyon."

"Lock them in, Commander," Morgan ordered. "Standby Bravo and Charlie Batteries."

Those were *Defiance*'s paired plasma lances and her batteries of hyperfold guns.

"I can't, sir; I don't have a lock," Nguyen snapped. "I don't have a large enough magnetic field to target the plasma lances."

Plasma lances used a magnetic guidance tube to contain their burst of artificial star-stuff. The tube would follow its target once established, nearly guaranteeing a hit, barring extreme measures.

The only way they wouldn't be able to lock on to the strange contacts was if they had almost no metal in their structure.

"Give me something, Commander," Morgan told her subordinate.

"I can scattergun the hyperfold cannons and I'll hit something, but our sensors and computers are failing to register the damn things, even *with* those engines."

A thousand kilometers per second squared was an incredible acceleration, but the contacts were still barely up to five percent of lightspeed as *Defiance*'s crew continued to try and analyze them.

"Are they a threat?" Morgan asked. They were almost in hyperfold-cannon range now. She didn't want to fire first, but...

"If they weren't firing off the most powerful fusion engines I've ever seen, I'm not sure I'd be convinced they *exist*," Nguyen replied. "I don't know, sir, but..."

A plasma cannon wasn't quite a lightspeed weapon. *Defiance* had just over three-quarters of a second's warning before over two dozen bursts of plasma hammered into her shields.

"Shields are failing," Rogers snapped from secondary control.

"El-Amin, evasive maneuvers *now*," Morgan ordered. "Nguyen?!"

"Firing."

A spray of white pinpricks appeared on the holographic display as Nguyen used twenty-four of the most advanced weapons in the Imperium's arsenal like a planet-scaled shotgun. Several of the engine signatures cut out as the blasts of energy hammered into their targets.

"Hit them again," Morgan ordered. "All batteries clear; engage with whatever works."

Missiles joined the second salvo as the Alpha Batteries came to life at rapid fire. Every six seconds, *Defiance* flung missiles down-range at eighty-five percent of the speed of light. More of the ghost icons disappeared, but another salvo of plasma answered.

Morgan felt her ship's scream in her bones as the shields went down. Plasma bursts slammed into the cruiser's armor, and she was once again grateful for her father. It had been Elon Casimir, after all, who had realized the potential of the mistake one of his production techs had made while producing exotic matter.

Compressed-matter armor was far short of the true neutronium the news liked to label it as, but it was tough, *tough* stuff.

"Breaches on multiple decks!" someone reported and Morgan inhaled a curse.

What the *hell* were they facing?

"El-Amin, open the range," she ordered. "Maximum speed."

Six seconds. With the drive online, it took six seconds to change the direction of their velocity vector in any angle they wanted.

In those six seconds, the ghost-like contacts accelerated another two percent of lightspeed toward *Defiance* and fired again. Most of the shots missed this time, but more red flashes appeared on Morgan's damage-report diagram.

The plasma pulses were burning clean through her compressed-matter armor, *vaporizing* the super-dense material and stabbing into her ship. The armor was minimizing the true damage so far, but *Defiance*'s armor was being peeled away, section by section.

More of the ghosts vanished under the pounding of *Defiance*'s weapons. Over half of the drive signatures were gone now—but *Defiance* was outright running now too.

"Get me thirty light-seconds, El-Amin, then match their velocity," Morgan ordered as another hit—the only one of this salvo—rocked *Defiance*. "Engineering, get me my shields back."

Each of the blasts paled in comparison to the two ship-killing plasma lances that ran the width of *Defiance* to support their wing-tip emitters, but *Defiance* had been hit at least fifty times now.

"Salvo dissipating before contact," Nguyen suddenly reported. "Hostile range appears to be about twenty-two light-seconds." She paused, then continued grimly. "I estimate ten contacts remaining. They're continuing to accelerate toward us, Captain. What do we do?"

"Finish them off," Morgan ordered. "Are the IDMs able to target them?"

"Negative, we're guiding them in by remote, which is a bitch at this range," Nguyen admitted. "None of our systems can register them as a target; we're aiming at the area *around* the engine flare."

They were still inside the minimum range of their hyperspace missiles, too. At this range, only her interface-drive weapons could reach the targets, and their hit ratios were sucking. She watched an entire salvo of missiles dive into the pursuing swarm. Targeted on a single one of the ghosts, Morgan wasn't sure any of them hit.

The following salvo was more effective and a ghost's engines went silent. Nine pursuers.

"Sir, that contact on Beta-A is moving," Nguyen reported. "They're heading away from us, point-five-five light."

And keeping the ghosts between themselves and *Defiance*. Morgan could take the ghosts easily now she was out of their range, but if she went around them, she'd never catch the freighter.

If she tried to take *Defiance* through the ghosts, they'd rip her ship to pieces.

"We have to let her go," Morgan decided aloud. "Continue to maintain this range and tear them up with missiles. Even if it takes three salvos apiece to kill these buggers, we have the missiles to burn."

In a straight missile engagement, after all, it was estimated that it would take *Defiance* ten to twelve salvos to take down a modern destroyer—and her missiles were *far* more capable than those the Imperium had possessed even twelve years before in the Taljzi Campaigns.

Another ghost vanished and Morgan shivered. *Ghost* was feeling particularly apt. At least twenty of the strange ships were already gone, and they clearly couldn't catch *Defiance* before Morgan's ship destroyed them.

All their deaths would achieve was protecting the freighter's escape, but they didn't even seem to be blinking. What kind of crew would fight that suicidally in those circumstances?

Just who were these people and what were they protecting?

CHAPTER ELEVEN

!LAT'S SKIN WAS PURE BLACK WITH FEAR, THE A!TOL administrator pressed into the corner of the upstairs office the prisoners had been stuffed in. Unless Rin was misreading his boss's skin color and body language, the A!Tol was done.

The squid was going to need serious help to be able to function again in the future, let alone run an archeological expedition outside technically known space.

To his own surprise, Rin was handling the situation relatively well. There were three members of the admin staff who'd been in the building with him and !Lat when the Marines had landed, and they had all been stuffed in one of the offices next to the data center.

"Be calm," he told them. "The Marines are here, which means it's only a matter of time until we're rescued. It's all going to be fine."

The building was soundproofed to make communications cleaner, and he could still hear the distant sound of plasma fire. At least some people with serious weaponry were in the building.

"They use...as hostages. Kill to buy time," a young Pibo with pale gray skin replied in halting English. "Marines can't rescue from that."

"Tova...it's Tova, right?" Rin asked. The Pibo neuter made an affirmative gesture with their hand. "The fighting is already in this building. That means the Marines have the camp. Our friends are fine and the Marines are already here. There isn't time for hostage-taking."

The sound of heavy footsteps in the hallway gave the lie to Rin's words. Shouted words in a language he didn't recognize without a translator echoed into the corner office. He glanced around desperately.

There was a desk. That was it. The strangers had even taken the chair out to make sure it wasn't used as a weapon. He suddenly found himself regretting !Lat's catatonia for a new reason: even an A!Tol male was physically stronger than most of their captors.

Rin certainly wasn't, but he took up a position behind the door anyway. Tova looked at him with big black eyes...and then made the same affirmative gesture with their hands.

The door swung open and Tova screamed. Rin had never heard anything like it. The Pibo was only about a hundred and forty-five centimeters tall, but he'd have expected that sound to come from a machine the size of a tank.

Whoever was entering the room paused in sheer shock at the noise, and Rin slammed the door into them. When he still heard them moving, he did it again. And again. Finally, a hand grabbed the door.

A cloaked human, the hood knocked back onto his shoulders, dragged himself around, looking for his attacker with angry but dazed eyes.

Rin punched the man in the face. As he recoiled, the scientist slammed the door into the stranger's head again. That sent him reeling backward into the wall.

He stopped moving as Rin stepped forward, breathing heavily. He'd never even *hurt* anyone before in his life. Gulping air, he checked the man's pulse. It was ragged but present. Unconscious, with potential brain damage, but alive.

"Tova, tie him up," Rin ordered as he carefully extracted the plasma pistol the man had been carrying. He looked at the weapon with distrust as the Pibo set to work.

"You know how to use this?" he asked. "Kosel?"

Kosel was a broad-shouldered amphibian with dark brown fur whose dryness warned of dire health consequences if the Indiri didn't get to a pool soon.

"I...count," he said in English even more halting than Tova's. "No shoot."

"God, do I miss translators," Rin muttered.

"I no better," Tova told Rin. "He...not good."

That "he" was !Lat, a sentiment Rin could only agree with.

"We can't move him," he told the others. "We can't leave. Get back in the corner," he ordered as he found the safety on the gun. Imperial weapons had heavily adjustable grips and controls, but this one had been set for a human male of much his size.

"I'm pretty sure I can shoot through a door, if nothing else," he said grimly as he took cover behind the desk. "Let them try and take us hostage. Beyond that, we wait for the Marines."

A distinct echo of plasma fire continued to hold out hope of rescue.

"KARL!" an accented voice shouted down the corridor, followed by a spiel in a language Rin didn't recognize.

"Anyone know the language?" Rin asked. He was glad his companions understood English without the translator. He could fumble through written Pibo if he had to, but his understanding of Indiri was limited to "sorry" and "where's the bathroom?"

From the blank looks he got back, neither Tova or Kosel was catching the language any better than he was.

"Karl?" the voice demanded from outside the door, and Rin took a deep breath, steadying the pistol with two hands and trying to remember a long-ago lesson from a date at a gun range.

The door shifted, and the voice said something confused and angry before flinging it wide open. For a moment, the cloaked form of what Rin thought was an Ivida stood framed in the door, glaring in. Whatever the pirate was expecting, it wasn't to have Rin pointing a gun at him.

That gave the archeologist a critical second to process the situation before the stranger went for their gun. The desire not to die overwhelmed hesitation, and Rin pulled the trigger three times in rapid succession.

He missed twice, but the second of the three shots hammered into the stranger's chest. The Ivida jerked backward, their own weapon falling from their fingers as they stumbled...and fell.

"My god," Rin whispered. He'd just killed someone. He was a *scientist*, a student of ancient history and the Precursors, not a soldier.

"More coming," Tova told him. The Pibo neuter had better hearing than he did. "No panic. Fight."

The gunshots had drawn attention, and the people he could see running down the corridor beyond the open door were carrying weapons. Heavier ones than the pistol in Rin's hand, but they still weren't sure what was happening yet.

He *was* sure and lifted the gun again. It had a lot less kick than the chemical burners his teen boyfriend had dragged him out shooting—and Rin hadn't been good at shooting those, either.

Lacking in accuracy, he made up for it in enthusiasm. Lining up the gun as cleanly as he could, he pulled the trigger and *kept* pulling it until the gun stopped shooting.

Three cloaked strangers were down, but a new figure appeared behind them...and Rin realized it didn't matter that he was out of charge for the gun. If the tiny pistol in his hand could threaten power armor, he didn't know how to change the settings.

The armored figure was unmarked, its surface changing color as they advanced down the corridor. They were carrying a plasma weapon but weren't firing it. Instead, something on their left gauntlet started to glow—and then the entire front of the suit of armor lit up red-hot like forging metal.

The armored stranger fell forward, revealing a second suit of armor that had emerged from the corner behind them. That figure stepped forward, studied the bodies, then turned a featureless helm toward Rin.

Rin helplessly pointed the gun at them, hoping to somehow intimidate them. Instead, the armored figure held up a hand, palm forward. A second figure appeared, conferred silently, and then proceeded into a different corridor as the first suit of armor approached.

The scientist kept the empty pistol trained on them, and to his surprise, the soldier locked their weapon to a rack on the back of the armor and put their hands up.

These *had* to be Marines. Before Rin found the nerve to say something, a third armored figure arrived by the efficient method of smashing through the building wall from the outside. This one had already locked their gun in place and studied Rin like a raptor studied a field mouse.

Their helmet retracted with an audible *thunk*, and the scientist looked up at a tall, dark-haired man with hawk-like features.

"Dr. Rin Dunst?" he asked in a distinctively French accent. "You can put the gun down. It is generally a sign that things are secure when Marines start using flight systems. Flying soldiers make for easy targets."

Rin hesitated.

"My name is Battalion Commander Pierre Vichy, Doctor," the Marine told him. "I am the commanding officer of *Defiance*'s Marines, and for reasons I'm not cleared for, you are our primary target for extraction.

"The site is mostly secure, but my mission requires me to get you to a safe location and..." Vichy paused, then managed to visibly shrug in the armor. "Plasma fire is not conducive to sustained structural integrity. We need to evacuate this building."

"We...we have a prisoner," Rin said, almost feeling embarrassed to raise it. Vichy and his people had just stormed the entire compound, in the face of what Rin was pretty sure was at least fifty or sixty of the pirate attackers. What was one prisoner?

"Show me," Vichy ordered instead.

Laying aside the empty gun, Rin gestured for the Marine CO to enter the office and waved at their unconscious captive.

"I beat him in the head with the door," he said uncomfortably. "Might be brain damage; he hasn't woken up yet. Name's Karl, I think, but I don't know anything."

"Bien, bien. Très bien," Vichy told him. "Dr. Dunst, we have now fought these people twice in two systems. We don't know anything about them either, but I can tell you that we have less than a dozen prisoners because those cloaks are proofed against stunners.

"Karl here may provide answers the others don't have. I'll have Marines take care of him. Any damage you have done, we can treat. Certainly more easily than plasma burn-through, n'est-ce pas?"

"Vrai," Rin replied slowly, taking a moment to realize he was unconsciously slipping into French in response to the other man's scattering the language into his speech. "I need to check on the compound and the dig site if possible, Battalion Commander." He gestured to !Lat. "Administrator !Lat is in a bad way and requires medical attention, but this site is critical to what we're looking for here."

"There's a reason I'm in this room alone, Dr. Dunst," Vichy murmured. "I'm cleared for Lost Dragon, at least."

"Ah." That was helpful. "Then you understand that I need to check on the dig site. It is critical to the Imperium."

"I'll have Marines take care of your people. I will escort you to the dig site myself. C'est acceptable?"

"Oui," Rin replied. "Sorry," he continued. "My French is terrible and I don't have a translator set on me right now. They took them away."

"At least you try, Dr. Dunst," the Marine told him. "We'll have some sent down from *Defiance* once she's back in orbit."

"Back in orbit? What happened?"

"Our cloaked friends had a surprise we weren't expecting," Vichy told him. "I'd explain it, Dr. Dunst, but I don't understand it well enough myself to know if we're going to classify it or not."

CHAPTER TWELVE

Pierre watched the chubby archeologist out of the corner of his eye as they crossed the compound. The dark-skinned man at least made the attempt to speak French, which had endeared him to Pierre even if it was pointless on a battlefield.

And, unprepossessing as the scientist looked, he'd captured one of the strange raiders who'd seized the site, and killed several more with that man's weapon. Pierre was an Imperial Marine, a soldier born of generations of soldiers. Rising to that kind of challenge impressed him.

"These ruins, they don't seem like much," Pierre observed as they reached the edge of the dig site. His Marines were still clearing away bodies. Once again, few of the raiders had surrendered. Getting answers was looking harder by the minute.

"That's because they're fifty thousand years old, Battalion Commander," Dr. Dunst said in a vaguely distracted tone. "Our best guess is that the Alava had about a billion people in this system." He gestured to the overgrown ruins. "According to the documents that led us here, this was the administration center of the region, a city of sixty million or so."

Pierre studied the ruins again. Presumably, "Alava" was the actual name for what everyone else called the Precursors.

"Doesn't look like it," he said.

"Not to me, either," Dunst admitted. "We think the faction of Alava out here may have been at least partially rogue. Our files on them are vague, and we've already run into areas where they appear to be wrong."

"We have files on the Precursors?" Pierre asked. That was news to him.

Dunst paused and sighed.

"Fuck," he said genially. "I am tired and very stressed, Battalion Commander, and I am talking to ignore what has just happened. Please, do me the favor of forgetting you heard that."

"I was read in on Lost Dragon," Pierre told the other man. "We're a long way out on a random spike of exploration that appeared to be directed at finding this system. I presumed we knew something."

"What I just let slip is not covered under the Lost Dragon Protocol," Dunst told him. "I can't say more, Commander, I've already said too much."

"C'est bon. Aucun problème."

Dunst seemed to at least understand that as he nodded and stopped in place, shading his eyes against the sunlight as he examined the scattered array of tents.

"I think most of this was them, but your Marines didn't help," he noted. "Needs must when the devil drives, I suppose. I need to find something, Commander Vichy. Will you help me?"

"I'm just here to watch your back, Doctor," Pierre pointed out. The surprisingly sparse file they had on Rin Dunst was clear: so far as the Imperium was concerned, the man next to him was worth more than, say, one of Pierre's Marine companies. Probably not more than *Defiance*, but protecting the man was now *Defiance*'s primary mission in this star system.

Interestingly to Pierre, it was very clear that Dr. Dunst did *not* realize that.

"I can pull Marines in for a search detail, if that would help," Pierre offered.

"Can your Marines recognize an Alava regional star projection?" Dunst asked. "I know some of the soldiers on the Taljzi Campaigns have seen them before."

The Marine officer considered that for several seconds.

"I, Dr. Dunst, am only vaguely certain I know what you mean," he admitted. "I suspect the only member of *Defiance*'s crew who could recognize that on sight would be Captain Casimir, and she's busy."

Defiance still hadn't returned to orbit, though the updates on his tactical network suggested that most of the cruiser's small craft contingent was on its way over.

"That is fair. Then I will search and you will watch my back," Dunst told him. "What happens to us now, Battalion Commander?"

The scientist's switch in thoughts left Pierre blinking for a moment before he chuckled softly.

"We evac, Doctor," he told the archeologist. "We pull you out and fall back to Kosha. There, we go over everything we've learned and get your people the medical help they need."

"This is the most important Alava site we have ever found," Dunst told him. "We have so much work to do here."

"And you will be back to do it, I suspect," Pierre said. "But today you have wounded and terrified people who need to go home. We extracted some of your people from a slaver ship; they're in even worse shape in many ways."

Dunst paused again.

"You hadn't mentioned that before," he noted.

"It has been a busy day," Pierre observed. "That's what brought us here, Doctor. We encountered them attempting to make a transfer of artifacts and prisoners to another ship during our survey. The prisoners told us they'd captured this site, so we moved in."

"And thank God you did," Dunst replied. "The people they took are safe, then?"

"Thirty-seven people are safe," Pierre said carefully and specifically. "We haven't yet confirmed if that's everyone."

"I think it is," the archeologist said after a moment's thought. "A few were killed, but if you rescued thirty-seven from their other ship, I think we have everyone who is still alive."

He gestured toward a larger set of tents with his head. "This way."

Pierre followed. The whole situation was still confusing to him. The ground defense had been determined but underequipped to stand off a Marine landing. The anti-stun cloaks would have been effective against law enforcement but were almost nothing against a military force.

The reports were still coming in, but it sounded like they had less than a dozen prisoners, and most of them were wounded. Whoever these people were, they'd fought like tigers.

Ducking under the tent flap to join Dunst, Pierre involuntarily inhaled in shock. He'd thought he'd been entering a collection of tents roughly shoved together. Instead, it turned out that the tents had been intentionally attached to create a large covered space where the archeologists had seriously opened up a Precursor structure.

"Our analysis of the city suggested that this was the headquarters building of a military base on the perimeter," Dunst told him calmly. "The base itself is gone, mostly prefabs that appear to either have been moved or have completely decayed.

"This was the structure that would have been home to the Alava portion of the military contingent, in any case. We thought we'd find a star projection here and we were right, but..."

Dunst was down in the half-buried structure, moving chunks of debris with surprising strength.

"It's gone," he said with a loud sigh. "We'd only begun extracting it when they landed, Battalion Commander. They knew exactly where the ruins and the key locations were. They didn't know where we were initially, but the sensor data I was seeing showed them landing at our site and four others, two of which we'd flagged as high-value locations."

"They knew as much about the place as you did?" Pierre asked. That was bad news.

"More." Dunst shook his head in the dim light as he clambered out of the structure, far more slowly than he'd entered it. "They knew two sites we didn't. And...well, it's hard to tell the difference between fifty thousand years of decay and the unintentional damage of someone being careful, Battalion Commander, but we think someone was here before us and had just as clear an idea of what they were looking for as we did."

"Someone else already scavenged the place?"

"Surveyed it, at least. They didn't take much, I don't think. Little enough at this site, at least, that we thought we were being paranoid. Now...now I think these people, whoever they are, were here before us."

"And specifically came back to deal with you," Pierre said grimly. "That suggests security breaches to me, Dr. Dunst."

"Me too, and I'm not great at security, as we've established," the scientist replied.

Pierre chuckled.

"Doctor, your government file is sparse in a way that tells me you know far more than you've even suggested exists to me," he told Dunst. "Someone sent these people out here? When?"

"If it's from us, no more than twelve years ago," Dunst said. "And even that is more than I should say, Commander Vichy. I think further conversation on this topic should include Captain Casimir, at least. I believe she is cleared for more of this."

"Probablement," Pierre conceded. Casimir wasn't an acknowledged expert on the Precursors, but she'd been on the Taljzi campaign and dealt with a pile of Precursor crap more directly than anyone else on the ship.

"What is she even doing out here?" the scientist asked. "I would have expected her to be posted near the Duchy."

"I am not the Captain's confidant and it is not my place to speculate," Pierre told the other man. He had his own guesses, but regardless of his occasional displeasure with his Captain, she *was* his Captain.

CHAPTER THIRTEEN

"WE'RE MOVING IN ON THE TARGET. THIS IS WEIRD."

Lesser Speaker Alex Braddock's voice hung softly in *Defiance*'s bridge. The shuttle pilot was in control of one of *Defiance*'s multipurpose utility craft. Designed primarily for search and rescue, the utility birds were also used for minor repairs on the exterior of the ship.

The repairs the cruiser needed today were beyond the utility shuttles' abilities, but Morgan had another use for them.

Braddock's shuttle was less than a thousand kilometers from what they thought was the most intact of the ghost ships. Even locating one of them had been hard, the strange ships defying *Defiance*'s sensors even in death.

"I've got it dialed in on visual and I think we're good," Braddock's voice continued, her tone perfectly calm. "Target has a star-relative velocity of just over eleven thousand kilometers a second. Rotation is one hundred and seven degrees per second. Range is eight hundred kilometers, closing at ten kilometers per second."

Lesser Commander Nguyen was running the flight operation, but there was no way that Morgan wasn't going to be listening in.

The situation on Beta was under control, with the prisoners and rescuees being loaded into shuttles to return to *Defiance*.

There were answers she'd get there too, but right now her focus was on Braddock's shuttle and its target.

"Range is three hundred kilometers, maintaining velocity and preparing grapples," the pilot reported. "Visual is...getting more detailed. Are you getting this, *Defiance*?"

"Show me," Morgan ordered softly. "Main tank."

"We are receiving your telemetry, Speaker Braddock," Nguyen confirmed. "We're showing the Captain now. Maintain your approach unless you register a threat."

"Understood, sir. Expect grapple deployment in one minute."

The ship that filled the holotank looked like nothing she'd ever seen, yet something about it rang familiar bells at the back of her mind. It had been a smooth shape, a rounded teardrop that reminded her of nothing so much as the sperm model from high school sex-ed videos.

"Do we have a spectro on the hull material?" she asked.

"Carbon, calcium, some silicon," Nguyen replied. "It's nothing like any starship I've ever seen."

"With the spin, we should be able to get a full three-sixty-squared. Show me."

A few seconds of processing passed and the rotating image froze. Morgan studied it, tapping commands to rotate it to the angle she wanted, zooming in on what she thought she'd seen.

"We blew a fifty-meter-wide hole in this thing with the hyperfold cannons," she said quietly as she looked at the wound. "What do you see, Commander Nguyen?"

The entire bridge was silent as they stared at the hole. *Wound* was the right word. They could see inside their enemy now, and there were no decks, no crew, no technology.

The wound exposed muscle and bone and vacuum-dried flesh on an unimaginable scale.

"How big is that thing?" Morgan asked.

"Based off their thrust energy during the battle, it masses about four hundred thousand tons. Two hundred and forty meters long, a hundred and eighty meters wide at the widest point." Nguyen stared at the wound. "Is it *alive?*"

"Not anymore, but it looks like it might have been," Morgan said drily. "That spectrography. How does it line up with natural-formed shells?"

"I'll have to have my people run an analysis," Nguyen admitted. "They're *creatures?*"

"Well, I'm seeing what looks like muscle and bone instead of crew decks and conduits, so...potentially, yes," Morgan agreed. "Warn Braddock that she's looking at a *dissection*, not a salvage op.

"I suspect this is going to be messier than she was counting on."

THE "SHELL" was made up of thousands—millions, really—of overlapping scales, ranging from a few dozen centimeters across to a couple of ten-meter monsters on the edge of being shed. That made sense, Morgan supposed, compared to a single solid shell that would need to be shed before it killed the creature.

"So, it could get bigger?" Rogers asked as Braddock used her shuttle's manipulator arms to rip a section of the creature's hide off.

"The shell definitely wouldn't be a limitation," Nguyen replied. "More armadillo than lobster, though I don't think Earth life has an exact equivalent to this."

"Most Earth life can't survive thousands of gravities of acceleration, let alone *create* it," Morgan said. "You'd think if combative deep-space wildlife existed, we'd have encountered it by now."

"There are over two hundred life forms in the Imperial catalogs that live in asteroid belts and the rings of gas giants," Nguyen told her. "Not so many that really do the deep-space thing, and nothing we know of that does interstellar, but..."

"If this was native to the system, there'd be more of them," Rogers snapped. "The raiders brought them. Tame space wildlife?"

"I've heard stranger things," Morgan said.

"We're through the hull...hide, I guess," Braddock reported, her voice sounding slightly ill. "Not much in terms of bleeding, though there's definitely some vein-esque things here. It's very dead."

"I'd hope so. I prefer things I blow fifty-meter-wide holes in to die," Nguyen said. "We're getting good scan data, Braddock, but I want you to dig deeper. We know it has some kind of plasma-generation system. Let's find that."

"Yes, sir."

The metal claws dug deeper into the dead ship, excavating hundreds of kilos of flesh to float off into space as Morgan struggled with the sense of familiarity.

"Braddock, grab a flesh sample for the analyzer," she ordered. "This is starting to look familiar, and that seems weird to me."

There was a pregnant pause on the bridge.

"Yes, sir, that is weird," the pilot confirmed. "Grabbing samples and running them through. I'll keep digging for the plasma guts as the scanner analyzes. It's still warm inside the thing, but I'm digging toward the only active heat source I see."

The data running over Morgan's screen from the analyzer wasn't entirely readable to her—the university degree she'd been required to get to be a Militia officer was starship engineering, not biology.

She could read the high levels, though. The flesh was tough as all hell, tougher than anything that had evolved in an atmosphere. Humans had a reinforcing skeletal structure. This entire creature had been made of living tissue that was sturdier than human bone.

Now that she was looking at the cell structure, the sense of familiarity was even stronger, and she plugged an authorization code in as she told the ship's computers to search for comparisons. It wouldn't access Dragon Protocol–sealed data, but it would get the data from...

"My God," she whispered.

"Sir?" Rogers asked.

"It's Precursor," Morgan told them. "It's artificial. The cell structure is based on the same manufactured architecture as the cloning *thing* on Arjtal."

That living device had taken biomass and living creatures and spat out duplicates of the creatures by the hundreds. It had allowed the Taljzi go from a convoy of sixty thousand refugees to an empire of billions that would have destroyed the Kanzi if they hadn't accidentally picked a fight with Earth as well—and through Earth, the A!Tol Imperium.

These ships were built on the same core architecture. Artificial life forms, custom-built to do things no natural organic being could do. And, because they were *alive*, they'd survived the apocalypse the Precursors had unleashed on themselves and their technology.

"Is that even possible?" Rogers asked.

"Obviously," Morgan said grimly. "We were digging into a Precursor site here, after all. A biotech Precursor defense system would still be entirely functional."

"Why would they have fought to cover the retreat of the pirates, then?" Nguyen asked. "That doesn't make any sense."

"I agree, which suggests we don't have anything *near* all of the information," Morgan agreed. "Braddock, keep dissecting. Be careful. A natural organism probably doesn't have anti-tampering mechanisms, but an *artificial* organism..."

"Understood, sir," the pilot replied. "I've managed to get a few close-range scans of the ship that show useful data, too. I'm sending those back, and I think I've located the main plasma sac. It's...well, it's four times the size of one of our fusion reactors."

"And from the heat signature, it basically *is* one of our fusion reactors with a passive magnetic containment," Nguyen interjected. "Lesser Speaker, if you cut that open, it will explode in your face. Pull back. Let's put together a plan before we poke at something that combines the worst attributes of a fusion power plant and a stomach."

"Agreed," Morgan said. "Bring our toy into Beta orbit with us and we'll consider what to do with it as we bring the evacuees on board."

She shook her head.

"If I was remotely comfortable putting it in our cargo bay, I'd say we should haul it home," she admitted. "Somehow, though, I don't trust a biologically created passive magnetic containment unit to hold forever."

"I agree completely," Rogers said. "Let's dissect the thing around the plasma sacs and get as good a feel for what we're dealing with as we can—and then if we need open up the sacs, we can do it with a laser from a couple thousand kilometers away."

"I have to admit, sir, that part sounds *much* less stressful," Braddock told them.

"Tow it into orbit, Speaker," Morgan ordered. "My understanding is that we have some of the Imperium's top experts on the Precursors in this system. Let's see what they say about lab-grown warships."

CHAPTER FOURTEEN

MORGAN GREETED MOST OF THEIR RESCUEES INDIVIDUALLY AS they were brought aboard *Defiance*, shaking appendages and giving reassurances as each sentient left the shuttle. The prisoners didn't get the same respect, though she watched as Vichy's Marines offloaded them.

Between two systems and two battles, they now had a grand total of twenty-one prisoners. Unfortunately, Morgan didn't have any interrogation specialists aboard. It wasn't a skill that a ship on survey duty on the far end of the Imperium ever expected to need.

Vichy and Susskind both had some of the training, at least, but minimal experience using it. They'd do what they could, but she suspected they wouldn't get many answers until they got back to Kosha.

The Marine CO himself was on the last shuttle up, accompanying the two senior scientists from the expedition. Morgan was familiar enough with the A!Tol to know that Administrator !Lat wasn't going to be any use to anyone.

She hadn't seen that dull shade of black on one of the squids before, but the unchanging nature of the A!Tol's skin shade and the degree to which the two Marines escorting him were guiding him suggested that !Lat was in terrible shape.

Dr. Rin Dunst, on the other hand, was far more aware. A dark-skinned man of average height who looked like he'd make a good pillow, he was studying everything around him in the shuttle bay with a sharp, assessing gaze.

He also clearly recognized Morgan the moment he saw her and made a beeline for her, dragging Vichy in his wake. The Captain had a very clear impression of a perfectly coiffed French poodle—the full-sized war-trained man-killer kind, yes, but still a French Poodle—being dragged along by a big, friendly mutt with more than a bit of mountain dog in it.

"Captain Casimir!" he greeted her. "I wanted to thank you personally." He gestured around the bay. "We lost seven people, but dozens were hauled away to be slaves and the rest of us were prisoners here.

"We owe you our freedom at least and likely our lives. Thank you, again and again," he insisted. "If there is any way my people can assist you, you have only to ask."

"First, you can be good passengers for the ten cycles it will take us to reach Kosha," Morgan suggested. "With an extra hundred-plus people and the cargo we pulled from the raiders' ship, things will be more cramped than you're used to."

Dunst threw his hands up in an expressive shrug.

"You overestimate our transport out here, Captain," he told her. "I believe we will be fine—and I will make sure of it, yes." He paused. "You and I must speak in private, I think, on matters of security."

"I agree," Morgan told him. "We've found a few damned odd things out here that I'm hoping you can shed some light on. Not least your captors. Do you know anything?"

"Nothing. I hope the computers Battalion Commander Vichy's people found will be of use once your people get into them," he said. "I have a few cyber-archeologists who could probably be helpful at that, if you want. We don't like to draw too much attention to it, but the people who can crack alien hardware and operating systems are pretty good at encryption and security, too."

"I'm not turning down any help today, Dr. Dunst," Morgan replied. "We'll put your people in touch with our cyber team under Speaker Murtas once they've settled in."

"Of course, of course. If I may impose on your time more quickly, though?" Dunst asked.

"Shouldn't you rest, Doctor?" Morgan asked.

"The moment I stop working, Captain, I am going to have to process quite a bit of trauma, and I'm not certain how helpful I'll be for a bit at that point," Dunst replied. "Better to get the use out of me now before the last day or so breaks me."

That was both a fascinating and disturbing level of self-awareness.

"All right. Vichy? Meet with Susskind and start on the interrogations," she ordered. "I'm probably going to have to read you in on a few more classified items before we're done, but I'm going to *try* to keep things secret if I can."

"If you insist, ma Capitaine," Vichy said. Somehow, despite having just spent ten-plus hours in power armor, the man's hair was still perfect. "I serve at your pleasure."

"Then get to work," Morgan ordered. "Vite, if you please, Commander."

To her surprise, throwing one of his French drop words back at him actually got her a small laugh from the Marine.

MORGAN POURED coffee for both herself and Dunst, sliding the cup across the table as she considered him.

"System, seal the room under Lost Dragon Protocols," she ordered calmly. She felt the Faraday cage close, and a green light on her desk confirmed the room was sealed.

"We're now isolated from the ship," she told the archeologist.

"I'm aware you're cleared for Lost Dragon. I presume you're cleared for a number of other Dragon Protocols, and we could spend ten minutes sorting out what both of us know and don't know about the Precursors and the Imperium's blatantly illegal-by-galactic-law research into them."

"Is it illegal if the policeman who wrote the laws has retired?" Dunst asked. "Have you seen a Mesharom recently, Captain?"

She snorted.

"From my conversations with Interpreter-Shepherd Adamase before the Mesharom command ship left Imperial space, I don't expect to see another one in my lifetime, Dr. Dunst."

Adamase had been *the* Mesharom in the region. As Shepherd, they'd been tasked with responsibility for a large chunk of this arm of the galaxy. The failure of the Mesharom involvement in the Taljzi Campaigns had gutted their Battle Fleet. The Frontier Fleet units once used to enforce most of the treaties the Mesharom had convinced the rest of the galaxy to sign had been pulled back to Mesharom space to guard their worlds and borders.

Morgan wasn't sure how long the twelve-kilometer-wide Mesharom war spheres took to build, but she did know that the Taljzi had lured a fleet of forty of them into a trap and wiped them out. Reading between the lines, that had been something close to *half* of the Mesharom Battle Fleet, a force the galaxy's "wise elders" had never expected to lose.

Many of the treaties the Mesharom had once enforced were still backed by most of the Core and Arm Powers, creating the foundation of "galactic law," such as it was. The ones around studying Precursor tech, though...those Morgan suspected weren't being given more than lip service by anyone.

"Without the Mesharom, there is no one to prevent the Imperium from investigating Alava sites," Dunst told her. "We do so in secrecy, just in case, but those weren't even treaties the Imperium voluntarily signed."

Twenty-plus years earlier, while Morgan's stepmother had been pregnant with twins, Annette Bond had negotiated with the Mesharom to receive technology in trade for surrendering a Precursor scout ship to the Mesharom.

The alternative had, explicitly, been the destruction of the planet the ship had crashed on and humanity's fledgling first colony. The Imperium's technology then had fallen far short of the standard necessary to stand against any Core Power, let alone the oldest of them.

Twenty years had changed that, but even now, the Imperial Navy would hesitate to challenge the Mesharom.

"I think that's how most of the Arm Powers feel," she agreed. "The Mesharom and the Core Powers forced a lot of treaties on us without really asking our opinion. Now, well...the larger Arm Powers like us are joining the Core in enforcing the ones we agree with."

The A!Tol Imperium and the Kanzi Theocracy were the two major powers of the spiral arm of the galaxy humanity lived in. Morgan knew humans had visited most of the powers in the galactic Core and even into several of the other spiral arms by now, but that was individual ships at most.

"Hence covert security protocols on an archeological dig," Dunst concluded. "This is a mess, Captain Casimir, and one I'm not sure how best to handle."

"Right now, I'm taking all of you back to Kosha," Morgan told him. "That's not up for discussion, not even by you."

"I am merely the deputy administrator, Captain," he demurred.

"Bullshit," she said calmly. "You're flagged in my files as a Category Two Asset, Doctor. That's an 'all aid possible will be rendered, to be extracted from threats at significant danger' classification. You're not *merely* the deputy administrator."

Dunst was silent, taking a sip of his coffee as if lost in thought.

"I am the expedition's premier expert on the Alava," he finally conceded. "I am updated and cleared on, so far as I know at least, all of our information on them."

Morgan sighed.

"We're getting into the realm of things I don't officially know," she admitted. "You're one of four people we most readily refer to as the Precursor subject-matter experts, the ones cleared for everything we know if not necessarily how we got it."

She held up a hand as he opened his mouth.

"I'm not officially cleared for that," she reminded him. "So, don't tell me about the others."

None of the others were human. Rin Dunst was the only Precursor expert who wasn't a member of the Imperial Races, a telling sign of both humanity's involvement in the whole mess and the trust they now held in the Imperium.

"I'm unsure on what you are cleared for, Captain," Dunst said levelly.

"I, at least, am more sure of what you're cleared for," Morgan said cheerfully. Dunst had seen the Mesharom files on the Precursors, a massive archive of history and technology, but didn't know the source.

Morgan knew the source of those files—she had *been* the source of those files, arguably—but had never really had an opportunity to go through the Mesharom Archive before it was locked down.

"We were out in this corner of the galaxy because we knew the Precursors had been out here and we believed there were intact, unsterilized sites," she continued. "This was supposed to be a local admin center, yes?"

"It's more than that," Dunst told her. "Alava—Precursor—historical files are messy. I don't know the source of the archive, you're right, but it's very clear that it's mostly archeological data and third-hand stories.

"Putting together the pieces of the puzzle occupies a lot of very clever people. What I and one of those *other experts* you mention identified is references to what appeared to be a rogue Alava state. Not one opposed to their central Hegemony but one that the Hegemony had written off as a distraction.

"No resources flowed either way, but it looked like there were about a billion Alava and ten billion from the subject races out here, at least. A tenth of that was supposed to be here, but our scans and research so far suggest otherwise."

"Define *otherwise*, Doctor," Morgan said slowly.

"This was their original colony site out here, their admin center," he told her. "But it was maybe two hundred million people. We're missing a billion Precursors, and without the star projection, we can't even ID their local systems. The maps we have from the central Hegemony are off in many key ways."

He shrugged.

"If nothing else, they're from far enough away that they appear to be missing entire stars."

Morgan shook her head.

"The concept of rogue factions in a race whose local security detachment around Arjtal chopped up three star systems to build and supply a shipyard makes me nervous," she noted. "I'll admit to the occasional feeling of relief that they're dead."

So far as their research stretched, the Alava had been the ruling race of the multistellar and multispecies Hegemony the modern galaxy called the Precursors, with another dozen not-quite-slave-races underneath them.

The A!Tol, who had shown up with a fleet and forcefully vassal-ized humanity before uplifting them, were friendly parents handing out free candy in comparison.

"I have studied them more than any other human, at least, alive," Dunst said quietly. "I can't argue with that relief. These strangers, though..." He sighed.

"We had located the star projection in one of the secondary military bases on Beta," he told her. "It was destroyed by the raiders. Or taken; it's hard to be sure."

Morgan grimaced, tapping a command on her desk. A hologram duplicating a portion of a far larger model appeared above the smooth slab of wood.

"This is what we have for this sector from their files," she noted. "You say it's wrong?"

"Out of date at best, but some of our research now suggests that the faction out here was actively lying to the Hegemony," Dunst told her. "What I have learned here that wasn't in the Archive is that the faction was working on their own megastructures, something different than the rest of the Alava."

"Biological?" Morgan asked. "Like the thing on Arjtal?"

He exhaled.

"I wouldn't have drawn that conclusion from what I've seen so far, but it would fit what little we've got," he admitted. "Other than the cloner, we haven't encountered much Alava biotech, though."

"We did here," Morgan told him. A few commands brought up the scans of the ghost ships. "When the raiders' last ship fled, biological warships covered their retreat. Twenty-eight of these attacked *Defiance*. We took a lot more damage than I'm admitting to the rest of your people, Dr. Dunst, which is why we're returning to Kosha."

He studied the teardrop shape.

"I swear I saw that shape in some of the diagrams we found," he told her. "But the raiders had my notes and artifacts."

"And once we crack their files, you'll have theirs," Morgan said. "I don't suppose that's going to give us any new answers?"

"I don't know," Dunst admitted. "I don't know what was going on out here or what these people wanted.

"I do know that there were eleven billion Precursors here when they died."

He paused, as though unsure how to continue.

"They had the nervous-system implants out here as well, I presume?" Morgan said delicately. "They died?"

The Alava and all of their servant species had used internal cybernetic systems to a far greater extent than any modern race Morgan knew of. The Mesharom had resisted...which was why the Mesharom had survived.

The Alava had built their technology around one set of laws of physics...and in an attempt to accelerate their FTL drives, they'd set up a massive experiment to *change* the laws of physics.

They'd carefully avoided most things that would impact living creatures, but they'd been aiming at things like conductivity—and they'd broken it. Suddenly, universal laws of electrical resistance and hyperspatial resistance had changed. All of their technology had stopped working, including the device that had changed the universe...and the implants tied into the autonomous nervous systems of every Alava and their subjects.

"They died," Dunst agreed heavily. "I didn't know you were cleared for that."

"I'm cleared for Fallen Dragon, but that's mostly because the people setting it up knew I already knew about it," Morgan told him. "The Mesharom told me. My knowledge of a lot of this mess predates us neatly dividing it all into buckets we could individually classify, Doctor."

"I see," he allowed. "It's rare for me to be able to have a mostly open conversation about this, Captain Casimir."

"I know the feeling," she with a smile. "Do you have any idea what was going on with the raiders?"

"They'd been on Beta before. They knew where to look for us and what was going on." He shook his head. "I think...two things. I think Lost Dragon itself was breached and someone told them we were there.

"I also think the Dragon Protocols overall may have been breached a long time ago. I suspect they were investigating these sites years before we were. I don't know what they found, Captain Casimir, but they seemed prepared to die to protect it."

"I know," she agreed. "I hope Commander Vichy gets some useful answers out of them, because this situation is making me nervous. I don't like not knowing what I'm digging through, Dr. Dunst."

"Nor me, Captain." He shook his head. "I must admit, I don't like the whole 'doctor' title. I can't even do basic first aid. Call me Rin, Captain."

She chuckled and offered him her hand.

"As the senior civilian aboard, I suppose you can call me Morgan," she allowed. "Just not in front of my crew!"

CHAPTER FIFTEEN

"WELL, WE HAVE AN ID ON THIS ONE," SUSSKIND TOLD PIERRE, gesturing at the image hovering above his desk.

"That is the one Dr. Dunst knocked out with a door?" Pierre asked, studying the blond man in the hologram.

"Exactly," the military police officer told him. Gerard Susskind was a small man with dark hair and piercing green eyes, currently focused on the hologram. "Dr. Dunst got a first name for him. It's not much, but it was enough."

"So who am I looking at?" Pierre asked.

"Karl Aafjes, thirty-eight years old," Susskind reeled off. "Place of birth, Amsterdam in Franco-Germany. No current residence on record. He acquired a merchant officer's certificate from the Frankfurt Ducal Merchant Academy at age twenty-two, signed on as junior watchstander on a ship named *Matronymic*, and left Earth forever."

"Family or crew?"

"He's not registered as crew on any ship in the Imperial records," the MP replied. "No marriage or children on record, either. Neither of those is a solid guarantee. Even officer positions are only registered when the ship needs something from the government or the bank."

"And even the father being around does not always mean children are on the paperwork, oui." Pierre shook his head. "But most likely single and quite possibly operating in gray shipping."

"It's a clean record, which means we're the first to catch him," Susskind said drily. "I've sent a request off for more detailed information. I could easily be missing his marriage licenses or his kids' birth certificates. I'd definitely know if he'd got another shipper's certificate or a criminal record somewhere."

"But he's definitely not a known pirate," the Marine concluded. He shook his head. "Ça n'a aucun sens. An officer slip and a decade-plus experience? There's a thousand freighters begging for a man like him. Unless he got blacklisted for something that wasn't criminal, there's no reason for him to be out here playing pirate."

"You can ask him. That we have a name and an ID bumps him to the top of my list for interviews," Susskind pointed out. "We don't have many people qualified for interrogation aboard. Really, it's just me."

"And enough of this is classified that Captain Casimir wanted me involved," Pierre told him. "Come on, Speaker. Let's go talk to Mr. Aafjes."

***

DEFIANCE'S MEDICS had very clearly focused on fixing Aafjes's potential concussion over such niceties as his black eye. There were clear marks where regeneration matrix had been used to rebuild shattered bones in the man's face, and those only added to the bruising.

The two burly MPs who'd handcuffed him to the chair stood by the door as Pierre and Susskind took their seats across from the blond prisoner.

"We will be fine," Pierre told them. "Leave us."

"I want to see a lawyer," Aafjes told them calmly. "The Imperium recognizes the right to counsel."

"The situation is more complicated than that, Mr. Aafjes,"

Susskind replied. "You were taken in active combat with Imperial forces and arrested in the act of piracy. Plus, we have evidence tying your operation on Beta to slavery.

"So, you see, Mr. Aafjes, you are *not* a civilian prisoner. You are an *Imperial military* prisoner. Your rights ever so subtly change in that case. Most notably, you do *not* have the right to counsel."

Pierre managed not to shake his head. By not bringing in counsel —a necessity, given that *Defiance* didn't carry civilian defense lawyers on board, for some reason—they also limited themselves to questions directly related to the circumstances Aafjes had been detained for.

Of course, they also had more than enough evidence to jail the pirate for the rest of his life, even if this interview got thrown out in court.

"I am not a pirate," the prisoner snapped.

"You were part of an illegal armed operation that attacked and seized an Imperial archeology site in a system claimed by the Imperium," Susskind laid out. "You illegally detained over one hundred employees of the Imperial government, and the operation attempted to transfer thirty-seven of those employees into the slave market.

"We can prove all of that, so I'd save your breath," the MP concluded. "I am not sure what label to apply to you other than *pirate*, Mr. Aafjes."

"I am not a pirate," he repeated. "I am bound to a higher law and a higher calling."

"Really."

Susskind's single-word response hung in the air unchallenged.

"Then who do you work for?" Pierre asked. "What *higher law* authorizes your actions?"

Aafjes smiled, shaking his head like a teacher dealing with a slow student.

"I am of the Children," he said. "We obey Her commands, and secular law and lord pale in comparison to Her will."

"The Children?" Susskind asked. "That's an astonishingly vague phrase, Mr. Aafjes. Would you care to expand?"

"We are all Children of the Stars, Speaker," Aafjes replied. "You don't yet know what you fail to understand. I obey Her will, the will of our true God."

"I am uncertain how a god's will leads to the murder and kidnapping of an Imperial research team or the vandalism of a historical site of near incalculable value," Pierre said. "You are a merchant officer, Mr. Aafjes. The Imperium is rich in opportunities for a man like you. What brings you out here and to these...depths?"

"You do not know what you fail to understand," Aafjes repeated, a small smile playing around his lips. "This is all proceeding according to Her plan."

"Really," Susskind said. "And who is She?"

"The Mother of All, the Womb of Existence," their prisoner told them. "She cannot be explained, only experienced. Cannot be described, only touched. I have walked in the presence of God."

He shrugged.

"What power do you wield that could scare me now?" he asked. "It was clearly Her will that I be here to attempt to explain your failures."

"If we wished to be...initiated into this wonder, where would we go?" Pierre asked.

Aafjes laughed.

"You are not ready and you are not worthy. If it is Her will that you join her Children, you will be shown ways. It is not my place to speak for the Divine Mother."

"You realize, Mr. Aafjes, that the Imperium does not recognize religion as grounds for murder?" Susskind noted. "Your crimes are more than sufficient to condemn you to hard labor for the rest of your life. Assistance in tracking down your colleagues may buy you clemency."

"Her will was that I was here to tell you of Her existence," Aafjes told them. "Anything more is not my task from Her." He smiled that small smile again. "You can ask whatever questions you wish, but I believe I will wait for that lawyer before I answer them."

He closed his eyes and leaned back in his chair, leaving Pierre with a grim certainty that they weren't going to get much of use out of him.

"How did your people know about the expedition?" the Marine demanded.

Only silence answered him.

He traded glances with Susskind, who gave him a "go ahead" gesture.

It didn't look like they were going to get answers, but that didn't mean they didn't have to ask the questions.

CHAPTER SIXTEEN

"Most of what we pulled from their computers is just our stuff, boss," Lawrence told Rin. Given several days of attention from *Defiance*'s medical staff and real food, she looked much better than she had in the cell.

"Information security or just...?" he asked. The two archeologists were sharing a meal in the corner of an officer's mess. It was better than the main crowded messes straining to feed an extra hundred-plus bodies, but not by much. Still, it had some level of quiet and privacy built into its design.

"I'm not sure and neither are *Defiance*'s techs," she admitted. "It looks like most of what we've got our hands on are secondary machines. If they had a central server on Beta, they slagged it so hard, the Marines didn't ID it as a computer."

"That's not reassuring, Kelly," Rin said. "These people scare me. We know nothing about them."

"We got a name out of the files," she told him. "The Children of the Stars. That's what they call themselves. A bunch of what we got looked like...first-draft religious texts."

"First draft?" Rin asked with a chuckle.

"Yeah," she confirmed, clearly thinking it through as she spoke. "You see the stages when you do historical research, the initial revelations, the follow-on texts, the first-draft analysis and compilation—and then later, the rationalizations, the standardizations and purges of texts outside the accepted structure.

"These are in the follow-on-text mode. Maybe even some of the initial revelations, but there's enough intentional vagueness that I think we're seeing a specific selection of stuff." She shrugged. "Between that and the fact that I found three variations on the same text, I stick with 'first draft.'

"We're looking at a cult, boss. I'd leave guessing size and threat level and such to the soldiers, as my expertise ends there." Lawrence shook her head. "Classic human mystery cult, to be honest. The aliens are new, but the style is familiar."

Rin nodded his understanding while taking a bite of his meal. One of the advantages of being on a ship intended to be crewed by one race was that there was actual real food aboard. In a multispecies setup like the Lost Dragon expedition, they'd been living off Universal Protein. While that substance was inoffensive at its worst, it took skill to make it taste good. The chicken curry the officer's mess was serving had actual chicken in it and tasted amazing after months of UP.

"A cult worshipping the Alava," he guessed. "That's going to be trouble."

"No shit," Lawrence agreed. "I mean, I can kind of see it. Some of the things the Alava built...they're beyond awe-inspiring. I've never seen an intact megastructure firsthand, but I can't help but wonder how it feels. Especially when you didn't know what was coming."

"Their awe became my terror, so my sympathy is limited," Rin said drily. "Did we get anything useful from them? What kind of crap is in these religious texts?"

"A lot of stuff about the Mother and the Womb, their God who created all reality," Lawrence told him. "Some of it's probably allegorical, but I'm guessing some of it is referring to an Alava structure of

some kind. I mean, if the Taljzi hadn't already had a religious structure to slot the cloner into, I could see it taking a shape like this."

"The last thing we need is for someone to start treating the Alava
as gods and their ruins as holy sites," Rin said. "Everything I've seen
suggests they weren't anyone we'd want to meet, let alone worship."

"And the fact that if a big-enough group started worshiping them,
we'd have problems getting clearance to excavate their ruins isn't a
factor at all, is it, boss?" Lawrence asked with a chuckle.

"There's that," he conceded. "Digging into Alava tech is one
thing. The Imperium is never going to stop doing that, dangerous as it
occasionally is. We don't *need* to excavate their cities to do that,
though it helps lead us to their actual technological sites.

"I just wish we had a more complete set of records for out here.
This particular branch of the Alava seems to have left even *their*
leaders scratching their heads. I don't suppose any of the images we
took of the star projection are in what we retrieved?"

"Looks like everything on the star projection was destroyed," she
admitted. "Reading between the lines of the religious texts and other
notes, they originally found one on Beta-A. 'Sacred answers hidden
in yellow fog,' according to the religious texts."

Beta-A was less pressurized than Venus, but the air would still be
toxic to humans. That it had a living ecosystem was probably going to
be fascinating to lots of people. Rin wasn't one of them—he was more
interested in how the Alava sites had survived fifty thousand years
of it.

"So, this cult knows more about what we're looking for than we
do." Rin sighed. "What a mess."

"We got one thing from that, though," Lawrence told him. "I'm
not a hundred percent certain, but the Navy techs I was working
with clammed up pretty hard at one point. I think they had more data
on what the cult ships were doing than I did and it lined up with
something we found."

"The cult ships?" Rin asked. "Wait, you think the Navy knows
where they went from D-L-K-Six?"

"Quite possibly, so I'm surprised we're not headed there right now," Lawrence admitted.

Rin nodded slowly. From his conversation with Casimir, the only place *Defiance* was going was a repair yard. The cruiser had come off far more roughly from her encounter with the Alava bioships than the Captain was letting the civilians know.

Part of the problem with having that information was that she was clearly trusting him not to disseminate it.

"I don't think Casimir wants to go into a possible battle with civilians on board," he said instead. "She'll drop us on the colony at Kosha and check in with her commanders. There's a Navy base at Kosha, too. She'll pick up reinforcements."

He patted the table.

"*Defiance* is an impressive ship to you and me, but she's still only a midweight warship at best," he concluded. "And no Captain is going to turn down reinforcements when facing the unknown."

CHAPTER SEVENTEEN

KOSHA WAS ONE OF THREE SYSTEMS OUT THIS FAR WITH A NAME. It was named for the neuter caregiver of the Pibo officer who'd originally surveyed the system, a cheap concession from the colonization corporation to the Navy when they'd bought the rights.

Now, the broad rolling plains of Blue Heart, Kosha's third planet, were home to just over five million of the centaur-like crocodilian Rekiki. About half a million members of other races, mostly human and Pibo, lived in the capital city and in orbit.

Morgan's records suggested about ten thousand of those were officers and enlisted of the A!Tol Imperial Navy. The system was a direct satrapy of the Imperium, with an appointed colonial governor and a single seat in the House of Worlds.

There was only one large space station in orbit above Blue Heart. It served as a transfer station for cargo going to the surface, a refueling and resupply depot for civilian ships, and a fully stocked Imperial Navy logistics base.

Most critical for the current state of Morgan's command, Kosha Station had a repair slip that could fit *Defiance*.

"We're cleared into the repair slip, sir," Nystrom told her. "Lord

Davor has requested a direct line with you as soon as possible but has already authorized our repairs and transport for the civilian passengers."

"Understood." Morgan skimmed through the status reports. *Defiance* was still intact in every significant sense, but she was more than a bit battered around the edges. She'd need several sections of her compressed-matter armor completely replaced.

Fortunately, Kosha Station had the replacements. Her ship would be in good hands in a few minutes.

"I'll be in my office if I'm needed," she told Nystrom. "You have the watch, Lesser Commander."

"Yes, sir."

Nystrom was the most junior department head on the ship and usually stood the watch with a more senior officer as backup. Morgan was reasonably sure the young woman could get the ship through a thirty-minute flight to a docking bay in friendly space.

"ECHELON LORD DAVOR," Morgan saluted. "It's good to speak to you in real time."

Hyperfold communications had an odd timing lag. Anything inside about a light-month was real-time or near enough to make no difference. A light-year, on the other hand, took just under an hour to cover. It rose linearly with the number of light-years after that up to about eleven light-years, where it jumped a hundredfold again.

The Imperium, like most powers with hyperfold coms, used relays spaced ten light-years apart to transfer messages as effectively as possible, resulting in an effective long-range communications speed of about nine thousand times lightspeed.

Those relays led back to starcoms, which *were* instantaneous anywhere within the galaxy. Starcom transmitters were massive and complicated devices that had to be built in place and never moved. Starcom receivers were, thankfully, more easily transported. Kosha

Station had one, which cut Echelon Lord Davor's com loop with the Imperial government in half.

"It's good to see you, Captain Casimir," Davor told her. The red-faced Ivida officer didn't show any sign of that, but Ivida faces didn't show emotion. Morgan couldn't see quite enough of the alien woman's form to truly read her body language. "*Defiance* appears in almost worse shape than your reports suggested."

"We're bruised and battered, Echelon Lord, but I think Kosha Station should have us cleaned up and ready for action in short order," Morgan promised. "We made some interesting discoveries while we were in hyperspace. My staff has prepared an update."

"With regards to these pirates?" Davor asked. "I was hoping we had some answers."

"Not as many as we'd like," *Defiance*'s Captain admitted. "We now know we're looking at a cult of between ten and twenty thousand members. They appear to be Precursor worshippers and had access to Dragon Protocol–secured information on this region long before we started even planning our current operations.

"Potentially, they were at D-L-K-Six around the initial colonization of Kosha," Morgan told Davor. "They've been poking at Precursor sites in the region for a while. They call themselves the Children of the Stars, and they seem to be worshipping something they call, variously, the Womb, the Mother, or just plain God."

"Precursor worshippers talking about a *Womb* makes me nervous when I consider the Arjtal creature and your encounters," Davor noted. "That's surprisingly limited data, too, Captain."

"We basically have their personal computers from their occupation of the dig site, sir," Morgan said. "There's no real details or deep information in them beyond a few extra notes on the site itself. Our prisoners have been uniformly unhelpful though quite willing to talk about the basic theology of the Children." She shrugged. "I think some of them were hoping to make converts."

"I presume and hope they failed," Davor said.

"Entirely," Morgan confirmed. "But between what the prisoners let slip and what we pulled from the files, we've managed to ID another Precursor system in the region that we believe the Children are actively operating out of.

"At the very least, sir, it needs to be investigated."

Davor snapped her teeth in one of the few, rather disconcerting, pieces of facial body language the Ivida had.

"I'm running out of ships to follow up on this, Captain Casimir," she said. "My entire command is scattered across almost as many star systems as we have vessels. A destroyer in D-N-E-Five, a destroyer in D-L-K-Six, *Defiance* in for repairs..."

"I understand, sir," Morgan said. "I feel that this needs to be followed up on, but it should be able to wait until *Defiance* is online or one of the destroyers gets back. I've seen no evidence to date that suggests that the Children have access to hyperfold communicators beyond the one at the Beta dig site."

"That alone is problem enough." Davor snapped her teeth again. "Commander Isk is also on his way back. *Serene Guidance* will need to restock and resupply, but she'll be ready to deploy before *Defiance* is."

Shel Isk was a Yin officer, one of the blue-feathered humanoid avians who had been the most recent acquisition of the Imperium until humanity came along. His *Serene Guidance* was an older destroyer, small and under-armed compared to *Defiance* but capable enough for her size.

"I have to admit, sir, I'm not in command here and even I'm feeling the lack of hulls," Morgan said.

"I've sent messages up the chain, and the Fleet Lords agree," Davor replied. "We're being sent another squadron apiece of destroyers and cruisers."

The current force around Kosha Station was a mixed squadron of twelve destroyers and four cruisers, with *Defiance* the newest and largest vessel by a significant margin on both counts. Another sixteen of each type would triple Davor's hulls and more than triple her firepower.

"I'm glad we're being taken seriously, sir."

"I want to know what we're facing, Captain," Davor told her. "Hopefully, *Serene Guidance* can get in and out without too much difficulty, but I'm not expecting Commander Isk to engage them himself."

Morgan nodded. Her own first command, almost ten years earlier now, had been *Hawkwing*, a sister ship to *Serene Guidance*. She wouldn't have wanted to take the destroyer against a flotilla of the Precursor bioships, and she doubted Isk felt any differently.

"I'll sit with my staff and prepare a briefing for Isk," she offered. "How much of this is he cleared for?"

"Include everything relevant," Davor ordered. "My understanding is that Lost Dragon is going to be expanded to include all of this dark water, and we'll be reading every Captain on station in."

"That's risky," Morgan noted.

"The secret of the expedition is already compromised, Captain Casimir. Preventing a similar attack and making certain we control the source of these bioships is more critical at this juncture. I don't think anyone is expecting it to leak back to the Mesharom at this point."

"Or that the Mesharom will do anything if it does," Morgan muttered.

"Exactly, Captain. Get your ship into dock; get the civilians offloaded and the repairs started. Pleased as I am with what the Navy is promising me, those squadrons are coming from the frontier with the Wendira. We're looking at thirty cycles at least before we're reinforced.

"I want *Defiance* back in space long before then."

"Understood, sir. We'll make it happen."

CHAPTER EIGHTEEN

Pierre watched the prisoners shuffle across *Defiance*'s loading bay with a cautious eye. Uncooperative as the Children of the Stars had been, he wasn't expecting a sudden escape attempt now —but he wouldn't be surprised by one, either.

There were more Marines in the loading bay than prisoners, maintaining a solid barrier between the Children and the research team that would be offloading shortly. Only a handful of the Imperial troopers carried plasma rifles today. The weapons would make a mess of *Defiance*'s internal structure and shouldn't be needed. Without the cloaks they'd been captured in, the Children weren't immune to stunners now.

"Battalion Commander Vichy? Report to the main airlock, sir," the voice of one of his squad leaders sounded in his headset. "We might have a paperwork problem."

Pierre buried a sigh.

"Comtois, take over supervising," he ordered. "I need to go investigate what merde we've dug up this time."

He was walking away before Comtois could reply. The Company Commander was *already* watching his Marines work.

Pierre's presence in the loading bay was likely redundant, but the Marine CO had wanted to watch the Children get offloaded with his own eyes.

They'd been an emmerdeur, a pain in his ass, since they'd come aboard. If there was a problem getting them off his ship, he wanted it resolved.

The squat gray-skinned alien in the formal white-and-blue robes waiting for him was his worst nightmare. Even on Earth, lawyers had mostly adopted a version of those robes. They were expected for making arguments in Imperial Court, and the practice had inevitably filtered down.

"Battalion Commander, I'm hoping you can deal with this individual," the Marine at the door told him. The prisoners were still aboard *Defiance*, a thin line of armed Marines in unpowered armor between them and the station.

There was, thankfully, a detachment of Marines from the Kosha Station detail waiting for them—but the tiny gray Pibo lawyer stood between them like an unbreakable object.

"What's going on?" Vichy asked, as calmly as he could.

"I am Kosha Station's Senior Public Advocate, Lako," the lawyer told him. "I have an authorizing writ for suspension of imprisonment and guarantor of appearance for your prisoners. They were seized without warrant and will be released into my custody."

Bail. The Children had apparently posted *bail* before *Defiance* had reached Kosha Station. That had all kinds of implications, but also was less meaningful than the Advocate thought.

"I need to see your writ, Advocate Lako," Pierre told the Pibo.

"Everything is in order," the lawyer told him huffily. It always amazed Pierre how much of the tone and emotion carried through the computer translation. The Pibo was speaking his own language, translated by the earbuds Pierre and every Imperial military officer wore, but Pierre understood not only his words but also his tone and intent.

"Je présume," Pierre agreed genially. "But I need see the writ regardless."

Lako huffed again, gaining a centimeter or so of height in his false indignation, but handed over the physical document. An electronic transmission accompanied it, but the paper was the official document.

Pierre made a show of reading through the entire writ, but he was really skimming it, looking for three key sentences. None of them were there and he handed the writ back to Lako with a smirk.

"Someone has wasted your time and the Judge's," he told the lawyer. "These are not civilian prisoners arrested in a sting operation or on accusations of copyright violation, Advocate. These are pirates seized in the acts of piracy and slavery, in open combat with Imperial Marines. No warrant was present or called for in that kind of active intervention on our part, which renders the fundamental basis of your writ invalid.

"Secondly, these prisoners are explicitly under Imperial military jurisdiction, and Judge Amitan's writ would need to be counter-authorized by the Navy chain of command. In this case, as Kosha Station does not possess a significant military judicial presence, by Echelon Lord Davor. This writ has no such authorization."

Lako was trying to gain another centimeter or two as Pierre looked down at him and continued to smirk.

"Thirdly, as these prisoners were taken in open combat with Imperial personnel—my Marines in this case, though a similar rule takes effect in case of prisoners taken by police in these circumstances —the writ would require an active proof of either a risk-mitigation plan or a reason why the prisoners are not expected to be a risk now."

Pierre folded the document up and handed it back to the lawyer.

"Your writ is invalid, Advocate Lako," he told the Pibo. "You are more than welcome to provide these citizens with their right of advocacy, but they will not be released from Imperial custody. Your meetings will take place at the Naval detention center."

Lako was trying to be indignant, but he was mostly managing

stunned. At Pierre's gesture, he stepped aside with the Marine, allowing the Marines to begin the prisoner transfer.

"Someone just tried to use you, Advocate," Pierre said, his voice very soft to make sure no one else heard him. "Your dedication to your role is admirable, but these prisoners are actively dangerous."

"They still have rights," the lawyer snapped.

"Oui." Pierre smiled. "And your job is to make sure we respect them. My job is to make sure they don't harm anyone else while we sort out what to do with them."

Lako turned, watching as the prisoners were escorted past him.

"They don't look like much," he told Pierre.

"Seven dead Imperial researchers, three dead and fifteen wounded Marines suggest an alternative interpretation," Pierre said grimly. "Once the transfer is complete, they are Battalion Commander Ir!Lan's problem."

"And mine," Lako replied.

PIERRE WAS glad to see the last of the prisoners off his decks. The writ worried him, though. For it to have been put together and authorized before *Defiance* began offloading prisoners, someone had almost certainly been waiting for them.

Someone on the station was working for the Children of the Stars. That raised all kinds of problems.

"Comtois, Hunter, on me," he ordered. He considered for a moment, then tapped a few more commands on his communicator. "Speaker Murtas, are you available? We have a security problem I desire your input on."

"I can be free in half a twentieth-cycle," *Defiance*'s intelligence and cyberwarfare officer replied. "I'd prefer not to leave this project in the middle of a compilation cycle."

"That's acceptable," Pierre told him. "Meet us in my office then."

A few taps on his communicator sent the same time slot to

Comtois and Hunter. Alpha's Company Commander was already halfway across the loading bay to him, so he gestured the other French officer to continue his approach.

"What's going on, sir?" Comtois asked.

"C'est un énorme merdier," Pierre admitted. "We entered the system less than four hours ago, Company Commander. The Advocate was waiting for us with a writ of suspension of imprisonment the moment we tried to move the prisoners."

"Well, shit," Comtois replied. "That usually takes a few days to get drafted and authorized. Someone was waiting for us?"

"We left Beta eleven days ago. If someone was using the expedition's hyper communicator to talk to someone in Kosha, then they could have been ready." Pierre shrugged. "Or, bien sûr, the Public Advocate office on Kosha Station could just be incredibly efficient."

"They only handle, what, two hundred thousand people of mixed species and an attached naval base, right?" Comtois asked. "I'm sure they have spare capacity to draft writs of suspension for pirates in under two hours. Might even have a template for getting pirates out of custody!"

The Battalion Commander chuckled—then gestured Comtois to drop the topic as he spotted Rin Dunst approaching them. To Pierre's surprise, the archeologist didn't slip in the sarcasm that had to be puddling on the floor.

"Commander Vichy, Commander Comtois," the archeologist greeted them with a small bow. "I am accompanying the rest of the expedition onto Kosha Station." The soft-looking man smiled.

"I will be staying longer than most of them, I suspect," he admitted. "Most of my expedition members are almost certainly going to need to go home and take a vacation before getting back to work.

"I will have to talk to the Institute and see about putting together a new expedition. There are a great many questions still unanswered out here, and I will probably need to keep my hands in what is going on with these Children," the civilian said cheerfully. "I am at your and your Captain's disposal, Battalion Commander

Vichy. I do not believe you are likely to find a better expert on the Alava out here."

"You'll need a new figurehead for a new expedition," Comtois muttered. "Can't have anyone realizing you're actually in charge."

Dunst put his hand to his heart in not-entirely-mock shock.

"Administrator !Lat was not a figurehead," he countered. "It simply wasn't necessary—or, really, practical—for him to be fully briefed on everything we knew of the Alava. So long as I was present to inform him of anything that became relevant, the setup worked just fine."

"And we shall rely on a similar structure, I believe," Pierre decided. "When I have questions, you will hear from me."

"And I shall endeavor to have answers, Battalion Commander. The Alava left us many mysteries, and it is my life's work to solve as many of them as possible," Dunst told them. "These Children are both a clue and an obstacle. I look forward to working with you to take advantage of the clue and neutralize the obstacle."

"THERE WAS no leak from *Defiance*. It is not a hundred percent certain, but a hundred percent certainty is impossible," Speaker Toma Murtas told the gathered Marine commanders. The tall and swarthy intelligence officer was leaning back in his chair in a way that made Pierre's spine twitch.

All three of the Marines in the room were sitting in nearly identical positions, rigid spines perched on the edge of their seats. The intelligence officer was almost sprawled backward in the chair in front of Pierre's desk.

Pierre took a certain degree of pride in what he thought was a solid compromise between small luxuries and an apparent spartanness to his office. The furniture and equipment were the same prefabricated plastic and metal as any other officer's space on the ship, but he'd added smart cushions to the chairs, and there was a crystal decanter of brandy on the prefab shelves.

The only true decoration was a plaque-mounted sword behind him, a cavalry saber forged for a young noble in the regiments of King Louis XIV, the Sun King of France. That saber had seen action through two hundred years of service with the various French armies —until the day the last scion of Pierre's family to use it as a weapon had died in one of the suicidal cavalry charges of the First World War.

It had been rescued from that battlefield, somehow, and had spent the ensuing three hundred years mounted on that wooden plaque as an heirloom of Pierre's family. His father had insisted it go with him on his deployments, which led Pierre to suspect it was as much a luck talisman as an heirloom now.

"I did not expect *Defiance* to be the source," Pierre told Murtas finally. He sighed, rising and filling glasses from the crystal decanter. They were all still technically on duty, but a finger of brandy wasn't going to hurt anyone.

"My guess, but I have no way to validate this, is that someone in the Advocate office was provided a fully prepared writ within minutes of us exiting our hyper portal," he continued. "Combined with the information that we had a group of prisoners taken in a complicated situation, the natural desire of Advocate staff to help people would get us to where we ended up."

"Nobody works for an Advocate office to get rich," Murtas replied. The intelligence officer probably had less interaction with the law than any of the Marines. "It's not that they're incorruptible; it's that there's no point. Idealists and white knights, the lot of them."

There was a pregnant pause in the room.

"Which is far from a bad thing," Hunter finally noted. "Most of the people who take that kind of shit job are good people, at least at the start. I get grumpy seeing them used, sir."

"So do I, Commander," Pierre agreed. "Which is why I asked Murtas to be here. Officially, there is no way we can find out where that writ originated. The Advocate office is, quite sensibly, forbidden from providing that information."

"What are you suggesting, Battalion Commander?" Murtas asked, straightening to something approaching military bearing for the first time.

"Echelon Lord Davor has her own intelligence apparatus on Kosha Station," the Marine CO noted. "I would be surprised to discover that they did not have a means of sourcing that writ. I would hope that as a professional courtesy, they would be willing to do so for you."

"It's not that simple," Murtas said slowly. "I'm a combat analyst and a computer geek, plus I'm Navy. The people you're talking about? They don't really regard me as a peer, sir. I can ask, but there's no guarantee of a friendly response."

"The Captain has a long list of strings to pull, Speaker Murtas," Pierre pointed out. "If we can trace the local end of the Children, it's useful, but it's not necessary. Ask them. It can't hurt, can it?"

"Unless our own spies *are* the local branch of the Children," Comtois muttered. "*Someone* gave them classified intel to start this whole mess, after all."

Pierre found himself wishing that Comtois had kept that thought to himself.

CHAPTER NINETEEN

"WE HAVE COMPLETED THE MAJORITY OF THE STRUCTURAL repairs, Captain," the Rekiki shipyard master told her. Takakek was a larger member of the species' noble caste, which made him a crocodile with an upright torso and sharp toothy jaws that outweighed Morgan around five to one.

Unfortunately for Takakek's intimidation factor, Annette Bond had kept a squad of Rekiki among her personal guard for most of Morgan's childhood. While she wasn't going to do anything silly, her initial reaction to large Rekiki was still mostly "mobile playground!" not "oh god, monster!"

"So, we could deploy now?" Morgan asked. She'd never actually spent this long with a ship in drydock before. *Hawkwing* had gone in for a refit at the end of her tour of duty aboard the destroyer, but she'd been transferred to the light cruiser *Fleeting Wrath* within hours of handing her command over.

Takakek laughed at her question.

"We have replaced or repaired the structural girders and supports of your ship, so I suppose so," he allowed. "You'd still be short a tenth of your beam weapons and have gaping holes in your armor, but *Defiance* could accelerate and maneuver at full speed."

"I'll wait for the armor and guns, I suppose," Morgan allowed with a laugh of her own. "How long?"

"Another six to eight cycles," the Rekiki told her. "It's not a fast process, sizing compressed-matter plates, Captain."

"I know."

She also knew that they'd been in the drydock for six cycles already and *Serene Guidance* had left three cycles earlier. The destroyer was scheduled to arrive at her destination in another three cycles. If *Defiance* wasn't ready to deploy, there was no backup for Commander Isk's ship if something went wrong.

Of course, backup six cycles away wasn't much more useful than backup six cycles away that couldn't leave for six more cycles.

"Everything is repairable, though, right?"

"Without question," Takakek confirmed. "She's a sturdy, well-built ship. The Indiri did a good job building her, and we'll have her back to full fighting stride before you take her out again."

"Good. Those hits were worse than I expected," Morgan told the shipbuilder. "You've seen the damage now. Anything we can do to minimize it?"

"Don't get hit," the shipyard master said. "Near-c plasma is hunter shit and I don't know where you ran into hatchling plasma lances, but in many ways, they're just as bad for damage as *Defiance*'s own heavy plasma beams.

"We've got a bit of information on the beam material that we've sent to the Echelon Lord's staff for analysis. We can do a bit with tuning the shields specifically against these beams, but mostly? If they hit you enough times, your shield goes down and even compressed-matter armor isn't going to do more than limit the damage."

Morgan nodded her agreement, glancing out the window at her abused ship.

"Don't get hit," she repeated. "I'll try my best, dockmaster."

"You're a warship Captain," Takakek replied. "Don't make promises you can't keep."

———

MORGAN WAS LEAVING Takakek's office when her communicator pinged. The ubiquitous devices took on a lot of different forms, even aboard military ships. Her own preference, inherited from her father and stepmother, was a scroll-like device based on the old UESF communicator.

It folded up to two cylinders, each the size of her thumb, but those easily extended to any length up to forty centimeters. The two cylinders then slid apart, held together by a flexible but strong material that acted as screen and keyboard.

If needed, it could create a forty-centimeter-by-forty-centimeter working and viewing surface—and then use hologram projectors to extend that. Morgan's default was a ten-centimeter square that acted as a handheld video phone.

She was surprised to see the caller identified as Rin Dunst, however, and took a moment to get into a quiet corner inside the main shipyard office before answering.

"Dr. Dunst, how can I help you?"

"Ah, Captain," he replied. "Did I catch you at a bad time, Morgan?"

She caught herself smiling at his remembering to use her first name. For a moment, she started to shut the smile down behind the "Captain Mask," then she remembered she was off-ship and in an only quasi-military office.

Morgan let the smile reach her face and was rewarded with an answering smile from Dunst. *Interesting.*

"A surprisingly good time, actually," she told him. "I was just finishing up my appointment at the shipyard, where I learned that I don't have nearly as much to do right now as I'd like. So, like I said, Rin, how can I help you?"

"I think I might be able to help you, actually," he replied. "Now that I'm in one place and have access to the proper Archives, I think I've learned a bit more about what we're looking at out here. I'd rather go over it in person. May I buy you dinner?"

Morgan studied the man's image carefully for a moment. She was quite sure that he was being both entirely aboveboard and had the expected unspoken hopes that came along with a dinner invitation.

"I'm free right now if you are," she told him. "How about a working lunch instead?"

She wasn't *quite* ready to shut the good doctor down, not without a bit more prodding, anyway. If nothing else, she wanted to know what he'd found in the Mesharom Archive.

She'd heard the capital A when he'd been speaking, and she doubted that was unintentional.

"Lunch sounds perfect, Captain," Dunst told her. "There's a sushi restaurant near the naval shipyard that's good for both food and security. It is, after all, next to the only military shipyard for sixty light-years."

Morgan chuckled.

"Sounds perfect," she echoed back to him. "I'll grab a table and discuss our security needs with the staff, and you can meet me there?"

KOSHA STATION SUSHI RESTAURANT might not have been particularly imaginative in its naming, but its owners had been very imaginative in supplying the necessary materials of their trade. Half of the menu was explicitly sourced from Blue Heart's oceans, but the rest were specifically un-gene-modified Terran fish.

No engine in the galaxy would allow fish to be delivered to a sushi restaurant three hundred-odd light-years away in the "proper" state for sushi, so Kosha Station Sushi had gone one step further.

They'd imported breeding stocks of several key fish for their menu and raised them in carefully designed farms on the station itself.

The water served double duty as part of the station's reservoirs, and two of the station's walls were explicitly one-way windows into the fish farms. Between the massive effort made to create an appropriate artificial environment for the fish and the fish themselves, it made for an incredible decoration.

And then Morgan was introduced to the secured dining room the owners kept for military officers.

"*Inside* the tank?" she asked, making sure she'd heard the host correctly.

"There is an access tube," the young woman—who appeared to actually be Japanese despite being this far from Earth—assured her. "But the water augments the security systems and renders the space as secure as possible."

"All right. Lead the way."

The access tube was standard, but the dining room Morgan was ushered into was amazing. The wall with the tube was covered in a hologram to make it appear to be as transparent as the other five walls...which *were* transparent.

The room was suspended inside a space currently pretending to be a well-lit lake somewhere on Earth. Like the windows from the restaurant into the tanks, the glass was one-way. The fish couldn't see the humans, but the humans could see the fish.

"We will bring your guest when he arrives," the host assured her. "I suggest you peruse the menu while you wait; even if you are familiar with sushi, we have our own variations here that take advantage of the opportunities presented by both Blue Heart and, well, the fish tank."

"Thank you, Ms..."

"Atsuko Ikeda, ma'am," the young woman told her. "This is my mother's restaurant."

"Your mother has done an incredible job," Morgan said. "Thank you, Ms. Ikeda. I'll take a look at the menu while I wait for Dr. Dunst."

"Of course, Captain Casimir," Ikeda told her. "Only the best for the Duchess's daughter."

Morgan let the woman leave before letting her frustration show on her face as she sighed. Hundreds of light-years from home, she couldn't escape her stepmother's shadow. There were humans throughout the Imperium now, and humanity's influence was out of scale with their size and recent entrance into the A!Tol's sphere.

The shadow of Terra stretched *far*—and Duchess Annette Bond's shadow stretched just as far. Morgan had spent her entire life in both of those shadows, and she wasn't entirely sure how she'd escape either of them.

She loved her stepmother. Her biological mother had died in childbirth. Annette Bond had been her father's lover when she'd been very young, and then her father had become Ducal Consort when Morgan had been barely more than a toddler.

The Duchess *was* Morgan's mother, so far as she was concerned, and she'd been a good one. But Morgan didn't want to be defined by her Duchess mother or her trillionaire father. She wanted her own story, her own legend.

She knew that was egotistical of her, but she was a *warship captain*. Ego came with the job.

A knock on the door pulled her attention back to the moment as Ikeda brought Rin Dunst in.

"I like your suggestion, Rin," she told the scientist. "Let's take a look at the menu and see what they have before we talk business, shall we?"

CHAPTER TWENTY

THEY SENT THE WAITER—A YOUNG BLACK MAN WHO PROBABLY wasn't related to the host and owners—on his way with their list, then Morgan picked up her tea and straightened in her chair, away from the table.

"You said you had some new data on our cultists," she reminded Dunst. "What did you find?"

"Not so much on the cultists, to be honest," Dunst admitted. "I'm leaving what's going on today in the capable hands of your military analysts. I did find something familiar as we were digging through what the Archive had on this region, though."

Glancing at the door, he laid his communicator down on the table and opened up a hologram. The projected image was only two-dimensional, a file photo filtered through fifty thousand years of memory.

The Mesharom had survived the fall of the Precursors, but their *technology* hadn't. Most of the records they'd preserved had been written down immediately after the fall, much of it carved into stone tablets to make certain it was saved.

The image on the stone was a familiar fat teardrop shape.

"Is that one of the bioships?" Morgan asked.

"I think so," he confirmed. "Unfortunately, either the Mesharom were unable to translate the text that went with it, or it isn't in the copy of the Archive we have. There's a few references to their biotech throughout the Archive, but I came away with a surprising evaluation:

"The Alava Hegemony didn't *trust* biotech." He shrugged. "They used it in extremely controlled environments, often with electronic or nanotechnological control and kill switches installed."

"Even ignoring what we're seeing here, we found the cloner at Arjtal," Morgan countered. She didn't necessarily disbelieve what he'd found, but she wanted to know how that linked together.

"That wasn't in the Mesharom files," Dunst said. "My guess is that it was a private science experiment on the far edge of their borders—and it might well have had an electronic control system at one point. When they killed their tech, they'd have killed that, too."

"So, if they didn't like biotech, where are these ships coming from?" she asked.

"I think these ships would be the main Alava state's worst nightmare," he replied. "They're either self-replicated or being created by a primary biological source. They could control nanites and anything they had to build, but they didn't trust that they could control biology. There was a fundamental fear in them of things they couldn't control."

"That lines up with a people who killed themselves trying to take control of the *laws of physics*," Morgan replied. A chime on the tube warned her that the staff had accessed the far end.

The room was supposed to be one hundred percent secure, and the warning was part of that. She still took a moment to check that the security-field generator she'd set up was running.

"So, do you make it back to Earth often?" Dunst asked slowly, changing the subject as the waiter returned with the first tray of raw fish. From the size, they'd likely get three more, so casual conversation was probably the right choice.

"Once a year, when I can," Morgan told him. "Not, to the occasional frustration of the Navy's personnel department, once a long-cycle."

A long-cycle, the time-frame around which the Imperium ran such things as assigning leave, was one hundred and ninety-five days. Technically, the leave allotment for an Imperial officer was ten cycles per long-cycle.

"That's...got to take some work," Dunst said. "We're a long way from Sol here. It's not like you can take most of a long-cycle off to go home for Christmas."

"I've spent a good chunk of my career closer to Sol, where I could jump aboard a Navy courier and be home in three to five days," Morgan replied. The new Navy couriers were the first recipients of the hyperspace-current-manipulating technology the Imperium had also acquired from the Mesharom.

"It's harder now, but that's part of the point," she admitted as she selected several pieces of sushi to try. "My girlfriend is about to get married, and I want them to sort out what the hell they want before I reinsert myself into that mess."

Morgan took more than a passing delight in the moment of sheer confusion that crossed Rin Dunst's face there. Confusion, followed by disappointment, followed by more confusion.

She finished off three pieces of sushi while he marshaled his thoughts.

"Your girlfriend is getting married?" he finally asked. The chime announced that a second wave of food was arriving.

"Yeah. Victoria and I have been together since the Taljzi Campaigns, but it was never fair to ask her to wait when I was out of the system fifty-plus weeks of the year. We decided to try an open relationship around...year five or so?" Morgan shrugged. She couldn't actually remember anymore.

"She and Shelly have been together for six years. *Technically*, I was still Victoria's primary partner, but I was only there for two weeks a year."

There'd even been an attempt to make it work as a triad at one point, though that had fallen through. Morgan found Shelly attractive enough, but the spark needed to maintain things over year-long separation wasn't there.

"Shelly actually asked me if it was okay before she proposed," the Captain concluded. It had stung more than she was going to admit to anyone, even if Victoria and Shelly's marriage explicitly included her as a secondary partner.

"That sounds like it gets complicated," Dunst said as the third set of food arrived. They'd already demolished the first two, and the waiter removed those trays with a silent bow.

"Not as much as you'd think." Morgan shrugged. "I spent fifty weeks of the year on a warship I'm in command of, Rin; my opportunities to take advantage of an open relationship are limited."

The archeologist actually blushed. Morgan had suspected he'd been hoping to make this dinner more personal than business, but she still hadn't expected to actually get a *blush* out of a man closer to forty than thirty.

The rotund scientist was about as much Victoria Antonova's opposite as was physically possible, but that was just fine by Morgan.

"Dr. Dunst, you are blushing," she told him with a laugh. "I thought this was supposed to be a *professional* lunch."

"I, I, uh..." He trailed off as the waiter arrived with the last set of food, and she continued to laugh.

"Let's be specific, shall we?" she finally asked as the waiter bowed out again. "I am in a long-term open relationship where I was recently downgraded to a secondary partner—with my full consent, but still a downgrade—and am a minimum of two months' flight from my girlfriend.

"I *am* available and open to the idea of a date, if you are interested, but this was still primarily a working lunch. Does that answer enough of the questions you weren't sure if you could ask?"

He was still blushing, but he was laughing now, too.

"Touché, Morgan," he conceded. "I do still have some more data on what was going on out here, now that the waiters should stop coming quite as often, but yes, I was hoping to get to know you better."

"All right," she allowed. "You may have one actual date, Dr. Dunst, and then we'll reevaluate, yes?"

"Do I get a formal report card, or is this more of a small-group evaluation?" he asked with a grin.

"That will depend on how you do, won't it?" Morgan replied with a wink. "That's a conversation for later, though," she continued more seriously. "What else did you find out?"

He nodded slowly, marshaling his thoughts as he inhaled another piece of sushi.

"This is really good," he noted aloud.

"I figured when the restaurant was *in* the fish tank," Morgan replied. "The Alava?"

"The Alava." He nodded. "The people out here were Alava and they brought a whole working population of the subject races, but they weren't part of the Hegemony. Not really. They weren't officially seceded, but they were sending only the minimum data home.

"The Mesharom didn't record much about this region because the central stars didn't know anything. Ten billion people two hundred light-years away from the nearest Alava system. They weren't out here because they liked how the Hegemony ran things."

"So, they might have been out here to do research and development the Hegemony didn't like? Like biotech?"

"From what we've encountered, almost certainly," Dunst agreed. "My concern, though, Captain, is that they only reported the one system to the central archives. Population growth for the time frame we're looking at suggests we should have seen a world of twelve to fifteen billion.

"There were maybe two hundred million people on D-L-K-Six-Beta," he told her. "So, ten-plus billion sentients were somewhere else. Different systems...or construction projects that called for billions of workers."

"Megastructures," Morgan concluded with a sigh. "That appears to have been the Alava style from the moment they had enough resources to build the damn things."

"It does speak to something fundamental in their psyche, I think," Dunst agreed. "But...more than megastructures, Morgan. Any Alava group is going to build something of a scale we'd regard as excessive and stupid. We saw that around Arjtal.

"These people almost certainly built *something* like that...but they also appear to have left the Hegemony to work on research the Alava main culture would not permit."

"I'm not liking where that leads me, Dr. Dunst," Morgan admitted.

His response was interrupted by the chime announcing the waiters, probably coming to remove the plates. He exhaled a long sigh and nodded to her as they waited.

No waiter materialized but the warning light was still on. Glancing at her companion, Morgan felt a chill of paranoia and rose to her feet.

"Something's wrong," she told Dunst—and then was thrown from her feet as an explosion tore through the tube connecting them to the station.

CHAPTER TWENTY-ONE

"Situation Threat-Actual, we have an active threat on *Defiance*-Actual."

"Merde."

Pierre's response hung in the air of his office for several seconds as he processed the situation. Even as he was swearing and thinking, he was pulling up the map of Kosha Station and grabbing the location of his Captain and her protective Marine detail.

"Lance Aniston, report," he snapped. "What is going on?"

"I'm not sure yet, sir," his team leader, Lance Emily Aniston, replied. "The Captain and Dr. Dunst were in a secured dining room suspended in part of the station's water supply. We had secured the entrance in cooperation with the restaurant, but it looks like we missed an explosive being carried by a waiter.

"The access tube has been severed. Status reports for the dining room suggest it is maintaining integrity, but I'm assuming there is a second component to the attack and I'm attempting to locate the nearest entry point to the tank."

"Understood. I'll have additional Marines on their way immediately," Pierre replied swiftly. "Are you patched into Station Security?"

"Yes, sir. They're the ones—yes, I have the nearest entrance. I am requesting Station Security secure the restaurant, and we are moving to the tank."

"Move, Lance," Pierre ordered. Leaving the channel open so Aniston could reach him if needed, he muted his side of it and started bringing up other channels.

"Speaker Qadir, we are Threat Actual; are you in motion?" he asked the woman in charge of his Alpha-Three Platoon, the current ready detachment.

"We are. Two squads are on the station in power armor and navigating to the restaurant and the water-reservoir access. One squad is reequipping for underwater combat and will follow under my command," Qadir replied.

That was the biggest problem they faced, Pierre knew. The bodyguards had breathers, but their plasma carbines wouldn't function underwater without prior preparation. Only their stunners were waterproofed enough to function underwater.

He hadn't expected to have a firefight in the station's water reservoirs, but he doubted whoever had just turned a waiter into a probably unknowing suicide bomber had expected that to be the end of the situation.

"Standard armor-carried plasma guns *will* function," Pierre noted. They'd only do so in one mode and it would be terrible for anything around them, but they'd work. "Send them in as soon as they have access. Our Captain is uncovered."

"They're on their way, sir," Qadir repeated. "But they knew this was coming and we didn't."

"I know," the Battalion Commander conceded. "En avant, Speaker."

He left that channel in the same semi-open status as his link to Aniston and switched to a third channel.

"Captain Casimir, what is your status?" he demanded. He wasn't sure she'd be able to answer him, but he had to at least try.

There was no answer and he checked the scanners. The entire space his Captain had been eating in was secured against communications to stand bugs off. Even with Navy coms, she almost certainly couldn't communicate out now that the hard link had been severed.

"Comtois, take over the watch," he ordered as he opened a new channel. "*Defiance*-Actual is dark and I am moving in myself."

"Is that wise, sir?" Comtois asked.

"I don't know, but our *Captain* is in danger, Company Commander," he replied. "We will do everything we can. Begin scrambling the rest of the battalion for me."

"Yes, sir."

Pierre strode purposefully to the half-closed bookshelf next to the plaque holding his ancestor's sword and swung it open. The bottom shelves were missing, replaced with a weapons safe that readily yielded to his codes.

None of the weapons in the safe were modern, but the twenty-second-century battle rifle his father had used for the Franco-German Army had the unique qualification of being a high-velocity battle rifle designed to function in any environment. *Underwater* had been third on the design criteria after *regular combat* and *vacuum*, but it had been considered.

Even Pierre had thought keeping ammunition on hand for the obsolete antiques in that safe was being excessively paranoid—but he'd still done it.

"BATTALION COMMANDER VICHY, this is Battalion Commander Addaka," a new voice sounded in Pierre's ears as he ran through the station. Qadir and her underwater-equipped Marines trailed in his wake, creating a large degree of chaos as twelve Marines set up for swimming and fighting underwater charged through the crowds.

"Do you have sensors on my Captain, Addaka?" Pierre asked the Rekiki officer.

"Not close-range, no. Someone has disabled the sensors in the fish farm tanks," Addaka told him. "Other Station internal systems strongly suggest we're looking at multiple divers in the tank, but it appears they've underestimated the restaurant's security measures. That dining bubble is more heavily armored than it looks, and there's a secondary security hatch that appears to be frustrating their efforts so far."

"Do you have anyone in there yet?" Pierre demanded. This was at least as much Station Security's mess as his.

"The farm tanks are somewhat intentionally hard to access," Addaka said grimly. "A course for the herd that made sense at the time, I'm sure. It mitigates theft, but my divers have commented on it before. It appears that they were correct."

"If my people aren't in the tank by the time I get there, we are going to start cutting walls," Pierre warned.

"With the blessings of the herd, Commander Vichy," the Rekiki replied instantly. "There is an emergency retrieval mechanism for the dining pod as well. It has also been sabotaged, but my people believe they'll have it online in a few minutes at most. The pod's armor should hold that long."

"I don't want to hang my Captain's survival on *should*, Commander Addaka."

"I agree. Water Management is screaming at me, but I'm opening several portals that aren't supposed to be opened. Your people *will* have access." The Rekiki paused. "And the fish will have an exit, but that's tomorrow's problem."

Directions popped up onto the HUD projecting to Pierre's contacts. It was a different access route now, but one that would get his people into the water sooner and about the same distance *through* the water as before.

"Thank you, Commander Addaka."

"I'd hurry, Vichy. We're registering explosions in the tank, and I don't know how long the bubble's armor will hold."

"Sir, it's Lance Aniston," the NCO leading Casimir's bodyguard cut in. "We're in the tank and are engaging the hostiles. They appear to be shielded against stunners and used explosives to throw my people away. Everyone's alive, but most of my team is injured, and I'm evacing two whose breathers have been damaged.

"Without better gear, I can't get to the Captain. I'm sorry, sir. There's nothing my team can do except get shot."

"Understood, Lance," Pierre replied. "Establish visual if you can and guide the relief teams in. We need to get the Captain out."

He muted all of his channels and stared down at his feet as he continued to run.

"Merde."

———

POWER ARMOR COULD FUNCTION underwater without problems, though the guns were more complicated. There were modules that could make the armor function underwater *better*, including everything from adding stabilizing fins to adding water jets to provide propulsion.

The eleven suits of power armor with Pierre had managed the quick and dirty version of that. No one had expected to be needing to fight inside the station's water reservoirs. Most of the time, almost everyone tended to forget that most stations and spaceships were something like thirty percent water by volume. It was required for life and it made a handy storage medium for both oxygen for breathing and hydrogen for the fusion reactors.

And now his Captain was free-floating in those tanks while some *connards* were trying to kill her.

Pierre's power armor hadn't been fitted out with the underwater gear, so he hadn't even bothered to grab it. He had grabbed an unpowered underwater deployment ensemble and had been strapping it on as he ran, with some help from Qadir.

By the time they reached the access point and he dove in, he had the same stabilizing fins and water jets as his Marines. He was far less armored than they were, but he suspected that the sixty-year-old slugthrower he was carrying was a far better underwater weapon than a plasma gun.

The water was *cold* and Pierre was wishing he had his armor even before he was fully submersed. Regardless of his desires, he turned on the water jets and shot forward toward a navpoint projected on the faceplate of the breathing helmet.

Icons told him the Marines were right behind him, their more powerful jets offset by the far greater mass of the armor.

"Form on the Commander," he heard Qadir order. "Watch your fire. Even on these settings, the corona of the plasma beams is a lot worse down here and your range is much shorter than you think."

The irony of potentially being vaporized by his own men not being careful enough wasn't lost on Pierre, and he listened to Qadir's unspoken suggestion, falling back into the formation so the Marines with plasma guns weren't shooting past him.

"Commander, this is Addaka." The Rekiki security officer—also an Imperial Marine, despite his current ignominious role—cut into Pierre's feed. "We have the retrieval mechanism working, but it looks like the attackers might be nearly through the armor.

"We're almost out of time. I show you on the edge of the tanks; I'm dropping targeting icons to your team. I can't guarantee they'll work, but I know you need to start shooting *now*."

Eight amorphous red blobs appeared on Pierre's faceplate, each marking a heat signature that he was too far away to pick out himself. Hopefully, the station computers weren't setting them up to accidentally blast the Captain with plasma.

"Marines, we have targets. Fire at will!"

He lined the rifle up carefully, surprised when the breathing helmet managed to interface with the obsolete weapon's computers.

He knew damn well he was out of practice with a projectile rifle, but he also didn't think the plasma beams were going to make it.

He didn't compensate for the recoil well enough on the first shot and fell farther back among his Marines as they charged forward. New heat icons for the plasma beams were confusing what limited sensors he had, and he focused on the targets Addaka was giving him.

The second shot was perfect. So was the third. The fourth was a bit off, but Pierre was in a rhythm now. Single shots at the center of the targets, using the jets to close the range and not even worrying about hitting his Marines.

There was no way an Earth-built, pre-Annexation, slugthrower was even going to *scratch* his people's armor. It was going to do a lot worse to the poor bastards he was shooting at.

He was most of the way through a thirty-round magazine when Addaka came back on the coms.

"We have the pod and it's moving to retrieval," the Rekiki reported. "I've sent the location to your non-underwater-equipped Marines; they'll be more useful there. Pod integrity is holding; I think you might have got them all, Battalion Commander."

"We'll move in and make sure," Pierre replied, shaking himself from his shooting zen state. "Qadir, did we take any return fire?"

"A bit, but more like your toy than anything that can threaten the suits," she said. "I'm not showing motion larger than a fish; I think we're clear."

"Move in and secure the pod," he ordered. "Relay me targets if you tag anything. I suspect this *toy* is more effective in this environment."

Qadir chuckled.

"I'm pretty sure we killed a lot more fish than you did, sir," she replied. "But...you're probably right when it comes to actual terrorists."

CHAPTER TWENTY-TWO

THE DINING ROOM CHAMBER SHIVERED AROUND THEM AS Morgan regained consciousness. Her head was pounding and she was cataloging concussion symptoms half-consciously as she forced herself to her knees.

"Rin?" she asked. It was dark except for flashes of light in the distance. Plasma fire. The hell?

"I'm here," he told her. "I want to know who manufactured this dining room for the sushi restaurant. I believe I want to buy shares."

"What?" she demanded, blinking away dizziness.

"My com says you've been out for just over five minutes," he said. "We need to get you to a doctor; that's not a good sign for a head injury."

"No shit. What's *happening?*"

"Someone detonated a bomb in the access tube," Dunst told her, his distracted voice suggesting that Morgan wasn't the only one who'd need a doctor. "Then half a dozen individuals showed up outside with what are either plasma cutters or short-ranged underwater plasma guns and have been trying to open us up like a can of fish."

Morgan suddenly realized she was wet. The floor of the bubble was covered in a layer of water several centimeters deep.

"They have failed so far, but I don't think that's going to last much longer," he told her. "Despite the state I was in when your Marines first encountered me, I am not particularly good with weapons and did not bring one. I'm afraid we are in some trouble."

There were definitely flashes of light closer in, too. Morgan could just make out shadowy figures carrying weapons through the transparent windows, but the plasma wasn't directed at them.

"So are they," she said with some satisfaction, then winced as her head pounded again. "Two sets of flashes of light tells me the Marines are here, so these guys are—"

One of their attackers slammed bodily into the pod, their flailing body smearing a long streak of blood across the transparent armor.

"Fucked," Morgan concluded. That hadn't been a plasma beam; those self-cauterized. What had they been shot with?

An echoing *bong* washed over the chamber, an impact that drew her attention to the entrance hatch. The hologram that had covered it was gone now, revealing a solid metal wall with an extra security hatch over the exit. It appeared that it was the connection between that wall and the "glass" of the rest of the pod that was now slowly leaking.

"We're moving," Dunst told her. "I doubt your inner ear is entirely functional, but I think we just got grabbed by something." He looked out. "The shooting seems to have stopped and we appear to be being rescued, but given today's events, I have to ask: are *you* carrying a weapon?"

"Yes." Morgan drew her plasma pistol and stared down at its vague, blurry shape. "I see two of them, so I probably shouldn't be firing it, but I have a gun."

"May I, Morgan?" Dunst asked, holding out a hand.

Morgan nearly dropped the gun passing it to him and forced a chuckle.

"Definitely looks like you're going to be the better shot," she agreed, her words audibly slurred even to her. "And I'm not a great shot to begin with. Set for max disp, max fire."

Maximum dispersion, maximum rate of fire. The gun wasn't set up to do much against power armor, but it would act as an automatic plasma shotgun at close range.

"I didn't know that was an available setting," Dunst said faintly. "Thank you. Now stay upright," he ordered firmly, one hand suddenly against the small of her back. "We might be rescued, but this pod is filling fast and we can't wait once we make contact."

"There'll be more," Morgan told him. "I wouldn't...only send one batch of assassins."

"I'm no tactician, but I was expecting much the same," the archeologist agreed. "That's why I asked for the gun."

She chuckled.

"You might have already earned that second date," she slurred at him.

"That's a future conversation, I think," he told her. "Let's get out of this alive first."

CONCUSSION OR NOT, Morgan was very capable of recognizing the sound of plasma fire when the hatch opened. It was close and she only heard a handful of shots before things fell silent.

"It's secure. Move quickly; we've lost too many Children today," a voice shouted, her translator calmly turning it into English for her. "The Mother demands the death of the Captain and the archeologist. *Finish it.*"

She could check the language that was being spoken, but that would have required movement and checking her communicator screen. Neither was feeling overly possible as more nausea overcame her.

"Need to stay in here," she told Dunst. "There's... there's..."

"I heard them too," he told her, maneuvering her with delicate hands to lean against the heavy metal wall. "Wait here."

"What are you *doing*?" She had enough control to grab the scientist before he charged out of the pod. "We *both* wait here."

"They're..."

"*Marines*," she hissed. "Coming."

Footsteps were approaching and Morgan steadied herself against the wall and gestured to Dunst. He wasn't the best man for the job, but he was the only one of them able to fight.

He flattened himself against the wall, holding the plasma pistol in both hands and taking heavy breaths as the footsteps grew nearer.

"Captain Casimir, we're here to get you to safety," a voice said in accented English. "You and Dr. Dunst are in danger here, and we need to move you off-station ASAP."

Dunst looked over at Morgan and she shook her head. She didn't recognize the voice and she knew perfectly well that the people after them would want them to come out where they could be more easily shot.

She had not expected Dunst to step around the side and shoot the speaker. The plasma pistol *crack*ed three times in rapid succession before the doctor cleared the door. Several blasts of plasma answered his shots, hammering into the back of the pod and potentially accelerating the leak.

"Black cloaks, face masks, definitely not friendlies," Dunst told her aloud. "Try that again, idiots!" he shouted out the door.

Several more plasma shots answered, and Morgan was glad that whatever explosives and grenades their enemies possessed appeared to have gone with the underwater team.

In answer, Dunst stuck the gun around the corner and randomly fired several times. With the dispersion cone, he might have even hit someone, but Morgan's concussion-addled brain only told her that the gun had limited ammo.

She wasn't sure she'd know how many shots it got in her default mode normally, but the headache was making it hard to think.

"There's at least five of them," Dunst whispered. "If they rush, I'm not sure what I can—"

A Marine's power-armor-carried heavy plasma gun had a very distinct sound from other plasma weapons, an echoing CRACK-*hiss* that Morgan had rarely heard outside a training range. At least half a dozen guns fired repeatedly for several seconds, and then another strange voice shouted down the hall.

"Captain Casimir, this is Lance Baudelio Seppänen," shouted a voice with a faint Scandinavian accent on the standard enunciation taught to Earth-trained officers. "We have secured the hallway. I can provide identification if you wish, but I think the situation is sufficiently in hand for us to wait for someone you recognize, sir, before you enter the station."

"Captain Casimir is injured, Lance Seppänen," Dunst replied. "Sooner is better, and I'm not sure she'd recognize Duchess Bond at the moment. What have you got for that ID, son?"

"Dr. Dunst?" the young NCO asked. "We shared a meal in the general mess for three of the days you were on *Defiance*. You liked our lasagna but hated the spaghetti, said the cooks did something incomprehensible with the spices. I believe you may have used the phrase 'what Lovecraftian monstrosity did they make this out of?!'"

Morgan hadn't been there for that meal, but the phrase certainly sounded like Dunst—and his chuckle suggested that he did remember that exact conversation.

She had enough time to reflect that that was a good thing before she slumped farther down the wall into blackness.

CHAPTER TWENTY-THREE

"ARE YOU ALL RIGHT, DR. DUNST?"

It took Rin several long seconds to process that Battalion Commander Vichy had arrived, let alone that the dark-haired Marine was talking to him. The archeologist's attention was very much focused on Morgan Casimir, watching in near-shock as the medics loaded her onto a stretcher.

"Commander," he greeted the Marine, playing for time to regain his mental equilibrium. The swing from Morgan agreeing to go on a date to sudden violence and death had been harsh.

He coughed and shook his head.

"I'm uninjured," he finally said. "I remain uninured to violence, though. This...this was unexpected."

"It shouldn't have happened," Vichy told him. The Marine appeared to be removing fins of some kind? Apparently, the Marine CO had been in the water while Rin had been sitting in a dark bubble with an unconscious woman.

That was going to go down as one of the most unpleasant experiences of his life.

"Best guess is they used a multipart explosive whose individual components didn't flag our scanners," the Marine continued. "We'll never know, unfortunately. The water flow in the reservoir will already have wiped away any residue we could analyze."

"I'm sorry; I should have been able to protect her," Rin whispered.

The Marine laughed. It wasn't an entirely pleasant or happy sound.

"Captain Casimir was armed and is trained in the use of her sidearm," Vichy pointed out. "She would have expected to protect you, Dr. Dunst, not the other way around. Ce n'est pas de votre faute. Blame the Children, not yourself."

"We're sure it's them?" Rin asked. "That seems..."

"Unlikely?" Vichy finished his sentence. "I would agree, but they had the same anti-stunner gear."

"I heard...something about the Children and the Mother, I think?" Rin offered. "It wasn't clear; they were far enough that they didn't think we could hear."

"They shot four Marines assigned to Station Security to try and ambush you here," Vichy told him. "We took one alive, but..."

"But what?" Rin demanded.

"I'm not sure how much of this you're cleared for, Dr. Dunst," the Marine admitted.

"Then check your records," Rin snapped. "I have a higher security clearance than you do, Battalion Commander. I don't care to delve into why, but I *am* cleared for this mess."

"Suicide device," the younger man said flatly. "Listen to this."

The Marine CO tapped at several keys on a holographic keyboard Rin could only vaguely see, starting an audio recording.

"You have the right to legal representation. I am not that representation and anything you say to me will be recorded and can be used against you in a court of law."

The Imperium didn't have the same legal requirement as many Earth polities still did—that a prisoner had to be informed of their rights—but the prisoners still had those rights, and old traditions ran deep.

"The Mother is watching," a voice slurred. "She sees *everything*. She will come for you. She will consume your worlds, your suns, and birth a shining new era from the sustenance of your eternities. All will be darkness beyond Her light."

There was a sharp cracking sound and Vichy waved the recording to silence.

"Self-initiated cortical explosive," the Marine explained. "He killed himself to prevent questioning but felt the need to dramatically threaten us all. What do you make of it?"

"I don't know," Rin admitted. "But we're definitely starting to get a feel for something at the center of the Children's world. An entity of some kind, potentially..."

He looked at the Marines around them. Vichy was cleared for Lost Dragon, which was probably enough for this conversation. The rest of the armored humans around them...not so much.

"Potentially, this is a conversation we should have in a secured space, once Captain Casimir is back with us," he murmured. "I'm suddenly concerned about the ship I know Echelon Lord Davor sent out."

"If Kosha Station is penetrated enough for them to send a strike team after you and the Captain, they know *Serene Guidance* is coming," Vichy confirmed. "And with her in hyperspace for three more cycles, we can't warn her."

The silence that followed was interrupted by Rin's and Vichy's communicators chiming at the same time. Looking at the Marine questioningly, Rin pulled out his own.

"Echelon Lord Davor wants to see us," Vichy said aloud while the scientist was still staring at the message. "Come on, Doctor. You're not going anywhere without Marines now."

"What? You can't be serious," Rin said.

"Category Two Asset, Dr. Dunst," the Marine replied. "We shouldn't have let you leave the naval base on your own as it was."

Rin swore under his breath. No one had told him nearly enough about the downsides of becoming one of the Imperium's top experts on a godlike dead race.

RIN HAD KNOWN that he'd spent most of his time in the military portion of Kosha Station—that was, he suspected now, most of how he'd avoided picking up a Marine escort—but this was the first time he'd seen the Imperium lock that base down.

The accesses to the naval base had been guarded but open when he'd left. Now, he learned that every access to the Imperial section of the base was a full armored airlock. There were guards outside the airlock who validated their IDs before they opened the outer doors. They were cycled through efficiently enough, but the extra security was blatant.

"Does...does the base have its own life support?" Rin asked as Vichy grimly lead the way.

"Oui," the Marine confirmed, obviously falling further back into French as the situation calmed. "The only connection for the atmospheric systems is the transit passageways. The power systems and a few others are linked but severable, is my understanding. It's not a completely separate station, but it's capable of functioning separately from the civilian station."

A separate station might have been easier to build, Rin reflected, but there was a value to the convenience, he supposed.

Vichy either had some kind of guiding beacon Rin couldn't see or knew his way through the base already. The Marine led the way to Davor's office without slowing or hesitating.

They hit a second layer of security at their destination, armored four-armed Tosumi Marines who checked their IDs with extreme thoroughness.

"The Echelon Lord is waiting for you," the noncom in charge finally told them. "Go in."

There was a harried-looking Yin officer on the other side of the door, smoothing down his blue feathers as they entered.

"The Echelon Lord is waiting for you," he echoed the noncom outside. "Corridor on the left, doors at the end."

Even Vichy had waited for the instructions. Rin wasn't sure if that was respect for the authority of the desk or the junior officer behind it, or that the Marine didn't know where the flag officer's office was.

The left corridor led to double doors that opened into a large office with either a viewscreen covering the entire far wall or an actual window out over Blue Heart.

The massive desk at the center of the room appeared to be carved from stone, a rock so dark red as to be nearly black. It was the only visible furnishing in the room, though Rin recognized the patterns in the metal walls that suggested additional furniture could be summoned if the occupant wanted it.

Two chairs had been placed in front of the desk and Davor stood behind it, studying the two humans as they came in.

"Sit," she ordered.

Rin obeyed without hesitation. Glancing to the side, he saw that his Marine companion hesitated for several seconds.

"Captain Casimir is in the base hospital," Davor told them. "Her prognosis is good."

Morgan had been standing when the dining room was detached from its mountings and sent into an uncontrollable spin. Rin had seen her fly across the thankfully tiny room and smash her head into the wall. He'd been unspeakably relieved just to see her wake up.

"Which now leads us to darker waters," the Echelon Lord continued. "Such as, what in black depths *happened*?"

There were few creatures in the world more clearly designed for a barely habitable desert than Ivida. The usual aphorisms and curses of an Imperial Race sounded strange coming from one of them.

"The Children of the Stars is the organization that attacked the

Lost Dragon dig site," Rin said instantly. "They appear to have had more of a presence here on Kosha Station than any of us anticipated."

"My guess is that they had both Dr. Dunst and Captain Casimir on a list for targets of opportunity, and the two of them leaving the base for a meal together was an irresistible target," Vichy said bluntly. "The attack showed every sign of being a contingency plan activated on short notice. If they'd been more prepared, they'd have secured the retrieval mechanism for the pod before activating the bomb."

"How did they get a bomb past the Captain's escort?" Davor asked.

"I take full responsibility, sir," Vichy replied. "We were not expecting or prepared for high-sophistication bombing activities. Captain Casimir's detail was operating under standard security protocols.

"We had not increased our threat level to account for potential attack on Kosha Station. That failure is mine."

"In this particular, yes," the Echelon Lord agreed. "But it was a failure shared by many of us. We were treating this organization as a religiously motivated pirate squadron. No one, Battalion Commander, considered the possibility that the cult would have operatives on this station.

"In the passing of the waves, it becomes clear that they would have positioned resources at the closest source of Imperial power. We are fortunate, in some ways, that they targeted Captain Casimir and Dr. Dunst. Similar resources could have caused serious harm in the base."

Rin had no response to that, and from the silence, neither did Vichy.

"Your response was rapid and appropriate, Commander Vichy," the flag officer finally told them. "Station Security's armorers took over three times as long to reequip any suits for underwater deployment. We expected to have more warning. Your technical team's speed and competence are commendable."

"Thank you, sir."

"Now. Dr. Dunst. You are one of our top experts on the Precursors and have spent more time looking at these Children than anyone else. Is there a weight to the current they follow?"

It took Rin a moment to parse the translated idiom.

"There might be," he admitted. "Lost Dragon is specifically about what appears to be a rogue faction of the Alava that was researching deeply into biotech like what we saw at Arjtal. The presence of biological starships built on the same basic architecture as the cloner suggests that something is making them.

"It's possible that there is a self-supporting population of these bioships out here somewhere. A detailed-enough dissection to confirm whether the creatures are capable of reproduction will take experts we don't have and time we haven't taken."

"Reproduction," Davor echoed. "You think these ships are breeding somewhere?"

"It's one of two possibilities, yes," Rin confirmed. "I'm no biologist, though. Based on my studies of the Alava, I can't see them creating anything that self-replicates. The cloner at Arjtal, for example, could duplicate almost any organic creature that entered it so long as it had been fed sufficient biomass but could not reproduce.

"If anything was going to be able to create a duplicate of itself, the cloner would be a good candidate. So far as we can tell from the few records the Taljzi found, it was intentionally designed to never be able to.

"The Alava did not trust anything they could not control," he told the Echelon Lord. "That, to me, suggests a possibility that lines up disturbingly well with the Children's rhetoric: there is a single source. An Alavan artifact of some kind that the Children have managed to activate that is producing these bioships.

"Probably, it is another biotech construct, as those are the most likely to have survived the Alava's fall intact."

"An organic shipyard, basically," Davor concluded. "We will know soon enough, I suppose. Commander Isk will arrive at the other system we know the Children operate out of within a few cycles. He will almost certainly be outgunned from the sounds of it, but he knows not to fight."

Rin had nothing to say to that. He didn't know Commander Isk, so he had to trust the Echelon Lord's opinion.

"If Kosha is compromised, the Children may know Isk is coming," Vichy suggested.

"I had followed the same currents, Battalion Commander," Davor admitted. "But we cannot contact *Serene Guidance* by hyperfold until she exits hyperspace, and none of my ships are large enough to mount starcom receivers."

"Sir, if we are looking at a large-scale Precursor artifact, should we be requesting heavier firepower?" the Marine asked. "My understanding is we're expecting reinforcements, but...not capital ships."

The office was silent and Rin looked down, carefully studying the stone of the desk. Unless he was mistaken, it was true Ivaran blood-stone. Common enough on Ivara, the Ivida homeworld, but to have it shipped all this way would have been insanely expensive.

No wonder Davor didn't have anything else in her office. The stone desk the Ivida carried with her was probably most of even a flag officer's mass allowance. A reminder of a home Davor clearly didn't expect to see again soon.

"No one is officially telling me there are no ships to spare, but I can see the undercurrents," Davor admitted. "A fleet remains at Arjtal, guarding the Taljzi. Multiple fleets stand watch over the Kanzi border in case their civil war spills our way. Another set of fleets has been moved to cover the Wendira, with the largest force positioned on their border with the Laians."

The Wendira were a Core Power, still far richer and more powerful than any Arm Power. So, however, were the Laians—and the oddities of the galaxy were such that the Imperium had ended up absorbing the descendants of the losers of the Laian civil war.

Somehow, the fight over that—and it had been an actual fight, with an Imperial task force getting mauled by a Laian war-dreadnought—had resulted in first a nonaggression agreement and now a tentative defensive alliance.

But the Wendira-Laian border was a wall of dead systems where the two powers had unleashed dozens of starkillers. The Imperium didn't *want* to get dragged into a war between them—and from what Davor was saying, it sounded to Rin like they were expecting to.

"With all of those commitments in play, my understanding is that there are no capital ships to spare," Davor told them. "That doesn't leave this room. Captain Casimir is already aware of everything I am and has likely followed the same currents.

"We must deal with this situation with the resources we have, as best as we can. I'd like a full briefing on everything your people have discovered about these rogue Precursors and the Children, Dr. Dunst."

Rin nodded. He'd have to check the Echelon Lord's clearances first, but he wasn't going to *say* that. He'd been warned when he'd been read in on the Dragon Protocols that telling people, especially military officers, that you had secrets you couldn't share was a bad idea.

He wasn't always good at that part, but he knew better than to accidentally argue with a flag officer!

CHAPTER TWENTY-FOUR

"I GOT YOUR NOTE FROM KOSHA STATION," VICTORIA Antonova's holographic image told Morgan. "What have I told you about getting yourself hurt, Morgan?"

The tall blonde Militia officer—executive officer of an orbital battle platform above Mars these days—looked good to Morgan. She was also sporting a new diamond ring on her left hand, but Morgan was trying not to think about that too hard.

"We'd send a care package if we could, but we're a long damn way away," Victoria continued. "Shelly and I send our love. Keep us up to date, okay? Both of us can swing vacation if you end up on medical leave somewhere; there's rules for that kind of thing."

Morgan snorted. Even if Terra law hadn't improved on handling consensual polyamory before the Annexation, *Imperial* law had to handle species that required as many as five different sexes to have children. Not to mention cultural differences like, for example, the Laians regarding monogamy about the same way humans regarded incest.

Victoria was formally and officially married to Shelly now—

Morgan wasn't sure if Shelly had taken Victoria's last name, but the message header showed Victoria hadn't changed hers—but she and Morgan were still registered as long-term partners with both of their services.

"We missed you at the wedding," Victoria said softly. "I...I know it's hard for you, but I still wish you could have been here. This posting, at the other end of the damn Imperium...it's not good for any of us, I don't think."

She shook her head.

"Only Megan attended out of your sisters, even. I *think* they all understand, but they were grumpy enough that they didn't prioritize it over the ten billion and one duties your mother gives them. Leah and Carol sent a card and a gift. Alexis...isn't speaking to me."

That got a laugh from Morgan. She was always hesitant to open Victoria's messages these days, so the laugh was good. It wasn't really funny or good that Morgan's not-quite-twenty-year-old youngest half-sister wasn't speaking to her girlfriend, but Victoria's plaintive, exasperated acceptance was still charming.

Morgan wasn't even sure that Alexis was cold-shouldering Victoria over the wedding. The youngest of the Bond daughters, Alexis was in many ways the most mercurial of Morgan's four half-siblings—*and* buried in the middle of a triple degree in business, law, and art.

"Look, I'm pretty damn sure that you took a posting at the ass end of nowhere to give me and Shelly space," Victoria continued. "Someone had to do the job, yes, but I know the Imperium prefers not to take people quite *that* far away from their registered partners if possible.

"So you volunteered. I know. I understand. I just want *you* to understand that I still love you. Just as much as I love Shelly. It's just...she's here and you're not. Next time you're back, I'll *prove* to you that nothing has changed, okay?"

Morgan had to smile at that. She and Victoria had spent a large portion of their communications over the years reassuring each other that things were still good and still going to work out. It didn't seem like that was going to change just because one of them had married.

"And since I know you *very* well, and we're all quite clear on what's allowed," Victoria continued, "I think you need to tell me about this archeologist you got shot at for."

"WELCOME BACK, SIR."

"I didn't go anywhere, Commander Rogers," Morgan told her executive officer as she crossed the bridge. "What's the daily?"

"The morning report from the yards says they're making faster progress than we dared hope," the redheaded First Sword told her boss. "They've carved a full cycle off the estimate, and we're looking at two more cycles at most before we're ready to fly again."

"Do we have our armor back yet?" Morgan asked.

"Not yet," Rogers admitted. "All of our guns are back online, and they're mostly working on cleaning up the damage they made to fix the damage we already had at this point."

"Isn't that how it goes," Morgan said with a sigh. She'd had to get her hair recut to cover the bald spot the doctors had shaved away to insert a probe into her skull. Nanites and regeneration matrix were wonderful things, but they needed to be injected close to where they had to work.

"Any news from *Serene Guidance*?" she asked as her First Sword rose to give up the command seat.

"Nothing," Rogers said quietly. "They're not officially overdue, hyperspace being what it is, but we're into the ninth sigma for possible emergences."

Which meant they were into the final half-cycle countdown for declaring the destroyer overdue. Ships did sometimes just go missing in hyperspace. Sometimes. Morgan was aware of seven incidents in the Imperium's entire history.

"Isk should have transmitted the moment he left hyperspace," she said aloud. "And he should be there. Even if they knew exactly where *Guidance* was going to emerge, she should still have transmitted."

That was one of the many advantages of the hyperfold communicator, after all. When Morgan's stepmother had been actively involved in warfare, they wouldn't have known what Isk had found until the destroyer returned. Now, though, the Yin should have reported in the moment he arrived at the target system.

Morgan brought up the map and stared at it in frustration.

"Two cycles till we're combat-ready, huh?" she asked.

"That's the current estimate. I wouldn't count on anything less than three, really," Rogers warned.

"And twenty-one cycles after that before we get reinforcements," Morgan murmured. "I miss *Jean Villeneuve* now." She chuckled. "Both of them."

Her one and only executive officer role in the Imperial Navy had been aboard the superbattleship named for her honorary uncle. She'd take the actual Jean Villeneuve back at any opportunity, but the twenty-megaton warship with a full arsenal of hypermissile launchers would probably be more useful today.

Probably.

"What do we do, sir?"

"Nothing, for two cycles," Morgan replied. "In those two cycles, I'm going to talk to the Echelon Lord and get clearance to take *Defiance* out. If something stopped *Serene Guidance* from reporting in, then there is something there and we need to investigate it."

She shook her head and studied the star chart grimly.

"And while Isk is a perfectly competent officer, *Defiance* is two generations newer and six times the size of *Serene Guidance*. If nothing else, I'm confident *we* can get a message out."

"IT'S good to see you up and well, Captain Casimir," Davor told her. "How are your waters?"

"My head still itches in places I'm not used to feeling *anything*," Morgan admitted. Terran regeneration technology had been near-miraculous even before the Imperium had arrived. It had been good enough, in fact, that the entire concept of the self-growing "regeneration matrix" had actually been poached and was now used across the Imperium.

Combined with Imperial nanotech to fix fractures and tears, it was a near-perfect package for the repair of most physical traumas. Less so for illnesses and wonky genetics, sadly, but if an Imperial doctor got to someone before they passed, very few injuries would be fatal.

But the psychosomatic side effects had to be experienced to be believed.

"And your ship, Captain?"

"*Defiance* is less than two cycles from deployment readiness, according to the yardmaster," Morgan replied instantly. "Close enough, sir, that I believe we should be discussing her next mission."

"I *want* to hold *Defiance* here, to cover Kosha Station," the Echelon Lord admitted. "With the attack on you, I will admit that the waters around here are looking darker and more dangerous than I would prefer."

Kosha Station did have two escorting defensive platforms and a small defensive constellation. The presence of HSM launchers on both platforms meant the setup was more dangerous than it looked, but Morgan was still comfortably confident that *Defiance* could take the station without much difficulty.

"Have you heard from *Serene Guidance*, sir?" she asked.

"No. Commander Isk and his ship are officially overdue and assumed lost," Davor admitted, the translator picking up the sad tone. "One hundred and eighty-six sentients, Captain. If they are dead, which is the most likely situation, these Children will pay."

"Agreed, sir. *Defiance* is our most readily deployed mobile asset."

Not least because the available lighter ships were dealing with the leftovers of her first two encounters with the Children. Morgan didn't envy the Captain tasked with hauling several of the bioships back to Kosha Station for expert dissection.

"Yes." Davor's single word hung on the channel as the Ivida tapped her fingers rapidly on her stone desk. "I don't like it, Captain. We don't know what happened to Commander Isk, and *Defiance* is also our most valuable asset.

"The failure to communicate is the most concerning aspect. Unless they were ambushed immediately on emergence, Isk should still have been able to transmit home."

"I think we need to build an early dropout into the next investigation," Morgan suggested. "If we check in a cycle or half-cycle before we reach the system, you'll at least know it was the target system that was the problem."

"I would still rather not lose one of the Imperium's most modern heavy cruisers and the clan-child of a Duchess," Davor said drily.

"I am more than Duchess Bond's daughter," Morgan snapped before she could stop herself. "I am an officer of the Imperial Navy, sir, and I can see my duty here."

"Your duty is to follow my orders," the Ivida replied with a harsh snap of her teeth. "But you are correct. I cannot make my choices based on your parentage; I apologize."

"Then *Defiance* will deploy?" Morgan asked.

"I will have the orders drafted and we will discuss." Davor raised a hand. "Given the situation and the likelihood of an encounter with Alava artifacts, I believe you will need an expert on hand."

Morgan managed not to point out that she was one of the better experts the Navy had on the topic, having been in the heart of the Taljzi Campaigns and being either cleared or aware of everything to do with the Mesharom Archive. She was silent because she knew there was a better expert on hand—the only person she'd ever known to regularly refer to the Precursors by their name. Like Echelon Lord Davor just had.

"I will speak to Dr. Dunst and, if he is willing, I will assign him to you as a civilian advisor."

It wasn't a question and Morgan agreed with the logic. It might cause her some personal awkwardness, but that was life. Hopefully, the doctor could be both understanding and patient.

It seemed likely.

CHAPTER TWENTY-FIVE

"Here's where we leave you, Doctor," the Marine standing at Rin's left side told him.

Three Marines had accompanied Rin every day since the attack. They'd rotated out, obviously, but he was still surprised at Lance Winchester's announcement. He'd assumed that the Marines, human to a one, had been detached from *Defiance*'s detail.

"Lance?" he asked.

"We're from base security," Winchester told him, nodding toward the *Defiance* Marines surrounding them. They were holding an extended perimeter around the access tubes to the heavy cruiser, even inside the naval base.

"*Defiance*'s Marines will take over your security now, under Battalion Commander Vichy's orders. Our AO ends at the airlock."

Technically, Rin was relatively sure that the Area of Operations for Vichy's Marines *also* ended at the airlock, but no one was blinking at the squad spread out around the entrance to their ship.

"All right," he allowed. "Thank you, Lance Winchester, Marine Pek, Marine Gupta. If you could pass my thanks on to the other Marines, I'd appreciate it."

"I can do that, sir," Winchester confirmed, passing Rin's luggage —a single wheeled case—over to one of *Defiance*'s Marines without asking.

"The doctor's an easy-enough package," he continued to the *Defiance* Marine. "Don't make his life too hard."

"If his life gets hard on this trip, we have much bigger problems," the Lance from Rin's destination said with a chuckle. "You're expected, Dr. Dunst. If you'll come with me, someone is waiting to take your bag and show you to your quarters."

Rin bowed slightly.

"Of course, Lance," he agreed affably. It seemed that *civilian advisor* ranked a significantly better standard of care than *senior civilian of the evacuees we're stuffing anywhere they'll fit.*

He followed the Marine through the airlock and access tube, envying the ease with which the woman stepped through the slight shift between Kosha Station's gravity and *Defiance*'s gravity.

Rin himself nearly fell into the wall on the same step, even knowing where the line was.

"Sorry, sorry, I'm fine," he told the Marine, levering himself back to standing. "Some day, I will get used to gravity shifts, but until then, I swear I'm going to overcompensate every time."

"Take a moment, Doctor," the Lance said. "It's not far and we're in no hurry. *Defiance* isn't shipping out for a twentieth-cycle."

Seventy minutes. That was probably enough to get him to his quarters and settled in before the interface drive tried to steal his stomach.

Once the ship was moving, he'd be fine, but there was very little about the process of getting aboard a ship in dock that Rin Dunst found enjoyable.

"CAPTAIN CASIMIR SENDS her regards as well and requests that you join her and her senior officers for dinner this evening once we're underway," the earnest young spacer told Rin once she'd delivered him and his baggage to his quarters.

"Thank you," Rin told the woman. "I presume there is a map of the ship in the data systems?"

"Of course, Doctor. You should be activated with the same profile you had last time," the woman assured him. "Do you need anything else?"

The vibratingly eager young woman left Rin tempted to try and find something to ask for, just to make the human puppy feel *useful,* but he really didn't need anything.

"No, that's everything, thank you. I can find my own way to dinner, unless I need to have an escort?" Rin asked.

"I don't believe so, Doctor," she said. "Battalion Commander Vichy should let you know shortly if you're expected to be escorted while aboard ship."

Rin presumed that the current lack of Marines probably meant no. Not least, he trusted Vichy to be competent enough to have told him by now if he was expected to be guarded aboard ship.

The young woman saluted—Rin knew perfectly well that Imperial Navy rules said she shouldn't, but she did anyway—and vanished back out his door, leaving the archeologist to look around his quarters.

Unless he was severely mistaken, it was the same room they'd put him in before. He was experienced enough aboard starships in general and warships in specific to know it was a large single room, probably the most luxurious quarters they had for passengers. *Defiance* wouldn't have flag officer or diplomatic quarters sitting empty.

From what Rin understood, that was an intentional lack of the design. Most ships of the *Armored Dream* class's size would have been equipped to act as flagships, but the Imperium had crammed so many weapons into the hull of their new cruiser, there'd been hard choices to make.

Actual details of what those choices were were beyond Rin's civilian understanding of the ship. His clearance would probably allow him to get that information, but it wasn't relevant to him.

Opening his traveling case, he removed the portable computer and the privacy-shield generator. The portable computer was a solid block of electronics thirty centimeters square and three centimeters thick. Far more powerful than his wrist communicator, it was also far more secure and actively lacking in the usual wireless connections.

This particular one would refuse to turn on unless the privacy shield was activated. His quarters didn't have a full Faraday cage, but the shield would block anything short of advanced Core Power spying tech.

Between the computer and his implant, Rin had downloaded everything in the Mesharom Archive on this region and a large amount of general information on Alava biotech and their reaction to it.

Plus the usual files on Alava tech and megastructures. Rin wasn't quite sure what kind of artifact the Alava had left behind there, but he doubted it was going to be small. The Alava just didn't *do* small by the time this region had been settled.

He checked the time. Someone had updated his personal calendar with the exact time of the dinner invitation, and he shook his head as he looked at it.

Dinner with Morgan "and her officers" wasn't quite what he'd been hoping for in the immediate future, but duty called for them both. He wasn't entirely sure he was comfortable with the whole situation with the Captain and her girlfriend and said girlfriend's wife. Polyamory was common enough, but that struck him as a level of complication that was asking for trouble.

It wasn't his trouble right now. But if he continued to pursue Morgan Casimir, it might become his trouble, and he wasn't quite sure how he felt about that.

TO RIN'S SURPRISE, there was a chime on his door admittance buzzer thirty minutes before dinner. His emotions attempted to imitate a three-ring circus for several seconds, expecting it to be Morgan Casimir.

Instead, he found Pierre Vichy standing on his doorstep in a plain black undress uniform and an openly worn sidearm.

"Bonsoir, Doctor," Vichy greeted him. "We will not be escorting you around the ship normally, but I presumed upon myself to make certain that you didn't get lost on your way to the Captain's mess."

"My current record suggests I'd stumble into a secret cabal of Children aboard the ship if I did get lost," Rin said with partially forced humor. "Just how dressed up is this affair?"

The Imperial Marines' undress uniform—for humans, at least—was the black full-body suit of a standard day uniform with a twenty-first-century-style formal business jacket over it in the same black.

Boards had been added to the shoulder of the jacket to sport decorative insignia, but the marker for Vichy's rank remained the two gold pips on either side of his bodysuit collar.

Rin suspected the underlayer suit could act as an emergency vacuum suit. Either way, the jacket was far more formal than his own slacks and a shirt.

"Throw a jacket on and ça va," the Marine told him. "You *have* one, right?" He studied Rin carefully for a moment. "I don't have anything that will fit you, but we may find something in the ship's stores."

Rin managed not to flush in embarrassment. His bulk didn't normally bother him, but compared to the spare and athletic form of the Marine CO, it was hard not to feel soft.

"I have a jacket; give me a moment," he said. He hadn't unpacked yet, but the jacket was supposed to survive being stored just fine.

Fortunately, it lived up to its advertising and the few wrinkles vanished after a few shakes. Slinging the dark blue jacket over his shoulders, he turned back to Vichy.

"Well, Commander, shall we?" he asked. "I have no idea of the etiquette for this. My only dinners with Imperial officers, well...they weren't human Imperial officers."

And he really didn't want to make a fool of himself in front of Morgan Casimir right now.

"You will be fine," Vichy assured him. "Come."

CHAPTER TWENTY-SIX

"Officers and guests, I give you the Empress, the Houses, the Duchies, the Imperium!"

"The Imperium!" Morgan's guests chorused back.

The toast wasn't actually part of the Imperial tradition. The first human officers in the Imperial Navy, like Morgan's honorary aunt Fleet Lord Harriet Tanaka, had made it up to continue an old *human* tradition.

The opening meal of any voyage was always a sprawling affair that ended up larger than Morgan would ever have wanted. If *Serene Guidance* hadn't been overdue and missing, *Defiance* wouldn't be leaving yet—and tonight was when she'd penciled in a potential date with Rin Dunst.

The galaxy didn't wait on the romantic dreams of mid-thirties polyamorous women, however, which left her with a job to do. Civilian and out of the chain of command or not, Morgan had to step very carefully around Rin aboard her ship.

But she had him at the dinner, along with her senior officers. The fierce-souled archeologist was sitting next to Battalion Commander Vichy, speaking to the Marine in slow but functional French.

On the other side of Dr. Dunst was Lesser Commander Nguyen, whose French was obviously worse even from three seats away. She was gamely trying, though, and was very clearly earning points with Vichy for the attempt.

Past her was Commander Rogers, who was leaning back in her chair and sipping her wine with a sharp gaze. Morgan met her First Sword's gaze and offered a second silent toast. The other woman returned it, so she presumed things were fine.

Engineering, Navigation, and Communication took up the other side of the table. Nystrom and El-Amin were comparing being raised in Scandinavia as a Tibetan-in-exile to being raised on Mars in one of the early Muslim colonies there.

El-Amin was hardly a typical Muslim, with his tightly wrapped woman's headscarf and soft tones, but Morgan's understanding was that New Cairo had diverged from its home religion in rapid and fascinating ways.

Past them and sharing Rogers's silence was Lesser Commander Gary Liepins, the cruiser's Eastern European engineer. Morgan had never even heard of Latvia before Liepins had been assigned to her command, and she'd thought her knowledge of Earth geography was good.

Morgan let the conversations run over her. She could understand the three-way conversation on her right far better than she was going to admit to Vichy, but since it was currently focused on harmless discussions of French wine, she didn't need to engage.

There was a lull in both conversations, and she tapped a nail against her glass to draw everyone's attention.

"All right, everyone, a bit of business before we go fall over to digest that dinner," she told them. "We portal out in just over a tenth-cycle. Then it's six cycles to K-Seven-Seven-D-L-T-Three. We'll be dropping out of hyperspace for a few hours one cycle short of D-L-T-Three to report in and make sure that Echelon Lord Davor knows we're alive before we stick our heads into the hornet's nest.

"We don't know what to expect at D-L-T-Three, but we know

the Children fled there from D-L-K-Six. We also know that *Serene Guidance* never even sent out a communication. We have to assume that Commander Isk was ambushed and destroyed almost immediately on emergence."

She let that hang in the room, reminding her people that their destination had already eaten a warship without a metaphorical sound.

"Given that information, my intention is to emerge from hyperspace on the far side of D-L-T-Three, avoiding a direct vector and any location that the Children would be expecting us to arrive in. I also intend to emerge roughly one light-hour out to get a scan of the system before we are detected."

She shook her head.

"I don't like playing games and sneaking in the back door," she admitted. "*Defiance* is the most powerful warship of her mass in the Imperium. But we know one of our ships died here, and we won't share *Serene Guidance*'s fate; I swear it."

"Depending on what we find, we can easily make an in-system hyper transit to close the range after the scan, too," El-Amin suggested. "That could give us an extra chance of surprise."

"A light-hour puts us out of tachyon-scanner range," Nguyen pointed out. "Everything we see is an hour out of date, not real-time."

"That we're up to a full five light-minutes of tachyon scanner range is handy but not essential," Morgan replied. "Data that's an hour old is better than plasma beams that are brand new. These people killed a destroyer before Commander Isk could even send a message.

"I have to assume we're facing overwhelming force, which means we run a maximum survivability scouting mission. We act like we're facing battle squadrons, people. Otherwise, we risk sharing *Serene Guidance*'s fate, and that will not happen."

No one was arguing with her. Even Nguyen's comment was just that. But she needed to make sure her people knew the stakes.

"We have six cycles," she told them. "A hundred and forty hours. Let's be as ready as we can be.

"Our most likely opposition is freighters retrofitted into armed pirates and more Precursor bioships," Morgan continued. "Given that analysis, I can see why Commander Isk took a riskier approach that was more likely to provide detailed information.

"My fear, people, is that we have drastically underestimated how big and dangerous those bioships can get." She shook her head. "Commander Nguyen, I want you to work with Dr. Dunst and see if we can get a mock-up for what a superbattleship-sized one of those things will look like in terms of threat level."

"It's always going to be mitigated by their engine and their weapons," Nguyen pointed out. "I wouldn't want to fight a big one, but so long as we can control the range, all they've got is a plasma cannon."

"All we've seen so far is a plasma cannon," Morgan corrected. "I don't think we know enough about Precursor biotech to assume we understand its limitations, Lesser Commander. Get me that mock-up."

"Of course, sir."

"The rest of you." Morgan looked around the room. "I want us to disaster-proof this mission as much as we can. If we have the ability, we will do a closer scouting pass. But right now, I want us to plan to get the most information we can with the absolute least risk.

"Everyone on board with that?"

MORGAN WASN'T in the slightest surprised to see Dunst lingering as everyone else drifted out. Vichy, who'd escorted him to the party, seemed to be waiting for him.

"Pierre, s'il vous plaît, nous avons besoin d'un peu d'intimité," she whispered in his ear as she stepped up next to him.

Her use of French completely threw the Marine, probably at

least as much as her request for privacy. He glared at her for a moment.

"Vous parlez français?" he demanded.

"Parfaitement," Morgan confessed. "Now, get going, Battalion Commander. I'm sure Dr. Dunst can make his way to his quarters unescorted."

That got her a *spectacular* eyebrow-raise and some muttering in French that she very carefully did not hear.

"Bien," he finally agreed. "Good night, Captain."

He saluted and left the room, leaving Morgan and Dunst alone with the now cleared table.

"I believe I just burned any chance of a reputation for subtlety with my Marine commander," Morgan pointed out to the archeologist. "Do you know I managed to avoid speaking French to him for almost a whole year?"

Dunst was studying her with a gaze that sent a flush of warmth down Morgan's spine.

"Why?" he asked.

"Because he was being a pompous French ass and it amused me," she admitted. "I tolerate it because he's good at his actual job and his Marines *adore* him. When they aren't calling him even less polite things."

The stewards had left the last wine bottle on the table. That had probably been intentional on someone's part, and the half-full bottle produced two glasses of wine with ease.

"You weren't hanging around to talk about Pierre Vichy," Morgan said as she passed one to Dunst. She realized as she did so that she wasn't sure if the scientist had the alcohol-control treatments any Navy officer got by default.

She shrugged mentally. He was a big boy and could make his own choices.

"No, I wanted to talk to you," Dunst admitted, then laughed. "Not even about anything in specific, I have to admit. Just wanted a chance to talk."

That was significantly less problematic than Morgan had expected—even if part of her had been hoping for an attempt at seduction, the smart part of her knew she'd have to shut Dunst down.

"Aboard this ship, I have to be very careful what I say and do," Morgan warned him. "Even with the hyperfold com, we are out of communication with higher authority a lot of the time. When operating independently, I am the master of this ship. I can't risk weakening that authority."

"I figured something of the sort," he admitted, his tone sad. "And I'm quite capable of being a good boy, Captain Casimir."

"You can still call me Morgan, Rin," she told him with a chuckle. "At least when we're in private like this. And you're still going to get those dates unless you find a new way to dig yourself into a hole over the next couple of weeks."

"Good to know," Dunst said with an answering chuckle. "I have spent at least as long on a dig site excavating and cleaning a single important artifact. My career requires patience."

"Mine requires both patience and the ability to recognize when to act instantly and with unhesitating commitment," Morgan said drily. "Unfortunately, that doesn't always work well in personal life, especially when duty gets in the way."

"Career can do much the same," he agreed. "And that was before I agreed to become one of the Institute's top experts. I don't think I really understood just what I was signing on for when I took that role on."

"Brain implants?" she guessed. Her files hadn't given much detail on just what kind of cybernetics Dunst had, only that he *had* some and that any doctor treating him had to know that. There were extra files that would only be unlocked by a combination of Morgan's and the ship's doctor's authorizations.

"Basically," he admitted. "I know more about the Alava than any other human alive. I imagine there are people in the Core Powers who know more, but I spent three years obsessively studying everything we had before I went back into the field. The implant is additional memory, an augment rather than a replacement for what I already know."

"I was surprised to learn we did any neural implanting," Morgan admitted. "I know humanity's twenty-first-century experiments... didn't end well."

At best, they'd proven impossible to control without self-hypnosis. At worse, they'd driven their recipients irretrievably insane.

"And then there's the fate of the Alava," Dunst agreed. "For me to access the files requires me to assume a specific physical position and basically self-hypnotize. That allows me to pull more detailed files that basically become part of my memory."

He shrugged.

"It's possible—and both easier and safer—for me to access the implant's databases via my communicator or a portable computer," he admitted. "That's my usual method, honestly. But even in those circumstances, I have to engage in some mental frameworks to unlock the data.

"It's as secure as it can be. It can't be retrieved if I'm dead, and given how hard it is for me to access the data in the first place, I can't imagine I can access it under duress."

"Quite the setup," Morgan murmured. "And here I just...know most of it."

"You're cleared for a lot of things, Morgan, but we've spoken about things you're not on the list for," Dunst said quietly. "Given that the Children seem to have access to some of the same data, I have to wonder where you learned it."

That was a *fascinating* way to phrase the question without accusing Morgan of leaking it, she reflected. He clearly didn't think she'd told the Children but was worried they had the same source as she did.

"Have you been told how we got the Precursor data we have?" Morgan asked.

"I'm not cleared for that," Dunst said instantly. "The...shape of the data implies much of it came from the Mesharom, but not all.

Officially, the archives I have access to are purely Imperial research, but I can tell that's bullshit."

"If you don't know, I can't tell you," she said. That was an easy enough line to draw. "But to answer your question, I'm responsible for how we acquired much of that data. I know where it came from; I know a lot of what it says.

"Add to that that I was in the middle of the Taljzi Campaigns and saw multiple star systems the Precursors had turned into machines. I have a very good understanding of who and what the Precursors were.

"I know how they died. I know what they did, and I know what level of neural implanting they had to allow for that to kill them. I'm not technically cleared for about half of that, but I'm the *source* for some of it." Morgan shrugged.

"Which I guess means I'm cleared? I never asked; I was just told not to tell anyone what I knew unless they were explicitly cleared for it."

She took a long sip of her wine and shook her head.

"And while this room is secure enough, we really shouldn't go into more detail than that," she told Dunst. "So, tell me, Rin, how *does* one end up one of the Imperium's speciality subject experts?"

CHAPTER TWENTY-SEVEN

"Emergence."

If someone dropped a pin on *Defiance*'s bridge, Morgan suspected it would have been stopped in midair by the tension before it was heard in the silence. The previous jaunt out of hyperspace to report that they were a cycle out from D-L-T-Three had been calm enough, but data from several light-years away wasn't going to tell them anything.

"Portal locus confirmed; we are sixty-three light-minutes from K-Seven-Seven-D-L-T-Three," El-Amin reported, his voice calm. "Holding position for further orders."

"Nguyen, what do we see?" Morgan said.

They had some limited data on the physical geography from long-range scans from Kosha, but that data was almost two decades old due to the distance. They knew that D-L-T-Three was a large F-sequence star with fourteen planets, six of them gas giants and one in the habitable zone.

D-L-T-Three-Delta had a high chance of being a good candidate for human colonization, depending on its atmosphere and surface water. Before the current mess, it had been scheduled for a survey in around two long-cycles.

"I'm not detecting any obvious artificial structures or energy signatures," Nguyen reported after a few seconds. "No megastructures, no secret colonies."

"Would an inactive megastructure be easily discerned at this distance?" Dunst asked.

"You tell me, Dr. Dunst," Nguyen replied. "Most of my data suggests that they should be."

Given the archeologist's role on this mission, Morgan had stuck him in the bridge's solitary observer chair. She'd served on ships with an entire peanut gallery, designed with the thought of carrying diplomats or flag officers who weren't in immediate command.

Like most of *Defiance*'s compromises, it was another way in which she was designed as a pure weapons platform. The survey work Morgan was supposed to be doing out there was one of the few non-conflict roles the *Armored Dream* class was capable of.

In the long run, she suspected that limitation would be the doom of the class. Even *Armored Dream* wasn't built along the most practical lines, with the wing-arches projected from her core hull, but the A!Tol required *multiple* functions to go with the form of their ships.

A cruiser that could not act as a flagship or a diplomatic vessel was eventually going to be replaced by a ship that *could*. For now, however, the Imperium still needed the maximum number of HSM launchers in the fleet.

"Most of them should be," Dunst agreed. "Would we detect something like the shipyard ring from the Taljzi Campaigns, though?"

That had been a massive space station wrapped around an entire super-Jovian gas giant, using the station for fuel and a planet-carving mining operation in a nearby star system for raw materials.

"Fifty-fifty," Nguyen admitted. "It depends on power levels, of course." She turned her attention back to Morgan.

"We're getting more refined data every second," she told her boss.

"But I'm not seeing any power signatures or any sign of *Serene Guidance.*"

"I wouldn't expect to see much of Commander Isk's ship until we get much closer," Morgan admitted. "But nothing at all?"

That seemed unlikely.

"Nothing we can detect from over a light-hour away," Nguyen corrected. "Minor installations on the planets, ships with drives down in occluded positions, anything with any kind of stealth field...there are a lot of things we could still be missing."

"What we have managed to analyze from D-L-K-Six suggests there was an Alava facility here," Dunst told them. "Very little detail, though I wouldn't read the information as suggesting a colony. More one of their refueling stations."

The Precursors—the Alava—had used a very different FTL drive from the current galactic civilization. A range-limited instantaneous jump, it had been much more fuel-intensive than hyperspace, and the Precursors had scattered glorified "truck stops" throughout their territories. The refueling stations were little more than a starcom and a set of cloudscoops on a convenient gas giant, but they were the most common type of Alava settlement anyone had found.

"If nothing else, a refueling station should have a local star map, unless the Children have already vaporized this one as well," Morgan replied. They'd found Arjtal by chasing those maps, after all.

"Agreed. I believe my role here is to give advice?" the scientist asked carefully.

"It is," Morgan allowed.

"If there is an Alava refueling facility, it is the most likely place for the Children to have set up operations and may provide us with valuable details on Alava operations in the region either way. Confirming its presence would be valuable."

Morgan nodded. She'd been thinking much the same, but having the confirmation from the civilian side was useful.

"What are we seeing on Delta?" she asked Nguyen.

"Whoever bought the colonization rights is going to be kicking themselves," the tactical officer replied. "Habitable zone, clearly a functioning biosphere...but under ten percent atmospheric oxygen and less than two percent surface water.

"Even the *Ivida* are going to find that one a hard place to settle. It's probably going to be worth more as a case study for the biologists and terraformers than as a potential colony."

That was in character for the Precursors. The Alava themselves had apparently been more adaptable than any known current galactic race, capable of adjusting to temperatures and oxygen levels that would kill a human in minutes. They'd used that to set up colonies where their subject races had to live in climate-controlled barracks and the Alava could survive outside.

"All right, people," Morgan told her bridge crew. "Hold the ship at battle stations. I'm making a transmission upstairs, and then we're going in closer."

She waited a moment to see if anyone raised intelligent objections. In the absence of a reason not to carry on her mission, she activated the privacy shield around her chair and began recording.

"Echelon Lord Davor, we have arrived in the K-Seven-Seven-D-L-T-Three System," she reported. "We have detected no sign of *Serene Guidance*, but we are scanning from far enough out to prevent detection of drive trails or sufficiently diffuse debris fields.

"From a distance of just over one light-hour, we have detected no signs of hostile activity or Precursor structures. Dr. Dunst's data suggests there is a refueling station on the fourth planet, which will be the likely location of any Children base.

"In the absence of a clear and present threat, I will be carefully moving *Defiance* deeper into the system to investigate further. My intention is to report in every half-cycle in the absence of new information or an immediate threat."

It wasn't much of a report, but it was all she had right now. She hit the TRANSMIT button and began to raise the privacy shield.

Then she noticed a warning icon next to her transmission request.

"Commander Nystrom," she said slowly. "Check your systems. Do we have a live hyperfold link? To anyone?"

The tension in the bridge tightened again.

"Negative, sir," the green-eyed officer said softly. "All hyperfold transmissions are failing. The system isn't even able to tell me why. It has a closed-circuit transmission test with a receiver at the opposite end of the ship from the transmitters, and that receiver isn't picking up our transmissions."

"We're not transmitting?" Morgan asked. "Or what?"

"We're transmitting, but it doesn't seem to be going anywhere," Lesser Commander Nystrom reported. "In the nine hundred and twenty-two meters of the closed loop, something is dampening the transmission to the point where it isn't registering at all.

"There's no way our long-range transmissions are getting out."

"Well, that explains why we didn't hear from *Serene Guidance*," Morgan said grimly. "Would Commander Isk's ship have had a similar test circuit?"

"*Serene Guidance* is two hundred and eight meters long, sir," Rogers interjected, the First Sword listening in through a dedicated intercom channel. Everyone in Secondary Control saw and heard everything on the bridge unless Morgan actively blocked them.

"It's entirely possible that the transmission is still clear enough after a two-hundred-meter circuit for *Guidance* not to have realized she wasn't transmitting."

"At which point, Commander Isk would have proceeded in-system without ever knowing that he was shouting into the void unheard," Morgan concluded. "Any idea how far this effect reaches?"

"Less than three light-years, since we had no problems at our check-in stop," Rogers suggested. "We have no records of such an effect nor any idea how such a phenomenon could be produced."

Neither, so far as Morgan knew, did the *Mesharom*. That...wasn't good.

"Sir, we should withdraw and report," Rogers suggested. "Even the existence of this phenomenon is critical intelligence."

"We also give up any chance of surprise if we leave and return," Morgan countered, but she knew her First Sword was right. "On the other hand, we arguably have already lost that. Nystrom, did any of our messages get through?"

"I'm checking now... Wait, that's funny."

"Commander? 'Funny' is not a useful status report," Morgan told her subordinate drily.

"Sorry, sir. We set up an automated arrival report to make sure that we sent a transmission even if we were attacked on arrival. *That* transmission went out without any problems. It looks like we were blocked about thirty seconds afterwards."

There was no way the lightspeed data from their arrival had reached a Children position at that point—it *still* hadn't reached any of the system's planets—which suggested that they had detected the hyperfold transmission itself.

"That also needs to be reported," she concluded with a sigh. "Commander El-Amin? Plot us a course to get out of here. Let's try one light-month to start—at a right angle to the direct course back to Kosha."

She smiled grimly.

"After all, we're not going back to Kosha."

She turned to Nguyen.

"And while El-Amin is plotting that, Commander Nguyen, I need you to power up the hyperfold cannons. Something is smothering our hyperfold transmissions. I need to know what's happening to the *guns* that run on the same principles."

MORGAN HAD to conceal a sigh of relief as they shot through the portal back into hyperspace. There'd been nothing in the system to present an immediate threat, but a jamming system the Imperial crew couldn't identify, let alone counter, left the back of her neck crawling.

"Nguyen? Those tests didn't look great," she told her tactical officer. "What have we got?"

"The guns are a powerful-enough and short-ranged enough pulse that they're not being stopped; that's the good news," the petite woman replied. "The bad news is we're losing about a quarter of our range and nearly half our hitting power at any given range.

"That dampening field is a nightmare."

"So, we have a new objective," Morgan said. "We need to retrieve that dampener. Potentially, our scientists can work out a way to counter it if we have a copy."

"Or perhaps even a way to tune it so we can still use *our* hyperfold systems, as we can do with our jammers," Nystrom suggested. "If we could shut down everyone *else's* coms and guns while still having ours at full power, that could be useful."

Morgan shivered at the thought. That kind of trick would have its limits—any peer power would duplicate the system eventually, but it would make for some one-sided fights the first few times it was deployed.

"It's potentially Alavan technology," Dunst reminded them. "That means it may be harder to duplicate than we think."

And it was almost certainly not working as designed. The fragments of Precursor tech that still worked often did so in ways dramatically different from their original intent. The supernova-inducing starkillers in the arsenal of every major power had been originally born as attempts to duplicate the Precursor star drive, after all.

"I could live with never running into active Precursor tech ever again," Morgan noted. "For now, El-Amin, what's our ETA?"

"Hyperspace is pretty dense here," her navigator replied. "Another few minutes."

"We'll stay at battle stations, then," she decided aloud. "Just in case something *really* weird is going on here."

Her crew turned their attention back to their consoles, a grim calmness spreading over the bridge as they watched their screens.

"Nothing in hyperspace near us," Nguyen told her after a

minute. "I'm seeing a few distortions that suggest there have been people out here, but there's nothing out here right now."

"So, our only problem is in that system," Morgan concluded. "That gives us a starting point."

"Portal in twenty seconds," El-Amin reported. "Hang on."

A countdown appeared on the main display, ticking away the seconds before *Defiance* lunged back into ordinary space.

Those seconds passed in silence, and Morgan watched her reports as the cruiser's exotic-matter emitters woke again, tearing a hole back into reality.

"Emergence."

They plunged back into realspace and Morgan checked the scanners immediately.

"Screens are clear," Nguyen reported. "No contacts, no contacts."

Defiance's Captain concealed a sigh of relief. The dampening field was making her twitchy. If Nguyen said they were clear, that meant there was nothing within the five-light-minute real-time range of the tachyon scanners.

"Nystrom?" she asked.

"Transmitter...clear," Lesser Commander Nystrom replied. "Tests are green; we can transmit at your command."

"All right. Take us down from battle stations, Commander Rogers," Morgan ordered. "Nystrom, Dunst—I want the two of you to put together a full report on everything we can sort out on that dampener and if it ties back to anything we know of in Precursor technology.

"Everyone else, we're going to take one watch, a quarter-cycle, to rest. Then we're going right back to D-L-T-Three loaded for bear. Check in with your departments and make sure you have a refreshed team ready for combat at the end of the watch.

"We might not have seen anything there yet, but I doubt that dampener just *happens* to be jamming coms out of a useless system."

CHAPTER TWENTY-EIGHT

THERE WAS NO LURKING AROUND AT THE EDGE OF THE SYSTEM this time. *Defiance's* hyper portal opened exactly four light-minutes from K77DLT3-Delta, the heavy cruiser plunging into regular space at a distance where she'd have real-time data on her most likely destination.

"You know, that moon is giving me flashbacks," Rogers observed as they studied their destination. Delta had a large moon, smaller than D-L-K-6-Beta's but still comparable to Earth's Luna.

"At least it isn't habitable at all," Morgan replied after a glance at the data. No atmosphere, no biosphere. Just a dead rock.

"Doesn't mean it's harmless," her First Sword replied.

"Agreed. Nguyen, focus your scanners on Delta, but let's not ignore the moon. Do we have any signs of hostiles?"

"Negative," her tactical officer replied. "Delta local space remains clear." She paused. "We *do* have signs of recent combat; I'm picking up diffuse patterns suggesting plasma fire and the signs of a drive trail."

"So, *Serene Guidance* made it this far," Morgan replied. "Can we locate her? Or her debris, at least?"

"Working on it."

"El-Amin, take us in closer," Morgan ordered. She studied the world in front of her. An uninhabitable desert, it still had a biosphere and an atmosphere. Just not one that any species she knew would like living in.

"Any signs of our bioships?"

"They've been here and they shot *Guidance* to hell," Nguyen said grimly. "If she took out any of them, the corpses have been moved or destroyed."

"Or buried," Dunst suggested. "The Children appear to have built their religion around the source of the bioships; they might well have some kind of veneration for the creatures themselves."

The range was dropping slowly, El-Amin bringing them in at a paltry twenty percent of lightspeed.

"Sir, I have a contact on the surface," Nguyen reported. There was no urgency in her voice, only sadness. "It...appears to be *Serene Guidance*. I'm pinging her black box, but it looks like she went down and went down hard."

With an interface drive, a vessel's velocity was a property of the drive field and not the ship. A missile worked by explosively releasing that velocity energy in an impact. Planetary gravity wells screwed with the drive as well, rapidly reducing maximum velocity as the surrounding natural gravity increased.

If *Guidance* had catastrophically lost her drive field and then continued to be fired at, she could still have gone down at hundreds or thousands of kilometers per second. The impact would have killed everyone aboard, artificial gravity or not.

"Black box is not responding," Nguyen continued. "We're getting better data of the impact crater, and it doesn't look good for anyone."

The bridge went very quiet as the big holotank filled with information and computer-generated imagery.

"It looks like she hit at just over two percent of lightspeed," the tactical officer said softly. "Even her electronics would have been nearly liquefied, and the debris cloud..." She shook her head. "If that planet was any less of a shithole to begin with, I'd say the biosphere was doomed. As it is, it *might* survive."

A five-hundred-thousand-ton ship impacting at two percent of lightspeed made even Earth's dinosaur-killer look like a toy. Two tera-tons of explosive forces. To call the impact site a crater was under-stating things. On a more oceanic planet, a *continent* would have been obliterated.

It was easy to forget just how much energy was wrapped up in even a small modern starship at any given moment.

"Make sure your data is being saved," Morgan said quietly. "This planet was different enough that it's worth something."

And it didn't look like anyone *else* would be getting any images of Delta's biosphere as it had been.

"Hold us at thirty light-seconds, El-Amin," she ordered. Nine million kilometers was still out of range for *Defiance*'s energy weapons and, hopefully, out of the effective range of the bioships. So far, twenty-two light-seconds had been the maximum range they'd seen, but that was assuming the Precursor creatures didn't have bigger siblings somewhere.

"Nguyen, focus our sensors on the moon. Nystrom, any luck tracing the source of the jamming?" she asked.

"It's hard to say for sure, but it's definitely somewhere in the Delta planetary system," the com officer replied. "If it's on the planet, it was unaffected by the impact."

"Everything I'm seeing suggests the moon," Rogers said quietly. "Where would the Precursors have put a starcom there?"

The Precursor starcom had been a smaller and more easily built installation than the one available to modern races, but it had still been fundamentally the same. The layout and structure were identi-cal, but the materials and scale had been different.

"We've seen them built into the ground before, but it would still be on the highest point they could find, probably on a side facing away from the planet," Dunst reeled off.

"Then I think I've got it," Nguyen reported. "There's a series of large impact craters on the far side of Delta's moon that combine to create a series of peaks almost twenty kilometers tall. I have what might be artificial materials at the top of several of those peaks."

"Launch a drone pattern, get me clearer data," Morgan ordered. "And tell Vichy his drop is go."

She had her suspicions about what was going to happen next, and she and Vichy had drawn up a plan. The stealth shuttles flashed on her scanners as they dropped away from *Defiance*, their launch hopefully lost amongst the twenty drones launching at the same time.

The drones oriented and shot toward the moon at seventy percent of the speed of light. They didn't have instantaneous coms, but they were still sending more detailed information than *Defiance* could get from nine million kilometers away.

"Confirm that; I have definite Precursor installations in those peaks," Nguyen reported. "And— *Contact!*"

"Report!" Morgan snapped as red icons began to appear on her screen, flashing up to meet her drones at eighty percent of the speed of light.

"There is a modern installation using the peaks for cover from scanners from anyone who isn't at *exactly* the right angle," the tactical officer told her. "They've opened fire on the drones with point-eight missiles."

Point-eights were old and obsolete weapons—but still effective enough when shooting down sensor drones that Morgan had intentionally not bothered to hide.

"Partial contacts are following," Nguyen continued after a moment. "Activating ECM systems on remaining drones and ordering them into evasive patterns. They should keep us informed."

"Understood. Partials are our ghosts?" Morgan demanded.

"Yes, sir. At least twenty, but more are launching from around the peaks." The Vietnamese woman paused for a moment, swallowing hard. "I'm reading at least thirty contacts comparable to what we saw before, but the second wave is only six...and my sensors are estimating them at almost triple the size of the others."

"Well, then," Morgan said calmly. "Commander El-Amin, please open the range. Commander Nguyen? Target those big bastards with our hyperspace missiles. All batteries are clear; fire at will."

She wasn't in range of the bioships today—and she had *no* intention of letting that change!

CHAPTER TWENTY-NINE

DEFIANCE'S TACTICAL TEAM HAD HAD OVER TWENTY CYCLES TO refine their data on the bioships to the point where they could target the strange creatures. As they fired their first salvo, Morgan was forced to the conclusion that there was only so much they could do.

The twenty-gigaton antimatter warheads of the hyperspace missiles certainly made an impression, lighting up the skies of the planet and the moon like newborn suns, but only one of their targets actually died.

The HSMs scored the only kill of that first salvo. As the sublight missiles swarmed toward the bioships, the creatures opened fire on them. *Defiance* had a limited number of interface-drive-missile launchers, an intentional compromise in favor of hyperfold cannon and HSM launchers.

The creatures pursuing her shot down most of the missiles. A handful made it through, but the hostile bioships were tough. They didn't have shields, so they had to *feel* those hits, but somehow they were still coming.

"Rogers, I need an analysis," Morgan said calmly as she watched.

"Are any of the ships we're seeing too large to be transported in the freighters we've seen the Children using?"

Defiance shivered as a second salvo flashed into space. Only her missiles were in range, but if Morgan tried to bring the cruiser's energy weapons into range, she'd let the hostiles into their range of her.

"No," Rogers said softly. "The bigger ones would take most of the capacity of the ships we've seen and require some refitting, which might explain why there are fewer of them."

"The Children are carrying the bioships around with them," Morgan concluded. "Presumably, they've worked out how to base and feed the things. What does a million-ton living starship even eat?"

"Organic compounds, elemental carbon, elemental hydrogen, and as many types of metal as you could find," Dunst suggested. "The cloner on Arjtal required organic biomass, but even waste matter from normal farming was enough.

"I'd imagine these guys need a metal-heavy diet, but they do have to eat."

"Rocks and dirt, most likely," Rogers suggested as their third salvo crossed the distance. "Appetizing to them, if not to us. I just wish they were as dumb as I'd like them to be."

New and ever-varying evasive patterns had been added to the bioships' maneuvers, costing them a measurable percentage of their forward acceleration—but they were still accelerating at nearly ten thousand gravities.

"I'm guessing they lost at least one to *Guidance*'s missiles," Morgan said. "She didn't have HSMs, so they're improvising a defensive response to that. Which isn't helping them as much as they'd like."

Nguyen had been adjusting her fire concentration as the strange ships pursued them. Her second salvo had been more of a test than an actual attempt to take down the bioships.

Her *third* was a different matter entirely.

Morgan could see now that the last HSM salvo hadn't even been intended to hit anyone. Nguyen had been herding the bigger bioships into a specific position, slightly farther back than the rest of their swarm.

Now six HSMs bracketed each of the four trailing monsters, and there was no chance they could evade. Armored and tough and big though the trailing bioships might be, they couldn't stand up to being trapped amidst multiple twenty-gigaton explosions.

One of them survived. Somehow. Even from this distance, it was clearly leaking fluids in a way that Morgan wouldn't have expected a regular ship to survive, let alone one that was definitely alive.

As the swarm recoiled from that loss, the sublight missiles arrived. Two dozen missiles flung themselves through the creatures' defenses, their electronic-warfare systems cycling through a dozen different programs as *Defiance*'s tactical team continued to try and find a trick that would work.

This time, they were targeted on a single bioship, charging forward like homesick meteors. The ship had slipped forward from the rest of the swarm, a difference of a few dozen thousand kilometers at most.

It was enough to degrade the shared defense, and six of Nguyen's missiles made it through. *That*, it turned out, was more than the natural compressed-matter scales could take, and the target vanished.

"Well done, Commander," Morgan told her tactical officer. "Keep it up. El-Amin, are we going to have a problem?"

"That depends on whether they've got the delta-v and the armor to get up to point six c," the headscarfed navigator replied. "Right now, it would be easier to leave them behind than to stay in range, but they're gaining speed fast."

"How much fuel can they even carry?" Rogers asked. "They'd have to have...half or more of their mass as fuel to pull that off and have a chance of slowing down."

"Assuming they care about slowing down or can't coordinate with the Children to pick them up," Morgan replied. "Plus, based off even our crude autopsy? They might just contain that much fuel...and those scales are compressed matter."

Her senior officers turned their attention back to the tactical display as a fourth set of HSMs tore through the last surviving large bioship and shattered several of his companions.

"The problem, sir, is I'm not sure I'm killing them fast enough," Nguyen admitted on the command channel. "There's still over thirty of the smaller units left, and I've burned a sixth of our hyperspace missiles already.

"We've got interface-drive missiles for days, but they're just ignoring everything I can throw at them in terms of ECM. Whatever they're using for sensors, it isn't fooled by any of the tricks our missiles can pull."

"We keep drawing them out until we've expended half the HSMs," Morgan ordered. "We have to assume there's more threats in play than this."

"Surely, we can finish them off with another eight salvos of HSMs?" Rogers asked. "The big ones were taking six each..."

"And the little guys are still taking six each," Nguyen replied as another salvo blasted out. Four of the smaller bioships disappeared. "It's more reliable, but it's still not guaranteed we're going to finish them off before they start catching up."

"They're not trying to catch us, anyway," Morgan reminded her people. "The bioships might think they can take us—they're being smart enough to improve their survival chances but not necessarily smart enough to know they can't win—but the Children have to know better by now."

"If they're not trying to catch us...the Children are running, aren't they?" Rogers asked.

"It had to be a toss-up for them," Morgan admitted. "If we'd come in closer, like *Serene Guidance* did, the bioships could have jumped us while they were already in range. The bigger units could potentially have gutted her at close range.

"As soon as we turned this into a stern chase, the bioships

couldn't win. After *Guidance* came through, unless they're idiots, they had a backup plan."

Another four bioships died. Nguyen wasn't even using the IDMs to try and kill them anymore, Morgan noted. Now the timing had changed so the sublight missiles came in as the FTL weapons arrived, sweeping through space to limit the swarm's options and keep them in the target zone for the hyperspace weapons.

"They're going to run," Dunst concluded, the civilian catching up. "They're just using the Alava ships to get us far enough away."

"We've been falling back for nearly four minutes, and those things are getting damn close to our own speed," Morgan said. "We're over two light-minutes away now, and if they've got a decent drive on a ship, they can outrun anything except HSMs already.

"I expect to see them rabbit in the next minute or so," she concluded with a shrug. "Even with half the bioships gone, we can't charge *through* the buggers. Their range envelope is still too dangerous for us to enter, so our options are limited. We can shoot them when they run, but they know we're bound by peacetime rules of engagement *and* they're technically criminals *and* we want to ask them questions.

"They're quite correct to assume I'll attempt to pursue rather than blow them away, and with the bioships in play, we can't intercept or even get into hyperspace fast enough to chase them. It's the same plan they pulled at D-L-K-Six."

"So, it works and they just get away?" Dunst asked.

"No, it doesn't, does it, sir?" Rogers said after a moment as Morgan grinned. "You were expecting this."

"It seemed very likely," Morgan agreed.

"Contact!" Nguyen snapped. "I've got a new ship launching from the moon. Freighter—big freighter, one of ours."

"*Ours*, Lesser Commander?" Morgan asked.

"Military-built fast support collier; hauls ten megatons of cargo at point-five-five c," the tactical officer replied. "She's big, she's fast. Even without the bioships, I'm not sure we could catch her."

"And that, Dr. Dunst, Commander Nguyen, is why Battalion Commander Vichy is in orbit of the moon with six stealth shuttles," Morgan said calmly.

"Let's finish off these bastards, Commander," she continued. "I trust Vichy to do his job. Let's do ours."

CHAPTER THIRTY

"Et nous voici," Pierre Vichy said cheerfully. "Viens dans mon salon."

If Company Commander Comtois thought his boss was insane, he was wise enough to keep his mouth shut.

"That is a monster of a freighter," he noted instead. "Do we have a plan?"

"The plan, Commander Comtois, is to take her," Pierre replied. "Suffisant, oui?"

"I was hoping for something more substantial," his subordinate noted, the shuttle around them vibrating as it began to move. "If she's what the database says she is, she's *fast*."

"If she's what the database says she is, we have full schematics," the Marine CO responded. He'd been working on a model only he could see while he teased his subordinate, and he threw it on the command channel with Hunter and Comtois.

"A *Rising Tide*–class civilian support freighter has its primary engine control *here*, its life support *here*, and its bridge *here*," he told them. "I performed a boarding exercise on a ship of this class when I was a Speaker. Those three points are almost impossible to move. *Armories*, d'autre part, are potentially easily moved but would be here, here, and here in the original design."

Six icons glowed on the model.

"We have six shuttles, three platoons from each company," he continued. "Commander Hunter, you will take your force and hit the bridge. It's well embedded, near the center of the ship, so you will face heavy resistance. We need prisoners, people, but anyone shooting at you is a valid target.

"Commander Comtois, one of your platoons will go for Life Support," he continued. "Once there, the platoon will see what they can do to make people sleepy."

The atmospheric makeup of a ship was entirely artificial. It would take some time for an adjustment to the O_2 and CO_2 to knock the crew out, but it was just as effective as stun fields.

Less *safe*, but he wasn't the one who'd issued stun-blocking cloaks to everyone.

"Your other two platoons will accompany the two of us as we punch straight for Engineering," he ordered. "While I assume at least some of these people don't want to die, their leadership has so far been quite willing to suicide and take everyone else with them.

"We want this ship intact. As many prisoners as possible, as many computers as possible," he concluded. "We have to assume they sanitized the ground sites, which means this thing is our only hope of finding out where the damn bioships are coming from."

"So, we take the ship, we capture the crew, and we ask all kinds of questions. Simple enough, non? Questions?"

"What if they have heavy weapons?" Hunter asked.

"Expect them," Pierre countered. "They have a military ship, people. Let's assume we're facing military hardware. But they won't have *Marines*, and they're not expecting us. We hit them hard, we hit them fast."

A moment of disruption rattled through the channel and he swallowed a curse.

"What was that?" Hunter demanded. Pierre was already accessing the shuttle's sensors to confirm what he expected.

"Multiple fusion-reactor overloads," he told his subordinate. "Plus nuclear bombs. They sanitized the ground site, all right."

The Children had *obliterated* the ground site. The sensors were showing at least thirty different explosions, ranging from fifty kilotons to several megatons. The latter had the telltale marks of fusion-reactor plants that had been specifically *designed* to go up like bombs when set to overload.

"That does increase the importance of taking the freighter, n'est-ce pas?" Pierre asked softly. "En avant, mes Capitaines. Le destin nous attend."

"Destiny can hang; let's do the damn job," Hunter replied. "Bravo Company, moving in now."

THE PLANNING SESSION had also served the purpose of letting the Children's escape ship get closer to the stealthed shuttles. Pierre's craft were moving at an easily hidden five percent of lightspeed, but the freighter was getting close enough to detect them.

The Children never had a chance. At six hundred thousand kilometers, the shuttles went from idling at five percent of lightspeed to charging at sixty percent of lightspeed.

They closed the range to the fleeing freighter in less than four seconds, specialty systems cutting the interface drive in the final instant before impact. Energy flares of collapsing drive fields blasted out behind the shuttles as they made contact, and plasma cutters woke up in the same moment.

The freighter's hull had a thin layer of compressed-matter armor, but Imperial Marine assault shuttles were designed to board *warships*. The Children's ship could have withstood missiles—or, at least, *a* missile—but against speciality tools it didn't stand a chance.

"We're in," Comtois told him. "Marines, forward!"

Pierre and the Company Commander were in the middle of the shuttle and in the middle of the pack as the Marines stormed onto the fleeing freighter.

"Remember, stun anyone you can," Pierre told his people. "We need prisoners."

Hopefully, the Children were less universal in wearing anti-stun gear aboard their own ship. Only time would tell.

"The schematics are matching up so far," the lead team reported. "Engineering should be this way. No contacts so far; we are moving in."

Pierre started to move after them and his suit sensors reported multiple flashes of stunner fire.

"Contact," the Lance in charge of the lead team reported. "Unarmored crew; we have successfully stunned them. Leaving them for the next team to secure; we are moving forward."

Pierre didn't need to give orders to the individual fire teams. At this point, even his company commanders didn't need to give much in terms of orders. His Marines were a well-oiled machine; they knew how to safely capture a starship.

Pierre's role would come in when things started going wrong. For now, he mostly let his power armor follow along with the platoon as he ran a tactical map of the entire ship in his HUD. Their initial contacts had all been pretty consistent: unarmored crew that either hadn't known the ship had been boarded or hadn't had time to get ready.

That wasn't going to last, especially as they pushed closer to the critical sections of the ship. His Engineering force was going to reach their destination first, which both made them likely to encounter real resistance first—and gave them the best chance of reaching their destination *without* resistance.

"Incoming!" someone snapped, and Pierre narrowed the map to focus on the battle around him.

He readied his own weapon as red contact icons flashed up on his HUD.

"Multiple contacts around the main access to Engineering," a Marine reported. "They have plasma weapons but minimal armor. We are advancing."

He could hear the plasma fire as well as see it on his screen as the lead elements of his force charged into the teeth of the defenders' fire.

The crackle died down after a few seconds, the red icons fading out on Pierre's display.

So did one of the blue icons representing his Marines. A tap on the hologram brought up the biometrics, and Pierre grimaced and mouthed a silent prayer.

Even Imperial medicine couldn't do much for what looked like a mostly vaporized head.

"We're moving into Engineering," a new voice reported. "Lance Braden is down, KIA."

"Understood," Comtois replied. "Second squad, move up. Keep them in your sights."

"There isn't enough space, sir," the point Marine replied grimly. "Not until we're into the Engineering spaces."

Pierre moved forward with the rest of the Marines, his hands tight on his own plasma rifle. The schematics told him that the point Marine was right, but he still had to see it before he let go of at least some of the guilt.

Even with eight Marines charging down the hallway, they'd had to go in waves. The space the Children had chosen to defend had allowed six of them to focus fire onto a space that only held three Marines abreast.

Lance Braden's body had been moved back out of the chokepoint, his armor leaned against a wall in the space the engineers had been firing from.

More plasma fire crackled in the distance and Pierre grimaced. He didn't say anything, though—his Marines knew the risks of firing plasma weapons in Engineering. If they were firing weapons, there was a reason.

"We have contact," a Marine reported. "Hostile power armor in the Engineering bays."

"Second platoon, move in," Comtois ordered. "Overwhelm them. Shoot straight, Marines."

Even with the sensors of multiple Marines in the relatively open space around the power reactors, the tactical map was still unclear on how many hostiles there were and where they were. By the time Pierre entered the space himself, hustling along with Alpha Company's first platoon, it was clear that the Children were making a serious push to hold his people up there.

There were at least twenty enemies in power armor in the space, and they had *serious* gear, the same heavy plasma rifles as his people.

"Sir, get down," Comtois snapped at Pierre. "Take cover—behind something they won't shoot, preferably!"

Pierre swallowed a chuckle as he ducked behind a heavy-duty power conduit. In this kind of fight, there wasn't much that would stop any of the weaponry in play. There were, on the other hand, a *lot* of things in the Engineering space that neither side could afford to shoot.

He had a three-to-one numerical edge on the defenders, and he knew in his bones that his Marines were better. It was a question of how bad his Marines got hurt—and the answer wasn't looking pretty.

Studying his HUD for a moment, he locked a target in and stepped out from behind his cover. His weapon fired a high-intensity beam of plasma that hit a Children defender as the fighter left their own cover, burning clean through his target's chest plate and sending them reeling backward.

"Push them, Marines," he barked. "We need control before someone rigs the whole place to explode."

Back in cover, his armor's computers were analyzing all of the data to make sure no one was doing that...and flashed a bright red warning. One of the armored figures was kneeling behind the main antimatter power core. No one was shooting anywhere near them—antimatter needed and received a lot of respect in this kind of fight—

but they were interfaced with the power core's systems, and that was definitely a bad sign today.

And even Pierre didn't want to shoot at them. The fight was swinging toward his people, but his people were busy fighting it. If the Child working at the console was doing what Pierre feared, there was no time.

"Comtois, cover me," he ordered.

He barely registered his subordinate's spluttered curses before he dove from his cover, hitting the ground running as he charged across the freighter's Engineering deck. Four of the ship's eight power cores were there, including the only antimatter plant on the ship.

The backup fusion cores located elsewhere could be shut down completely from there, and the antimatter core was the easiest one to induce a catastrophic failure in.

Antimatter earned every gram of the respect it was given.

For the first few steps, no one even seemed to notice that someone was mad enough to charge the full length of the open deck. After that, it felt like every one of the Children was targeting Pierre.

The Marine fired on the run, shooting at the defenders in his field of view. He wasn't sure he hit any of them, but that wasn't the point. He couldn't shoot at his target; the engineer had chosen their position far too well.

Fortunately for Pierre's longevity, Comtois had a far better field of fire and was just as good as his boss was counting on him being. Shooters that came close tended not to get a second shot, the Company Commander peppering their hiding spots with fire to keep their heads down.

Pierre hoped that his distraction was buying his people the opportunity to take down more of the Children, but his focus was on the antimatter core. The engineer had to know he was coming—the crescendo of plasma fire around him wasn't subtle—but they continued to focus on their work.

A plasma bolt slammed into Pierre's armor from behind. Integrity warnings flashed up on his HUD, and he hit a command he never thought he'd actually use.

He tossed his plasma rifle aside as the hydrogen reservoirs in his suit that fed it vented themselves. There were multiple spots he could vent the high-pressure gas, which meant he sent it all out the back of his suit, turning an emergency ammunition dump into an improvised rocket.

A stray plasma bolt ignited the hydrogen cloud and he suspected he made a hell of a show as he blasted across the last dozen or so meters, his armor's force blade snapping out as he flew.

He used his suit's actual jets to control his course at the last minute, using every scrap of his momentum to swing the meter-long blade into his target and cleave the engineer in two in a single blow.

Pierre hit the ground exactly like a quarter-ton suit of armor. He managed to roll onto his feet, the contortion leaving him wincing in pain as he came up on one knee and activated his armor's stun field.

The weapon wouldn't do much against anyone in armor, but the pulse of energy screwed with everyone's targeting systems, allowing him to close the distance with the engineer again, severing the connection between the dead Child and the antimatter core.

No one was shooting at him now. He was in the same "don't shoot the *fucking antimatter*" safe zone the engineer had been relying on, and he linked his own armor into the console. If he was *very* lucky...

"Assez!" he snapped aloud.

The ship was still using the Imperial Navy–issue operating system. Which meant that Pierre could now see that the engineer had mostly succeeded. The antimatter and hydrogen feeds were already turned all the way up.

The engineer hadn't managed to turn off the containment fields, but they'd been plugging in the authorization codes to do it. Pierre focused on the engineering console, closing out the battle as he fought with the software to save *everyone's* lives.

He wasn't an engineer, but the Imperium trained their Marines in how to stop this exact situation. Some parts of the OS were suffi-ciently generic that his codes worked. Others...weren't.

He'd stopped the containment field shutdown, but he didn't have the control to slow the feeds. The core could only handle a reaction of a certain intensity, and the system was giving him warnings.

Pierre couldn't stop it. The core was still going to overload, unless...

"Stand by for lights out," he barked on the main command chan-nel, and used the strength of his armor to tear the surface of the console off. He assumed there were easier ways to take it off if you had tools, but he had powered-armor gauntlets.

The cover was designed to come off, and nestled in the middle of the circuit boards was what looked like a glorified valve control. Grabbing it in the two armored fingers that would fit around it, Pierre pulled the emergency shutdown control out of the console, rotated it ninety degrees, and slammed it back down.

The feed for every single reactor on the ship stopped in the next second. The lights went out a moment later, the system automatically focusing on using the power reserves to keep up the reactor contain-ment until the reactions ended.

Emergency lighting began to switch on after a few seconds as Pierre breathed a long sigh of relief.

"Speaker Qadir," he said calmly. "Life support should have emer-gency power, but I'd appreciate it if you can confirm that once you are in control. En avant, Speaker."

The room around him was dimly lit and he realized the shooting had finally stopped.

"Engineering is secure, sir," Comtois's voice said in his ear. "Did...what I think just happened just happen?"

"That engineer had the antimatter core set to overload and I'm no hacker," Pierre said calmly. "Emergency shutdown works, n'est-ce pas?"

"Yes. Yes, it does," his subordinate agreed.

CHAPTER THIRTY-ONE

Rin hadn't really *ASKED* if he should be going over to the captured Children ship. The cyberwarfare experts—the Imperial Marines' polite name for hackers—he'd been working with aboard *Defiance* had loaded up to go with the second wave of Marines, and he'd shrugged and gone along.

He'd seen bigger ships than the freighter they were pulling up alongside, but he'd done a lot of work and study in A!To, a star system guarded by multiple squadrons of superbattleships. The freighter was the size of a standard battleship, though, which made her the largest ship he'd seen this far out.

Fortunately, almost none of that size and mass had gone to weapons.

A Marine Speaker was walking down the rows of seats in the shuttle, checking everyone's gear. They stopped in front of Rin and looked down at him. The power armor allowed even average-sized humans to loom quite effectively, and the archeologist quailed a bit.

"Dr. Dunst," the man greeted him calmly. "I'm not even going to ask if the Captain has approved this. I'm not turning this shuttle around for one civilian."

Rin returned the faceless helmet's regard as levelly as he could.

"I'm Speaker Lebeau, Bravo-Five-Actual," the Marine introduced himself. "You realize, Doctor, that we are going aboard a recently secured hostile vessel? That may or may not still have active Children operatives aboard?

"Most importantly, we are boarding a vessel that currently has its atmosphere set to induce minor hypoxia in anyone without proper breathing equipment," Lebeau concluded drily. "Spear Vaquero! Get me an unpowered armor set with atmo gear." He studied Rin very specifically for a few seconds.

"Size seven; we'll need to cinch it down, but I am not letting the civvie wander that ship without armor and an O_2 mask!"

Another armored Marine—presumably Spear Vaquero, the platoon's senior noncom—appeared a few seconds later with a full combat suit, an open-down-the-back neck-to-toe armored garment, and the attached helmet.

They studied Rin for a few seconds, then retracted their own helmet, revealing an androgynous face with short-cropped black hair.

"All right," Vaquero said brightly. "I've got this, Speaker. He'll be armored and masked before he enters the ship."

"Make certain of it," Lebeau ordered, then raised an armored finger at Rin. "I'm assuming you have a reason to be here, Doctor, but you don't go aboard that ship until Spear Vaquero clears you as armored up—and you don't do it without a fire team of Marines around you. If any of that is a problem, said fire team of Marines will *sit on you* to make sure you don't leave this shuttle.

"Am I clear, Dr. Dunst?"

"Entirely, Speaker Lebeau," Rin confirmed with a grin. He unstrapped himself from the chair and reached for the suit. "These people have been stealing and wrecking Alava artifacts across the region. I want to see what they keep on hand for themselves.

"I'll be a good civilian, I promise."

Lebeau snorted and continued on, leaving Rin with Vaquero.

And the armored suit, which did not look like it was going to be comfortable to put on.

SEVERAL EXCRUCIATINGLY UNCOMFORTABLE minutes followed as the shuttle docked, and most of the Marines trooped off to join their fellows in making sure there were no Children with oxygen masks hiding in corners.

Finally, they had the armor cinched in around Rin so it was snug against him in the places it was supposed to be, and he had the mask on.

"Straightforward enough, I suppose," Vaquero observed.

Rin stared at them like they'd grown a second head.

"That was *straightforward*?" he asked.

"I graduated the A!Tol's bodyguard course," they told him. "I have put everything from doctors to diplomats to children in armor, including members of eleven different species. It's easier to do it with someone who shares your basic physiology, and it's much easier to do it with someone who's smart and cooperative."

Vaquero grinned and closed their helmet.

"And now I shall leave you to the tender mercies of Lance Sanderson," they told him, gesturing to one of the four suits of power armor still in the shuttle. "I have a platoon to help organize. Chop chop, Dr. Dunst. We all have work to do."

The Marine NCO was gone before he could think of a response, and he shrugged helplessly as he turned to Sanderson.

"I need to rendezvous with Speaker Murtas," he told the Marine. "Is his location flagged?"

"He's in the main computer center with a stack of people who can make my armor dance with me in it," Sanderson replied. "We can get you there."

"Let's get moving, then," Rin told his escort. "The sooner we're mixed in with everyone else, the less danger we're in."

"You're in no danger, Doctor," Sanderson told him. "I'm authorized to put very large holes in this ship to keep you safe."

"Yes, well, I'd rather not put holes in the ship until we've determined which parts we might need!"

Someday, Rin Dunst was going to get used to the fact that the Navy and Marines regarded him as an asset on par with their entire starship. Someday.

All evidence suggested that day was definitely not today.

RIN WAS EXPECTING to find the freighter's data center a hub of activity, with the computer experts and hackers plugged into consoles and holographic systems all over the place as they tore into the files they'd extracted from the freighter's computers.

Instead, he found a half-assembled portable computing setup surrounded by bored-looking techs. The only lights in the room were portable lamps the *Defiance* contingent had set up themselves, and they shone on dull and unpowered spikes of molecular circuitry and blocks of cheaper computer servers.

For a moment, he thought it was a power problem—but then he spotted a portable power generator in the corner. Murtas had come prepared for this.

The Speaker in question was sitting on the power generator as Rin approached him, his masked chin resting on his hands as he studied the computer center.

"Speaker Murtas?" Rin greeted the man via a private channel. The masks didn't leave much ability to be heard.

"Dr. Dunst. If you were hoping to get useful information from my dive into the ship's computers, you're going to be sadly disappointed."

"What happened?" Rin asked.

"I'd hoped that when the Marines threw the ship into emergency shutdown, they'd done so before anyone had initiated a purge protocol on the computers," the gaunt and pale-haired intelligence officer replied. "I suppose the fact that the bastards were already trying to overload the antimatter core should have told us their assessment of how this was going to end."

"The data's gone?"

"We powered up the molycirc cores, at least; they've been wiped," Murtas confirmed. "There isn't even an *operating system* left. It's possible we can retrieve some data if we restored an OS, but it's impossible for us to make certain that our installation doesn't write over the very data we're trying to save."

"Can we extract the cores and analyze them elsewhere?" Rin asked.

"That depends on whether we want to move the ship or not," the Navy officer said. "That's Captain Casimir's call, not mine. If I pull every box and molycirc spike in this room and haul them back to Kosha, we should be able to retrieve *some* data. Everything was deleted; it's a question of how much was properly hashed before the power went down."

"Any idea?"

Murtas coughed.

"We could be lucky and retrieve as much as fifty percent," he admitted. "Or...we could find that ninety percent of the contents of the computers are hashed and the ten percent that's left is just the OS and the code doing the hashing.

"It's a complete throw of the dice at this point, and to get it, we're leaving a freighter that costs as much as a pair of destroyers a lobotomized hulk drifting in the middle of nowhere."

"There have to be other ways to move that don't require its own computers, right?" Rin asked.

"There probably are," the Speaker admitted. "And were I a line officer or an Engineering officer, I'd probably already have the solution to my problem." He gestured around the room. "I'm a tech geek and an intelligence wonk, Dr. Dunst. *I* can't fly this ship without all of its original hardware and software.

"I have a copy of its original software on *Defiance*, but if I install that, I risk losing everything I'm here to access. So, right now, Doctor, I'm feeling pretty damn useless."

"What do we know about this ship, Speaker?" Rin asked. "I was hoping to get at the files, but my *plan* is to go through the stash of Alava artifacts I figured they had aboard."

"I know her name: *Child of the Great Mother*," Murtas told him. "I know her schematics and I have a message in the queue to dig through the builder's files and see if we can track who bought her.

"I'm guessing the news *there* is going to suggest things I don't want to know."

"I'm...not sure I follow," Rin admitted.

"This is a military ship, Doctor," the Speaker told him. "Not a warship, but it's got nearly warship-grade interface drives and warship-grade hyperspace emitters. She's not a military courier with classified hyperspace tech, but she's still packed with tech that's not supposed to be sold to anyone other than the Imperial military.

"So, my five marks says the builder's records are going to say she was built under order for the Navy or another government branch, everything entirely aboveboard. And somewhere between her being taken into the Imperium's service and her showing up out here, she went astray—and that, Dr. Dunst, makes me wonder what the source of our little cult problem actually is."

Rin wasn't even sure how to respond to that.

"That makes no sense, Speaker," he told the intelligence officer.

"My job is to be paranoid, Doctor," Murtas replied. "I'm still assembling my data, and I'm starting to spot the holes. Some of those holes are just things I'm not cleared for. Like, I'm pretty damn certain both you and the Captain knew we'd be finding Precursor structures out here and that's why the surveys have stretched so far in this direction.

"There are other bits like that, where I'm pretty sure everything's legit, but I'm not cleared." The man shrugged. "And then there's holes that don't make sense. A military-grade freighter in the hands of a religious cult that clearly knows more about Precursor bullshit out here than we do—but didn't necessarily need to to get started."

"You think someone in the Imperium sent them out here?" Rin asked.

"It's a possibility. A ship like this would make the perfect base for a long-range covert survey expedition. If it went silent because of *something*, well...then we'd need real force, and that's most easily deployed by pointing a major survey effort in this direction."

"I wish I could believe that was as paranoid as it sounds," the archeologist replied. "I like that option better than what I thought you were saying."

Murtas snorted.

"Even I, Dr. Dunst, hesitate to consider the possibility that the Children are being actively managed by a conspiracy within our own government. I mean, our overlords can't even *lie* worth shit."

"That's not actually true," Rin admitted quietly. "They just have to focus on a different emotion when doing it. Determination to keep a secret works pretty well. They can't sustain a long-term deception, but keeping a secret in the face of random questioning? The A!Tol can manage that.

"It's nearly impossible to have corrupt A!Tol politicians, but it's merely *difficult* for them to conceal a conspiracy."

"And the difficult we do immediately," Murtas replied, almost automatically. "That's not helping my paranoia, Doctor."

"Your paranoia is a professional benefit," Rin said. "For the moment, though, I want your guess on that schematic we were talking about. If there was a stockpile of artifacts of historical and religious importance on this ship, where would you put it?"

"The big cargo bays wouldn't be the right ones," the analyst replied instantly. "Those are probably hauling the bioships. The ship has a few smaller, more heavily secured storage compartments. They're where we'd put things like spare molycirc cores and similar high-value, low-cubage cargo."

"Sounds about right. Can you flag them on my map? I'll take my escort and check them out. We might find something useful there."

"More than I'm finding here," Murtas agreed. "I'm about to move on myself. We've got enough prisoners that we need to start processing them, and for my sins, that falls on Intelligence and the Marines."

CHAPTER THIRTY-TWO

"THE GOOD NEWS IS THAT OUR HYPERFOLD COMS ARE BACK UP and our guns are working properly again," Rogers reported to the gathering of the senior staff.

Defiance was now less than ten thousand kilometers from *Child of the Great Mother*, with shuttles flying back and forth every few minutes. Most of Vichy's Marines were still aboard the captured freighter, but a number of Morgan's Navy crew were over there now as well.

"We've sent in a full report to Kosha Station and requested information on *Child*," Rogers continued. "She's a military ship, so we're hoping we can ID when she went missing."

"Our best guess at this point is that she was taken by pirates some years ago," Morgan noted. "There is a possibility that she was sent out here intentionally ten to twelve years ago on a covert pre-survey of the region.

"If so, we can assume that survey went very, *very* wrong," she concluded drily. "As for *Child* herself, I dragged Commander Vichy back aboard to brief us. His efforts appear to be the only reason we retrieved her intact."

She wasn't going to admit just yet that the report had included a recommendation that the Battalion Commander be awarded one of the Imperium's higher awards for valor. The French officer *still* annoyed her, and it hadn't *really* been his job to make the crazed charge that had prevented *Child* from self-destructing, but he'd done it.

They'd lost eleven Marines KIA and another thirty wounded taking *Child*, but the antimatter core would have killed all of the hundred and eighty Imperial personnel on the ship. Along with the hundred and fifteen Children aboard as well, though Morgan cared somewhat less about them.

"*Child of the Great Mother* is currently lobotomized and power-less," Vichy told *Defiance*'s officers. "We killed her power, but they wiped her computers. My understanding from Lesser Commander Liepins"—the Marine gestured to *Defiance*'s Chief Engineer—"is that both life support and the power systems run on local operating systems that appear to still be intact.

"Certainly, we have control of *Child*'s life support and have restored her atmosphere via the use of portable generators. Commander Liepins has a team aboard that is studying whether we can overwrite their software and security and bring at least the secondary power cores back online."

"It's looking promising," the Latvian engineer interjected. "But from Speaker Murtas's analysis, we have very little functional aboard the ship to feed power *to*."

"We could restore her operating systems and take full control, but we'd risk losing everything in her files if we do so," the Speaker, the most junior person in the room, told them all. "If at all possible, I'd like to bring her computer cores and servers to Kosha Station untouched. With the resources at the station, we should be able to do a full dump of the data without damaging it.

"*Defiance*'s computers simply don't have the capacity to take a full copy of an entire starship's computing network," Murtas admit-ted. "We need the Station and the Navy base's computers to do that."

"Understood," Morgan allowed. She didn't like drawing on her stepmother's experience, but thanks to Annette Bond, she knew the answer to this problem.

"In one memorable moment of my stepmother's career, she used a hyper-capable survey ship as a substitute control center for a crippled freighter," she reminded them all. "In that case, the entire bridge and power supply were gone. *Of Course We're Coming Back* was providing power to the ship's existing exotic matter emitters.

"If *Child* can provide her own power, we can load the hyperspace navigation software into one of our shuttles and wire it into the ship's control systems. Then we should be able to use the shuttle to control and fly *Child* without risking the data we want to use.

"Liepins? Is it doable?"

The engineer was silent with a thoughtful look on his face.

"The biggest problem will be trying to insert the shuttle into the drive and hyperspace emitter control links," he admitted. "We'll need a team at Engineering managing the power core no matter what, but I think it should be doable.

"We are probably far safer having *Defiance* escort the freighter for the trip, though."

"I was planning on it," Morgan agreed. "Is there anything else in this system even worth us taking the time to study?"

"Dr. Dunst is still nose-deep in the pile of artifacts he found aboard *Child*," Vichy reported. "But from the time he and I took to look at the surface installation, we don't think there's anything left even worth looking at. They nuked it *very* thoroughly."

"Someone is very determined to keep their secrets," Morgan noted. "Did our interrogation get us anything of value?"

Vichy and Murtas shared a look, and the Marine CO made a conceding gesture to the much more junior intelligence officer.

Murtas glanced around the table at the people he shared a room with. Five department heads, the First Sword, the Captain, and the Marine CO. Seven other officers, most of the people on the ship senior to him.

The ship's surgeon didn't sit on these meetings, and the Marine company commanders were busy aboard *Child of the Great Mother*.

Murtas had answered questions before but he seemed less ready for this particular bomb to get dropped on him. Morgan made sure to keep her face calm and inviting as she gestured for him to proceed.

An intelligence officer wasn't likely to become a starship commander, but Speaker Murtas was the juvenile form of the kind of sentient whose intelligence would dictate the deployment of entire fleets. He'd need to be ready to share his conclusions with his seniors.

If building that readiness required Morgan to be more patient than she'd like, that was part of the job she'd taken when Empress A!Shall gave her a ship.

"Most of *Child of the Great Mother*'s senior crew is dead," Murtas finally began. "They were the ones with the weapons and ready access to air masks and anti-stun armor. They fought with the same fanaticism we've seen out of what I now suspect might have been specially selected units on D-L-K-Six and Kosha Station.

"The handful of senior cult members we have in custody have been as hard to interrogate as anyone we've taken previously," he continued. "The usual vague phrasings around the Mother and the Womb. A couple of threats around the Mother consuming light that isn't hers, that kind of thing."

He laid his hands on the table, levering himself to a straight-backed sitting position.

"It was in the interrogations of the more junior members of the crew that we finally began to find *context* for what those statements mean. I've been putting together pieces, but there are some key points I think we all need to know.

"First, the Womb is a place and a creature. Every one of our cultists has seen it and touched it. One used the phrase 'I have walked on the skin of my God,' which to me suggests a living Precursor structure of some size.

"Secondly, the Womb is a stellarvore."

Unused to briefings he might be, Murtas knew to wait for his audience to process just what that word meant.

Sun-eater.

"You cannot be serious," Rogers exclaimed.

"I am," Murtas said levelly. Morgan made a mental checkmark. It might have taken the young Speaker—the man was still a few years shy of thirty—a few extra seconds to get going, but he'd found his footing.

"I am not certain of exactly what scale this entails," he continued. "There are a number of different ways our prisoners described it, but it was quite clear in the aggregate that we are talking about a biological creature in close orbit of a star, drawing on both the heat energy of the star as well as its physical mass to sustain itself and to create the bioships we've encountered.

"The Children call the bioships Servants. Holy Servants, Grand Servants, Her Servants..." Murtas shrugged. "A lot of different descriptors but always the same core name. The Womb eats bits of stars and births the Servants. The bioships are not, so far as the cultists know, self-reproducing."

"They're also not much of a threat at this point," Nguyen pointed out. "We can outmaneuver and outshoot them, even if they're still hard to target. If one cruiser can take out a swarm of fifty or so, they're no threat to a real fleet."

"That's when we control the battlefield," Morgan countered. "We couldn't do what we did here if a swarm of fifty of them was heading toward Kosha Station. To defend something, we'd have to stand and fight. And those things can demonstrably make a goddamn mess of our shields and armor.

"They're slow and short-ranged, which means they make solid defensive assets and could make for a terrifying juggernaut if pointed at something we have to defend," the Captain said grimly. "Murtas, do we have any idea what kind of numbers we're looking at?"

"Large," he said simply. "It's clear that the limit on how many Servants they could deploy was a question of transport and feeding rather than supply. Similarly, it sounds like there are definitely larger Servants guarding the Womb itself."

"Do we know where the Children are based?" Rogers asked. "Even if these Servants are dangerous, they are limited by their need to be transported through hyperspace by modern ships."

"At the Womb itself," Murtas said. "And no, I have not managed to identify the location of the Womb. None of the individuals who are providing us with useful information even know. If we have any prisoners that do know, they're not telling us."

"So, we now understand the scope of the threat," Morgan said calmly. "The Womb and its Servants are a severe but contained danger on their own. It is the Children that make them a threat. If they're based at the Womb, then we must locate it.

"The only answer I see lies in *Child of the Great Mother*'s files. It will take some time to refit *Child* to interface with one of our shuttles and enter hyperspace, so we will wait for that process to be complete and to receive new orders from Kosha Station.

"At last report, our reinforcements are at least twenty-one cycles away. Hopefully, by the time those squadrons arrive, we will have located the Womb and potentially have a better idea of what we're looking at there.

"*Defiance* has handled swarms of dozens of these Servants," Morgan concluded. "I have full faith in the ability of an entire squadron of modern warships to handle whatever this Womb has created to defend itself."

And if it was a sun-eater, well, *Defiance* at least possessed a final answer to the problem.

"Commander Liepins, let's get started on that refit. We should hear back from Kosha Station in the next few hours, and I want to be on our way as soon as possible."

She smiled thinly.

"I think we've all seen more than enough of this particular star system."

CHAPTER THIRTY-THREE

THE CHILDREN OF THE STARS HAD DONE EVERYTHING IN THEIR
power to protect the storage bay against intruders. The storage area
had been designed as a secure vault even in the original schematics, a
thirty-thousand-cubic-meter area with its own layer of armor and
only two entrances.

The Children had added a triple lock to each of those entrances,
requiring not only a physical key but a genetic sample and an authen-
tication code.

Unfortunately for the Children, *Child of the Great Mother* was a
military ship. Its systems had built-in overrides available to certain
clearances and certain ranks. Vichy had had a long list of those codes.

The degree to which they'd almost all failed had been disconcerting. From the French Marine's expression when he activated the
override that *did* work, he wasn't necessarily supposed to have it.

The vault had been a Cave of Wonders for Rin Dunst, though,
and he knew he'd barely surfaced from it to sleep and eat, let alone
shower or collate reports. The Children's members had clearly
included people trained by the Imperial Archeology Institute, but
their organization was intentionally obfuscated.

It had taken Rin an entire day just to work out the substitution key they were using on the IAIS categorization system. The sheer scale of their effort and research had begun to sink in after that.

This vault was clearly not the primary storage place for the Children. Many of the items Rin encountered had a flag that said they were duplicates, a second item where multiples had been found.

Many he recognized as having distinct stylings that marked them as from D-L-K-Six. Not only had the Children visited his dig site before him, but this ship had. Many of the secrets he'd been investigating had been discovered, labeled, and stuck on these shelves.

What he didn't have was the research that could link things together. Still, there was an answer in the room. He knew it.

When he found the code telling him there was a star projection in the vault somewhere, he cheered aloud.

"Sir?" one of the Marines asked from the door. "Are you okay?"

"There's a star projection here, Marine," Rin told them. "We might just have some answers."

"Uh. Yes, sir."

He *knew* the Marines understood more than they were letting on, but they were also probably trying to avoid getting drafted as research assistants. Their job was to protect him as he tried to sort through multiple museums' worth of Alava artifacts for his answers.

Going from the single reference to try and locate the star projection took him over thirty minutes. Part of the problem was that he was expecting, well, the suspended metallic orbs of an intact Alava star projection.

Instead, he found a box. He stared at it for at least a minute before he opened it and swore.

Every one of the orbs and their hanging threads and everything to set up the projection was in the box. Without the three-dimensional map that they were supposed to mimic, they were useless to him—and if he *had* that map, he wouldn't have needed the projection.

"Damn you bastards," he muttered. "If you worked for me, I'd fire you all. You *dismantled a star projection?*"

Closing the box, he pushed it backward and dislodged something else. Instinct sent him diving for the computer tablet before it hit the floor, and he stared at the black square with questioning hope and horror for several long seconds before he straightened up.

"You didn't," he murmured. He checked the date on the label. It was recent—they'd loaded this box onto the ship within hours of *Defiance*'s arrival in D-L-T-Three.

The plan, presumably, had been to put a holographic copy of the star projection there...but if the tablet had been abandoned and forgotten in the crisis, there were all kinds of possibilities.

Rin's hands were trembling as he settled cross-legged on the floor and pulled out his communicator. He'd have to find Murtas's people if he was right, but he might have just struck solid gold.

"IT'S A SEPARATE NETWORK," the intelligence officer told him several hours later. After Rin had confirmed there was live data on the tablet, Murtas had turned out to be aboard the military freighter.

He was apparently *in command* of the ship, since Rin had completely missed that they'd left the D-L-T-Three System a full two cycles earlier. The archeologist wasn't entirely sure how the freighter was being flown, but they were in hyperspace and following *Defiance* back to Kosha Station.

Murtas had brought six noncoms with him, equally split between his Navy Intelligence hands and the cyberwarfare specialists from Vichy's Marines. They were sweeping the secured vault with extremely sensitive scanners and had already produced three more tablets and a cubical personal computer.

"None of these machines were linked to the main ship network, so the purge order didn't affect them," Murtas continued. "They were encrypted and secured, but the code is old. We're in, Dr. Dunst."

He handed the tablet back to Rin.

"My people are going to track down the remaining tablets, and we're already taking a download of everything," he noted. "You're welcome to keep one of them and access the network, but I'd ask that you not edit anything."

"Please, Speaker, I am at least somewhat familiar with the concepts involved here," Rin replied with a chuckle. "My preference would be that we copy everything to a personal computer we control and I dig into that, but for the moment, there is one thing I must see."

It took him seconds to find the file he was looking for.

The tablet's intended final form would have been a glorified holo-projector, with the single file that showed how to set up the projection stored in it. With the interruption of *Defiance*'s arrival, it had been left with a connection to the private network the cult's scientists had been running.

That connection had let Murtas track the rest of the machines. Rin doubted the working machines of the cult's archeologists would give them everything, but at the very least, they would explain what the cult had found on these particular artifacts.

Most importantly, though...

The holographic version of the Alava star projection filled the empty space above the table. Rin touched a few controls, adjusting its size.

"Can we bring the lights down in here?" he asked. "Someone?"

One of the Marines was already there, dimming the lights to make the holographic chart visible.

"These things have always been traps," Murtas noted drily. "All we find in them is death and confusion."

"Well, most of the ones we've seen before used a pretty standard iconography," Rin pointed out. "Silver was fueling stations, gold was colonies or major projects, copper was known autochthonous civilizations."

He stepped back to study the projection, and Murtas stood next to him.

"I'm not seeing any of those, Doctor," Murtas said quietly.

The stars in the projection all looked the same at first glance, plain steel ball bearings hung in the air.

"That doesn't make sense," Rin replied. "The whole point of these maps was to provide a physical local chart of their assets."

The projections had actively updated too, with computers controlling the positions of each of the tiny orbs until their power cut off fifty thousand years before.

"And this should also be showing how to rebuild the pile of thread and baubles they stuffed in that box." Rin poked at his communicator, accessing the tablet's files remotely and looking for the build instructions. Skimming through them... "Wait; I'm changing the contrast."

It was a theoretically tiny change, but the Alava had possessed superior vision to humans, at least. As soon as the numbers included in the instruction set took hold, the difference was clear.

"Some of the stars are marked in titanium instead of steel," Murtas concluded. "That feels...wrong."

"They would know the difference, but anyone from the main Alava Hegemony wouldn't know what was important. The people out here needed a map of their systems, like any other Alava, but they didn't want the other Alava to know what was important to them."

"How rogue *were* these people?" the taller man asked, looking at the model. "My rough count gets over a hundred stars flagged as titanium, Doctor. This isn't a few rogue colonies. This is an entire rogue *empire*."

"Helps answer where ten billion Alava and servants went, doesn't it?" Rin asked. "If they scooped up a new race or two of servants without telling the main Hegemony, they could easily have built a new state out here.

"But why? They focused more on biotech than the main Hegemony, but the degree to which the Hegemony didn't know about this is strange. We didn't name the main Alava state the Hegemony by random choice, Speaker. The Alava were an extremely homogenous state. They weren't a monolithic culture, but they were closer than most the Imperium has encountered.

"I'd have said they didn't *go* rogue," he concluded. "Except now I'm wondering how much of that was just the Hegemony's view of the galaxy. And how many rogue hundred-star states were hanging around the Hegemony's periphery, concealing their true extent from the empire we assumed contained their entire species."

"Well, that sounds like we're going to find all kinds of weird shit on the edge of the galaxy, aren't we?" Murtas asked. "Helps keep us employed."

"Us and the rest of the Arm Powers," Rin agreed. "Most importantly right now, Speaker, is that I don't see an answer in this map about where the Womb is. I was hoping they'd have marked their megastructures in gold like the Hegemony did out toward Arjtal."

"I figured," Murtas said. "Even a hundred star systems isn't an insurmountable obstacle, Doctor. Once our reinforcements arrive, we'll start scouting the nearer ones and work our way out.

"It might not be a big glowing LOOK HERE sign, but it's definitely a step in the right direction."

"I'll keep looking through these files," Rin promised. "There *has* to be an answer in here."

"No, Dr. Dunst, there doesn't," the Navy officer told him. "There might be, but we've already got more out of this museum vault than I was expecting. You can keep going through it all, but as the acting captain of this ship, I am going to give you very specific orders.

"Is that going to be a problem, Doctor?"

Rin turned to look at the other man and arched a questioning eyebrow.

"You are going to get the fuck out of this vault, *shower*, eat a meal, and sleep for at least twelve hours," Murtas told him. "Because according to the Marines, you've gone six days on ration bars and a *total* of thirty hours of sleep.

"If you convince your bodyguards you can continue your studies while taking decent care of yourself, I'll let you. Otherwise, your time in here is going to start being specifically restricted by the Marines. Am I clear?"

"I...I can do that, I suppose," Rin admitted with a chuckle. "There's just so much here."

"And it will still be here when you're showered, fed, and rested," Murtas replied. "And my Captain will kill me if I deliver you to Kosha Station in your current state, Dr. Dunst."

Rin looked at the officer in surprise. It took him a moment to realize none of the noncoms were close enough to have heard that, and he watched Murtas put a finger over his lips.

"I'm an intelligence analyst, Dr. Rin," the younger man noted. "My *job* is to read patterns. So, you can do your research, yes, but I'm not delivering the man who owes my Captain a date to the station as a disheveled, smelly mess.

"Are we clear?"

CHAPTER THIRTY-FOUR

"A HUNDRED STARS?"

Defiance might not have hyperfold communications, but they were close enough to *Child of the Great Mother* to carry on radio communication. So long as the two ships were within a light-second of each other in hyperspace, they could see each other and talk to each other.

So, Dr. Dunst's discovery had been sent over, leaving Commander Rogers staring at the hologram of a Precursor star chart and questioning the sheer size of their search area.

"One hundred and seven," Morgan confirmed. She was looking at the notes as she sat behind her desk, the chart hanging over the plain metal surface between her and her First Sword. "We're also not actually clear on which star system this particular chart came from, so the first priority I'm going to drop on Nguyen's team is matching this up to the real world."

Fifty thousand years of stellar drift made that hard enough even when you had a defined point in the central star. Without that, it could easily take Morgan's tactical team days to map the star chart to realspace.

"It's something," Rogers admitted. "More than we had before we hit D-L-T-Three. Still feels pretty sparse to have lost lives for."

"We neutralized a major Children position and captured what I suspect is their most capable vessel, even if *Child* is not a warship," Morgan said. "We did well at D-L-T-Three, Commander Rogers.

"I want you to work with Commander Nguyen on this chart," she continued. "We need to locate all of the stars the Precursors flagged in this area. Some will just be fueling depots. Some will be colonies. Some might just be points of interest—but some of those will be local intelligent species, and we have obligations there under the Kovius Treaty."

Kovius was a Mesharom star system. The treaty signed there, around when humanity had been working out how to build pyramids, protected "younger" species from existing powers. Morgan had to flag a forty-light-year radius around a new species' homeworld that couldn't be exploited.

Those stars would be reserved for the species in question. Imperial policy was to watch undeveloped races and not to interfere until they'd developed hyperdrive on their own.

Of course, at that point, they were to be semi-voluntarily annexed. Membership in the Imperium came with many privileges, but no one was going to pretend the A!Tol had given any of their uplifted vassals a *choice* in the matter.

"Somewhere in those hundred and seven stars is apparently a biological shipyard attached to a star," Morgan concluded. "We find that, we find the Children and we end this damn mess."

"Any idea for hints?" Rogers asked, looking at the star chart.

"Not a one right now," Morgan admitted. "Let's get the chart mapped to our charts and see what we're looking at. Some answers might fall out that aren't obvious right now."

"Fair enough." The First Sword studied the map and shook her head. "I'm glad we're getting reinforcements. For the first time since we started talking about this, I think we might be better off *without* battleships."

"If they'd sent battleships, we'd have a division of battleships and an echelon of cruisers coming," Morgan agreed. "It would take a lot longer to sweep a hundred stars with ten ships than with thirty."

"Exactly. I still wish we had at least one battleship in the region."

"Echelon Lord Davor has us," *Defiance's* Captain told her First Sword. "*Defiance* is more powerful than any battleship in the Imperium's service was when Earth was annexed. Three decades makes for many changes."

"I was born in an Imperial colony, sir," Rogers reminded her. "I don't know if Hope would have been colonized soon enough for that without the A!Tol. Things change."

"And our job is to make sure those changes don't hurt the people of the Imperium," Morgan said. "*Defiance* isn't a capital ship by a modern standard, but she's still one of the most capable vessels of her size. We'll carry the brunt of what comes, First Sword."

"I know, sir. And we'll carry it well; you have my word on that."

"I DON'T SUPPOSE you had any sudden inspiration on the star chart you didn't share in the report Murtas sent over?" Morgan asked the man in her screen.

Dunst looked freshly rested, showered, and shaved. From the rumblings she'd been getting up unofficial channels, that had probably required someone to sit on him. The security vault on *Child* had been his dream and nightmare combined.

"Not yet," he admitted. "I haven't been back in the vault since that was sent over. I, ah, had been overdoing it and needed to rest."

"You're no good to us if you work yourself to death, Rin," Morgan told him. "We're still three cycles out of Kosha Station. We have time for you to find a miraculous answer."

"I have some ideas that I didn't have before I rested," he admitted. "We've been focusing on the 'official files' on that network, but I'm curious to see what a clearly Institute-trained archeologist was writing in their private notes about the cult they'd ended up surrounded by."

"Do we know who she was?" Morgan asked.

"We know who *they* were," Rin corrected. "Catatch sterile named Al-Ka. They were the one rigging the antimatter core to explode, so I know that Al-Ka bought into the whole cult. Which, given that I would expect Institute training to inure someone to being caught by a cult, I find rather concerning."

"What do we know about Al-Ka?"

"Not much yet. We IDed them after we entered hyperspace. I'll request their Institute file when we arrive; that might help us trace more of just how an Imperial military freighter ended up out here with those kinds of people on board."

"Parts of this stink," Morgan agreed. Murtas had raised his conspiracy theories with her, but she'd told him to keep the theories to himself for now. She still wanted her people's eyes open.

And while Rin was definitely *not* one of "her people" in a specific and valuable sense, he was still part of this mess.

"I'm going to go through their private files and see if there's anything useful in there," Dunst concluded. "That's the extent of my brilliance at the moment. We'll see what shakes out."

"So we shall," Morgan agreed. "For my part, Nguyen's team is working on mapping that star chart. Without a reference point, it's harder than you might think."

"I've done it with a reference point, and that was bad enough," Dunst admitted. "I'm *extremely* appreciative of Commander Nguyen's efforts."

"I'll let her know," she promised. "One more thing, Doctor."

"Yes, Captain?"

"If you have time, feel free to research the restaurant listing for Kosha Station some more," she told him. "You do still owe me dinner. The first night back while everyone else digests our various time bombs sounds right to me."

He chuckled.

"I'll see what I can do, Captain Casimir," he promised.

CHAPTER THIRTY-FIVE

OFFICE POLITICS CROSSED SPECIES AND CULTURAL BOUNDS LIKE nothing else, in Rin's experience. Dr. Al-Ka, a scientist with a list of qualifications to easily match Rin's own, spent most of their journal complaining about their fellow Children, stooping so low as to call the bridge crew "a collection of hormone-addled seeders and breeders."

Rin had needed to look up the meaning of that. Apparently, the Catatch reproduced in litters of twenty-plus children, all born as steriles like Al-Ka. A randomly selected set of the litter would be treated with hormones to become biologically male and female to create the next generation of Catatch.

The *Imperium* treated all three Catatch genders as equal. The Catatch emancipation movement was *politically* acknowledged but still fighting an uphill social battle. "Seeders and breeders" were regarded as losing intelligence to the hormones that allowed them to reproduce.

The fact that the breeding sets had historically been kept locked away in specially built glorified prisons and deprived of even the most basic education had *nothing* to do with that, Rin was sure.

Most Catatch steriles wouldn't call someone a seeder or a breeder unless angry, though, and Al-Ka was apparently perpetually frustrated with *Child of the Great Mother*'s command crew.

Al-Ka had also drawn double duty as one of the senior engineers on *Child*, an apparently self-taught role. It wasn't clear from the journal what had happened to the ship's original engineer, but then, it wasn't clear where *Child* could have come from.

Only the last hundred or so cycles' worth of entries were in the electronic file, and Al-Ka clearly had a solid sense of operational security. The Children were determined to protect the location of their god, and the archeologists among their numbers had been fully on board.

Al-Ka had been studying the ruins at D-L-T-Three to see what information they could retrieve on the "birth of the Great Mother," presumably the original construction of the organic machine the Children now worshipped.

Most of their work had been cataloging the artifacts aboard the ship, and they had complained mightily about the degree to which they had been required to act as the freighter's engineer.

And yet the Catatch's faith in the Great Mother, their belief in the strange deity the Children had found, was unwavering in the text. The sheer *awe* Al-Ka wrote of the Mother with chilled Rin.

This was a sentient who shared his knowledge. Al-Ka had clearly been briefed on much of the Imperium's knowledge of the Alava—like Rin himself, they *never* referred to them as Precursors.

Al-Ka had known that what they'd encountered was a glorified machine, one built of flesh instead of steel, but still a machine. But they had touched it and all of their training in science and analysis had failed.

They had become a worshipper of a creation of the Alava. Rin had seen images of the Alava's creations, and he could understand awe, but to worship this Womb as a god?

There was something Rin was missing. Something he didn't understand—and if he didn't understand it, he feared that he and the rest of *Defiance*'s crew were just as vulnerable to the fate that had overtaken Dr. Al-Ka and their companions.

Then he found the drawings. Al-Ka had organized their files in such a way that Rin had missed them until he'd read through the entire journal, but once he found them, he realized that Al-Ka had truly missed their calling.

The sketches were also only from the last hundred cycles, but they were *spectacular*. The first one Rin found was of the Alava base in D-L-T-Three. Six peaks, broken fragments of ancient meteor craters, rose above a valley filled with the distinctive shapes of Imperial prefabricated structures.

The artificial tones and structures on those peaks had been picked out in digital pencil, giving Rin a perfectly detailed view of a place that no longer existed. The peaks and central valley that Al-Ka had drawn over the course of several cycles were gone now, vanished in the nuclear fire of the Children's security policy.

The level of detail and attention was awe-inspiring. Rin didn't know how long it had taken Al-Ka to put together the drawing, but they'd obviously taken at least several cycles to sit outside their base in an environment suit and sketch.

The next sketch was a clearly quicker piece, of a female Yin whose pose and clothing left Rin wondering whether *sterile* actually meant *no sex life* for a Catatch.

The next few sketches were more to Rin's interest. They were detailed work-ups of particular artifacts that Al-Ka had found.

And then Rin found it. The image in the drawing was an Alava artwork, the three-dimensional frescos the four-legged Precursor race liked to use for public imagery. Most likely, the original artwork had been vaporized with the base in D-L-T-Three, and the galaxy was worse off for it.

Al-Ka had titled the piece *The Birth of a God*. Rin didn't know what the Alava had called it, but it showed a creature that looked like a human heart hanging in space while ships orbited around it. The original artist had managed to catch the multiple different streams being fed into the open valves of the heart-like creature.

One was clearly physical fuel of some kind, probably something equivalent to Universal Protein or a similar source of biomatter. Another was a gas or a liquid, probably hydrogen.

The third was clearly live plasma, being created and delivered by a large ship that looked like nothing so much as a fusion reactor with thrusters attached, even to Rin.

At the bottom of the image was the edge of a star, but most important was *behind* the focus of the artwork. The stars were picked out in detail in the back of the fresco, and Rin knew the Alava.

No Alava artist would have put those stars in unless they were *exactly* correct. If they were in the background of the creation of the Womb, then those stars had been the constellations seen from that place at that time.

And that meant that Al-Ka's sketchbook had just undermined the security efforts of the entire cult of the Children of the Stars.

CHAPTER THIRTY-SIX

"WE'VE GOT IT," NGUYEN SAID IN AN EXHAUSTED TONE. SHE was one of the two other people physically present in the room with Morgan—the other was Commander Rogers. Dunst and Murtas were linked by hologram from *Child of the Great Mother*, where Vichy had been pulled out of a training exercise down in Marine country and was only linked in by voice.

Presumably, he looked slightly less than perfect, and that would have been unacceptable.

"Define *it*, s'il vous plaît," Vichy asked.

"We know where the Womb is," *Defiance*'s tactical officer told them. "We got the star chart mapped about half a cycle ago, shortly after Dr. Dunst delivered a sketch of what appears to be the initial activation of the Womb."

"The Alava had an obsession with stars, always," the archeologist said. "No Alava would have put incorrect stars in the background of an image of that much importance."

"And the constellations mapped to one of our target stars," Nguyen agreed. "I don't know what the Alava named it; we're flagging it as Target One."

"We'll have to discuss this with Echelon Lord Davor once we arrive," Morgan told her staff. "While our reinforcements should only be ten cycles away, we may want to move on this sooner rather than later to minimize the cult threat."

"Target One's current position is thirty-six light-years from Kosha," Nguyen noted. "We don't know as much about the hyperspace in that area as we'd like, but we're looking at a minimum of fifteen cycles' travel time by my calculation."

Hyperspace was *always* variable. If someone worked out how to predict a flight time perfectly, they'd be rich beyond belief anywhere in the galaxy.

Even the flight from Earth to Alpha Centauri, a relatively short flight through low-density hyperspace, could vary by as much as twelve hours. That was before a navigator took into account the currents that could be found, some of which could run ten times as deep as even the densest regular regions of hyperspace.

The Imperium was experimenting with technology to increase the local density of hyperspace. Stolen from the Mesharom, it was only mounted on the most critical of couriers so far. Even with that, though, travel time was unpredictable.

"What's Target One's name in our records?" Rogers asked.

"That's our current biggest headache," Nguyen told them. "Target One doesn't exist in our records. Part of what took so long to reconcile the Precursor map to our charts is that there are multiple stars that aren't in our records."

"Stars don't go missing as a rule," Murtas noted. "They called it a sun-eater. It can't have literally been eating *entire suns*, can it?"

"It seems unlikely," Morgan agreed. "But if it's grown large enough to eclipse large chunks of its star, it might not be as visible as we would expect from any given distance."

A terrifying thought all on its own. How big *was* this Womb?

"Our only real option is to scout where the stellar orbit calculations say Target One should be," she continued. "Echelon Lord

Davor will likely want someone to confirm the Womb is there before we start sending out entire squadrons of cruisers to deal with it."

"If it's big enough to eclipse a star at that kind of range, are cruisers going to be enough?" Dunst asked.

The conference was silent.

"We expended over half our munitions against the bioships in D-L-T-Three," Morgan said quietly, "and I am still in possession of over a hundred twenty-gigaton antimatter warheads, Dr. Dunst.

"I am confident in the ability of a squadron of Imperial cruisers with modern hyperspace missiles to deliver sufficient firepower to obliterate anything short of a star itself."

The question was whether that squadron could manage to reach its target to do so. Everything they'd seen suggested that there were large numbers of the Servants around the Womb, plus whatever warships or armed freighters the Children themselves still possessed.

The Children had always been willing to run so far. They'd have ships on hand, even if they'd probably fight at Target One. That was the home of their god, after all.

"We might get sent on a scouting jaunt before the main strike, but believe me, everyone, we will be going after Target One with a real strike force. The Children will be given a chance to negotiate—what they've learned could be of great value to the Imperium—but if they are determined to be a threat, they will be destroyed."

If nothing else, Murtas was right that the evidence pointed to *Child of the Great Mother* being sent out there under her original name as home to an Imperial survey project. That project had gone *very* wrong, but hopefully not so wrong that Morgan was going to have to blow away all of what appeared to be a crazy Imperial science team.

"We're back in Kosha in a cycle. We'll see what our next mission is then—we may not need repairs this time, but we definitely need more missiles!"

CHAPTER THIRTY-SEVEN

THE A!TOL IMPERIUM MIGHT BE RUN BY AMPHIBIOUS SQUIDS taller than any human and contain nearly thirty different species, but some rules were apparently universal. One of them was that militaries ran on "hurry up and wait," which resulted in Morgan cooling her heels in the reception area near Echelon Lord Davor's office.

She'd arrived in system to orders to report in person as soon as physically possible. Now she was waiting for the flag officer to be available after she had hurried to be there.

The young Rekiki officer behind the desk twitched in response to a chime that Morgan couldn't hear. Her response was also behind the privacy screen, but she gestured Morgan over to her a moment later.

"The Echelon Lord sends her apologies for the delay," the Speaker told her, "but she wants to show you First Fleet Lord Tan!Shallegh's message."

Morgan swallowed hard, hoping she'd at least managed to conceal her surprise and concern from the junior officer. Fleet Lord Tan!Shallegh was as A!Tol as the A!Tol came, a nephew or some equivalent—A!Tol family relationships were odd—of Empress A!Shall herself.

He was also a *male* A!Tol who had overcome his species' long-standing sexism to rise to the pinnacle of his career, his position as First Fleet Lord marking him as *the* senior officer of the Imperial Navy.

He was also the fleet commander who'd first conquered Sol and then saved it from the Kanzi.

Morgan's stepmother regarded Tan!Shallegh as a personal friend. Morgan most emphatically did not know him well enough to do the same.

"Thank you, Speaker. I presume the Echelon Lord hasn't moved offices?"

"Double door at the end of the hall, Captain Casimir," the Rekiki told her.

With a firm nod, Morgan set off down the corridor. She wasn't even sure why the First Fleet Lord was speaking to Echelon Lord Davor, let alone why he wanted to speak to Morgan.

Dreading it would only make it worse, so she tapped the admittance button as soon as she reached the doors. They swung open automatically and she stepped into the office.

Nothing had changed in Davor's space. The Ivida flag officer was seated behind her desk, looking at a holographic image of the tentacled A!Tol that had clearly been scaled to put Tan!Shallegh at eye level with Davor.

"Come in, Captain Casimir," Davor ordered. "Take a seat."

Morgan obeyed, watching as the hologram shifted so Tan!Shallegh was now more clearly visible to her than to Davor.

It wasn't a live hologram—the Kosha System didn't have a starcom transmitter. They could *receive* a live transmission from Tan!Shallegh, but their inability to reply would limit its use. The nearest starcom was sixty-five light-years away, which meant any answer they sent back would be sixty-five hours old by the time Tan!Shallegh saw it.

"I've reviewed the summary of your new information," Davor

told her. "Unfortunately, the circumstances have changed since you left D-L-T-Three." She gestured at the hologram and started it again.

"A Laian war-dreadnought was jumped by powers unknown near the Wendira border," Tan!Shallegh's voice began, Morgan's earbud translators automatically linking in to the holoprojector.

"The dreadnought and its escorts were destroyed, but not before they got a message out. Not enough to identify their attackers, but enough to warn the Republic that they were under attack."

The A!Tol's skin was a determined and concerned dark green.

"The Republic is assuming the attackers were Wendira and has summoned the Grand Swarm's representatives to explain themselves. In the meantime, their entire fleet has gone on alert and they have activated our mutual defense treaty."

The world was doing its best to fall out from underneath Morgan. It was the general assessment of the Imperial Navy that its most heavily upgraded ships—*Defiance*'s *Armored Dream* class and that generation of designs could go up against Core Power ships on an even basis.

But they only had a limited number of ships upgraded to that level. The previous generation had better weapons than most Core Powers—the A!Tol Imperium remained one of a very small group of powers in possession of a working hyperspace missile—but their shields and electronic warfare systems fell well short of those deployed by the Wendira Grand Swarm.

And the one advantage the Core Powers still unquestionably had over the A!Tol was production. They often had more ships and they also usually had *bigger* ships. If the Imperium was dragged into a war between Core Powers...

"Given the new alert levels along the Coreward frontier, we've drawn on a number of nodal deployments I'd rather not have drawn down. Most relevant to you, I'm afraid, is that I have halted the tide of your reinforcements.

"Division Lords Ibo and Assendorp have already received their updated orders. The majority of their ships are returning to the Wendira border. Captain Kelik's destroyer echelon will continue to the Kosha System."

Tan!Shallegh fluttered his tentacles.

"I know this news darkens the water," he conceded. "I have seen the reports on what these Children of the Stars may have found, and they make me nervous. I cannot spare modern cruisers from the potential war, but not everything in the Navy has been upgraded sufficiently to be worthy of this fight.

"A division of battleships under Division Lord Bo-Ta will be on their way from the Lirip System within the next two cycles. Their ETA will be between fifteen and twenty-one cycles, I'm afraid, and they are older ships retrofitted with minimal hyperspace missile and hyperfold cannon armaments, but they are battleships with compressed-matter armor. We are trying to break free escorts from the Lirip System as well, but I wouldn't expect more than an echelon of older cruisers and destroyers."

The First Fleet Lord's dark skin tones warned of the depth of the situation. Even disregarding the three-cycle transmission time, it was clear to Morgan there would be no argument.

"The situation you have uncovered represents a grave potential threat, but this 'Womb' has existed for fifty thousand years. It is unlikely to become an immediate threat tomorrow, and a potential war with the Wendira will be an existential threat to the Imperium.

"You will continue to receive standard briefings from the usual channels, Echelon Lord Davor," Tan!Shallegh concluded. "But I wanted to advise you that I was stealing your reinforcements myself. I will be leaving A!To within the next cycle, taking two squadrons of superbattleships to a nodal base near the Wendira border.

"If we are lucky, the Wendira and the Laians will sort this out. Her Majesty has ambassadors in place to mediate the discussions, so I have some hope that we will avoid outright war. But that potential must be my focus.

"Smooth waters to you, Echelon Lord Davor."

The holographic recording ended and Morgan slowly shook her head.

"Relying on the Wendira and the Laians to even *talk* to each other, let alone come to an agreement, is always a risky game," she said quietly.

"As I understand the waters, the Laians bear some resemblance to the Wendira Worker caste," Davor replied. "And the Wendira Royals are unimpressed by their lack of deference. They are, however, impressed by the swathe of dead stars between their territories.

"Fear of mutual annihilation should provide some incentive to their talks."

"We can hope," Morgan agreed. "Where does that leave us, Echelon Lord?"

"My plan, Captain Casimir, was to wait until our reinforcements arrived and use them to scout the sixteen closest systems of these rogue Precursors," Davor told her. "In the absence of those reinforcements, I greet the identification of a target system like the spring fish schools."

"*Defiance* needs a few hours to restock and rearm, but we should be able to deploy within the cycle," Morgan replied. "Sir, the scale of what we might be facing...it may be eclipsing the star it is feeding on.

"It isn't small and it won't be undefended."

"I do not, Captain, expect you to assault the Womb," Davor clarified. "I want you to confirm its presence. We will wait for Division Lord Bo-Ta to arrive with their battleships and move against it with real force.

"While *Defiance* alone carries as many hyperspace portals as Bo-Ta's ships do combined, there is much to be said for the weight of a real capital ship. Those bioships will have a harder time penetrating the battleships' shields, and we will retain the range and speed advantage."

Not as much of one as *Defiance* had, since the battleships would have to close to interface-drive-missile range to do real damage. But still, Davor had a point. Morgan was definitely more willing to go in against the Womb with twenty million tons of capital ships than with three million tons of cruiser.

"The situation on arrival may prove to be more dangerous than we anticipate," she noted. Despite the rudeness, she pulled up her communicator and checked something.

"Captain?" Davor said, her tone questioning.

"My apologies, sir," Morgan told her boss. "I had to confirm that you were cleared for information sealed under the Final Dragon Protocol. You are, thankfully, and I am obliged to remind you that *Defiance* does carry Final Dragon–class strategic weapons."

The office was deathly silent for at least ten seconds, to the point where Morgan registered that Ivida breathed quietly compared to most species.

"No," Davor finally concluded. "Final Dragon remains one of the few tools we have that exceed even most Core Powers' capabilities. I will not authorize its deployment to deal with a Precursor leftover."

"As Captain of a Final Dragon–equipped ship, you inevitably have a great deal of discretion around the weapons' use," she noted. "As much as the currents of our law allow it, I am *forbidding* you to deploy strategic weapons against the Womb. Am I clear, Captain?"

"You are, sir," Morgan said crisply. "I'm not exactly eager to fire one."

"Some would be," Davor replied. "Some would be."

"And they didn't pass the psych tests to command an *Armored Dream*–class cruiser," Morgan stated. She was briefed or aware of a lot of things she wasn't technically cleared for, and even *she* hadn't known why she was being subjected to an entire new and intrusive set of tests before she took up her new command.

"So I must hope," her CO agreed. "We have no choice but to investigate the Womb, Captain, and the grim truth is that even if I had Captain Kelik's destroyers here, there would be little point in sending them with you.

"You and your crew will take two cycles to rest while Kosha Station's people rearm your ship," she ordered. "Then, you will proceed to Target One and confirm just what in darkest depths we are facing out here."

"Understood, sir."

CHAPTER THIRTY-EIGHT

THIS TIME, RIN HAD MADE SURE THAT THE RESTAURANT HE'D booked was inside the security perimeter of the Kosha Station Navy Base. That had limited the quality of the places he was looking at, but he'd left a few dozen friends behind in the base when he'd followed Casimir off into the dark.

Kelly Lawrence swore by the Rekiki restaurant attached to the hotel she was staying in. Despite the chef not being human, he apparently had a wizard's touch with Universal Protein.

The crocodilian centaur at the entrance didn't blink at a pair of humans showing up, either.

"I have three reservations and four open tables set up for bipedals," she told them instantly. "Do you have a reservation?"

"We do, under Captain Casimir," Rin replied with a smile and a glance at the Captain next to him. She seemed withdrawn this evening, which he suspected meant she'd received the kind of news she wasn't allowed to share with him.

"Of course, with the extra security requirements," the hostess noted. "This way, please."

Rin and Casimir followed the sentient into the restaurant. It was about what Rin had expected, the kind of mildly upscale décor and furnishings that any hotel trying to not look terrible tended to lean toward.

The effect was undermined, from his perspective at least, by being put together for Rekiki esthetics. A lot of the colors were shades of red and brown that human eyes couldn't easily distinguish, turning the hunting murals into muddy mixes of paint to him.

Someone had spent a lot of effort and probably quite a bit of money to make the restaurant look better but had focused on a style that would only look good to about a quarter of the Imperium's species.

Of course, since the planet beneath them was primarily a Rekiki colony, it made sense.

The room they were taken to was better in some ways; it had been painted a light brown and left undecorated beyond that. A single table filled most of the small private room, and Rin's teeth itched at the privacy field.

He and Casimir took their seats, and the Rekiki leading them flourished a pair of menus out of what Rin wanted to call saddlebags.

"We have a human-tailored set of Universal Protein offerings, and we currently have a human-compatible special, listed on the last page. Your waiter will be with you shortly."

The Rekiki hostess withdrew, leaving Rin and Casimir alone with the menus.

"Four Marines at the door," Rin's date finally said with a sigh. "At least another four running a patrol through the surrounding station sections, and that's just *Defiance*'s Marines."

"I appear to have been handed back to Station Security," he noted. "Two of their Marines are at the door. They've probably found yours and are commiserating already."

"That is what they do," she agreed, flipping the menu open. "*Human-compatible* does not, apparently, mean *appetizing*."

"Do I *want* to know?" Rin asked.

"Well, if I'm reading this right, the meal is still *alive* when served," Casimir replied with a chuckle. "Any idea what I should be looking at?"

"A friend of mine is staying in the hotel this place serves," Rin told her. "She swears by their UP and pasta, of all things."

"Spaghetti and bolognese sauce with UP and actual tomatoes, I see." She was smiling. "My understanding is that Rekiki can eat tomatoes, actually. I remember Dad talking about how they had become one of our biggest export products.

"Potatoes and soy make great raw material for UP, but tomatoes are entirely edible for Rekiki and they *love* the things. So, Italian food at a Rekiki restaurant makes a surprising degree of sense."

"I did not know that," Rin admitted. "I spend most of my time off-Earth eating basic UP." He coughed. "I'm not known for paying that much attention to what I eat."

"Murtas had some...*commentary* on your working habits aboard *Child*," Casimir agreed with a chuckle. "Do try to take better care of yourself. I do look forward to getting to know you better."

"That's good to hear," Rin admitted. "Professional captain face left me wondering."

"That's work," she agreed. "While I'm aboard *Defiance*, I am her Captain and I cannot really be anything else. Morgan Casimir the woman gets subordinated."

"I'm familiar with how that works," he said. "Though, of course, for me it results in working for several days without necessarily sleeping."

"Which is more dangerous in some ways than getting shot at, Rin," she said with a soft laugh. "I'm glad you found what you did in the Children's files. You're going to have weeks to go over it all now, I suspect."

"That's the plan," he agreed. "You'd know better than I what the plan is for dealing with them, but I heard we had reinforcements coming."

He caught the moment the mask came back up, and he sighed.

"What's wrong?" he asked.

The waiter arrived at that moment to collect their orders, distracting from her moment of concern.

"Something's been bothering you since we met up," he told Casimir after the Rekiki left. "What's going on?"

"I can't tell you a lot of things; you're just going to have to live with that if anything is going to come of this," she told him, waving a hand over the table. "*Defiance* is going back out in another cycle, thirty hours or so.

"Everyone is on leave while the station crew sweeps and tidies. This is all we get for now, Rin."

"Back out?" he asked. "But with more ships coming..."

Rin might not be a military officer, but he was a student of history and a smart man.

"There are no more ships coming," he concluded. "The reinforcements got diverted to a crisis the Imperium isn't publicly talking about yet. Given everything going on...the Wendira and the Laians are spear-rattling again, aren't they?"

She stared at him.

"You know damn well I can't answer that question," she finally said with a chuckle. "And apparently, I need to learn that you're *dangerous*, Rin Dunst. There's no way you should have put together that *hypothesis* from what I said."

"Despite my predilections and obsessions, I do keep up to date on Imperial politics," Rin told her. "I am an employee of the government, after all, and politics help decide what gets grant money and what doesn't."

And wars tended to result in *nothing* getting grant money, but he was a historian. As a student of dead civilizations, he found it was wise to be aware of things that could take one's own civilization into that category.

"And where do *I* fall on that list, Dr. Dunst?" Casimir asked with a chuckle. "Am I a predilection, an obsession, or Imperial politics?"

He laughed.

"A point of curiosity, so far," he told her. "An intriguing individual with so much potential, both for myself and for the Imperium."

"You are attempting to flatter me, Rin," she replied. "And again, I need to realize that you are a dangerous man."

"I am, at best, merely mostly harmless," he told her. "Nebbish archeologist of the finest stereotype, Morgan. If I flatter, it is only through the intent to speak the truth."

She laughed and reached across the table to lay her hand on his.

"You're adorable, is what you are," she told him. "Did you intentionally book a restaurant attached to a hotel, Rin? Were you so sure of yourself as to book a room?"

That thought had never even occurred to him and the joking warmth he'd been projecting disintegrated into a moment of pure anxiety.

"Wait, what? No! I wouldn't..."

Morgan was laughing at him as he felt his cheeks flush.

"You're even *more* adorable when you blush," she told him. "That was probably the best answer you could have." She winked at him. "Though I will admit that *I* checked to be sure there were rooms still available for tonight."

DESPITE A DISTINCT LACK of complaints the previous night, Rin was still self-conscious enough about his body to cover himself with a sheet while he watched Morgan very nearly dance around the hotel room as she collected her things.

She hadn't gone so far as to put any of her clothes back on, which made the view extremely pleasant and distracting. Eventually, she stacked her clothes on the dresser and dropped back onto the bed.

"You're awake," she said with a smile, and proceeded to kiss him thoroughly.

Rin had definitely had worse mornings, and he had a hard time thinking of better ones.

"Have been for a bit," he confessed. "Watching you is extraordinarily pleasant."

He kissed her this time and they were both distracted for a few moments.

"Flatterer," Morgan said. "I don't have to get going straight away. There were a few questions in my inbox, but most of my crew is off-ship. That limits how many disasters are going to land on me in the next, oh, six hours."

"What happens in six hours?" Rin asked.

"That's when everyone is supposed to report back aboard *Defiance*. So, in six hours, I start to get the reasons why people are late and have to decide if I believe them or send Speaker Susskind's MPs after them."

"You're going out after the Womb, aren't you?" he asked softly.

"I can't tell you that," Morgan told him.

"I'm cleared for *that*, at least," Rin countered. He was cleared for more than that, he was sure, but Morgan tended to err on assuming he wasn't. She was an incredibly attractive and smart woman, but that particular tic was going to start annoying him sooner rather than later.

"Fair." She shrugged, probably *intending* to distract him. "Yeah, we're doing a scouting run. No one is going to actually go after the Womb with just one cruiser."

"You have to take me, Morgan," he told her. "There's nobody more qualified to judge what we're looking at here. A biological Alava megastructure? Even most Alava wouldn't have known what to make of it."

"I do."

"You realize that this"—Morgan's gesture encompassed her nakedness, the bed and, presumably, the previous night's festivities—"doesn't happen aboard ship?"

"That has nothing to do with why I need to come with you," Rin countered. "I'm not some hormone-addled college student, Morgan. I am *the* expert on Alava structures and history in this region."

"And I've read the entire Archive you're drawing on," she told him. "I know more than you think I do, Rin. I know enough for this. It's not like we're picking a fight or trying to kill it on this op."

"Morgan, please," he said.

She was off the bed now, straight-spined and looking down at him.

"It's not your call, Dr. Dunst," she said formally. "It's mine. *Defiance* is running a scouting operation, and there's no reason to risk our subject-matter expert on a scouting run, is there? The answer is no."

For a moment, he considered arguing further—but he also realized that continuing the argument wouldn't change her mind and *would* result in her leaving the room.

He shook his head and said nothing. She sighed, her posture softening.

"My job, my call," she told him as she took a seat next to him again, her arm wrapping around his shoulders. "Okay?"

"Okay," he conceded. Her fingers running over his skin sent a shiver through him, and he looked at her sharply.

"What?" she asked innocently as her hands continued to explore. "I already told you, Rin, I don't need to be anywhere for *hours* yet!"

CHAPTER THIRTY-NINE

Rin stopped outside the main office complex of the Navy base in an uncharacteristic moment of hesitation. His watch said that *Defiance*'s crew would be returning aboard the cruiser as he waited, which limited how much time he had if he was going to do this.

He knew perfectly well that the moment he asked for the appointment he wanted, any chance of things continuing with Morgan Casimir was dead. That was the only thing holding him back —but he also knew that he knew the Alava better than anyone else in the region.

And that included Morgan Casimir, oddly well informed as the Captain was. She had a better idea of what she was taking her ship into than most, but the Alava's leftovers were dangerous. Even she was safer if Rin went with her...and *Rin* needed to be there.

There was no way they should be going after what had to be the most active Alava artifact left *without* one of the Imperium's experts aboard. He couldn't be sure if she'd refused him out of a desire for glory, a desire for control, or a desire to keep a new lover safe.

Regardless, she'd been *wrong*.

Or so Rin told himself, anyway. He was self-aware enough to

know that his desire for glory and knowledge was definitely a factor in his thinking.

Hesitation or not, he'd made his decision. He walked through the sliding doors and up to the Marine NCO holding down the front access to the administration center.

"Lance Millicent," he greeted the human woman. "I need to speak with Echelon Lord Davor as soon as possible. It is of critical importance."

"Uh-huh." She studied him for several seconds and Rin returned her gaze levelly. He doubted his unprepossessing form and plain suit were impressing the Marine, but that wasn't the point.

"And you are?" she asked.

"Dr. Rin Dunst of the Imperial Institute of Archeology," Rin told her. "The Echelon Lord knows who I am."

"Sure she—" The Marine cut herself off as she plugged Rin's name into her computers.

"Step over here and validate your ID, please, Doctor," she instructed a moment later, the vague dismissal replaced with sharp attention.

Rin obeyed, placing his left hand on a scanner and tapping in a numeric code with his right.

"Hold on one moment, Dr. Dunst," Lance Millicent told him. She raised a privacy shield and starting speaking into a channel.

"All right," she told him, dropping the shield. "A Marine will be here momentarily to escort you to the flag offices. The Echelon Lord is not immediately available, but her staff will find a place to stash you until she is. Please wait there."

She pointed to a seat near one of the doors leading deeper into the admin center. Rin nodded and took the indicated seat. He was amused, if unsurprised, by the very clear assumption in the Marine's tone that Rin no longer had a *choice* in this. From the moment he'd leaned on his status as a "Category Two Asset" to get a meeting with the local flag officer, he wasn't getting out of that meeting if he changed his mind.

Fortunately, that was just fine with Rin.

"DR. DUNST, I'll admit that I didn't expect to see you again so soon," Davor told Rin as the archeologist took a seat, studying the Ivaran bloodstone desk.

He'd taken a few moments to research the stone before coming back to Davor's office. It was rare to have undecorated bloodstone off of Ivara. The stone's significance to the Ivida was one of the few fragments left of their original culture. It rarely left the planet and almost never without being made into items of astonishing beauty.

Davor's desk was even more unusual than he'd thought at first pass and appeared to exist only because the Echelon Lord's family ran one of the largest bloodstone quarries on the planet. Its lack of decoration was as much a statement as anything else, speaking to the wealth and power of the Echelon Lord's family.

"With everything going on, I wanted to speak with you before *Defiance* left," Rin told the flag officer.

"I presumed as such," Davor replied. "That's why my staff made time for you before you leave. I apologize for cutting the time as short as we did, but these are rough waters we swim in."

It took Rin a moment to parse Davor's intent. Then he grimaced.

"Echelon Lord, that's what I want to talk to you about," he admitted. "I'm not currently leaving with *Defiance*. I spoke to Captain Casimir and she feels she is sufficiently briefed on the Alava to handle the artifact without my assistance."

The office was quiet for a few seconds.

"That is her decision to make," Davor said cautiously. "I was not aware of Captain Casimir being so well-informed on Precursor matters."

"I do not know her sources, but she knows a lot about them," Rin admitted. "But I know more, sir. I am one of the Imperium's top experts on the Alava, and we are about to investigate what might be the most important Alava artifact we're going to find.

"She *needs* my support, Echelon Lord. But more than that, the *Imperium* needs an archeologist and a historian there to document what we find. I understand that it may be necessary to destroy the Womb—in that case, it is utterly essential that we learn as much about it as possible before we do."

Davor snapped her mouth in a twitch-inducing sound. Humor, Rin thought.

"I would expect you to argue against destroying the Womb," the Echelon Lord noted calmly.

"It is an artifact of the Alava, and those tend to be dangerous beyond our worst fears," Rin replied. "Plus, this particular one we *know* is creating biological warships that appear to be under control of a cult that is delving into everything from slavery to terrorism.

"I accept that its destruction is probably necessary, in which case I want to study it beforehand, both so we know as much as we can and so that we can more safely destroy it," he concluded. "I need to be on *Defiance*, Echelon Lord.

"I need you to overrule Captain Casimir."

And now he'd said that, he knew he'd just killed any relationship with her. He regretted that—a lot—but he had to do his job.

"You understand, Dr. Dunst, that what you are asking me to do may well have serious consequences for both Captain Casimir's career...and yours," Davor warned him. "For me to formally overrule her would hang over her as a black mark for long-cycles to come—and no officer of the Imperial military will be comfortable working with you again.

"Leaving aside the *personal* consequences for you and Captain Casimir," the Ivida concluded.

Rin was taken aback...and then realized he probably shouldn't have been. He'd had a Marine escort that reported to the Echelon Lord the previous night, after all.

"The personal consequences will fall as they will, Echelon Lord,"

RELICS OF ETERNITY   273

Rin said quietly. "Duty drives us, even when personal affairs would interfere. I suspect she will understand better than most...eventually.

"I would prefer not to cause her long-term trouble, but I need to be there. The Imperium needs to be there."

There was another long silence.

"I agree." Davor studied him. "I don't believe that Captain Casimir has formally banned you from her ship so much as declined to invite you as a civilian advisor under her own authority.

"Since there is no record of her refusing you, I see a solution that should serve all of our needs...but that, as you say, Dr. Dunst, serves the Imperium above all other waters."

CHAPTER FORTY

"All departments, check in," Morgan ordered from the central seat on *Defiance*'s bridge. "Are we ready to go?"

"Tactical is green," Nguyen reported. "All magazines are full, all weapon systems reporting green on unpowered self-check."

"Navigation is green," El-Amin reported from the front of the bridge. "All tanks are full, all engines are green."

"Engineering is green, all systems check out at ninety-eight percent operating efficiency or higher," Liepins reported.

"The Marines are ready to be bored out of our minds for the trip," Vichy said. "I've picked up some new training sims and some playing cards."

"All tanks and supplies are topped up," Trifonov, the Logistics officer, added. "We're behind on paperwork, but when aren't we?"

"We'll catch up on the trip," Morgan promised her junior-most department head. The paperwork exchange was almost traditional, in her experience.

"I've heard that before," the young man replied.

There was a silence where Morgan was expecting her last department head to check in.

"Nystrom?" she asked. "Does coms have a reason we should be holding off?"

"Apologies, sir, yes, sir," Nystrom told her rapidly. "We've received a hold request from Echelon Lord Davor's staff; we are apparently having a civilian team added to the mission, and they haven't reached the dock yet."

"A civilian team, Commander?" Morgan demanded. Her suspicions raised a spike of anger in her gut. Would Rin Dunst have seriously gone over her head like that?

"Yes, sir. The Echelon Lord has detached several experts on Precursor artifacts and technology, including two cyber-archeology specialists familiar with Precursor computer systems, to support us. Dr. Dunst appears to be in charge?"

"I see," Morgan replied, keeping her tone level. The traditional humor and jokes of a starship underway were gone now. For a few seconds, she seriously considered ordering El-Amin to take *Defiance* out anyway.

It was, at least theoretically, her right to refuse a team like that. But she'd end up spending a lot of time explaining why—and since her own access to knowledge around the Precursors wasn't covered under the current classification rules and breakdowns, that explanation would get messy.

It wasn't that Morgan wasn't supposed to know what she knew. It was that most of the people under the current rules weren't supposed to know *why* Morgan knew what she knew. Her clearance level had been retroactively labeled "Old Wyrm" and was held by several dozen people who'd learned about the Precursors and the Mesharom before they started carving up the Mesharom Archive.

Most of the people who were cleared for the Old Wyrm Protocols had been involved in stealing the Archive in the first place. Explaining that Morgan didn't need Dunst and his people would be hard enough—explaining that she didn't want to risk *everyone* in the system who knew anything about the Precursors would risk all kinds of questions about personal entanglement.

Probably valid questions.

"El-Amin, hold us until the civilian team is aboard," she ordered with a concealed sigh. "Trifonov, find quarters for them. In a block, if you please. They'll be restricted to quarters for operational security until I say otherwise. Get Susskind to provide MPs to enforce that."

"Yes, sir," Trifonov replied instantly. "I'll have someone meet them when they come aboard."

"Thank you, Commanders," Morgan said, her tone less distracted that she felt.

She'd had damn good reasons to keep Rin Dunst off her ship. The Imperium needed an expert present when they reached the Womb, yes, but she was entirely capable of being that expert.

They also needed an expert in place to take over if something happened to *Defiance*. An expert on Dunst's level shouldn't be going anywhere near a high-threat environment. His presence aboard her ship would limit her options in ways she hadn't wanted to deal with.

And if she'd also potentially wanted to keep an adorable but squishy man out of the line of fire, that hadn't been part of her official reasoning. And her official reasoning had been enough.

It seemed Echelon Lord Davor hadn't agreed.

MORGAN WASN'T ENTIRELY surprised when Rogers stepped into her office several hours later, shortly after *Defiance* entered hyperspace.

"First Sword," Morgan greeted her as the other woman dropped into the seat across the desk.

"You want to talk about it?" Rogers asked bluntly.

"Talk about what, Commander?" Morgan replied.

"Why we have the same civilian advisor we had for our last cruise aboard, but this time he's restricted to quarters?" the First Sword said. "Was he *that* bad in bed?"

Morgan glared at her subordinate, who met her gaze calmly.

"Marines acting as bodyguards keep a lot of secrets from a lot of people, but they don't keep who the Captain is sleeping with from the First Sword," Rogers told her bluntly. "I doubt they've even told Vichy that, but they did tell me.

"Because that's part of their job, and managing the Captain is part of mine. So, just why is the man who knows more about what we're flying into than anyone else *and* is sleeping with my Captain locked up again?"

"I would argue that having *slept* with your Captain does not imply a continuing arrangement," Morgan countered. "I'd need different permission from my girlfriend for that."

Which she explicitly had, but that wasn't Rogers' business.

"Honestly, I'm only concerned about the personal part because it appears to be spilling into the professional part," Rogers said. "What's going on, sir?"

"What's going on is that I explicitly told Dunst that he wasn't coming on this trip, because the Imperium would be better served by him checking out the Womb from the observation deck of a battleship," Morgan said flatly. "He's one of our top experts on the Precursors. We already accidentally took him into one battle with the Servants and the Children; he's too valuable in what is inevitably going to be a high-risk scouting run at a hostile megastructure."

"And he went to the Echelon Lord," Morgan's XO concluded. "Okay. Damn."

"Yeah. So he went behind my back and over my head to get on *my* ship on a mission he's too damn valuable to be risked on," Morgan replied. "We need a Precursor expert for this, yes, but *I* know almost as much about this as he does.

"Now we probably have the only four people in fifty light-years who can tell you who the Alava's primary subject races were on board this ship. We almost certainly have the only people who can recognize Precursor biotech from cellular analysis.

"The restriction to quarters isn't *necessary*, but neither is allowing civilians the run of the ship," Morgan concluded. "If they wanted privileges, they shouldn't have *pissed me off*."

She'd looked at the list of who Dunst had brought with him. If the suggestion had been raised instead of imposed, she'd have been perfectly happy to bring Kelly Lawrence or one of the other cyber-archeologists with her.

The concentration of knowledge now aboard *Defiance* was what she'd wanted to avoid. Only even more so.

"Make sure that they have a lab with proper sensor access and so forth when we reach Target One," Morgan told Rogers. "We've got them, so we'll use them, but I'll be *fucked* if I pretend I like having them aboard."

Her First Sword swallowed something that sounded suspiciously like a giggle.

"What?" Morgan snapped.

"Phrasing, sir," Rogers finally said. "My understanding is that 'getting fucked' would definitely be among the reasons to like having Dr. Dunst aboard."

"That is *not* happening, First Sword," she said flatly. "Even if a certain male hadn't just decided to ignore my own authority over my own ship, I would not be sleeping with *anyone* aboard a ship under my command."

"Oh, I know," Commander Rogers agreed swiftly, then shook her head. "I'll touch base with Dr. Dunst and his team and see what they need for a lab."

"Thank you." Morgan raised a hand as Rogers turned to go. "And, Commander Rogers?"

"Yes, sir?"

"No matchmaking. Rin dug his own bloody grave on this one."

"Of course, sir."

CHAPTER FORTY-ONE

In Pierre Vichy's considered opinion, his Marines were most likely going to be completely useless on this trip. They had zero data on what kind of structure they were looking at in the case of the Womb and even less data on what kind of facility the Children would be operating there. He was running his people through a series of boarding and intrusion scenarios, but without data, it was just generic training.

That didn't make it a bad thing; it just meant it wasn't going to change their effectiveness against the target on the board much.

Despite his best efforts, he hadn't even acquired any new stealth shuttles. The report on his screen was his almost complete review of their performance with feedback from his Speakers and NCOs.

The executive summary was "get me more." The stealth shuttles had been instrumental in taking *Child of the Great Mother* at all, let alone taking her intact.

Their whirlwind return to Kosha Station had barely given him time to have his shuttles fully serviced, let alone try and poach stealth ships from the station.

He was still staring at the screen, considering how best to incorporate the phrase *these save lives* into the final paragraphs when his com chimed.

"Battalion Commander Vichy," he responded instantly.

"Commander Vichy, this is Dr. Dunst," the familiar voice of the archeologist greeted him.

"Ah, Doctor. Comment ça va?" He'd known Dunst was aboard, though he hadn't seen the man yet.

"Bored," Dunst said drily. "I'm restricted to the quarters we've been assigned, but I was wondering if you'd be willing to join me for dinner. I think my fellow scientists and I might kill each other if we don't get a distraction shortly."

"I didn't realize you were restricted," Pierre admitted. That would have been an MP task, he supposed, with his Marines only being called in if needed. He doubted that Dunst or the other archeologists were causing trouble, though.

"Oui, eh bien, je sais pourquoi," Dunst told him in atrociously accented French. As he said, he obviously knew why and was tolerant of it.

Pierre didn't know why, but he doubted the scientist wanted him to ask over the intercom.

"I could break some time for dinner tonight," he told the other man. "We're still barely halfway to Target One. C'est un long voyage."

Eight cycles in, at least six or so more to go. Target One wouldn't have been in the first wave of systems the Navy would have scouted on their own, as Vichy understood it.

"Je sais," Dunst agreed. "Don't get me wrong, Battalion Commander; I like the people I've brought with me. But I spent a week in a cell next to Kelly Lawrence, for example. We ran out of things to talk about a long time ago."

Pierre chuckled.

"Dinner it is, then," he promised. "I'll see you shortly."

DESPITE THE CURRENT "NOT QUITE WELCOME" status of the civilian team, Pierre was unsurprised to see that the steward staff were still being entirely helpful and cooperative with Dr. Dunst. The archeologist had made a generally positive impression on *Defiance*'s crew.

That meant that the dining room attached to their rooms had been done up with proper tablecloths and such, and that the stewards had put together a meal that looked surprisingly appetizing.

Pierre himself had brought a bottle of wine from a French vineyard—owned by some cousin; even *he* couldn't keep track of his cousins upon cousins without a spreadsheet some days—as a gift.

"Commander Vichy," Dunst greeted him brightly. "Please, come, have a seat. You, after all, get to leave this little corner of the ship once dinner is over."

The Marine placed the bottle carefully on the table and glanced around. He wasn't familiar with the other two scientists at the table. One was a four-armed Tosumi with deep blue and green feathers, their vestigial wings hidden beneath a simple toga-like wrapped cloak.

The other was a familiar-looking woman with short black hair and brown eyes he could easily see someone getting lost in. It took him a few moments after he took the seat to even recognize her anymore.

"Miz Lawrence, I apologize, I didn't recognize you," he admitted. "You look much better."

The cyber-archeologist had been ill and starved when he'd first met her. She looked *far* healthier and better at a proper weight.

"I don't believe you've met On Rai," Dunst gestured to the other person at the table. On Rai's meal looked almost identical to the carefully arranged rice dish the humans had been served, which suggested major effort on the stewards' part.

Defiance wouldn't have been equipped to feed a Tosumi anything but Universal Protein and vitamin powders. The ship's storage would have been filled with human food—food that would have been actively poisonous to Tosumi metabolisms.

"I have not," Pierre confirmed, bowing slightly to the avian alien. "A pleasure, On Rai. I'm aware of Dr. Dunst and Miz Lawrence's specialties. You're another computer expert?"

"If you call poking at rocks that should never have carried electricity and trying to determine if they were computers or just rocks *being an expert*, yes," On Rai rumbled. The only nonhuman on the ship, they'd taken the unusual courtesy of attaching a translator speaker to their shoulder.

"Sometimes, we can sort of make Alava computers work," Lawrence agreed. "Sometimes, we're pretty sure we're poking at what was supposed to be decorative sculpture that just *looks* like a computer."

"Some of their tech definitely works," Pierre pointed out. "I heard stories of the star cannon out by Arjtal."

"I was on the expedition that finally shut that down," On Rai admitted. "Even cutting in dangerously close through hyperspace like the Fleet did when rescuing the Mesharom, it was *still* a month's flight in realspace to reach the platform."

The "star cannon" had targeted any vessel with an operating interface drive. No one in the Imperium was used to operating with spacecraft that measured their maneuverability in meters per second squared.

"And six weeks to work out enough of the system to shut it down," Lawrence pointed out. "I did most of my Master's on your work there, On Rai. It sounded amazing."

"You've done enough of it now to know it's really just boring," the Tosumi replied. "Our work involves a lot of swimming in place, changing things ever so slightly and seeing what happens."

"Mine is generally more...active," Pierre told them with a chuckle. "I apologize for the restriction right now. We're often cautious about where civilians are allowed aboard warships."

"We understand," Dunst said with a wave of dismissal. "We've been transported on warships before, Battalion Commander. We've been promised a lab for examining the Womb when we arrive; I'm honestly content with that."

There was something else going on, Pierre suspected. Dunst didn't strike him as the type to blithely accept what even Pierre thought was an odd level of restriction unless he thought he'd done something to deserve it.

"Have you spoken with Captain Casimir?" Pierre asked. "While this is not nonstandard, necessity required us to give you more freedom when we had the entire expedition aboard."

Dunst was silent for a few moments too long, and Pierre *finally* worked out what was going on. Not all of it, he was sure, but there was definitely an extra layer of personal tension between Dunst and the Captain.

"I see no reason to impose on the Captain," Dunst finally said. "She's given or promised us all we need to do our work. We're here as civilian advisors, Commander, to help where we can.

"We're just bored, and I hoped to impose on you for conversation."

Pierre laughed.

"Mais oui," he replied. "You feed me, I bring wine, we talk into the night. It is very French."

"Oui, le vin. D'où cela vient-il?" Lawrence asked in perfectly fluent French. She had a distinctly British accent to the language, but it was faint and almost adorable.

The woman now had Pierre's *undivided* attention as he answered her question about the wine.

CHAPTER FORTY-TWO

"Portal open. Emergence in five. Four. Three. Two. One. Emergence."

Defiance flashed through the portal she'd torn in reality at a quarter of the speed of light, every weapon system active and every scanner sweeping the space around them.

"Report," Morgan ordered grimly after a moment.

"Nothing to report," Nguyen replied, her voice sounding almost twisted. "There's nothing here, Captain. *Nothing.*"

Morgan was about to counter that there was never truly nothing in a star system—and then the sensor sweeps updated the main hologram.

They weren't *in* a star system.

"I'm guessing that we're not looking at an eclipsed star at this point," she finally said.

"No. There is no star here," Morgan's tactical officer replied. "No planets...every calculation says the star the Womb was built at should be here, but we're in empty space."

"Were the stars on that image wrong?" Morgan asked. She was

irritated with Dunst still, but she doubted that he'd have been *that* far off. "Did they send us to the wrong place?"

"Even if the stars were incorrect, we still used them to identify a star in the Precursor charts," Nguyen replied. "El-Amin? I'm assuming we're in the right place?"

"I'm validating as best as I can," the navigator replied. "It threw off our final arrival calculations when there wasn't a mass here, but we're certainly within a light-day or so of our intended destination."

A sick silence fell over the bridge as everyone considered that.

"Did the sun nova?" Morgan asked.

"Even if the star novaed, there'd be a stellar remnant," Nguyen replied. "Permission to deploy maximum VLA? We're looking for everything at this point, and we need better resolution."

"Granted. There's nothing out here to stop us getting our drones back," Morgan said.

A Very Large Array used hyperfold communicator–equipped drones to create a virtual telescope hundreds of thousands of kilometers across. The drones lacked some sensors their mothership had—they weren't big enough for the widely dispersed receivers of a tachyon scanner—but the different receivers could dramatically expand *Defiance*'s eyes.

Dozens of robotic spacecraft spilled out from their launch bays and zipped away at seventy percent of lightspeed. It only took a few minutes for the VLA to take form.

Minutes Morgan spent trying to guess what had made a star *disappear*.

"Commander Rogers, while Nguyen gets the VLA online, I want you to look at the gravimetrics of the area," she ordered. "We're looking for sequential shock patterns."

"You think someone fired a starkiller?" her First Sword asked. "We're a long way out for *that* to have happened."

"Or something equivalent," Morgan replied. Even the Precursor experts she'd stuffed in a lab in the belly of her ship weren't cleared to know about the source of the starkillers. An attempt to duplicate or activate a Precursor engine could have had messy results.

"Gravimetrics are clean," Rogers reported after a couple of minutes. "I guessed. Even a starkiller leaves a stellar remnant. I've never heard of a star just vanishing."

"What do the gravimetrics show?" Morgan asked. "Deep space? Or..."

"No. This was a star system," Rogers confirmed. "Gravitational echoes remain. They're the weirdest I've ever seen, but then I haven't spent much time looking at the ghost of a star system before."

A shiver ran down Morgan's spine.

"I've seen *dead* stars," she said quietly. "But this is something else. Nguyen?"

"There's...scraps here," the tactical officer said slowly. "Like someone blew the planets into pieces to better use them as raw materials."

"That would fit Precursor methods," Morgan noted. "They did like to carve up entire worlds for their cores."

"This was rougher and left a lot more debris behind," Nguyen concluded. "It looks like anything of real value was used up, but that left a lot of dust. None of it registered on our first scanner pass, but we're picking it out now.

"Most of it's just a heterogenous cloud, maybe half an Earth mass spread across a star system's worth of space. But..."

The young Vietnamese woman trailed off.

"Lesser Commander?" Morgan demanded.

"It gives us something to hold a trace," Nguyen answered. "And there's a distortion pattern here—radiation, waste hydrogen, an eddy in the dust—that suggests something moved through the dust cloud after it had taken form."

"Define 'something,' Commander; this mystery is making me nervous," Morgan ordered.

"I don't know, sir," the tactical officer replied. "Just the fact that I can still pick it out after what looks like tens of thousands of years? It was big, sir. Made war-spheres look like toys."

"Can we trace where it went?" Rogers asked.

"I can't," Nguyen admitted. "That's not...that's not something I'm trained to do. This trail probably predates some Core Powers. We need..."

"We need an archeologist," Morgan concluded, sensing several meals of crow in her future. "Conveniently, we have three. Send everything you have down to Dr. Dunst's lab and link his people in to the sensors."

"Full access, Commander Nguyen." She swallowed a sigh. "Trust me, Dr. Dunst has the clearance for it."

She rose from her seat and gestured Rogers over.

"Commander Rogers, you have the bridge," she told her First Sword.

"Where are you going, sir?" her XO asked.

"To go brief Dr. Dunst on just what we've found and what we need from him," Morgan replied.

The apology that was required wasn't anybody else's business.

"SO, THAT'S WHAT WE HAVE," Morgan told the three archeologists in the temporary lab. *Defiance* had very few unused spaces—that was part of why evacuating the expedition from K77DLK-6 had been such a pain—but she did have *redundant* spaces. The "lab" was a secondary sensor control room.

It wasn't an overly spacious room for its intended purpose, but it was intended for an operating crew of ten. Removing the seats had allowed several tables of additional equipment to be added, which had resulted in an even more cramped space.

"You already know the answer," On Rai said bluntly. "We have assumed in our currents that the Womb was closer to a space station than anything else. This new evidence is that it is self-mobile."

"That explains the path in the dust," Morgan replied. "It doesn't explain what happened to the star."

"It does," Dunst said. His voice was very small and tired-sounding. "The Womb took the star with it. Or had already completely consumed the star by that point. What you're seeing isn't dust as we think of it.

"That cloud, Captain Casimir, is a coprolite on a massive scale. Your target *ate* a star system. Presumably with Alava assistance at this stage, but the evidence is clear."

"That is impossible," she argued. The sinking feeling in the pit of her stomach made all the counterargument she needed, though.

"The facts do not support it being impossible," he reminded her. "We stand amidst the remains of an entire star system. No worlds. No star. Only debris.

"I agree with Lesser Commander Nguyen's assessment that the Alava destroyed the worlds first," he continued. "We have evidence that they occasionally used a system similar in some ways to our hyperspace missiles for demolition on a planetary scale."

"I've seen planetary-scale plasma cutters," Morgan said. "I haven't seen that one, though I vaguely remember something?"

"Teleporting a multi-teraton antimatter charge into a planetary core was wasteful by Alava standards," Dunst told her. "They did it when they were in a hurry. My guess would be that they didn't care much what form of raw material the Womb was fed, only that it was fed."

"So, they blew up entire planets and fed the wreckage into it?"

"Basically," he agreed. "Then, at some point after the Alava died, the Womb ran out of food in this system. So, it left."

"That implies both more intelligence and more flexibility than I was expecting of the Womb," Morgan admitted. "That I might be facing an *intelligent* megastructure wasn't something I'd expected."

"It would explain quite a bit about the Children themselves, though," the other woman in the room told her. Kelly Lawrence had been digging into the sensor data since Morgan had arrived, mostly ignoring the conversation.

"If they *spoke* with it, saw it, touched it...if this thing is half the size and power I'm starting to suspect, the argument that it is a god would be very compelling in those circumstances."

"It is not a god, and it is potentially a serious threat," Morgan said. Not, perhaps, as serious as a war between the Wendira and the Laians, but serious enough for this far into the middle of nowhere.

Even her worst-case scenarios couldn't see any way more than *Defiance*, at worst, could be threatened. But she was considering the possibility of needing to reassess those scenarios.

"Have we learned anything we can work with?" Morgan continued.

"We can revise further if we keep working, but I've got an initial probability cone of where it might have gone," Lawrence told them. She waved it up above a holoprojector on one of the tables.

The star chart was readily recognizable to Morgan, and the pale orange cone covered far too much of it. Including, to add to her nightmares, the Kosha System.

"Do we have *anything* to narrow it down?" she asked. "Do we even know how fast it's going?"

"There's nothing in this data to give us that," Dunst said slowly. "But we have a lot of information from the Children. I think we might even have copies or digital scans of most of the artifacts they used to find the Womb in the first place."

"Keep at it," Morgan instructed. "Whatever it takes. That cone" —she gestured at the hologram—"includes Kosha System. I'm not leaving *this* system until I either have a destination or know for sure that all of this was a waste of time."

"We'll find an answer, Captain," Dunst assured her. "The Children found it and I'm certain we have more information than they did at this point."

"I hope so," she told him. "I really hope so."

CHAPTER FORTY-THREE

RIN WAS ACTUALLY SURPRISED AT THE DEGREE TO WHICH Casimir had changed her mind on the spot the moment she realized she was wrong. Suddenly, his team was no longer restricted to quarters and had access to anything they might need.

Most tellingly about the professionalism of *Defiance*'s crew and Captain, he supposed, was that the only real difference between *restricted to quarters* and *access to anything you need* was that he didn't have an MP escorting him around the ship.

They'd already been providing him with everything he needed for his work equipment and data. If he'd needed the ability to pace while he thought, well, even he understood that was hard to provide while keeping his mobility restricted.

Now he was pacing the corridor outside their lab, trying and failing to divine just how the Children had managed to find a creature that had left its last known location forty-five thousand years earlier.

Between the bits of information they'd picked up in their whirlwind return to Kosha Station, he now knew a bit more about how

Child of the Great Mother and her crew, the original Children, had ended up out there.

Both the ship—commissioned as *Child of the Rising Storm*—and the identified scientists and crew-beings had been Imperial, all right. All of the scientists had been either Archeology Institute members or Navy researchers. The ship had been built fifteen years before and served in the A!Tol's survey corps.

Then, four years later, the files for every single identified individual and the ship itself simply vanished, lost beneath a security block that Rin's authorizations and clearances hadn't sufficed to open.

Presumably, people *with* that access were now going through the data under those seals to work out what had happened. Assuming they weren't distracted by a potential war, anyway.

Rin knew enough to put together the pieces now. Freshly in possession of a bunch of information on the Alava, a covert Imperial project had been launched to investigate a region the A!Tol suspected the Mesharom hadn't cleaned up yet.

A ship capable of long-range independent operation and a select team of scientists. They'd come out there, dug through K77DLK-6, and then gone on to Target One. Most likely, there'd been something at K77DLK-6 similar to the fresco he'd found at K77DLT-3.

So, the expedition that would become the Children had ended up right there, orbiting a dust cloud that had been a star system and wracking their brains to work out where the Alava creation they were hunting had gone.

He reached the end of the corridor and turned on his heel. The sight of someone coming up the corridor stopped him in his tracks, and he shook his head to clear his thoughts as he recognized the ship's First Sword.

"Commander Rogers, how may I help you?" he asked. "If you're hoping for answers, I don't have any yet."

"I suspect that if you had answers, I'd already know them," she admitted. "I did want to talk with you, Doctor. Is this a bad time?"

"I'm just wearing holes in the flooring and my brain alike," Rin told her. "What do you need?"

"The flooring is the same ceramic composite as the interior bulk-heads," the Commander said. "It takes more than a few hours of pacing to cause noticeable wear."

"Give me a couple of days," the archeologist replied. "Because I suspect I'll wear through it before I *do* have any answers."

"I probably don't have any useful contributions," Rogers said, leaning against the wall and crossing her arms. "I'm here for a completely different problem, one where you probably do have the answers and can help my ship get back to proper efficiency."

That was sufficiently outside Rin's expectations that he caught himself nearly staring at the Navy officer.

"All right, Commander, you've managed to get my attention," he admitted with a chuckle. "Care to explain?"

"You. My Captain. This bullshit," the XO replied with a gesture around them. "*One* of you is going to have to apologize. You're *both* in the wrong and *neither* of you is really going to be working properly until you get it sorted out."

"I'll admit, Commander, I was regarding that as a 'future-Rin' problem," he confessed. "Captain Casimir made it very clear that anything personal between us ceased the moment the two of us were aboard her ship—and I have no illusions about the amount of damage I did by going over her head, either.

"And the advantage of polyamory, as I understand it, is that dumping my ass doesn't leave her without a support network," Rin said. "Everyone involved is an adult, Commander Rogers."

"And you're fine and she's fine and I bloody well know that chorus, Dr. Dunst," she said. "And I'm back to 'You. My Captain. This *bullshit.*'"

"I'm lost."

"It's in what you expect to see, Doctor," Rogers told him. "Each of you is determined to present a certain face to the world. She's a starship captain. You're a team leader, an expedition vice-director. You're both familiar with authority and consequences of losing face.

"And you're playing the same game of masks and expectations with each other. It's in *what you expect to see*."

"So, I expect to see Morgan being the stern mistress of her command and angry at me, so that's what I see?" Rin asked.

"Exactly. And all of that is true and honest and all of it is a lie," the XO said bluntly. "I'm her First Sword, her executive officer. It's my job to know what she thinks, Dr. Dunst, and right now, she thinks she's an idiot.

"She's not, and she had reasons to bar you from the ship. She was wrong in the end, but that doesn't negate those reasons, does it, Doctor?"

"No," he admitted. "I'm still not seeing your point."

"Talk to her, Doctor. Outside the meetings and the data transfers and the mission. She's still allowed to be human; she's just not allowed to show that to the crew."

"Because it's not what they expect to see?" Dunst asked.

"Exactly. My job means I need to see what's there, not what I expect to be there. In this case, I can tell you that right now, my ship is going to run at ninety-eight percent when we finally find this thing.

"And that if you and my captain sort out this bullshit, that goes right back up to a hundred percent, where it belongs. Because while my captain is very good, she's also still human."

"And she's also seeing what she expects to see?" Rin asked.

"Exactly. And she thinks you're mad at her."

He chuckled.

"I'm not," he admitted. "I needed to be here, Commander. But I knew what that was going to do to any *personal* matters. She took it better than I expected."

"So apologize," Rogers instructed. "And get it sorted out."

"I'll...think about it," he promised. "It sounds like a distraction for us both right now."

"And again, that's what—"

"I expect to see," Rin cut her off as it hit him. He stared blankly at the wall. "I'll think about it," he promised again, "but right now, I need to talk to my team."

"You have an answer?"

"It's all in what we *expect to see*."

———

"KELLY, I need you to put up a map of the stars in the probability cone as the Alava star projection had them," Rin ordered as he barged back into the lab. He barely even registered Rogers coming in behind him and leaning against the doorframe as she watched the conversation.

"Doctor?"

"Do it, quickly," he told her. The holographic star chart flashed into the air, multicolored icons in the orange cone marking the stars.

"Now, flag those locations in white," Rin continued. "And overlay our *current* star chart, highlighted in blue."

"Other than Target One, they should be the sa..."

"We knew they weren't," Rin told Lawrence after she trailed off. "It's why Nguyen had problems with mapping the Alava star projection to current charts, because some stars were wrong and some were missing."

There was a small green dot marking *Defiance*'s location, next to the white-highlighted icon for the star that *had* been Target One. There was no blue icon there. As they had now seen at close range, there was no star at all.

"There," Lawrence said softly. "Another missing star. Six light-years from here, close to the edge of the probability cone."

Rin walked around the hologram to study the star. They didn't have details from the Alava projection as to what type of star any given icon represented.

"Why this one?" he asked aloud. "It's not the closest, it's not... Wait. *Was* it ever the closest?"

Lawrence dug into her computers.

"Yes," she confirmed. "If the Lesser Commander's calculations are correct—and I don't see why they wouldn't be—K-Seven-Seven-D-I-Four didn't come closer until forty thousand years ago. If the Womb left before then, that would have been the closest star."

"So, what would have been the closest stars to here when the Womb finished eating it?" Rin asked grimly.

The lab was deathly silent.

"That one," Rogers said, stepping over to join him and pointing at a star. "It's on our charts, at least, but look at it."

Rin studied the icon. He wasn't quite sure what Rogers was indicating, though. It was off position, he supposed, but even the best calculations were often off by a bit when talking about stars.

"Miz Lawrence, can you focus on this one?" Commander Rogers asked. "K-Seven-Seven-D-K-J-Nine."

The entire display shifted.

"It's just a little thing," Lawrence said. "Energy levels are barely above white dwarf range."

"That's why no one has scouted it," Rogers said. "It's at least a light-year out of position, and our closest scan is from five light-years away. No one has paid a lot of attention to it."

"It's only ten light-years from Kosha," Rin said quietly. "That's closer than I want a sun-eating Alava creation to anything I care about."

"It's a white dwarf on scanners, but the spectrography is all wrong," Rogers said. "Why did we never flag this?"

"Because we have one colony out here that only really exists to help conceal the investigation into the Alava ruins," Rin admitted. "No one was paying attention to subdwarfs and white dwarfs when they were looking for Alava sites and potential colonies. We had dozens of main-sequence stars to look at; even astronomers didn't have the time to look at oddities in something this small."

"Well, this 'small star' looks like our answer to me, Dr. Dunst."

"Because it's *not* what we expect to see," Rin said, echoing

Rogers's words back to her. "We need to brief Captain Casimir. I don't think we're going to learn anything from this far away."

He didn't know the math well enough to guess the flight time to the system they'd flagged, but he doubted it would be quick. Fifteen cycles to get all the way back to Kosha, and the Womb was two-thirds of the way back to their home base.

It wasn't, at least, *headed* to Kosha.

Thank all that was holy for small mercies.

CHAPTER FORTY-FOUR

"I HAVE TO ADMIT, THE CONCEPT OF THIS THING HAVING EATEN two stars is somehow making me even more uncomfortable," Nguyen said as Rogers and Dunst finished their briefing. "And our best guess for its location is a star that is out of place?"

"Unfortunately, it makes sense," Rogers told the junior officer. "If it is hopping from star system to star system, it is, well, bringing its food with it."

"My concern, Commander Rogers, is just how tough is a target that eats suns?" Morgan asked, looking at the star charts they'd been going over. "Is it even going to notice us peppering it with antimatter warheads?"

The twenty-gigaton warheads on her hyperspace missiles were probably the most powerful regular weapons *Defiance* had. Her point-eight-lightspeed interface-drive weapons had roughly a third of the impact energy of the big antimatter bombs.

"We simply don't know," Rogers admitted. "Dr. Dunst?"

"Commander Rogers has the essence of it," the archeologist agreed. "It's not an assessment I've ever had to do, but I would guess that the Womb is no tougher, structurally, than the Arjtal cloner. It's just going to be bigger. We're talking something gas giant–sized at least, attached to and manipulating a small star."

At least. That was a terrifying phrase in this context.

"How big can it have grown?" Morgan asked softly. "Some idea of what we're about to investigate would be useful."

"It depends on the creature's metabolism," Dunst said. "No one is qualified to judge that. We've never had an intact living Alava biomechanism to examine. So far, we have yet to encounter one that didn't require nuking for one reason or another."

She swallowed a chuckle, allowing a smile to reach her face. She'd done a lot of said nuking, including using a hyperspace missile launcher's hyper portal to deliver orbital bombardment munitions to the cloner.

Unfortunately, the cloner's final fate had been inflicted by a Marine assault shuttle pilot ramming his craft into it. There'd been a lot of posthumous medals given out that day.

"This one has been alive and mobile for fifty thousand years," Morgan noted. "It has eaten at least two star systems we know about. A mobile sun-eater, officers, represents a threat to the Imperium we cannot allow to stand."

"It's your ship, sir," Rogers pointed out. "What are your orders?"

"We do what every Captain has done since the dawn of time, Commander Rogers," Morgan told them. "We steer to the sound of the guns. In this case, a dying star pulled onto a new course.

"It might not be our prey—but if it *isn't* the Womb, then we have *two* things out here capable of bodily moving stars. Both hope and Occam's razor lead me to the same target, people. Target Two.

"It is not *Defiance*'s role to engage and destroy the Womb," she reminded everyone. "It is our job to locate the Womb, identify the Children's base, and call in reinforcements. This is a situation better handled by the battleships Echelon Lord Davor has been promised than by one heavy cruiser."

"If it's the size of a gas giant, will even two battleships be enough?" Nguyen asked.

"That's why we're scouting it, Lesser Commander," Morgan replied. "In fifty thousand years, the Womb has only moved thirty light-years. We can, if necessary, wait for more ships to be available."

If the crisis on the Coreward border resolved peacefully, then the Imperium could easily deploy several squadrons of modern *superbattleships*. The HSMs of two lightly refitted battleships and a modern heavy cruiser might not take down the Womb.

If the HSMs of forty-eight or more modern superbattleships couldn't, well, the Womb was slow and the Imperium still retained its arsenal of starkillers.

MOST OF MORGAN'S officers had left the briefing room before she realized that Dunst was standing just inside the door, waiting. At that point, El-Amin and Rogers were the last two officers in the room —and the Martian officer took in the waiting professor and glanced back at Morgan.

Any commentary or conclusion on El-Amin's part was overtaken by Rogers gently taking the man's shoulder and guiding him out, firmly sealing the briefing room's door behind them to leave Morgan and Dunst alone in the room.

"My First Sword has an *agenda*, doesn't she?" Morgan asked drily as she glanced around the empty room. "Commander El-Amin might well have had something he needed to discuss with me regarding our course."

"I can't speak to Commander Rogers's intent," Dunst noted, spreading his hands wide in a shrug. "*I* was only intending to ask if you could make some time for me later."

"It appears I have some time now, Dr. Dunst," Morgan replied. She knew she should probably be angry at her XO—setting this up was arguably a minor violation of protocol, though hardly a significant sin by any standard—but she was mostly amused.

And pleased? She interrogated her own emotions as she waited for Rin Dunst to speak, and found herself smiling and raising a hand to forestall his saying anything.

"I am *Defiance's* Captain," she told him. "Inside this hull, I am not supposed to be wrong. All the Captain does is correct by definition in the eyes of her crew, to be judged on return to port by her superiors and peers.

"Based, presumably, on the reports of crew members who were *not* blind to her flaws, which renders the argument of blind obedience somewhat false, doesn't it?" she continued. "But the fact remains that a Captain must present a front of infallibility."

She gestured around the room.

"My crew have intentionally left us alone, and *you*, Dr. Dunst, are very aware of my fallibility, I think. I apologize for restricting you to quarters. While easily justified, we both know I did it for pettier reasons."

"Thank you," he said instantly, then paused. "I apologize for going over your head," he said quietly. "I felt it was necessary. I still feel it was necessary, but I know it was a dangerous thing to do."

"Yes," Morgan told him flatly. "You could very easily have set up a fight between myself and my superiors that would have ended my career. Echelon Lord Davor, it seems, has a more delicate touch than others I've served under."

She shook her head.

"I know far more about the Precursors than you think," she said quietly. "I wanted to make sure that there was an expert on the scene and a backup expert at Kosha Station in case this scouting mission went wrong."

"You know about the Alava, but your focus is on your job," he replied, his voice equally soft. "The Alava are my life. You have access to the data, but you're not an expert the way I am. You needed me."

"I did," she conceded. "We would have muddled through in the end without you, I think, but we were better off for having you. You still shouldn't have gone over my head."

"I had to," he said. "I don't know how much you know about the Alava, Morgan. From what I can tell, nobody out here does. That leads to some fascinating questions on my part, but it also means that to anyone other than you, you were charging off to investigate an Alava artifact without an Alava expert.

"I think you needed my expertise, yes, but I also think that you needed me along to help keep the secret of what you know about them and how."

How much Morgan knew about the Precursors wasn't a secret that would break the Imperium. If the wrong someone started poking at how she knew it, though... The Mesharom had retreated to their own territories, pulling back the fleets that had once watched the galaxy on their behalf. But faced with evidence that she had copied the data core of a Mesharom war sphere...

"I don't think you even begin to understand the consequences of that secret coming out," Morgan said quietly. The Imperium was quietly incorporating reverse-engineered Mesharom technology into its warships—that tech underpinned the powerful new shields that protected *Defiance*, for example—but it was still a slow and careful process.

Their modern ships could fight the outer Core Powers on a reasonably even basis, but even the Laians and Wendira feared the Mesharom.

"I'll admit that was more Davor's reasoning than mine," Dunst admitted. "But I think it's something you overlooked. I'm sorry I went over your head, but it had to be done."

"And what, you expect me to forgive you and to carry on the path we'd started before?" Morgan demanded.

"I think both of us need to be focused on the Alava creature that eats suns," the archeologist told her. "I think that your First Sword, at least, thought us being angry at each other was a distraction you couldn't afford and wanted us to make up."

Morgan snorted.

"I suspect the phrase that my faithful executive officer would use is actually *kiss and make up*," she told Dunst. She sighed and shook her head, taking a seat in one of the chairs and gesturing for him to join her. Standing and staring at each other was starting to get old.

"You were right...*enough*...that I'm not really angry at you anymore," she told him. "But you could have seriously hurt my career if you'd done that with a different flag officer."

Dunst picked up the chair nearest her, turning it to face her and taking a seat in it. This close, she couldn't help noticing how warm his eyes were.

"I know. Davor made that point very clear," he admitted. "I didn't know that then. I'd have argued harder with you if I had."

"It wasn't exactly a circumstance where I was going to listen very well," she conceded. "You probably could have raised it again once I was back aboard ship, but I can be...stubborn."

"So can I," Dunst conceded. "I'm not expecting anything, Morgan. I wanted to make peace between us so that we can get the job done."

She chuckled. She wasn't even sure when he'd started using her first name again, but she hadn't corrected him and she wasn't going to now.

"I appreciate that," she told him. "It helps, of course, that my First Sword has apparently gone fully shipper-on-deck. I trust her judgment—I have to, or commanding a starship just doesn't work."

"She seemed trustworthy to me," Dunst admitted. "I doubt she'd hesitate for a second to knife me in the back and throw me out an airlock to protect the ship, though."

"Interesting definition of *trustworthy*," Morgan noted. "That's usually the *Captain's* definition of trustworthy for an XO."

"She'll protect her people above all else. Seems trustworthy to me," he told her.

Morgan glanced up at the sealed briefing room door, then glanced back at the time.

"I have to go," she finally conceded, a decision clicking into place as she did. "El-Amin will have his course plotted by now, and we need to get moving."

"Of course," Dunst agreed instantly. "Thank you for giving me the chance to apologize."

"I have a price for it," she told him, smiling slightly.

"Oh?" he said carefully.

"Captain's mess, eighteenth twentieth-cycle, Dr. Dunst. Your attendance is required," she told him.

They might not be able to make it work, but in a few days, they were going to be making a high-risk scouting pass at an entity that appeared to eat suns.

There was no *time* to let things dangle in the realm of possibility.

CHAPTER FORTY-FIVE

"I F YOU TELL ME THAT THE STAR ISN'T HERE, I'M GOING TO GET grouchy," Morgan said. There was an undercurrent of humor to her tone, but it wasn't *pleasant* humor.

"Then get grouchy," Nguyen told her. "It's not here. But we didn't expect it to be here, either, sir. We're at the last location we have it flagged, which is based on a cursory star scan done as part of a survey five light-years away, two years ago.

"So, our data is seven years old, and we know the star is moving."

"Well, I guess we know what direction it was going," Morgan conceded as she looked at the hologram in the middle of the bridge. They were in the middle of nowhere, but logically, the Womb should be a few light-months away at most.

It had only traveled twenty-five light-years in fifty thousand years, after all. Less than a tenth of a percent of lightspeed on average, though it probably had stopped to eat the planets of the stars it had consumed.

Because *that* wasn't a terrifying concept.

"Everything suggests that it should have been heading to the nearest star based on the positions maybe ten thousand years ago," Nguyen noted. "That would put it on *this* line."

An astrographic chart appeared on the main hologram, shrinking the standard tactical display. A white line appeared, from where the star should have been according to the Precursor charts and the expected target.

"And?" Morgan asked calmly.

"It's not on that line," Nguyen admitted. "We're doing a broader scan. It can't be *that* far away. I'd estimate around a light-month, maybe two. We know it was here seven years ago."

Morgan knew it wouldn't take long for them to locate it. Dim and distorted as Target Two appeared now, it was a star. Even if it was six times as far away as Nguyen estimated, they'd be able to locate it in short order.

"We've got it," the tactical officer announced. "My god...Sir, I'm putting the course projection on screen."

A new icon appeared on the astrographic chart, a red orb that glittered like an evil eye. A line stretched from that red orb, projected from the last known location to calculate both velocity and direction.

The line intersected another icon, nine and a half light-years from the icon's current location. The icon was a highlighted star, with a stylized planet and a stylized space station next to it.

The planet meant there was a colony there. The space station meant there was a resupply base there. And there was only one colony and one resupply base within thirty light-years.

"It's headed for the Kosha System, and it's up to an average velocity of seven percent of light," Nguyen said grimly. "Assuming a constant acceleration, it would have a current velocity of almost point-one-five *c*.

"That's still sixty years from reaching Kosha Station, but..."

"The course change represents a clear and direct threat," Morgan confirmed. "Commander El-Amin! Assuming it's followed that course and acceleration, our ETA to intercept? I don't want to get closer than a light-day at initial emergence."

"Local hyperspace is pretty stable, and there are no currents or unexpected dead zones," the navigator replied, clearly thinking out loud. "Eleven hours, roughly half a cycle."

The degree to which human Imperials intermingled Imperial time and date standards with Terran measurements could still amuse Morgan, even at the most dangerous times.

"All right. El-Amin, get us back into hyperspace heading after that thing," Morgan ordered. "Rogers, stand the ship down. Minimum watches, cycle for the next nine hours so everybody gets at least six hours' rest and sleep."

"And in nine hours, sir?" Rogers asked. She knew the answer, Morgan was sure, but it needed to go in the record.

"In nine hours, we go to battle stations. I don't trust the Children not to have some kind of watch in hyperspace, and I am so very done with Precursor surprises."

***

MORGAN KNEW she wasn't going to sleep, but she had to set an example. She retreated to her quarters, dimmed the lights, and started soft music playing.

There were a thousand things she could do. She could record a message for Victoria. She could talk to Rin or even drag him to bed with her, though that felt a little too much like taking advantage of her position.

None of them really appealed. She stared at the dim ceiling while the music played, but she kept running through mental scenarios again and again and again.

Finally, she got back up with a sigh and pulled up a tactical-simulator program on her computer. They had a pretty good idea of the bioships' capabilities. The real question was how many bioships the Womb would have to defend itself and whether the Children would have more modern vessels to assist.

No one had confirmed the existence of a covert scout expedition based around a long-range freighter, but she didn't need that confirmation. She'd seen the data Murtas had acquired around the known members of the Children and *Child of the Great Mother*.

A long-range military freighter with a Navy science team and a handful of Imperial Archeology Institute specialists to provide extra backup on the knowledge side. The problem she was facing was that the Imperium wouldn't have sent one ship.

Child of the Rising Storm would have been sent out with escorts. That could have ranged from a single destroyer up to multiple heavy cruisers, depending on how dangerous the A!Tol had judged this region of space at the time.

Morgan would have sent heavy cruisers, at least, along with any expedition that expected to meet Precursor technology. Given the time line, that probably meant some iteration of the *Thunderstorm* class, the first cruisers equipped with HSMs.

Defiance could handle any of her predecessors one-on-one, but even a two-ship division of cruisers could wreck Morgan's command in a straight-up fight. That was ignoring the bioships, and the computer was happily telling her there was no basis on which to calculate an upper limit on the number of those.

The Womb had the mass of three entire star systems to play with. The first one had been specifically blown into pieces by the Precursors to feed to it more easily, but the bioships, according to the simulation Morgan ran as she was thinking about it, could do a decent job of carving up a planet.

That carving would take longer than using the Precursors' teleported munitions. That potentially explained why the Womb was "only" twenty-five light-years away after fifty thousand years if it could get up to fifteen percent of lightspeed.

Most likely, moving the entire star at that kind of velocity was draining on both its energy and fuel reserves. Without a reason, the Womb wouldn't accelerate that fast.

That meant, of course, that the Womb was specifically targeting Kosha. It wanted the naval base and the colony, but for what?

Unless Morgan missed her guess and her math, the Womb would need to eat when it reached Kosha. To sustain itself, it needed to eat the planets and sun of each star system it arrived at. It was going to burn through most of the mass left to it in its captive sun just to reach Kosha.

But...sixty years. That wasn't quite the worst-case scenario, but it put the Womb's limits in perspective. To push an entire star's worth of mass, even ignoring whatever the Womb itself weighed, to that kind of velocity with a reaction engine...

It couldn't go that much faster; not with a glorified fusion rocket pushing a star. So, sixty years. Maybe fifty.

In a hundred long-cycles, the Imperium could move mountains. Build entire new fleets specifically intended to fight the Womb.

That it was headed for Kosha made it a *direct* threat to Imperial territory and Imperial citizens, but for all of its scale, power, and horrific diet...the Womb was far from an *immediate* threat.

Morgan would scout it out, and the Imperium would send a fleet. It would be handled and handled without any real danger to anyone.

So why did fear coil around her spine and keep her awake?

CHAPTER FORTY-SIX

DEFIANCE'S BRIDGE HUMMED WITH ACTIVITY. MORGAN SAT AT the center of that hum, a trained pattern of shifting attention keeping her aware of everything going on. Repeater screens on her chair arms let her pull up what any station on the bridge was looking at, and the main holoprojector showed the standard tactical display as well.

Everything was green. *Defiance's* weapons, engines, defenses and sensors were clear, and the minutes were ticking down toward the moment of truth. Even from six light-months away, there was only so much detail they'd been able to discern of a creature next to a star.

From the planned light-day, they'd be able to count its hairs. Assuming the Womb had hairs, that was.

"Emergence in five minutes," El-Amin reported. "Mass shadow is where we were expecting it." He paused. "It's bigger than I was expecting. I'm going to have to adjust our emergence."

"Understood," Morgan replied. "Tactical, be prepared for the unexpected."

"If anything out here twitches, it better flag an Imperial IFF fast or it's going to get shot," Nguyen said grimly. "Anomaly scanners are clear; I have no hyperspace contacts."

Morgan nodded silently as the seconds ticked down.

"I'm going to have to bring us out early, and I can't be certain of the range," the navigator told them all. "Mass shadow is significantly larger than expected. I'm not sure where the thing actually is."

"Understood," Morgan repeated. "Emergence, Commander?"

"Sixty seconds," El-Amin snapped. He tapped a command and opened a shipwide channel.

"All hands, this is Lesser Commander El-Amin. We are emerging early; stand by for portal translation."

Seconds ticked by and new icons popped up on Morgan's screens as power ran to her ship's exotic-matter emitters. They charged up, flashed on her screens, and then the main display showed them activating.

Outside of a combat situation, a portal was usually opened five to ten light-seconds ahead of a ship. It could be cut tighter if necessary, but the extra range gave a navigator time and a safety margin.

Safety margin if, for example, an unexpectedly variable mass shadow caused the portal to open three light-seconds closer than expected.

"Portal close, portal close!" El-Amin snapped. "Emergence!"

Despite the problems, *Defiance* slashed into normal space with most of her usual grace, the portal collapsing behind her as El-Amin twisted her through a ninety-degree turn to keep her from heading directly at their target.

The main holodisplay filled almost instantly, Nguyen's team standing by to pick up their prey, and Morgan felt the shock ripple across their bridge as they finally got a solid look at the Womb, the Great Mother —the alien artifact that an Imperial survey team had decided was a god.

Even in her worst nightmares, Morgan had envisaged the Womb as a parasite on the stars it consumed, a gas giant–sized tick or mosquito "drinking" the stars' plasma to consume it.

She was not prepared for the size of her prey. *Scale* wasn't a term she could apply—she had nothing to really give the Womb scale—but it was immense. It resembled its teardrop-like progeny in rough form, with a bulbous "head" that wrapped *around* the star, and a long tail, easily ten times as long as the star it was feeding on was wide, that extended out into space and presumably acted as a magnetic accelerator to turn starstuff into reaction mass.

"How...how big *is* that thing?" Morgan asked softly.

"It has the mass of an entire star system," Nguyen told her. "That's what screwed up El-Amin's calculations. We were expecting a subdwarf, maybe an orange dwarf. A tenth to a quarter of a solar mass.

"I'm reading just over *two* solar masses."

"It ate three star systems and metabolized them," Rogers said from secondary control. "Much of the stellar mass was expended as fuel, but that's still *three star systems*."

"How close are we? I can't tell from the display," Morgan snapped.

"Its size is confusing our systems... Maybe two light-hours. We came in far closer than we were planning," El-Amin admitted. "I am maintaining the range."

"It's two-point-three *million* kilometers from the top of the 'head' to the tip of the 'tail,'" Nguyen reported. "I'm not sure even our antimatter bombs are going to make a dent in that thing."

"They will if we bring enough of them," Morgan replied. "I need a confirm on the velocity vector."

Silence answered her as her bridge crew bent to their work. That wasn't a question that should have taken this long, but their scanners weren't designed for a creature with twice the mass and three times the size of Earth's sun.

"Vector remains on a direct line for the Kosha System," Nguyen finally confirmed. "Current velocity, eighteen-point-five percent of lightspeed. It is not currently accelerating or decelerating." She swallowed audibly.

"It is likely reserving what remains of the last sun it captured to sustain itself until it reaches Kosha and to provide deceleration at the other end," she concluded. "My god."

"People, *that* is a sun-eater," Morgan said as levelly as she could manage. "Its lack of speed contains it, but that is a clear and present threat to any and all civilizations near it.

"Our job is not to destroy it today," she continued. "As Lesser Commander Nguyen pointed out, our entire arsenal of HSMs would probably fail to kill it without far more precise targeting than we are capable of."

She smiled thinly.

"Which means, people, that our job is to get in close enough and get enough scan data that when we bring a real fleet to kill this thing, they *are* capable of that precision targeting."

Morgan gestured to El-Amin.

"Lesser Commander El-Amin, set our course for the sun-eater," she ordered. "In the absence of hostile activity, we will approach to one light-minute for detailed tachyon and lightspeed scans."

"You think it's going to let us that close?" Rogers asked.

"I think we're going to see how many bioships it has to defend itself in about two hours," Morgan replied. "We have the advantage in that they're not expecting us and they probably don't have hyper-fold-equipped sensor probes watching us.

"We will close in realspace at point-six *c*. At some point in the next three hours, we're going to encounter their defenders, and we'll see just what the Children and their 'Great Mother' are bringing to the party.

"I have no intention of risking this ship, people, but we need as much data as possible," she reminded them all. "The closer we can get, the better off we are. I am prepared to play cat and mouse with the Servants if that's what it takes, but if that thing has a weak point, I want to know."

Because she'd be far happier if they could take it out with two battleships in a few weeks than if they had to wait years to assemble a fleet.

Just because it was *currently* only traveling at eighteen and a half percent of lightspeed didn't mean that was as fast as it could go. Nine and a half light-years gave the Imperium space and time, but Morgan wasn't sure just how many risks she was willing to take with this kind of monster.

DEFIANCE'S JOURNEY toward the Womb was blisteringly fast by any objective standard, the cruiser's cruising speed of sixty percent of lightspeed crossing vast distances in moments.

The distance they were crossing was even more vast. Now that they understood what they were facing, Morgan knew that they could use a hyperspace jump to close the range—but speed wasn't the point anymore.

She wanted to see how the Womb—and the Children—reacted.

In two hours, they closed over half the distance to the Precursor monstrosity, but then the light of their arrival finally reached it. Their tachyon scanners didn't reach it yet, but the probes they'd sent ahead of them were twelve light-minutes closer.

Still not in tachyon-scanner range, but close enough that Morgan saw her enemy's reaction after thirty minutes instead of forty.

"Drones have contacts," Nguyen reported. "As expected, I'm seeing deployment of bioship Servants..."

Nguyen didn't need to continue her report. The red icons on the screen were visibly beyond counting, bubbling out of the Womb like an over-shaken soda. Not dozens. Not hundreds.

Thousands of bioships. Probably more. All of them accelerating toward *Defiance* at the same thousands of gravities as the Servants they'd encountered before.

"We can still evade them," El-Amin reported calmly. "I'm not sure we can get past them to get a decent scan of the creature itself, though."

"We are far more maneuverable than they are," Morgan replied.

"Nguyen. If there's a standard prefabricated base on that thing, how close would we need to get to detect it?"

"Like the one at D-L-T-Three?" her tactical officer asked. She paused for several seconds, everyone on the bridge watching as more Servants spilled out from the Womb.

"Within five light-minutes," she admitted. "And I couldn't be certain it didn't exist until about two light-minutes."

Thirty-six million kilometers. Morgan didn't bother to ask if tachyon sensors would help—the five-light-minute number told her that *was* using the tachyon scanners.

"At a thousand KPS squared, can they get into range of us before then?" Morgan asked.

"Easily," Nguyen admitted. "It will take us another fifty minutes to get that close. I'm not sure what their speed cap is, but they'll match our velocity in three minutes. Relative velocity gets *weird* at that point, but they'll intercept us about halfway."

"I don't suppose they're all being so helpful as to charge right at us like that?"

"Negative," the tactical officer replied. "Looks like 'only' about five hundred of them are headed straight for us. We've got about three thousand units spreading out in a cone around that, creating an interception zone we'd almost certainly have to pass through to reach the Womb itself."

"And how many are staying behind?" Morgan asked.

"About another four thousand," Nguyen said. "I've got about eight thousand Servants on the screens, and some of them are *big*. It looks like there's a core of battleship-sized units in the force hanging back to defend the Womb."

Morgan was silent, studying the situation. She could reverse *Defiance*'s velocity in six seconds, turn her headlong charge into a headlong flight. The cruiser could dance circles around the Servants in her sleep, but...

She shook her head.

"El-Amin, ninety-degree vector change, port and up," she ordered. "Let's circle for the moment and see what they do."

"They have the interior position, sir," Rogers warned over their private channel. "And enough acceleration to make sure we can't get through."

"I know," Morgan agreed behind her privacy screen. "But they can't force us into a fight, not with reaction drives."

"No. But we're twenty light-minutes out, and I'm not sure how much closer we can get, sir," her First Sword told her. "I'm not sure we're going to get into five light-minutes. The Servants are already starting to shoot down sensor probes."

Morgan checked the status of their forward probes and grimaced. Nguyen had set up several patterns at fixed distances from *Defiance*, moving her real-time sensor range forward, but the farthest pattern had now collided with the Servants and was getting picked off by precision plasma blasts from the living ships.

"We need to get closer," she said aloud. "If we cut around to the other side in hyperspace, that will at least leave this bunch heading in the wrong direction at a good chunk of lightspeed."

"We're only going to get one group of the things headed the wrong way, sir," Rogers warned. "They're too fast—and they're only going to fall for that once. We've scouted the target, Captain. It might be time to fall back and bring in bigger guns."

Morgan nodded, dropping the privacy screen and studying the screen again. There were a lot of bioships out there, and they seemed determined to chase her.

"Sir?" Nystrom's voice sounded concerned. No one had been expecting the communications officer to have much role in today's work, but her battle station was on the bridge.

"Lesser Commander?" Morgan replied.

"We just got pulsed with one *hell* of a radio wave," the coms officer told her. "Not a sensor pulse. A com transmission. It looks like a compressed data burst—I have it isolated on a secure server."

"A data burst? From who?" Morgan asked.

"Unless I'm missing my numbers, from the Womb itself."

Defiance's Captain exhaled a long breath.

"Can you translate it without risking it trying to run code on our systems?" she asked.

"Easily. It appears to be an audio-only transmission, but we have security protocols for this," Nystrom promised her.

"How long to translate it?"

"A minute or two at most," Nystrom said.

"Do it. I'm guessing that's from the Children, and I'm *fascinated* to hear what they have to say."

THE MESSAGE WASN'T from the Children of the Stars.

"*I. See. You.*" The clearly artificial voice echoed around the bridge. Morgan had kept the message playback limited to there, but as she watched the impact ripple through her bridge crew, she began to think she should have limited it even more.

"*You. Squirm. In. My. Space.*" The words fell like tombstones into a shocked silence. It wasn't translated, which raised disturbing questions to Morgan. Not only was the Womb able to talk to them, but it had known that *Defiance* had a human crew.

Or was it just that the main people it had dealt with had been human?

"*You. Hurt. My. Spawn. You. Tear. My. Space. You. Stink. Of. Energy. You. Stink. Of. Food.*"

"My god," Rogers muttered. "It hasn't encountered an MC unit before."

The power plant that drove *Defiance*'s engines and weapons was a matter-conversion core, converting mass directly to energy in a process that Morgan only loosely understood.

"It's seen antimatter, but not matter conversion. Fuck. We are a *perfect* target for it," Nguyen said, finishing the First Sword's thought.

"Come. To. Me. Join. Me. Yield. The. Food. You. Flesh. Mind. Not. Food. Yield. The. Food. You. Do. Not. Need. To. Die. Yield. The. Food."

Nystrom cut off the playback.

"I suspect it continues along the same pattern for a while," she said drily. "I assume we're not handing the sun-eating supermonster our matter-conversion power core?"

"Not a chance in hell," Morgan replied. "It's already dangerous enough. I don't want to think about what it could do using an MC core for additional power."

"What the—?!" Nguyen suddenly snapped. "Sir! The sun-eater!"

"What?" Morgan's attention snapped back to the main display and a chill ran down her spine. The Womb's speed hadn't changed, but its velocity *vector* had. Suddenly, it was moving at eighteen-point-five percent of lightspeed toward *Defiance*. It had flipped its vector one hundred and twenty degrees in a moment.

"That's not possible with what we've seen of its maneuvers," Morgan said grimly.

"I'm running the sensor history and I've got a blip of what looked like the mother of all interface drives," Nguyen told her. "Wait...there it goes again."

The sun-eater was now moving at *twenty* percent of lightspeed. No apparent acceleration.

"It has an interface drive?" Rogers demanded. "How? That thing is *huge*."

"I'm not sure it is an interface drive as we understand it," the tactical officer replied. "Liepins, does this scan data make any sense to you?"

"No..." the chief engineer replied on his dedicated channel. "What the hell am I looking at, Lesser Commander? This...this looks like an interface drive flaring and burning out. The entire life cycle of a missile in under a second, but on a scale..."

"On the scale required to create a device that would *push* a creature that contains a star," Morgan said softly. Another pulse flashed across their sensors, and the Womb was now moving at twenty-one-point-five percent of lightspeed.

"It couldn't build an interface-drive field that could encompass it. It *could* create an expendable push tug that uses a catastrophic field collapse to push itself. It's basically hitting itself with a giant version of our missiles just to move."

Twenty-four percent of lightspeed. The pulses were increasing in frequency and power, though not up to the original spike that had completely reversed the Womb's velocity.

"We need to move and we need to move now," Morgan ordered. "El-Amin, open a hyper portal. Get us *out* of here."

"There is a two-solar-mass object heading toward us at over twenty percent of lightspeed," her navigator said, his voice disturbingly calm. The calm that lay beyond terror. "I'm not even sure I can run the calculations to create a portal under those circumstances, sir. Certainly, it can't be done quickly."

"Then get us moving in realspace until you can," Morgan snapped. "Commander Nguyen?"

"Sir!"

"Stand by all weapons batteries. If that thing can build a tug to push itself, then..."

"Multiple interface-drive contacts!" one of Nguyen's senior NCOs suddenly barked. "I'm reading at least twelve battleship-sized interface-drive contacts, current velocity point-six-five *c*."

Morgan nodded and bowed her head.

"Like Wendira fighter craft, they aren't concerned about protecting the crew," she said softly. "They can outpace with interface drives, and the Womb itself is screwing with our hyperspace portal.

"Estimated time to range?" she asked.

"That depends on whether they have anything we're not expecting," Nguyen admitted. "We'll have HSM range on them in five minutes. If they've only got plasma guns upsized along with the rest of them and we turn to keep the range open, they won't bring us into plasma range for ninety minutes after that.

"But if they've got any other surprises to go along with the interface drives, your guess is as good as mine."

"El-Amin, keep the range as open as you can," Morgan ordered. "Hold back on our sprint capability for now. I don't know if the Servants know we have it, so let's keep it as a surprise."

She looked at the tactical plot again and swallowed a bitter sigh.

"Any sign of modern vessels or the Children at all?" she asked.

"If they're there, we can't see them behind eight thousand bioships," Nguyen admitted. "Womb is now up to thirty percent of lightspeed, sir. I don't know how fast it can get."

Morgan checked a note on the communication systems. Nine-point-five light-years meant nine and a half hours' hyperfold-transmission time. Any request for reinforcements would take ten hours to reach anyone. Another ten hours for even a *message* to get back.

At least three cycles for reinforcements, and Kosha Station had no reinforcements to send. They'd send telemetry uploads, but there was no help coming.

"El-Amin, how much distance do you need to jump us out?" she demanded.

"I don't know, sir," the navigator admitted. "We're trying to run the numbers, but our calculations, our nav computers...none of our models are designed to handle mobile objects with multiple stellar masses. We could need as much as a light-day of clearance. And it's still accelerating."

It seemed unlikely that the Womb could match her ship's sixty-percent cruising speed. It was almost certainly counting on its much faster progeny to bring her to heel—the big interface-drive Servants had passed the main swarm now, but the rest of the Servants were still accelerating after Morgan.

A light-day of clearance. Morgan was reasonably sure she could take out the big Servants chasing her. Interface drives made them more maneuverable, more able to avoid her hyperspace missiles, and their sheer size meant they could probably take a hit from the big antimatter warheads.

Maybe. Even a modern battleship could go down to a lucky HSM. While the weapons didn't count on it, it was certainly a *possibility* for them to emerge inside their targets.

"Assume our targets don't know about HSMs and won't start maneuvering until we hit them," Morgan told Nguyen calmly. "Also assume they're going to maneuver as much as we would facing an HSM-equipped ship as soon as we have hit them.

"Maximize your opening salvo, Commander. If we can punch half of those big bastards off the map in the first round, we've got a better chance of getting through this."

There were answers to the situation. The easiest was to run. Push the sprint mode as long as she could, to the point of making her crew sick and crippling her ship, to get them out. The most straightforward was to fight, to hit the big Servants fast and hard and swing out on a different vector, hoping the Womb couldn't completely change its velocity vector the same way again.

"Captain, Dr. Dunst is requesting to speak with you," Nystrom told her quietly. "He says it's important."

Now was not the time for her not-quite-boyfriend to be trying to talk to her, Morgan knew— but she also knew that Rin Dunst had a good sense for what was important. And the last time he'd thought something was important and she hadn't, *he'd* been right.

"Link him through," she replied. "Let's draw this out, people. This isn't a fight we can win, so let's make the Womb *pay* to bring it to us before we get the hell out of here."

CHAPTER FORTY-SEVEN

"Mo—Captain Casimir," Dunst greeted her.

The correction had clearly come the moment the scientist had realized Morgan didn't have the privacy screen up. She couldn't really, not with an active fight about to descend on her ship.

"Dr. Dunst. What do you need?" she asked. "It's not a great time."

"I'm running over the data you're getting," he told her. "I'm the guy who isn't tied up in the moment or trying to keep the ship alive, so that lets me look at the data in a way you can't."

"What did you find?"

"The interface drives on those ships? They're not an installation," Dunst said flatly. "The Children didn't build and install a modern interface drive on them. They grew it themselves.

"The Womb adapts faster and more effectively than our worst nightmares. It's not using tech built for it by the Children. It's grown its own interface drives *and* it's worked out how to get around the fact that the drive just can't move its entire mass."

"It's a much bigger threat than we think," Morgan said softly as what he was saying sank in. She'd been expecting decades—a lifetime, really—before the Womb threatened Kosha, but he was right. It was moving at over thirty percent of lightspeed now to chase her. Even if it failed to acquire *Defiance*'s matter-conversion core, it would reach Kosha in twenty years at most. Still time, but not enough time that it could be dismissed as a threat for later.

"You're not following it all the way through, Captain," Dunst said quickly. "The armor scales on the Servants? They're a form of compressed matter. For us, compressed matter is an inversion of the process for making *exotic* matter.

"It needs exotic matter for interface drives, so the Womb has obviously made that leap."

"Yes, I get that," Morgan agreed. "Doctor, this is not the time to play teacher and see if I can follow along. We're opening fire on the interface-equipped Servants in the next ninety seconds."

"If the Womb can build interface drives, it can build a hyperdrive."

The Captain's seat beneath Morgan seemed to fall away beneath her. A hyperdrive. Of course. The two technologies were inextricably linked—her father had developed humanity's interface drive *from* their hyperspace technology.

If the Womb could give its children interface drives, it could give them hyperdrives.

"That does increase the threat level of its progeny, yes," she said grimly. "Thank you, Dr. Dunst."

"Captain Casimir, even we could build a hyper portal big enough for that thing," the xenoarcheologist reminded her. "It would take more exotic matter than an entire *fleet* of superbattleships, but we could do it.

"That's what it's conserving that sun for, Captain. That's what it wants *Defiance*'s power core for. So it can create enough exotic matter to build a hyperdrive for itself. It's not a question of *if* it will; it's a question of *when*."

"And then of how many stars it eats before we can gather a fleet big enough to stop it...and how big it gets from eating them," Morgan finished. She stared at the creature on her screen and felt the weight of the galaxy settle on her shoulders.

"We need to call in heavy firepower," Dunst told her. "This is more important than we thought it was. More important than the wars we're watching. My god, Captain...the Alava wouldn't have designed it to self-reproduce, but given enough mass and enough power, it probably can. Life finds a way, and the Womb is alive."

"So, we have to kill it," she said, very softly. "We can't escape, Dr. Dunst. We're trapped right now. Our hyperspace portal emitters can't handle mobile objects of this magnitude in their vicinity. I can call for help, but I'm not sure I can escape."

The channel was silent.

"Morgan," he said, his voice nearly a whisper in the probably vain hope that no one else heard him speaking. "You *have* to destroy *Defiance* before letting it take her conversion core."

"It won't come to that," Morgan told him, her voice very calm, very level. "Thank you, Dr. Dunst. Your analysis is invaluable and has been critical in the decision I have to make.

"The bridge is now being sealed under protocols you are not cleared for. The situation *will* be dealt with."

The channel cut and Morgan felt every eye in the room focus on her.

"Computer," she ordered, her voice still far calmer than felt remotely reasonable to her. "Seal the bridge under Final Dragon Protocols."

ALL THAT HAS BEEN CREATED CAN BE recreated, and history turns in cycles.

Over thirty years earlier, Morgan Casimir's stepmother had earned humanity's Duchy by destroying a dozen miniaturized starkillers built by a terrorist faction and intended to rekindle the war between the A!Tol and the Kanzi.

The Imperium *now* knew those weapons had been reverse-engineered from a stolen Mesharom weapon that not even the Core Powers had been brave enough to touch. With access to the Mesharom Archive, the A!Tol hadn't needed to reverse-engineer the technology.

They'd simply built a small but growing number of exact duplicates of the Mesharom weapon, the Final Dragon–class strategic weapons. Each was approximately a third of the size of one of Morgan's assault shuttles, and each was just as capable of inducing a near-instantaneous supernova as the regular destroyer-sized weapons.

"Everything you see and hear from now on is classified under the Final Dragon Protocols," Morgan told her bridge crew. "If you breathe a word of what you are told or what we do now, you will face prosecution under Imperial law for violation of Dragon Protocol classifications."

Her people knew what that meant. The Imperium didn't believe in the death penalty, but part of that was that they had *worse* options. The Dragon Protocols protected secrets they needed to keep from the Core Powers.

The best case someone could hope for would be a lifetime imprisonment. The rarely deployed mind wipe was a distinct possibility.

Looking around, Morgan was certain her people understood.

"Commander Nguyen, I am releasing the performance specifications on our Omega Battery to your console," she continued. "With Commander Rogers sealed out in Secondary Control, I require your cross-authentication for the deployment of strategic weaponry."

A new chill ran through the bridge.

"Sir, this is... Sir."

"This ship is equipped with three Mesharom-designed miniaturized starkiller weapons," Morgan told her flatly. "I require your cross-authentication for their deployment. We will need to penetrate the Servant formation to a range of three light-minutes to deploy the weapons, but I believe that star still has sufficient mass that its nova *will* kill the Womb."

The bridge was silent, but Nguyen nodded and tapped commands on her screen.

"I agree with your assessment of the range, sir," she noted. "I authenticate authorization for the deployment of strategic weaponry."

"Confirmed. Omega Battery is released to your control," Morgan said clearly. She would have to defend this to an inquiry, probably one close enough to a court-martial as to make the distinction entirely academic.

But there was a reason that the Captain of a warship equipped with strategic weapons had the codes to fire them without anyone else's authorization. She entered those codes now, watching as an entirely new section appeared on the tactical display, three icons flicking to green as the deadliest weapons in the galaxy confirmed they were active and ready for deployment.

"Lesser Commander El-Amin, on my command, we will set our course directly for the Womb and engage full sprint mode," Morgan told her navigator. "Hopefully, the extra speed will confuse our targets sufficiently to get us close enough to deploy the starkillers.

"Lesser Commander Nguyen, you will program the targeting for the Final Dragon weapons yourself. Your staff will assume control of our primary weapons. All batteries are clear for fire at maximum rate until we are out of weapons.

"We need to punch a hole in, and we need to punch a hole out."

"Sir, I suggest we arrange some kind of decoys to cover the starkillers' approach," Nguyen said. "Interface drive missiles can help, but the starkillers will stand out as larger targets."

"Coordinate with Commander Liepins and Commander Vichy," Morgan ordered. "They can be cleared for this if necessary, but we need to commandeer Commander Vichy's shuttles.

"We get one salvo of three shots, people. Only one needs to connect, but we need to survive to fire, and at least one needs to get through."

CHAPTER FORTY-EIGHT

THE BATTLE JOINED AS ORIGINALLY PLANNED, THE TWELVE massive Servants entering range of *Defiance*'s tachyon sensors and her hyperspace missiles simultaneously. Nguyen's team took a few seconds to lock in the current course of targets that didn't know they needed to be dodging, and then fired.

Normally, an interior hit was pure luck—but this enemy didn't even know it was a possibility. Four HSMs targeted each of the leading Servants and at least one arrived inside each of them.

One moment, twelve battleship-scale biological warships were plunging toward Morgan's command at a relative five percent of lightspeed.

The next, Nguyen's six targets were expanding clouds of debris that Morgan didn't really want to see a close analysis of.

The surviving six were slow to start evasive maneuvering, but they were fast enough that the second salvo only got one interior hit. The other missiles made their close-range attack runs at a quarter of the speed of light, with over half missing or being shot down.

A second Servant died in a cascade of antimatter explosions, but Morgan knew that was their last easy shot. The third salvo didn't kill any of them, though leaking liquids and vapors were clear on the scanners.

"The shuttles will be prepped in five minutes," Nguyen said quietly. "If we turn now, we won't be in deployment range for seven. Your orders, sir?"

A fourth salvo lashed the Servants, and Morgan watched in silence. This was the safest part of the fight, and part of her wanted to draw it out. There were arguments both ways, too, but she wasn't sure how much of it was just to avoid the ravaging she knew her ship was going to take when she tried to punch through the expanding net of lesser Servants coming her way behind the interface-drive ships.

"I don't suppose the Womb is going to push through her guardians and leave itself exposed, is it?" she asked aloud.

"The sun-eater appears to have settled at forty-two percent of lightspeed," Nguyen told her. "The main swarm is holding velocity at half of light. Scans suggest they *can* go faster."

"They're waiting to see how the biggest and baddest do," Morgan concluded. The answer was *poorly*. A ninth Servant died under her ship's missiles, leaving only a quarter of the original squadron to continue their hopefully fruitless pursuit.

"We hold the course until the last of the interface drive units is dead," she ordered. "Or until they demonstrate they can threaten us at this range."

The range was still over a hundred million kilometers. They were outside the range of the *starkillers*, let alone the Servants' more conventional weapons.

Unfortunately, the need to deliver the weapon *into* a sun had negated using an HSM chassis to deliver the starkillers. The Mesharom, who used a missile that generated both of its own hyperspace portals, hadn't bothered. The Imperium, who generated the entry portal aboard the launching starship, couldn't fit the weapons through their current generation of launchers.

A realspace deployment was required. The weapons had a long range, but today, that range wasn't enough.

"Battleship Servants are improving their evasive maneuvers but not...enough," Nguyen reported. Only one remained. "They also appear to have not mastered retreat."

Twenty-four missiles flashed through hyperspace and bracketed the surviving bioship in an inescapable globe. When the half-*teraton* of explosions faded, only debris remained.

"Hostile squadron destroyed," the tactical officer continued. "Main swarm continues on course at fifty percent of lightspeed."

"Let's give them a moment to see what they do," Morgan ordered. "Come on," she murmured to her distant opponent. "You don't want me to get away. You want my power core and you've got an inner shell of defenders still. *Bring it,* you ancient bitch."

Silence reigned on *Defiance*'s bridge for several seconds.

"Main swarm is splitting," Nguyen reported. "We've thirty-five hundred units chasing us in a great big net, and they are breaking into two formations. Still a net big enough to catch our vectors toward the Womb, but half are maintaining point-five *c* and half are now accelerating toward us."

"A thousand KPS squared still?" Morgan asked.

"Yes, sir."

"Let them come," she ordered. She watched the velocity of her targets scream upwards. A hundred and fifty-five thousand kilometers a second. A hundred and sixty. A hundred and seventy.

A hundred and eighty thousand. Now they matched *Defiance*'s velocity and continued to accelerate.

"They can't slow down from this speed, can they?" Morgan asked softly.

"Best guess is they have a little over one-point-one *c* of delta-*v*," El-Amin told her. "Once they're over sixty percent of lightspeed, somebody's going to have to catch them."

"Or the Womb is writing them off to try and catch *us*."

A hundred and ninety-five thousand kilometers per second. Sixty-five percent of lightspeed, heading directly toward *Defiance*.

"Do they have a chance in hell of being able to target us as we interpenetrate?" Morgan asked.

"We don't with any of our sublight weapons," Nguyen admitted. "I can launch a spread of interface missiles as we close, but the only close-range weapon I can hit them with is the hyperfold cannons. Our plasma weapons are useless at that speed."

"Well, that does answer the important question, doesn't it?" the Captain said with a small smile.

"Lesser Commander El-Amin, Lesser Commander Nguyen...*execute.*"

SIX SECONDS. That was the time period necessary to completely change the vector of an interface drive.

One moment, *Defiance* was plunging directly away from the Womb at sixty percent of the speed of light, pursued by an immense swarm of bioships. Half of those bioships were slowly starting to gain on her, potentially sacrificing themselves for the chance to catch the Imperial cruiser.

Six seconds later, she was plunging into the teeth of that pursuing swarm at *seventy* percent of the speed of light.

There were a dozen reasons that no Imperial ship had a standard cruise speed of over sixty percent of light. It was energy-intensive and damaging to the engines. The dampeners used to contain the gravitic warping of an interface drive started to fail at those speeds, making it dangerous for the crew.

And, most relevant right now, at those velocities, even Imperial sensors started getting confused. Even though the interface drive didn't play fair with either Newton *or* Einstein most of the time, velocities measured in fractions of the speed of light did not add neatly.

Morgan's ship charged toward the bioships at seventy percent of light and they charged at her at just over sixty percent—but their *true* relative velocity was only around ninety-two percent of lightspeed.

That velocity still consumed the light-minutes between them with blistering speed.

"Targeting hyperfold cannon directly ahead," Nguyen reported. "Launching sublight missiles and allocating HSMs."

New icons appeared on *Defiance*'s plots as her standard missile launchers spoke. The missiles were fifteen percent of lightspeed faster than their mothership, and they plunged into the swarm ahead of her.

"Bogies are firing. I am evading," El-Amin said, his tone utterly flat. "Enemy targeting is badly degraded by relative velocities and their own dilation effects."

Morgan hadn't even considered that. *Defiance* didn't suffer from time dilation—a reduced degree of *distance* dilation, yes, but not time dilation—but the Servants were using reaction drives. They were fully subject to regular physics.

"They're still shooting down the missiles," Nguyen reported. "They're going to hit us."

"I know," Morgan conceded. "Liepins, keep my shields up. We'll cross the entire range envelope of the first swarm in under a minute. We have to survive that."

The first swarm was seventeen hundred Servants, averaging over a million tons apiece. The second swarm was eighteen hundred, averaging a little under a million tons apiece.

"The problem is the third swarm," Morgan murmured. There were still two thousand Servants directly accompanying the Womb, averaging over *two* million tons apiece. Some of them easily approached the ten-million-ton monsters they'd already smashed with the HSMs.

"We'll be on the right side of the first two swarms when we launch the starkillers," she noted more loudly. "The last defensive swarm is the problem."

"The decoy shuttles will help, but we have to draw their attention," Nguyen said grimly. "I'm not seeing a lot of ways to do that."

"I only see one," Morgan agreed. "El-Amin...we're not turning back once we launch the starkillers. We're going right past that thing and we're cutting through the range of the defensive swarm."

"We can avoid their range, sir," he argued.

"But they can almost certainly shoot down the starkillers, Lesser Commander, and nothing else in our magazines is going to take that thing out. We *have* to draw their attention."

And while she wasn't going to say it, Morgan knew that if came down to trading *Defiance* for the sun-eater, the Imperium came out ahead. She suspected the whole damn *galaxy* came out ahead.

"Entering estimated range of the first swarm in thirty seconds," Nguyen reported. "Engaging with hyperfold cannon on our target list." There was a long pause. "If I have to fight a battle outnumbered five thousand to one, can I at least fight an enemy that *doesn't* take my best hits and keep coming?"

"Keep your fire spread," Morgan ordered. "We're better off right now with fifty Servants who can't energize a full beam than with five who are vaporized."

"Maintaining fire spread," the tactical officer confirmed. "We're landing solid hits, sir, but it's taking at least half a dozen before they're even acting like we *touched* them. I miss our own plasma lances."

Almost in answer to Nguyen's words—their own long-range plasma weaponry required a metallic or interface-drive target to an extent that made the Servants immune to it—the bioships opened fire. Near-lightspeed blasts of plasma littered the empty void around *Defiance,* and El-Amin twisted the ship like an angry seagull.

Hits still landed, but Liepins was watching the shields. Sectors flashed red as plasma beams nearly overwhelmed them, only to quickly flash back to orange as Engineering rebalanced power from the surrounding sections.

It was robbing Peter to pay Paul, and it *worked*. Ten seconds passed. Twenty. *Thirty*, and *Defiance*'s shields were still up.

But the range was *nothing* now. They'd avoided the center of the net the Servants had cast, but they couldn't move far enough to avoid still having bioships on all sides. They just didn't have several *hundred* bioships in any given direction.

Part of Morgan had hoped the Servants were stupid enough to injure each other as *Defiance* penetrated their formation, but they showed no signs of it. They exerted a level of situational awareness and fire control she wouldn't have expected from less than an experienced Imperial fleet.

Nguyen had focused her fire from the beginning, continually opening a larger and larger hole of dead or crippled Servants. There were no functioning bioships within half a million kilometers of the point where the cruiser flashed through the Swarm—but half a million kilometers was bad enough.

The shields went down. Not individual sectors. Enough hits came in simultaneously that *Defiance*'s overpowered shields, based on a design stolen from the Taljzi and updated with select Mesharom technology, just...went down.

"Liepins!"

If Morgan's engineer replied to her barked challenge, she didn't hear him as warning chimes rang out around her, matching icons flashing across her display.

"We've been hit," Liepins said grimly. "Multiple breaches on multiple decks, armor integrity is down to under forty percent. Shields...shields are cycling. Why are we still alive, Captain?"

It took Morgan a moment to work out just what Liepins was asking. They weren't being shot at. They'd punched through the swarm...and now no one was shooting at them.

"Commander Nguyen?" she asked. "What happened?"

"They're having problems turning around," the tactical officer reported. "They don't have shields or interface-drive fields. At those velocities, there's enough particle density even out here to cause actual friction."

"They can't turn," Morgan repeated, studying the screen. The icons of the enemy units were clear, pointed in the same direction they had for the last few hours. Days? Minutes? Morgan's sense of time was getting messy.

"They can't turn quickly; that's for sure. We're...we're going to be out of range, I think, before they've flipped."

"Hold your fire, then," Morgan ordered. "Focus on the second swarm; stand by. We only have a few minutes until we hit them."

She turned to Liepins.

"Any way we can keep the shields up next time?" she asked. "I'm not sure we can take that again, Lesser Commander."

"We can't," Lesser Commander Liepins said grimly. "Blow a bigger hole? I'm not sure there's anything I can do, Captain."

"Understood."

Morgan shook her head and looked at the display. Less than two minutes until they entered range of the second swarm. That group was moving slower as well, adding another ten seconds to the time they'd be in range.

At forty percent of light, *this* swarm was going to be able to turn.

"El-Amin, can you get us farther from the center?" she asked.

"If I do, we move away from the hole Commander Nguyen is blowing with the missiles," her navigator pointed out.

A dozen or more Servants were already dead or crippled as Nguyen blazed her way through *Defiance*'s magazines.

"And I can't punch a new one," the tactical officer reported grimly as a new set of red icons appeared on Morgan's displays. "We are out of hyperspace missiles. They killed us a few hundred million tons of these things, but we're down to interface missiles and the hyperfold cannons."

"Then we go through the hole we've made," Morgan conceded with a sigh. "Any ideas, people?"

Defiance's bridge was silent as the seconds ticked away. The swarm they were charging toward was still six light-minutes short of the Womb itself. The immense Precursor creature continued to charge toward them at forty-two percent of light itself, seemingly eager to bring Morgan's ship within its grasp.

She didn't want to know what defenses the sun-eater could muster itself. At the minimum, she suspected the massive fusion thruster it no longer needed could function as the biggest plasma cannon in existence. It wasn't currently pointed at *Defiance*, though, and she doubted a creature that massed as much as two stars could turn quickly enough to aim that engine.

"I have an idea," El-Amin admitted. "It's a terrible idea and I don't know if it will work."

"Will it keep us alive?" Morgan demanded.

"It'll buy us about half a second," the navigator told her. "If that. But..."

"Based off the last punch, half a second might just save us all. Do it," Morgan ordered.

She didn't ask what his plan was.

She didn't really want to know.

CHAPTER FORTY-NINE

THE CHARGE TOWARD THE SECOND SWARM WENT MUCH THE same as the first. Plasma washed over the shields, but Liepins kept them up. It went so much like the first, Morgan *knew* the Servants were preparing something.

"They're conserving their fire and adjusting their positions," Rogers's voice said in her ear. "I don't know what you're planning, sir," her First Sword continued, "but I suspect that if we get hit with the full fire of five hundred Servants at the same time, it isn't going to happen."

Secondary Control's links to the bridge were now mostly open, a necessity for running the ship in a battle. Only the bridge crew had needed to be briefed on Final Dragon, which bought Morgan's executive officer a bit of grace.

Even if the bridge was destroyed—difficult to do without destroying the entire ship—the starkillers would launch now. Commander Bethany Rogers could never be held responsible for Morgan's decision.

The Final Dragon starkillers were, after all, one of the Imperium's most deeply held secrets. Morgan suspected she was about to fire a tenth of the Imperium's entire arsenal of the weapons.

"I'd like to live through my plan," Morgan conceded to Rogers. "So, I'm crossing my fingers for whatever El-Amin has come up with."

She had a pretty good sense what it was, and she had to admit she was in full agreement with her navigator.

It was a terrible idea and she didn't know if it was going to work.

"Penetration in ten seconds," El-Amin reported. "Portal formation in nine. Eight. Seven."

A hyperspace portal wasn't impenetrable, but by its very nature, what went through it went somewhere else.

Better, though worse from any perspective except this one trick, they knew that they couldn't manage a stable portal. The exotic-matter emitters would be pulsing rapidly, creating and losing multiple portals in a second as they tried to punch through a barrier too warped by the rapid movement of the Womb to allow a solid portal.

That would strain the emitters—but it would also provide *Defiance* with a shield that moved with her. For a bit.

El-Amin had guessed half a second. Morgan had privately estimated a third of that. They were both wrong.

"Unstable portal pattern in place," the navigator snapped, the words already taking longer than Morgan had expected to have the shield. "Maintaining in position—pattern lost, we've lost the pattern... we're through."

They were. The portal pattern had held for two and a half critical seconds.

"Shields are still up," Liepins reported. "Beaten to shit—we only blocked fire from one side—but the shields are still up."

"They focused everything on trying to hit us, and El-Amin scattered that across a few dozen light-seconds of hyperspace," Rogers said with satisfaction. "Can we do that again?"

There was a long pause while the navigator twisted the cruiser around the incoming fire as the swarm turned to ineffectually chase after them.

"Not if we want to leave," El-Amin finally said. "Liepins?"

"We lost the pattern when we blew one of the main emitters," the engineer said grimly. "I've got drones already moving out to repair it, but we only have enough parts to do that once. Blow another main emitter, and I need an asteroid and a week before we can open a portal."

"And we need to get out of here," Morgan replied. "Nguyen. Range?"

"Ninety seconds to three light-minutes. Do we...do we get closer before we launch?"

Morgan studied the map. The final defensive swarm was now accelerating toward her and would reach range at about ninety light-seconds from the Womb. She didn't know what the Womb had for defenses either, though she doubted it could accurately target her ship at almost thirty million kilometers.

"Hold to one hundred light-seconds," she ordered. "Then execute. El-Amin, I need to cut us close enough to the last defenders to draw as much of their attention as possible, but we need to be far enough out to hit the gas and get the *hell* out as soon as the starkillers are through."

"Yes, sir," the replies chorused.

Morgan leaned back in her chair and studied the display in front of her. *Defiance* was battered but unbroken. Her screens warned they'd fired off most of their interface-drive missiles at this point too, but her ship had made it as far as she needed to.

They could still fail. They could still *die*, even if they succeeded.

But no force in the universe could stop *Defiance* from launching her starkillers at this point.

"INITIATING LAUNCH SEQUENCE. Missiles in holding pattern. Drone shuttles deploying. First wave drone shuttles in holding pattern. Second missile salvo in holding pattern."

Icons spilled out of *Defiance* on the display as seconds ticked away. The announcement she was waiting for, the one that she had prayed to *never* hear in her entire life once she'd understood what *Defiance* carried, followed.

"Final Dragon authorizations processed. Final Dragon *Defiance*-One, deployed. First decoy wave forming up. Final Dragon *Defiance*-Two, deployed. Second decoy wave forming up.

"Final Dragon *Defiance*-Three, deployed. Holding for third wave of decoys to finish deploying."

Nguyen's steady sequence of reports belayed the tension in the bridge. They were back under Final Dragon lockdown, with secondary control still only getting half the information.

There was no way to hide what Morgan had just done, but the purpose of the secrecy wasn't to protect Rogers from *knowing* what had happened. It was to protect Morgan's XO from ever having to take *responsibility* for what had happened.

"All decoy waves ready. All Final Dragons deployed." The bridge was so quiet, Morgan was certain *everyone* heard Lesser Commander Thu Nguyen swallow before she hit the last button.

"Final Dragon launch complete."

The icons lit up with bright colors as all of them brought their interface drives online in a single moment. The shuttles' drives had been stripped of safety systems and overloaded to allow them to run at the same eighty percent of lightspeed as the starkillers.

The missiles had always been able to be stepped down to that speed. The starkillers were just too big to be propelled by the Imperium's latest point-eight-five missile drive.

"That's us, people," Morgan told them. "Whether we succeed is in the hands of God now. El-Amin, decoy course, if you please. Nguyen? Cover those missiles."

"We can only sustain the sprint for fifteen minutes at most," her navigator warned. "That...is unlikely to be enough to get clear."

"It will have to be," Morgan told him. "Take us through their formation, Commander El-Amin. Commander Liepins, keep those shields up no matter what. We're *going* to live through this, people.

"And then everything is going to be *so* classified, you won't even be able to tell the story for drinks!"

The laugh she got from her bridge crew was strained, probably forced in some cases, but it was there. It released at least some of the tension in the room, allowing people to focus on their roles as their plan unfolded.

"That's it," Nguyen said a few seconds later as the missile launchers flashed red on Morgan's display. "That's the last of our missiles, sir. We're down to hyperfold cannon."

"Do what you can," Morgan ordered. *Defiance* had now expended nearly every resource aboard that could be expended. Every shuttle, every drone—even the expensive new stealth shuttles— was acting as a decoy for the starkillers. Every missile had been fired. She couldn't even send her Marines to board a ship without delivering them with *Defiance* herself.

"Swarm is targeting the decoy groups, but they're focusing on us," Nguyen admitted. "We're losing decoys, but all Final Dragon munitions remain intact."

There was a moment of silence.

"Final Dragon units have penetrated the swarm and are moving toward the sun-eater," the tactical officer reported. "I repeat, *all* Final Dragon units have penetrated the enemy defense."

"And that, Commander El-Amin, is your cue," Morgan said with forced brightness. "Get us the *fuck* out of here!"

Defiance spun in space, rotating through a seventy-degree turn in seconds as she reoriented as directly away from everything as she could and went to maximum sprint almost directly opposite the sun-eater's vector.

"Range is opening at point-eight-six c relative," he snapped. "Time to contact?"

"Sixty seconds," Nguyen reported. "I have live data feeds from the probes in the decoy swarms— What the *hell?*"

"Commander?" Morgan demanded.

"I have three *Imperial* destroyers launching from the sun-eater," the tactical officer said swiftly. "Scanners make them *Unyielding Stance*–class ships. Warbook says older units, pre-Taljzi Campaigns, but they have full fourth-generation Sword and Buckler."

Sword and Buckler was the automated turret-and-drone antimissile system carried by every Imperial warship. Designed by Morgan's father with the help of data *acquired* during her stepmother's sojourn as a privateer, their installation had helped fuel the Duchy of Terra's rise to prominence in the Imperium.

The only good news was that the fourth-generation system was still a purely laser-based system, lacking the hyperfold cannons built into the *seventh*-generation system that *Defiance* carried.

Morgan's ship could take all three destroyers, even with her munitions expended—but to do it, she'd have to turn around and head right back through the defending swarm.

"Commander Nystrom," she said quietly. "We've been sending live telemetry back to Kosha Station this entire time, correct?"

"Yes, sir," her coms officer confirmed. "The relevant portions have been secured under Final Dragon Protocols, which I believe the Echelon Lord can access."

"She can. More importantly, the Imperium can."

Morgan watched in silence as the destroyers drove toward the incoming starkillers.

"There's nothing we can do," she finally concluded. "We can't get there in time to cover them. El-Amin, the moment you think you can open a portal, do it. Regardless of whether the sun-eater is dead or not. We've outmaneuvered them enough to escape, I think."

There were other Servants out there in a rough cloud around the

Womb, but the vast majority of them had been concentrated in the barrier *Defiance* had punched through and around the Womb itself.

If the starkillers failed, *Defiance* couldn't take the Womb or its defenders—but Morgan was sure they couldn't catch her now, either. Too many of them had expended too much of their fuel.

"Destroyers are engaging our salvos," Nguyen reported grimly. "They've deployed over a dozen Buckler drones—it appears they're starting on the shuttles."

"They know," Morgan concluded. "They've guessed, at least, but they have no idea what is actually carrying the starkiller."

Every eye on the bridge was locked on two things: the desperate attempt by the destroyers—presumably *Child of the Great Mother*'s original escort and manned by crews of Children cultists—to stop the starkillers; and the countdown until El-Amin thought he'd be able to open a hyper portal.

Morgan hoped the time estimate was conservative. Even at point-seven lightspeed, they couldn't outrun a blast wave traveling at point-nine-nine lightspeed for an entire day.

But that was the choice she'd made, and every second she ran from the sun-eater at full sprint was another two hundred thousand kilometers of space between them and the nova she was hoping to induce.

"Dragon *Defiance*-Two is down," Nguyen reported grimly. "Most of the shuttles are gone too, and one of them nailed the starkiller. Time to impact is... It's too late."

"Commander?"

"It's too late. Impact is *now*."

There was nothing. The icons vanished off the display and nothing happened.

"Commander Nguyen?" Morgan asked.

"*Defiance*-One hit the sun-eater itself, I have impact data reports coming back from it and the decoys," Nguyen said quietly. "I doubt the thing *liked* that, but..."

"And *Defiance*-Three?" Morgan demanded.

"Contact. We have coronal penetration and system activation," the tactical officer confirmed. "And...the destroyers have taken out the last of my probes, sir. We're down to lightspeed scanners for long-range data.

"It will be at least six minutes before we can confirm if the starkiller functioned as designed."

"Understood."

Patience was a virtue, but right now, Morgan was looking at a dead ship either way. A starkiller had connected. That should have been it. The star encased in the Womb was a half-eaten ragged thing, but it was still a *star*, a stellar furnace of unimaginable energy.

"El-Amin, watch your gravity scanners," Morgan ordered. "I think that the detonation pulse and the nova should do something."

"In theory, once it stops actively maneuvering and the mass starts dispersing, I should be able to more easily open a portal," her navigator confirmed. "I think. That it's moving away from us is also helping; we're getting...wake instead of bow wave, if the metaphor tracks."

"It does," Morgan agreed. The sheer kinetic energy of the moving Womb was screwing with the hyperspatial interface, but it was causing more havoc in front of it than behind it. The Womb probably didn't even know about the effect, but it made its pursuit terrifyingly deadly.

"I have Final Dragon impact on lightspeed scanners," Nguyen reported. "All signs...all signs..." She swallowed.

"Nova imminent," she reported grimly. "Standard estimate is one hundred eighty seconds from impact. That means it already blew, sir."

"No gravity wave along the interface yet," El-Amin reported. "A nova *should* show up on the interface before the shockwave gets here."

"Keep us in sprint mode," Morgan ordered. "It sucks for the ship and it sucks for us, but I'd rather have to treat everyone for bone cancer than get vaporized by a dying star."

Her navigator just nodded. The distance was continuing to

grow...and Nguyen had now added a probability-shaded series of expanding zones around the hopefully ex-star.

Morgan could only wait, watching as the zone of death expanded at lightspeed. Even weakened as the sun had been, her best guess was that *Defiance* wouldn't survive anywhere within a light-hour of the blast.

None of Nguyen's probability zones had them making it that far.

"Hyperspatial interface wave," El-Amin suddenly snapped. "Nova was at least two minutes ago. Hyperspace pulses repeating."

"Can we portal out?" Morgan demanded.

"Not yet," he replied. "Analyzing the cycle; we might be able to manage a destructive interference pattern with the interface wave."

Nothing smaller than the movement or death of a star would create ripples along the hyperspatial boundary. Enough starkillers had been fired over the millennia—even one by the Imperium, long before—that they knew how fast that ripple traveled: roughly three times the speed of light.

That meant the realspace shockwave was only a few minutes away.

"Cycling emitters," El-Amin reported. "Sir...I can't guarantee I'm going to be able to get us *out* of hyperspace."

"We'll deal with that later," Morgan told him. "Get us out of here."

"I have the cycle," her navigator announced. "Hold on; this is going to be rough. Portal close, portal *close!*"

Five light-seconds gave them a safety margin but also meant the portal had to stay open for five seconds.

Five hundred meters required no such allowances.

CHAPTER FIFTY

"The good news, everyone, is that we're still alive," Morgan told the gathered officers in *Defiance*'s briefing room. The cruiser's department heads were arranged around the long table in what looked like order of exhaustion.

Looking unexhausted—if terrified—Rin Dunst sat the other end of the room.

"The bad news is what everyone is in here to brief me on," she continued. "How about we get started with the broadest. Commander Liepins? How's *Defiance*?"

"We're still here, so better than I was afraid of," the engineer told everyone. "The emergency portal did a number on our power-distribution network, as we had to give Commander El-Amin far more power than those emitters are supposed to need.

"So, the bad news is that we don't have exotic-matter emitters anymore—well, technically, we still have *one*. We need eight to create a portal to realspace," Liepins concluded. "The other bad news, which I really hope doesn't become relevant, is that our power distribution is probably not up to combat demands at this point.

"I'm reasonably sure I can maintain the shields at navigational levels, but I'm not sure I can take them back up to combat levels, and I am absolutely certain I can't bring the shields up to combat levels *and* provide enough power to fire the hyperfold cannons."

"What about the plasma lances?" Morgan asked. "Hyperfold cannons aren't much use in hyperspace and, well, you already established we're not leaving hyperspace."

Liepins laughed bitterly.

"You might get one shot," he told her. "If you're okay with not having shields afterwards. Or, quite possibly, engines."

"Well, that answers that, doesn't it?" Morgan said. "The only place we're going is back to base. El-Amin?"

The headscarfed navigator bowed his head and sighed.

"I think I've got enough of a bearing to get us back to Kosha Station," he told her. "But I'm not certain. We could end up flying around in circles, praying we find someone."

"The good news is that Kosha Station has a permanent hyperspace installation," Morgan replied. "It's set up to detect anybody coming in, but it will also give us an idea of whether we're in the right place.

"We can't take *Defiance* back out on her own, but any other hyper-capable ship can open a portal for us. We're also capable of using the hyperspace launcher's portals to send messages into realspace, though we no longer have any shuttles to send through them."

At this point, Morgan had briefed at least everyone in this room on just what those shuttles had been sacrificed for. She suspected a lot more people knew than had been officially cleared on Final Dragon, which was a problem.

Conveniently, it was Speaker Murtas's problem more than hers right now.

"If Commander El-Amin can get us even close to the Kosha System, we can send a message through a launcher portal for Echelon Lord Davor to send someone for us," Morgan concluded. "That's better than I was afraid of."

"We still have sixty-five people in med bay," Rogers told her. "No deaths, somehow, but med bay is still feeling overwhelmed."

"The sooner we're back to Kosha Station, the better for everyone. Does anyone see any reason why we shouldn't be on our way? Liepins? She can take the trip?"

If *Defiance* couldn't take the trip back to the Navy base, they were in a lot of trouble.

"She can't do much else, but she can do that," Liepins confirmed. "We're going to be tied up for a while with repairs, sir."

"I know. I'm even pretty sure it was worth it," Morgan told them. "We did good, people. There was a very real chance the Womb was going to build itself a hyperdrive at some point in the next few years. At that point, it would have just shown up in Kosha—and we would never have been able to predict when."

"I have bad news on that front," Dunst said from the other end of the table.

He was mostly there to keep him in the loop on what had happened. He'd earned that much respect by making the connections that Morgan couldn't in the middle of the battle.

"I'm not busy checking on repairs and making sure the cruiser can fly," he reminded everyone. "That gave me a chance to go through our data from the battle. I had one of Commander Nguyen's NCOs double-check me, because I didn't even think what I was looking at was possible."

Dunst laid a projector on the table and opened up the standard tactical plot. The time stamps showed that it was literally in the final seconds before *Defiance* had opened her portal and fled into hyperspace.

"Here," he said quietly, pointing to a specific point on the plot. "Lesser Blade Pinheiro and I went over it several times. That's a hyperspace portal."

The briefing room was very quiet.

"It could have been one of the Children destroyers, matching up with the gravity pulses like we did," Nguyen suggested.

"I would guess the destroyers went through the portal, but it wasn't generated by them," Rin continued, his voice still soft. "They wouldn't generate a portal over a thousand kilometers wide."

"At least we know the sun-eater didn't make it out," Rogers said grimly. "But that sounds like it had built its own hyperdrive."

"We can't trace it in the current state of hyperspace here," Nguyen said after a moment's thought. "Whatever made it out is long gone. The chaos of the nova will prevent any useful tracking for a while."

"What are we looking at, Rin?" Morgan asked.

"Best case? The Womb used a partially constructed hyperdrive system to help the Children escape," the archeologist told them. "They'll be a pain, but I'm reasonably sure the Imperium can deal with three rogue destroyers."

Morgan remembered the warnings coming out of Kanzi space. The Theocracy's civil war was probably going to send more than three rogue destroyers into Imperial space.

"And the worst case, Dr. Dunst?" she asked.

"The worst case is that the Womb overcame the limitations of her design," Dunst told them. "The Alava would not have designed it to be able to reproduce—but they also would not have designed it to build interface drives or hyper portal emitters.

"It would have had to create the structure for a child from scratch, but I think we can be very certain that the Womb was *very* smart and that it had a *long* time to work out how to create a seed."

He shrugged helplessly, and Morgan understood the understated terror on his face now.

"So long as it took it ten thousand years to travel between stars, there was no point in it breaking the Alava restrictions on its ability to reproduce. Given a hyperdrive and potentially some kind of interface drive...it could very likely have decided that there was a purpose to it creating more of itself."

"If there's another one, we know how to kill them now," Nguyen said grimly. "Plus, it's going to take it at least a few hundred years to grow to its parent's size, right?"

"Probably," Dunst agreed. "But remember that this is not a stupid creature. This is a creature that, presented with an interface drive, learned how to duplicate it. Learned its limitations...and then worked out a way around those limitations for its own purposes.

"The Children called it a god. I am far from that generous, but it was a *terrifyingly* intelligent creature. Its child will be equally capable—and it will *know how we killed the first one.*"

Something Morgan suspected Dunst had worked out, even if no one had explicitly told them that *Defiance* had fired a starkiller into the Womb's captive sun.

"All of that will need to be written up and reported," she told her crew. "Right now, at least, that child isn't a threat. We have time to find it and time to deal with the Imperium's other problems.

"We'll pass on everything we have to High Command, and they'll decide what we do about the child. For now, let's get our people home."

CHAPTER FIFTY-ONE

"Welcome, Captain. Have a seat."

Morgan felt the doors to Davor's office swing shut behind her like the swing of the executioner's axe. She obeyed the gentle instruction, taking the solitary chair in front of the big red stone desk.

"I don't have much else to do, sir," she admitted with a small smile. "*Defiance* can't even enter hyperspace on her own right now. We appreciate you sending *Green Corona* to get us."

Green Corona was the second-most powerful warship under Davor's command until the battleships arrived sometime in the next few days, a *Thunderstorm*-D class cruiser built during the Taljzi Campaigns. Given *Defiance*'s current state, *Green Corona* was the only thing really standing between Kosha Station and anyone who wanted to cause trouble.

Of course, Morgan was reasonably sure she'd eliminated the only real threat to the base. For now, anyway.

"It's not often I see a ship crawl back home in quite that bad a shape," Davor said levelly. "Most ships that get that abused, Captain Casimir, don't make it home."

"We did some of the worst of it to ourselves getting into hyperspace at the end," Morgan said. "The Womb's effect on the local hyperspatial interface was unusual."

"And the Final Dragon weapons had their own effect, as I understand," the Echelon Lord noted. "I've reviewed the reports prepared by you and your senior officers, Captain. You do understand, yes, the problem for maintaining Final Dragon Protocol security that your actions create?"

"I do, sir," Morgan confirmed. She was staring at a point just above and to the right of Davor's bony shoulder. "It was made clear to me when I was briefed on the full armament of my command that any deployment of the Final Dragon weapons would need to be justified before a board of inquiry or equivalent."

"In addition to that, I must point out that you deployed strategic weapons in violation of a direct order," Davor said calmly. "Given the shortcomings of the Servants, it seems clear that, say, a squadron of superbattleships should have been able to clear local space around the Womb and enable a far closer examination of what remains perhaps the most intriguing Precursor artifact we have ever encountered."

"It did not appear that a squadron of superbattleships would be available soon, sir," Morgan replied. "And I agreed with Dr. Dunst's assessment that it was only a question of time before the Womb constructed a hyperdrive. The fact that it created a hyper portal to allow *someone* to escape at the end suggests we may have even been overestimating how long that would take."

"I read the report," the Ivida flag officer reminded her. "Though I did draw a conclusion from the reports that I'm not sure you did. You were concerned at the time and in hindsight over the potential for the Womb to capture your ship and use its matter-conversion core to accelerate its exotic-matter production or potentially augment its feeding cycle."

"Yes, sir. Capture of a modern warship could have led to...serious problems."

"You are assuming, Captain, that the Children of the Stars were able to provide their databanks to the Womb in a manner that could be read by a fifty-thousand-year-old organic brain designed to interface with a completely different communications and information systems technology base," Davor told her.

"More likely, in my opinion," the Echelon Lord continued, "is that the Womb duplicated hyperspace and interface-drive technology from sensor data and examination of the technologies in the hands of the Children. It is entirely possible, if that assumption were true, that the Womb would be able to duplicate our matter-to-energy conversion processes based solely on close-range scans of your vessel.

"Scans, Captain Casimir, that the Womb already had."

Morgan stared at her superior. That had never even occurred to her.

"You are correct, sir; I did not draw that conclusion from the situation we were presented," she admitted.

"Nonetheless, you appear to have made an overall accurate assessment of the threat," Davor told her. "The unpredictable arrival of two solar masses in the Kosha System would destroy the colony on Blue Heart, regardless of whether the Womb proceeded to eat Kosha itself.

"Given the data you had available, your decision to proceed with the deployment of strategic weapons was both within the authority granted to you as commander of a strategic weapon platform and entirely reasonable," the flag officer concluded. "There will be no inquiry, Captain Casimir. *I* have authorized your decision, and any consequences or penalties thereof will fall on me.

"Is that clear?"

"Sir. Yes, sir," Morgan replied. "Thank you, sir."

She paused.

"What consequences, sir?" she asked slowly.

Davor studied her, the Ivida woman's eyes unreadable as she analyzed Morgan.

"This does not leave this room," she finally told Morgan.

"Of course, sir. Everything we are discussing is sealed under Final Dragon Protocol."

"More than that, Captain. You did not hear this from me, or at all. Is that understood?"

"Yes, sir," Morgan said crisply. She was nervous now. That didn't sound right.

"I received both explicit fleet orders and clear back-channel personal messages informing me that under no circumstances was the Womb to be destroyed," Davor told her. "By the time I'd received them, we already knew you'd engaged the Womb. Passing them on would have been pointless; they'd have been ten hours too late by the time you got them.

"It is very clear to me, Captain, that someone in the Imperium suspected the Womb existed and was prepared to place the colonies under my protection at extreme risk to allow for study of it," the flag officer concluded.

"We know the Children were born out of a survey mission we can't find any record of," Morgan admitted. "Are you saying they may still have allies in the Imperium?"

"What we saw of the Children was a cult born out of an encounter with a mind-bogglingly powerful entity," Davor reminded her. "That does not mean that what we saw is all that there was. It is possible that the people who sent that first expedition out still had contacts with it.

"It is possible, Captain Casimir, that someone in the Imperium already knew what we found out...and those waters are dark and deep. They scare me, Captain."

"And me," Morgan admitted. "The A!Tol aren't supposed to be able to *do* conspiracy."

"Our overlords lie poorly," Davor noted grimly. "But they are far more capable of deception than they even perceive themselves to be.

"And even if the A!Tol are silent in this matter, twenty-eight species have members of sufficient power to have set this in motion. I will cover your back from consequences, Captain Casimir, but I'm afraid there is at least one I can already expect."

"Sir?"

"I cannot, given the orders I received while you were fighting the Womb, recommend you for the medals and honors you and your crew most richly deserve," Davor told her. "All I can do is protect you from those who would attack you for your actions."

"Protect my crew, sir, and I am more than happy."

"That, Captain Casimir, was never in doubt."

MORGAN HOPED that her running into Rin Dunst outside the naval base headquarters looked at least somewhat accidental. It hadn't been entirely planned, but she'd known he had a meeting there and she'd told him about hers.

Despite what she'd said to Davor, the two and a half cycles since she'd arrived back in the Kosha System had been hectic chaos. *Defiance* was now in the capable hands of Kosha Station's yards once more, and Morgan had time to breathe.

"Well, you're not in cuffs, so I take it that went well?" Dunst greeted her with a chuckle as he fell in beside her. "Lunch?"

"Maybe; let's walk for now," she told him. "I know at least some people who'd think cuffs would mean things were going *very* well."

"If nothing else, I don't believe you are the Echelon Lord's type," the archeologist replied as he walked beside her. "It went well?"

"It did," she agreed. "Some...worries," she admitted. "Not the kind we can talk about."

"That's how it goes," Dunst agreed. "You have the same problem with Victoria, I would guess?"

"Both ways," Morgan confessed. "There's things I can't talk to her about and things she can't talk to me about. Half the time, it turns out we both knew something but weren't allowed to talk to each other about it."

She shook her head.

"She'll like you, if we ever get you back to Sol," she predicted. "If nothing else, she'll think you're good for me. Keep me humble."

"She knows about me?" Dunst asked.

"Of course. She gave me permission before we even had a date," Morgan confirmed. "Anything else would be unfair to everyone, I think."

"Makes sense, I suppose," he allowed. "Still getting used to this whole concept."

"Is it worth it?" she asked. She was pretty sure of the answer.

"So far," he agreed with a chuckle. "Even if we occasionally butt heads."

"That won't change," Morgan warned him. "I'm on Kosha Station for a while as *Defiance* gets repaired, but after that...I go where the Navy sends me."

"And I go where the Institute sends me," he warned her in turn. "Though if you're looking for a place to crash while you're on Station, I do have an apartment here."

"Wait, seriously?" Morgan asked in surprise. They'd spent their night together on Kosha Station in a hotel, after all.

"I'm not expected to be on Kosha Station very much," he told her. "But we're looking at half a dozen potential digs in this sector, so it made sense to find some place to stick my stuff. You're welcome to use it while you're on station, even if I'm not."

"You disappearing that quickly?" Morgan said.

"Probably," he admitted. "A bunch of messages are flying back and forth, but even though we blew up one site, we identified several more. The list of places we want to dig into is expanding rapidly, and it isn't the Alava's nature to have only done one of a type of thing."

"You think there's more biological megastructures?"

"I know there are," Dunst said. "So, we'll keep poking at Alava sites until we find them, and we'll keep the Navy in the loop. I'm here for at least a few more cycles, but I expect to be gone long before *Defiance* is back in commission.

"But you're welcome to use my apartment while I'm gone," he repeated.

"And if Victoria comes to visit?" Morgan teased.

"Then she is also welcome to use the apartment," Dunst agreed with a chuckle. "Do I know how any of this is supposed to work? No! Am I willing to give it all a shot? Yes."

"Good. Because I *am* worth it," Morgan told him. "Victoria, for all of her continuing frustration with me, tells me so."

"So long as the Imperium recognizes your worth as well, I think you'll be just fine," he said.

That sent a chill down her spine as she considered Davor's warning.

Most likely, the sun-eating Alava creation she'd just killed had sent a child fleeing into hyperspace, with an escort of cultist warships. On top of that, those cultists appeared to have allies within the Imperium.

Now Dunst was warning there might be more Alava biologicals in the sector—because she needed more worries.

And beyond all of that, the Imperium stood on the edge of not one but *two* wars.

She shook her head.

"No lunch," she decided. "Show me this apartment, Dr. Dunst. I'm curious to see how well the Imperium keeps our premier archeologists!"

ABOUT THE AUTHOR

Glynn Stewart is the author of *Starship's Mage*, a bestselling science fiction and fantasy series where faster-than-light travel is possible–but only because of magic. His other works include science fiction series *Duchy of Terra, Castle Federation* and *Exile,* as well as the urban fantasy series *ONSET* and *Changeling Blood.*

Writing managed to liberate Glynn from a bleak future as an accountant. With his personality and hope for a high-tech future intact, he lives in Kitchener, Ontario with his partner, their cats, and an unstoppable writing habit.

VISIT GLYNNSTEWART.COM FOR NEW RELEASE UPDATES

 facebook.com/glynnstewartauthor

OTHER BOOKS
BY GLYNN STEWART

For release announcements join the
mailing list or visit **GlynnStewart.com**

STARSHIP'S MAGE
Starship's Mage
Hand of Mars
Voice of Mars
Alien Arcana
Judgment of Mars
UnArcana Stars
Sword of Mars
Mountain of Mars
The Service of Mars
A Darker Magic
Mage-Commander (upcoming)

Starship's Mage: Red Falcon
Interstellar Mage
Mage-Provocateur
Agents of Mars

Pulsar Race: A Starship's Mage Universe Novella

DUCHY OF TERRA
The Terran Privateer
Duchess of Terra
Terra and Imperium
Darkness Beyond
Shield of Terra
Imperium Defiant
Relics of Eternity
Shadows of the Fall
Eyes of Tomorrow

VIGILANTE
(WITH TERRY MIXON)
Heart of Vengeance
Oath of Vengeance

Bound By Stars: A Vigilante Series
(With Terry Mixon)
Bound By Law
Bound by Honor
Bound by Blood

TEER AND KARD
Wardtown
Blood Ward

CHANGELING BLOOD
Changeling's Fealty
Hunter's Oath
Noble's Honor
Fae, Flames & Fedoras: A Changeling Blood Novella

ONSET
ONSET: To Serve and Protect
ONSET: My Enemy's Enemy
ONSET: Blood of the Innocent
ONSET: Stay of Execution
Murder by Magic: An ONSET Novella

FANTASY STAND ALONE NOVELS
Children of Prophecy
City in the Sky

Made in United States
North Haven, CT
18 July 2023

39219084R00225